In the past three years, *New Yo*[illegible] Sherrilyn Kenyon has claimed the [illegible] extraordinary bestseller continues to top every genre she writes. With more than 25 million copies of her books in print in over 100 [illegible]ntries, her current series include: The Dark-Hunters, Th[illegible]gue, Chronicles of Nick, and Belador. Since 2004, she ha[illegible]d more than 50 novels on the *New York Times* list in all fo[illegible]ncluding manga. The preeminent voice in paranormal fi[illegible]ith more than twenty years of publishing credits in all [illegible]s, Kenyon not only helped to pioneer, but define the [illegible]nt paranormal trend that has captivated the world.

Visit Sherrilyn Kenyon's websites:
www.darkhunter.com | www.sherrilynkenyon.co.uk

www.facebook.com/AuthorSherrilynKenyon |
www.twitter.com/KenyonSherrilyn

Praise for Sherrilyn Kenyon:

[illegible] publishing phenomenon…[Sherrilyn Kenyon] is the [illegible]ning queen of the wildly successful paranormal scene'
Publishers Weekly

[illegible]on's writing is brisk, ironic and relentlessly imaginative. These are not your mother's vampire novels'
Boston Globe

'Whether writing as Sherrilyn Kenyon or Kinley MacGregor, this author delivers great romantic fantasy!'
New York Times bestselling author Elizabeth Lowell

Dark-Hunter World Series:
(in reading order)

Fantasy Lover
Night Pleasures
Night Embrace
Dance with the Devil
Kiss of the Night
Night Play
Seize the Night
Sins of the Night
Unleash the Night
The Dream-Hunter
Devil May Cry
Upon the Midnight Clear
Dream Chaser
Acheron
One Silent Night
Dream Warrior
Bad Moon Rising
No Mercy
Retribution

The Dark-Hunter Companion

The Belador Code

Blood Trinity
Alterant

League Series
Born of Night
Born of Fire
Born of Ice

Chronicles of Nick

Infinity
Invincible

By Sherrilyn Kenyon writing as Kinley MacGregor:

Lords of Avalon Series

Sword of Darkness
Knight of Darkness

Devil May Cry

Sherrilyn Kenyon

piatkus

PIATKUS

First published in the US in 2007 by St. Martin's Press, New York
First published in Great Britain in 2007 by Piatkus Books
This paperback edition published in 2012 by Piatkus

A CIP catalogue record for this book
is available from the British Library.

ISBN 978-0-7499-5641-7

Printed and bound by CPI Group (UK) Ltd, Croydon, CR0 4YY

Papers used by Piatkus are from well-managed forests
and other responsible sources.

MIX
Paper from
responsible sources
FSC® C104740

Piatkus
An imprint of
Little, Brown Book Group
100 Victoria Embankment
London EC4Y 0DY

An Hachette UK Company
www.hachette.co.uk

www.piatkus.co.uk

To Neco, who will always live in my heart. I miss you much and wish I could "holler at my boy" one more time. For my fans, the Kenyon Minions and RBL women whose love and support has seen me through countless storms. To Retta, Rebecca, Kim, Vic and Dianna for holding me up when I needed it most. To Kia, Jack, Jacs, Alex, Carl, Bryan, Soteria, Cee, Judy and Aimee for all the work you do. For Merrilee, Monique, Sally, Matthew, Matt, John, Brian, Anne-Marie and everyone else at SMP for all you guys do to get the books to the shelves and for not cracking my head when I'm late with a manuscript. But most of all, for my family for allowing Mommy her quiet time and for eating more pizza than the good Lord ever meant children to eat. To my baby brother, Steven, who really does mean everything to me and for writing a great song for Ash. Last but not least, my husband who is my anchor. Thank you for always being there. This one's for you guys. I hope you enjoy it.

Devil May Cry

PROLOGUE

Vengeance.

Some say it's a poison that infiltrates the soul and strips it bare. That its path only destroys the one who treads it.

But to others, it's mother's milk. It nourishes and thrives—gives them a reason to survive when they have nothing more to hold them to this world.

This is the story of one such creature. Born a god in the time before mankind even recorded their meager history, Sin, also called Nana, was the one who ruled the known universe. His pantheon was supreme and all around him paid homage.

And then the day came when other gods rose to challenge him. For centuries he fought the bloody war, and he would have been victorious had one act of treachery not robbed him of his godhood.

Stripped of his cabalistic powers, he was left to walk in the world of man as one of them and as something else. Something dark. Cold. Lethal.

But the game isn't over. Defeat does nothing but feed the part of the soul that demands a rematch. So long as there is life, there is hope. And so long as there is hope, there is determination.

And the need for vengeance that ever treads by the side of the defeated.

For centuries the ancient god has bided his time, knowing that his enemy's complacency and arrogance would bring her back into his circle.

Now the day of reckoning lies within his grasp . . .

CHAPTER ONE

"He needs to be destroyed. My preference is painfully and quickly, but any means that ultimately results in his death will work."

Acheron Parthenopaeus turned his head to see the Greek goddess Artemis approaching him. For centuries now the two of them had been tied together, and at times such as this the goddess actually believed she controlled him.

The truth, however, was very different.

Dressed only in black leather pants, he sat on the stone railing of her temple balcony with his back against one of the columns that lined it. The balcony was made of sparkling white marble that overlooked a breathtaking view of a rainbow waterfall and a perfect forest scene. But then one would expect no less on Mt. Olympus, where the Greek gods made their home.

If only the inhabitants were as perfect as the landscape . . .

With flowing red hair, unblemished porcelain skin, and sharp green eyes, Artemis would be beautiful if Ash didn't begrudge her every breath she drew.

"Why do you have such a burr up your ass all of a sudden where Sin's concerned?"

She curled her lip at him. "I hate it when you talk like that."

Which was exactly why he did it. May the gods forbid he ever do anything she liked. He had enough problems with *that* already. "You're changing the subject."

She huffed before she answered. "I've always hated him. He was supposed to die. Remember? *You* intervened."

She was seriously oversimplifying that sequence of events. "He survived on his own. I merely gave the guy a job after you fucked him over."

"Yes, and now he's gone insane. Did you not see that he broke into a museum last night, knocked out three guards in the process, and stole a high-profile artifact? How is that not exposing your precious Dark-Hunters to public scrutiny? I swear he did it on purpose, hoping to get caught so that he could tell the humans about all of us. He's a threat to everyone."

Ash dismissed her anger even though he did agree it was a reckless move on Sin's part. Usually the ancient ex-god had more sense. "I'm sure he just wanted to touch a piece of home. Hell, whatever artifact he took probably belonged to him or some member of his family. I'm not going to kill anyone because he was homesick, Artie—kind of like killing someone when he's on the can. It's just wrong."

With her hands on her curvy hips, she glared at him. "So you're going to dismiss it as trivial?"

"If by that you mean I don't think it warrants his immediate execution. Call me crazy, but yeah, I'm dismissing it."

She narrowed her eyes on him. "You are going softball."

Ash frowned until he realized what she meant. "Soft, Artie. You meant to say I'm going soft."

"Whatever." She moved to stand beside him. "The Acheron I remember would have sizzled him for half the infraction."

He released an agitated breath before he responded. "Fried, Artie, damn, learn to speak. I've got a headache from trying to figure out what the hell you mean most of the time. And at no time in my life would I have ever fried anyone for something like this."

"Yes, you would have."

He thought about that for a moment. But as usual she was wrong. "No. Definitely not. Only you would move me to that kind of violence over something so insignificant."

"You're such a bastard."

At least she got that right, in more ways than one.

He leaned his head back against the column so that he could look up at her. "Why? Because I won't do your bidding?"

"Yes. You owe me this. You made me get rid of my assassin and now I have no control over those creatures that—"

"That *you* created," he added, interrupting her angry tirade. "Don't forget the important part here. The Dark-Hunters wouldn't exist at all had someone, and for the sake of your missing intellect let me clarify that, *you*, not stolen powers from me that could bring back the dead. I didn't need the Dark-Hunters to help me fight against the Daimons and protect the humans. I was doing fine on my own. But you wouldn't have it. You created them and made me responsible for their lives. It's a responsibility that I take most seriously, so excuse me for banning you from killing them because you have reverse PMS."

She scowled. "Reverse PMS?"

"Yeah, unlike a normal woman, you're cranky twenty-eight days out of the month."

She moved to slap him, but he caught her wrist in his hand. "You haven't bargained for the right to hit me."

She wrenched her arm away from him. "I want him dead."

"I'm not your tool in this." And lucky for Sin, Ash was here. He was the only reason Artemis didn't kill Sin herself. They'd made the pact centuries ago, after she'd flambéed a Dark-Hunter for one erroneous comment, that she would never again go after a Dark-Hunter without Ash's approval.

Her eyes were still seething. "Sin's up to something. I can feel it."

"Of that I have no doubt. He's been plotting your murder since the day you stole his godhood from him. Lucky for you, I'm in the way and Sin knows it."

She narrowed her eyes on him. "I'm surprised you're not helping him kill me."

So was he. But in the end, he knew he couldn't be a part of that.

He needed Artemis in order to live, and if he were to die, the world would become an even scarier place than it already was.

Too bad that. 'Cause honestly, he wanted nothing more than to bid her ass goodbye and never look back.

Artemis shoved at his raised knee. "Aren't you at least going to ask him why he was at the museum? And why he assaulted those officers?"

A sliver of hope went through him. "Are you going to let me leave to do it?"

"You owe me three more days of service."

So much for hope. He should have known better. The bitch had no intention of letting him out of her temple until his two weeks were up. It'd been a bitter bargain he'd made with her: two weeks as her pet sex slave for two months of freedom from her interference. He hated playing these games, but one did what one had to.

Even when it seriously sucked.

"Then it looks like it can wait."

Artemis growled at him as she curled her hands into fists. Acheron was ever her bane. Why she put up with him she didn't know.

Actually, she did. Even in his stubbornness, he was still the sexiest man she'd ever seen. There was nothing she enjoyed more than watching him move. Or even sit, as he was doing at present. He had the most viciously perfect body any man had ever possessed. His long blond hair was braided over one shoulder as he leaned back with his arms folded over his chest and his bare left foot tapped in time to an imaginary beat only he could hear.

Powerful and bold, he bent to her will only when she forced him to it by blood and bone. And even then, he did so grudgingly and defiantly. He really was like a wild beast that no one could tame.

For that matter, he bit and snarled at anyone who tried to pet him.

And the gods knew she'd tried for centuries to either win him over or beat him into submission. But nothing worked. He was ever near and ever unattainable. It infuriated her.

She pouted at him. "You'd like for him to kill me, wouldn't you?"

He let out a small laugh. “Hell, no. I want that honor myself.”

How dare he! “You wretched—”

“Don’t insult me, Artie,” he said, cutting her words off with an irritable tone, “when we both know you don’t mean it. I get really tired of the lip service.”

A shiver went over her at his choice of words. “Strange. I never get tired of yours.” She reached to touch his lips. They were the only part of his body that was soft—like the petals of a rose—and she was ever fascinated by them. “You have the most beautiful mouth, Acheron, especially when it’s on my body.”

Ash groaned as he recognized the heat in her emerald eyes as she fingered his lips. It made his skin crawl. “Aren’t you ever satisfied? I swear if I were mortal, I’d be limping from our last go-round. If not dead. We really need to find you a hobby other than jumping on top of me.”

But it was too late, she was already pushing his knee down and straddling his thighs.

Grinding his teeth, Ash leaned his head back as she began to nibble his throat. He tilted his head, knowing what was coming while she lightly tongued his skin. Her heartbeat was already pounding as she slid herself closer to him.

And then he felt her sharp incisors piercing his skin an instant before she began drinking his blood . . .

“*Katra!*”

Kat Agrotera sat bolt upright in her bed at the shrill call in her head. “What did I do?” she asked, trying to figure out why Artemis would be angry at her now.

“Were you asleep?”

She blinked as Artemis appeared in the room beside her bed. The room was completely dark except for the eerie glowing blue light that radiated out of Artemis’s body.

Kat glanced down at the bed where she sat in her pink sock monkey pajamas with rumpled sheets and hair, then decided sarcasm was not the better part of sanity. “I’m awake now.”

“Good. I have a mission for you.”

Kat had to bite back a sharp laugh. “I hate to be the bearer of reminders, but you traded my service to Apollymi, remember? Now the big evil of Atlantis that you fear forbids me to do anything you say. She kind of finds it funny that she can irritate you that way."

Artemis's eyes narrowed on her. "Katra . . ."

"Matisera . . ." she said, imitating Artemis's agitated tone. "I didn't ask for this. You're the one who made the bargain with Apollymi that I have to live with. Personally, it irks the shit out of me to be traded like some Yu-Gi-Oh! card you got tired of having around the house. But trade me you did. So sorry, I'm playing for the other team now."

Artemis came forward then, and for the first time Kat realized she was actually afraid.

"Is something wrong?"

Artemis nodded before she whispered, "He's going to kill me."

"Acheron?" He was the most likely candidate.

"No," she said sharply, "Acheron would never hurt me. He just threatens it. Do you remember when you were a young woman?"

Well, given the fact that was about eleven to ten thousand years ago, it was a bit of a stretch for her. "I try not to, but some things are still crystal. Why?"

Artemis sat down on her bed before she took Kat's stuffed tiger and pulled it to her. "Do you remember the Sumerian god Sin?"

Kat frowned. "The one who broke into your temple eons ago and tried to take your powers and kill you?"

Artemis's hand tightened on the tiger. "Yes. He's back and he's trying to kill me again."

How was that possible? Kat had personally taken care of that enemy. "I thought he was dead."

"No, Acheron saved him before he could die and made him a Dark-Hunter. Sin thinks I'm the one who drained him of his powers and left him for dead." The terror in Artemis's eyes scorched her. "He's going to kill me, Katra, I know it. The entire world is going to end. We are coming up on the Sumerian *apokalypsi*—"

"I don't think they use that word."

"Who cares what word they use?" she screeched. "End of the world is end of the world regardless of whatever term you use for it. The point is, Sin is now going to try to overthrow me again and take my place. Do you know what that means?"

"There will be much rejoicing?"

"Katra!"

She sobered. "Sorry. I get it. He wants revenge."

"Yes, for something *I* didn't do. I need your help, Katra. Please."

Kat sat there for a moment, contemplating. It wasn't like Artemis to ask for anything. She always demanded it—that only told Kat how much Artemis feared Sin. But even though it was obvious the goddess was scared, Kat suspected there was more to this story than Artemis was letting on. There always was. "What aren't you telling me?"

Artemis gave her a blank stare. "I don't know what you mean."

"Of course you do." Artemis never told the whole truth about anything. "And before I commit myself to some disaster, I want to know everything about it."

Artemis's face hardened. "Are you telling me that you refuse to help me after all I've done to you?"

That actually summarized it well. "I think you mean 'for me', Matisera, not 'to me'."

"As if I care. Now answer me."

Wow. For a woman asking for help, Artemis had a wonderful way of expressing it. But then that was her nature, and Kat would be suspicious if Artemis was anything less than authoritative. "What do you want me to do?"

"What do you think? Kill him."

Kat was aghast. "Matisera! What are you asking?"

"I'm asking for you to save my life," she snarled, "which is the very least you could do for me. Especially after all I've given you. Sin will kill me if he gets a chance and take all my powers. Who knows what he'll do to mankind once his godhood is restored. How he'll make them suffer. I've already gone to Acheron and he has refused to help me in any way. You're the only hope I have."

"Then why don't you kill him yourself? I know you're capable of it."

Artemis sat back in a huff. "He has the Tuppi Shimati. You do remember what that is, don't you?"

"The Sumerian Tablet of Destiny, yeah, I remember it." Whoever held possession of it could render another god powerless. It could also be used to strip a god of their powers entirely and thereby allow the possessor to kill any god they chose. Not exactly something the gods wanted in the wrong hands.

Artemis swallowed. "Who do you think Sin will come after now that he has it?"

No-brainer there. Artemis. "And with that you have my undivided attention. Don't worry, Matisera. I'll get it from him."

Artemis actually looked relieved. "I don't want anyone to know our past. You of all people understand how important it is that it remain hidden. Don't fail me this time, Katra. I need you to fulfill your word to me."

Kat flinched at the reminder of the one and only time in her life she'd failed in her mission to Artemis. "I will."

Artemis inclined her head before she vanished.

Kat lay back in bed, thinking of what had just transpired. On the one hand, she had no doubt that Artemis was telling the truth about the Tablet of Destiny. Sin's pantheon had been the one who'd created it. If anyone knew how to find and wield it, Sin would be he.

But Artemis was still Artemis.

Which meant some important parts of this story were most likely missing and before Kat went traipsing off after another god, even a fallen one, she wanted to know as much about him as she could.

Reaching for her cell phone on the nightstand, she flipped it open and noted the time. It was one A.M. for her, but in Minneapolis it would be midnight. She pressed the 6 button and waited until she heard a soft, feminine voice answer.

Kat smiled at the sound of her friend's greeting. "Hi, Cassandra, how ya doing?" At one time, she'd been Cassandra's protector for Artemis. But since Cassandra had become immortal and was married to the ex-Dark-Hunter Wulf, Kat had been reassigned . . . and then traded off to the Atlantean goddess Apollymi.

Even so, Kat was still close friends with Cassandra and made it a habit of visiting her friend whenever she could.

"Hey, baby girl," Cassandra said with a laugh. "We're fine. We were just finishing up a movie. But I can tell by the tone of your voice and the time of this call that you've got something more on your mind than checking in with me."

Kat smiled at her friend's intuition. "Okay, I'm busted. There was a point to this call. Can you put the big guy on the phone for me? I have a couple of Dark-Hunter questions for him."

"Sure. Hang on a sec."

Kat raked her hand through her tousled curls as Wulf came to the phone. When she'd first met him, he'd been a Dark-Hunter. They were immortal protectors who'd sworn their service to Artemis in exchange for an Act of Vengeance. Their job was to kill the Daimons who preyed on human souls and to spend eternity in Artemis's service protecting mankind.

But Wulf had been granted his freedom and now he lived happily with his son and daughter and wife in Minneapolis. And he policed the Daimons only when the Dark-Hunters in his area needed an extra hand.

"Hey, Kat. You wanted to speak to me?" Even after all these centuries, his voice still held its thick Nordic accent.

"Yeah. Do you happen to know the Dark-Hunter named Sin?"

"I know a couple who have that name. Which one are you referring to?"

"Sumerian."

"The fallen god?"

"That would be he."

Wulf let out a speculative breath on the other end. "Personally, no, I don't. But I've heard rumors about him. They say he's crazy as hell."

"They who?"

"Everyone. Any Dark-Hunter who's ever been in his area. Any Squire who ever made the mistake of crossing his path. He's a vicious bastard who tolerates absolutely no one near him."

Well, that didn't sound promising. But it did corroborate Artemis's fear. "You know anyone I can call who knows him personally?"

"Ash."

Yeah. There were two problems with that. One, Artemis would flip out if Kat ever went near the Atlantean god, and two, Artemis would flip out if she ever went near the Atlantean god.

"Anyone else?"

"No," Wulf said firmly. "Let me reiterate that he's completely antisocial and will not interact with anyone. They say he once let a

Dark-Hunter die at the hands of a Daimon and laughed while he watched it happen. You can log into the Dark-Hunter bulletin boards at dailyinquisitor.com/bbs and see if you can find someone he might have let into his inner circle. I seriously doubt that from what little I know about him, but that would be your best bet."

Great. Just great. "Cool. Thanks for the help. I'll let you get back to your movie. You guys take care."

"You, too."

Kat hung up the phone and then grabbed her laptop from under the bed and followed Wulf's advice, but after a couple of hours on the bbs and on the Dark-Hunter.com Web site reading profiles, she gave up. They didn't tell her anything except Sin was a loner and a psycho.

Apparently, he didn't even go after Daimons. According to one story, he'd walked past a group of them once while they were feeding and didn't even grimace. There were also numerous stories of him inflicting burn wounds on himself and cursing anyone who came near him.

Boy, he sounded like a warm, fluffy bunny. She couldn't wait to meet him. Obviously he wasn't a people person, which was fine by her. As an only child, she didn't always play well with others either.

But the tales of his self-mutilation concerned her. What kind of creature was he that he'd continually do such a thing? Had his sanity been lost when he'd been drained of his god powers or had he always been like that?

Sighing, she closed her laptop and forced herself to get up out of her comfy bed and dress. It was only three in the morning . . . still a couple of hours before sunrise, which meant Sin was probably on the streets, wandering about aimlessly as he bypassed Daimons in need of death.

Kat closed her eyes and concentrated until she found what she was looking for . . .

Sin's essence.

But it wasn't where she'd expected to find him. Instead of being in Las Vegas, he was in New York . . . Central Park to be precise. She frowned at the sight as she shimmered in the shadows in a transparent Shade form. No one would be able to see her, but if the light were to hit her just right, it would catch a luminescent outline of her body. That was why she was keeping to the shadows—out of sight and reach of an insane ex-god.

Her research had said that Sin was stationed in Las Vegas. About half an hour outside of town.

What was he doing in New York in the middle of the night?

How had he gotten here and when?

But that wasn't the really important part. It was the way he walked through the dimly lit area of the park. "Stalking" would be a more apropos term. He was like a bloodthirsty beast trailing after the scent of its prey. He had his head bent low, his eyes barely more than a slit as he skimmed the area around him. Dressed in a long black leather coat that rippled and flared with his movements, he was an impressive sight. His shoulders were wide and his short, curly jet-black hair barely brushed the collar. Unlike other Dark-Hunters, his eyes weren't black. They were a golden brown—like the color of a lion's eyes. Topaz. And they glittered like ice against his darkly tanned skin.

His features were perfect in form, but since he'd been born a god, it was expected. As a rule, gods weren't ugly people. And even if they were, they usually used their powers to fix that. It went with the whole god-vanity thing that could be quite off-putting at times.

Appearing no older than his mid-thirties, Sin moved with a fluid, timeless grace. His black eyebrows were drawn together in a stern frown, and at least two days' worth of whiskers dusted his face.

Truly, he was exquisite, and a part of herself that she wasn't acquainted with took extreme notice of his dangerous masculine lope. Something about the way he moved went through her like a hot, heady wine. It made her dizzy and breathless.

Made her want to reach out and touch the very creature she knew would kill her if he had a chance. He was mesmerizing and engaging.

Suddenly he stopped dead in his tracks and cocked his head in her direction. Kat held her breath as trepidation pierced her heart. Had he heard her? Sensed her? He shouldn't be able to, but then he was a god . . . or at least had been one before.

Maybe he did have that power.

But as she saw the slight shadow to her left, she realized that he wasn't focused on her Shade form. He had his attention firmly rooted to the trees in front of her. And whatever was there was whispering in a language she'd never heard before. It was low in tone, with a sinister sound that was like some strange combination of grinding gears and a bone-chilling screech.

"Erkutu," Sin whispered in a voice that was laden with power. In one fluid motion, he dropped the coat from his shoulders to show a body so corded with power that it actually sent a shiver over her.

He wore a sleeveless black T-shirt and black leather pants with buckled biker boots. But what stood out even more than the deep, perfect indentations of his muscles was the set of knives strapped to his biceps and the ancient hilt of the dagger in his left boot. He had a silver vambrace on each forearm, and as he approached the shadows he unwrapped a long cord from his right wrist. On each end of the cord was a metal ball about the size of a golf ball. The balls flashed in the light and made a slight *tink* in the night as he walked.

It was obvious he was gearing up for battle, but there were no Daimons anywhere near them. If there were, she'd be able to sense them.

And still that strange whispering continued.

Kat crept through the trees, trying to see where he was headed.

Without warning, something was hurled at Sin's head. He ducked it and rose, twirling the cord over his head like a cowboy with a rope as he moved. The balls whistled in the air a moment before he released them and they flew through the foliage.

A scream tore through the night.

Kat froze as she saw what had caused it. At first it looked like a pretty human woman, until she opened her mouth and showed a double row of serrated fangs. But worse than the fangs was the blood that dripped from her chin. Human blood that matched the redness of the creature's eyes.

And she wasn't alone. There were three of them in total—the woman and two stocky men. Kat had never seen anything like them. They definitely weren't of the human species even though they had human bodies. They communicated with one another in that ferret-meets-Flipper language of theirs.

As one unit, they rushed Sin. He ducked and sent the first one to reach him flipping over his back. In a smooth, fluid move he pulled the dagger from his boot and sliced at the second male. The demon caught his arm and sank his fangs into Sin's hand.

Cursing, Sin kneed the creature in the stomach and twisted to confront the woman. The female demon jerked back a split second before his dagger would have slit her throat.

The first male pushed himself up and rushed Sin's back. Sin turned and hit the ground so that the demon would fall into the arms of the one who had bitten him. He uncoiled another string from his left arm, then rose and wrapped it around the throat of the female. She screamed an instant before her head fell free from her body.

Kat turned away and cringed at the grisly sight as bile rose in her throat.

The other two demons shrieked, then ran. Crossing his arms over his chest, Sin jerked the knives from his biceps and threw them straight into the backs of the fleeing beasts. The knives landed at the bases of their spines with an unerring accuracy. They fell instantly to the ground, where they writhed and screamed in agony.

After one last cry, they each went still. But continued to whine.

Kat was horrified by what she was witnessing. It was grisly and intense, and there was something about Sin that said he was enjoying it a lot more than he should. It was as if he took pride in inflicting as much pain on them as he could.

He's a sick bastard.

Sin watched the men for a few seconds more before he went to check on the human they'd been feeding from. But it was too late for her. Even from her distance, Kat could tell the human was dead as her glassy eyes stared up at the star-filled sky. Her entire body was ravaged from their kill.

The poor woman.

His face grim, Sin closed the woman's eyes and whispered an old Sumerian prayer for her soul to rest peacefully in spite of the violence that had taken her life. Kat was surprised by his actions. They seemed completely incongruous with everything she'd just witnessed from this man.

At least that was her thought until he retrieved a knife from the back of one of the demons. He made a ball of fire in his right hand to heat the blade, then once it was hot, he placed the blade over the bite wound on his hand. She cringed in sympathetic pain even though he didn't so much as whimper.

He merely stood there with his teeth clenched while the stench of burning flesh made her queasy.

But he wasn't through. Once his wound was cauterized, he went back to the human woman and then mercilessly cut her head from her body. Kat cringed in horror.

He's insane . . .

There was no other explanation. Why would he do something like that to their poor victim? It didn't make sense.

And still he wasn't through. He repeated the decapitation on the two male demons before he piled all the bodies together and burned them. His face completely stoic, he watched them burn. The flames illuminated his cold, emotionless features. The shadows darkened his eyes, making him look even more like a demon than the ones he'd killed.

He didn't speak a single word the entire time or show even a drop of compassion.

Once they were completely burned, Sin spread the ashes with the toe of his boot until there was no trace left of any of them. No one would ever know what had befallen the one poor woman.

Kat felt sick. How was it this man had been allowed to live given this kind of savagery? Did Acheron not know what Sin did at night? That he desecrated human remains? She couldn't imagine Acheron forgiving something so horrendous. It wasn't in his nature, any more than it was in hers.

Maybe, for once, Artemis was right. A man like Sin didn't need to be let loose on the world. He was too dangerous.

But before Kat went in there blazing to attack him, she needed to know what his powers were. From what she'd just seen, he could control fire and he was well versed with weapons and hand-to-hand tactics.

Taking him out would be tricky. Perhaps stasis would be a wiser choice. She could put him to sleep where he couldn't hurt anyone—it would be like death, only he would still be alive. Yeah, that might be her best bet instead of just outright killing him.

And while she contemplated his death, Sin headed for his coat.

He put it on with a flourish and then vanished into a shimmery mist.

Damn it!

Kat closed her eyes, trying to locate him again so that she could finish her mission.

But she felt nothing. No trace of him anywhere.

She frowned. How could that be? He had to have an essence, and that essence always left a calling card. She tried to locate him again, and again there was nothing. It was as if he were no longer part of the earth. She had no idea where he'd gone.

That had never happened to her before.

"Where are you, Sin?"

But the real question wasn't where he was. It was what he was doing . . .

CHAPTER TWO

Sin flashed himself back to his hotel room even though he could have just as easily taken himself home. Right now he didn't want Kish or Damien to bother him. He needed his space and time alone to prepare himself mentally for what he had to do.

He was coated in blood, and though there had once been a time when he would have reveled in it, those days were past. Now he was tired of the never-ending battles. Tired of fighting in a war he knew he couldn't really win.

There was only one person whose blood he wanted on his hands. One person whose blood would make him rejoice to feel its stickiness coating his flesh.

Artemis.

The mere thought of cutting her head from her body brought a smile to his face as he made his way into the bathroom for a long, hot shower.

After turning the water on, he dropped his weapons to the floor, where they landed with a heavy thunk, and stripped while he waited for the water to heat. As soon as it was scalding hot, he stepped inside and let the water rinse him clean. The fighting had left him gritty and covered with sweat and blood—his and theirs. Dipping his head down, he watched as all of it slid from his flesh to the tile and then circled down the drain.

The heat felt good against his sore muscles. But it did nothing to alleviate his troubled thoughts.

The Kerir or Reckoning, as some called it, was coming and he still had to find the Hayar Bedr or Forsaken Moon before the gallu demons found him and destroyed him. Without the Moon, Sin stood no chance whatsoever of beating them back.

Not that he had much of one even with the Moon, but that sliver was infinitely better than no hope whatsoever.

Sin ground his teeth as he envisioned the Kerir in his mind. At midnight on New Year's Eve as people rushed to celebrate, the seven Dimme demons that Anu had created to avenge their fallen pantheon would be freed. The only one who could fight them was Sin, and since he no longer possessed his god powers, he didn't have a hope in hell of succeeding in beating the Dimme back.

May the gods, ancient and new, have mercy on them all.

"Damn you, Artemis," he snarled. The stupid bitch. By one act of selfishness, she'd condemned them all. And she didn't even care. She thought her own godhood would protect her from the demons to come.

She was such a fool.

Why do you even bother? All fighting would do was prolong his own death. But it wasn't in him to just stand aside and do nothing while innocent people were killed. Do nothing while the earth was overrun and destroyed. No, he'd been fighting back the gallu demons for too many centuries to just cede the earth to them without taking out as many of them as he could.

They were hard kills, but the Dimme . . .

They would rip him apart and laugh while they did so.

Sighing, he turned the water off and reached for a towel. He paused as he saw the latest scar on his hand. Damn them for it. Unlike the Daimons the Greek god Apollo had cursed to live by stealing human souls, the gallu could turn humans into one of them. The poison in their bite could infect even Sin and make him a demon as well. It was why he had to burn the poison out every time it invaded his body. Why he had to make sure to behead the creatures and burn their bodies. It was the only way to completely destroy the poison and to keep them from regenerating.

They were prolific breeders. One bite, one blood exchange . . . that was all it took. They didn't have to kill humans to turn them into demons. But the gallu enjoyed the killing so much that they usually did it just for shits and giggles. Once infected, the deceased human quickly lost control of their id to the gallu, who could command the human to do anything they wanted. The humans then became mindless blood slaves.

Or worse.

Eleven thousand years ago, there had been designated warriors sanctioned by the Sumerian gods who had been trained to fight the gallu off. When the number of those warriors had fallen and they'd become all but extinct, Sin and his daughter and brother had trapped the gallu to keep them from preying on humanity. But over time, and after the death of the Sumerian pantheon, the gallu had begun working their way free of their prison. They'd also become smarter and more organized.

Now they were trying to find the artifacts Sin's brother had hidden to help awaken the Dimme, hoping that the Dimme would reward them for their loyalty. And the Dimme probably would.

Yeah, in three weeks' time it was seriously going to suck if you were human.

Sin towel-dried his hair. There was no use thinking about it tonight. He'd found the Tablet of Destiny. Tomorrow, he'd seek the Moon. Until then he needed a few hours of rest.

Completely naked, he tucked himself into the bed and tried to put the night out of his mind. But it was no use. He could picture the gallu gathering their forces. See them turning the humans into creatures like themselves. It wouldn't take them long to overrun the world. Mother would turn on child, brother on brother. Theirs was a blood hunger that knew no satiation. The ultimate weapon, they'd originally been created to combat the Sumerian pantheon's enemies.

Specifically, they'd been created to battle against the Charonte demons that Sin's father had been convinced would one day destroy them all. What his pantheon had never envisioned was the day when Atlantis would be destroyed and her Charontes along with her. With no other demons to keep them in check, the gallu had turned their attention and hunger on the humans.

They'd laid waste to entire cities before Sin, Ishtar, and Zakar had corralled them. Sin could still see the bodies of the slain humans rising up as mindless demons to fight.

But more than that, he could see his own children turning on him . . .

Sin growled as he banished those memories. They would do nothing but cut him more deeply. And he'd been cut enough. The past was gone.

He had a future to fight for and he'd need all his strength for it. Closing his eyes, he forced himself to think of nothing. To feel nothing. He couldn't let anything as petty as revenge or hate deplete him. He had too much to do.

K*at wandered through* the streets of New York, trying to get a bearing on Sin. He might not even be in the city anymore, but since he'd been here the night before, it was the most likely spot to search for him. A chill wind cut through her as she made her way through the holiday crowd.

Honestly, she loved visiting New York at Christmas. She could well understand her father's need to be in the city this time of year. True, it was cold, but there was a lifeblood here as people rushed through the streets, shopping, working, and living.

What she loved best was the decorated store windows and the fun themes their decorators chose. They were exquisite and made the hidden child in her giddy, especially when she saw other kids squealing in delight as they pointed to a window and then rushed to the next one, pushing past aggravated adults.

Kat had never been so carefree. Even though she'd been sheltered, her childhood had never been innocent. She'd seen things no child should see, and though she tried not to be jaded, it was hard not to be.

But those children who were laughing and giddy . . . the ones who had no idea how ugly the world could be—they were the ones she fought for. And those children were why she had to find Sin and stop him. He couldn't be allowed to prey on them.

Not after what he'd done last night to that poor woman. Why would he desecrate a human body? Kat still couldn't get over that. It hit her on a level so raw that she could do nothing but ache for the woman and her family, who would never know what had happened to her.

It was mean and it was awful. More than that, it was just wrong.

As Kat paused to let a little girl cross in front of her, a large man shoved her from behind. Kat scowled at him as he passed by her, mumbling to himself. He took one look at the child and hissed like a cat. Then he stared at the child speculatively . . . like a feral beast contemplating its next morsel.

But as he reached for the child, her mother snatched her back and chastised her for running away.

The man turned a hungry look on the pair that made Kat's blood run cold. It was unnatural. What's more, there was a flash of red in his eyes that wasn't human.

She'd never seen anything like it.

With one last sneer, he seemed to think better of attacking the mother and child before he continued on his way.

Curious about him and his intentions, Kat followed inconspicuously. If it weren't for the daylight shining so brightly, she'd think him a Daimon trying to find a human soul to steal to elongate his life. But that wasn't possible. Because of Apollo's curse on their race, none of the Daimons could come out so long as the sun was shining. If they did, they burst into flames.

What was he then?

More to the point, what pantheon did he belong to? If he wasn't human and he wasn't Daimon, some god had created him. The question was for what purpose?

Kat reached out with her powers, but all she could sense was his human spirit and his anger as he stumbled about.

Maybe he was simply insane . . .

He darted into a side street where there weren't any people. Something in her compelled her to ignore him and continue her search for Sin.

Kat didn't. It wasn't in her to just let such a thing go. If the man was up to no good, she was one of the few people who could stop him. She would never be like her mother and just ignore people's pain. Not when she could stop it.

So instead of walking on, she followed the man down the empty street. She didn't make it far before he turned on her with a feral snarl.

This time his eyes were a flaming red that swirled around his black pupils. He opened his mouth, showing her a double row of fangs before he grabbed her by the shoulders and threw her into the brick wall.

Stunned by his attack and appearance, she swung to hit him. He caught her hand, then grabbed her throat and shoved her back into the wall with a force so great, it rattled her to the marrow of her bones. Had she been human, it would have rendered her unconscious or dead.

As it was, it hurt like hell—and it seriously pissed her off.

"What are you?" she asked.

He didn't answer as he picked her up—something that was no small feat given the fact that she was six foot four and solidly built—and tossed her into a parked car so hard she bent the hood and popped the latch on it. The windshield shattered under her as the car alarm began wailing. She could barely breathe as she tasted blood in her mouth. Pain pierced her.

She tried to move, but her arm was broken and she seemed to be stuck in the bowed, shattered windshield. His eyes churning red, the man stalked toward her.

Just as he reached her, she saw something falling from the top of the building in front of her. Nothing more than a black blur, it hit the ground so hard, it splintered the concrete.

It took her a second to realize what it was, and what it was shocked her even more than the creature attacking her.

It was Sin, dressed all in black leather. Crouched low, he rose slowly to his feet, prepared for battle. His eyes were pinned on the man in front of her.

"Gallu," he said in a low, sinister tone. "Try picking on someone who can fight back."

The man left her to attack him. He swung at Sin, who raised an arm to catch the blow on his silver vambrace before he delivered a staggering blow to the man's chin. The man staggered back. Sin punched him hard in the chest, driving him back another step.

While the man wobbled from the blows, Sin pulled back his long coat to show a large dagger. The man came at Sin with his mouth open, trying to bite him. Sin dropped to the ground and swept the man's feet out from under him. The man hit the cement hard. Sin turned and drove the knife deep between the man's eyes.

The man screamed, writhing on the sidewalk as he flailed and kicked.

"Oh, shut the fuck up," Sin growled before he pulled the dagger out and stabbed the man again.

Kat slid off the car, cradling her broken arm, and before she could stop him, Sin decapitated the dead man and burned him right there on the sidewalk. She recoiled at the horror of it. They were in broad daylight and Sin didn't even seem to care.

Anyone could see this.

Before she could move, Sin was in front of her, grabbing her. "Are you bit?"

He didn't even look at her face before he started frisking her. She hissed as he touched her broken arm, but he didn't pause in his inspection.

When he pulled up her shirt to look at her stomach, she slapped his touch away. "Get your hands off me."

"Did he bite you?" he snarled, punctuating each word harshly.

It was then he looked up at her face and froze.

A heartbeat later, he grabbed her throat and started choking her.

CHAPTER THREE

Kat lifted her legs and kicked him back. Sin hit the ground with a *whoof* before he flipped to his feet and came after her again.

She pushed herself away from the car and ducked his hands, then sucked her breath in sharply as she hurt her arm—that only made her angrier. "Trust me, asshole, you don't want a piece of me."

His nostrils flared. "Oh yes, I do. I've been dreaming of strangling you for centuries."

What the hell did he mean by that?

All of a sudden, the sound of approaching sirens rent the air. Kat turned her head to listen, but the instant she did, he grabbed her.

This time when she went for him, he moved faster than was humanly possible. One moment they were on the street and in the next everything went black.

Sin smiled evilly as Artemis collapsed into his arms. It was true he lacked the bulk of his god-strength, but his brother had made sure after Artemis had drained him that he still had enough juice to protect himself.

Even against the gods.

He couldn't believe fate had been so kind as to throw the bitch right into his path . . . Now she was his and he was going to make her pay for what she'd done to him.

Smiling at the very thought, he flashed himself to his penthouse in Las Vegas. None too gently, he dumped his prisoner on his black leather sofa before he went to his bedroom to gather a few necessary items. Holding a goddess hostage was tricky business. Once she awoke she'd be pissed and wanting blood.

His blood.

Therefore, he'd need a few things to make sure she didn't use her powers to rip his heart out. Opening his closet, he moved to the back and shoved his clothes to one side. Hidden behind them was his vault. The door was made of tarnished bronze and held a hand and retinal scanner. Rather impressively modern, given the fact that he was an ancient Sumerian ex-god. But one had to make adjustments when one was locked in the hell that was the modern human world.

He opened the door and moved inside, where he kept the remnants of his own temple in Ur—what few things Artemis hadn't destroyed after she'd eliminated him. It wasn't much, a gold urn or two and the altar tray where his worshipers had once placed offerings. He'd also kept a few statues, but most of the vault's contents were taken from his daughter's temple in Ur. After her death, he'd tried to save anything that bore her image, and those were carefully preserved in the glass cases around him.

But that wasn't what had brought him here. What he sought rested in the far back corner, in a leather trunk that creaked eerily as he opened it. A sadistic smile curled his lips as he found the one item he'd saved all these centuries.

The *diktyon* that Artemis had used to tie him in place as she sucked his powers from him. Something in its composition rendered an immortal powerless. It kept them trapped and helpless.

He could still feel the humiliation of being at her mercy.

And once the bitch had drained him, she'd dumped him in the desert still wrapped in the net.

"Thanks for being so compliant. Now to pit the rest of your

pathetic pantheon against each other until they're all gone." Her laughter had rung in his ears.

Like a milk-whelp, he'd been forced to call out to his family for help. His father had laughed and then turned his back . . . as had all the others. The only one to show him pity had been his brother, Zakar. If not for him, Sin would still be lying in the desert.

Rotting or worse.

Of course their laughter had died out soon enough. Artemis had fulfilled her promise. Almost every member of his family had been disposed of by the Greek gods. The Greeks had either absorbed their powers and replaced them or turned them against one another until none were left. That had been three thousand years ago.

Now it was time to settle the score.

Grabbing the net, he headed for the couch where he'd left Artemis "sleeping".

She was still lying right in her spot, unconscious. Good. *You know, you could kill her right here. Right now . . .*

The temptation was strong. But then what fun would it really be? She was unconscious. She wouldn't feel it. Wouldn't know it. Besides, she was a goddess. To kill her while she still had her godhood would cause a rift in the universe.

The only way to destroy a god was to dispense or absorb their powers and then kill them.

Not to mention, he wanted to see her suffer. He wanted to look her dead in the eyes when he sucked her powers out and reestablished his godhood—wanted her to know the abject humiliation and pain of being completely vulnerable.

And that he could only do if she were awake and alive.

Damn.

With that in mind, he took his time cocooning her in the webbing. Let her be held down by her own weapon. It was only fitting. If he was lucky, she'd cry like a baby and beg for a mercy he had no intention of giving her.

Oh yeah, he could hear her now . . .

"Please, Sin, please let me go, I'll do anything."

"Bark like a dog."

She would, too. She'd be crying and hysterical. And he'd just laugh at her. He savored the very thought of it.

Sin paused as he secured her feet and glanced up at her face. To his deepest chagrin, he actually had to admit that she was beautiful—in a lethal, snake-like, venomous, bitch sort of way. In his murderous dreams, he'd forgotten exactly how graceful and attractive she was.

But here and now, he remembered things he'd buried three thousand years ago. He'd gone to her temple that day because she'd intrigued him. Granted goddesses were beautiful, but Artemis had been exceptionally attractive even by their high standards. She'd told him how lonely she was. How she wanted someone who understood her. He'd stupidly considered her a kindred spirit.

And like everyone else he'd ever known, she'd turned on him. Kindred spirit nothing. She'd laughed in his face and had reduced him to a pathetic immortal.

He didn't see anything beautiful about her now. But he did find it odd that she had blond hair instead of the vibrant red she was famous for. Maybe that was because she'd been in the human world and she was trying to pass as one of them for some reason.

Still, her body was the same. Tall, graceful, and well-built, she was put together like the goddess she was. Any man, immortal or otherwise, would kill to have access to a woman like this. And Sin remembered a time when he'd been so attracted to her that he would have done anything to make her happy.

Now all he wanted was to kill her.

"Hey, Sin?"

He paused as he saw his servant, Kish, coming into the room. Just under six feet tall, Kish appeared to be in his mid-twenties, but in reality the man was almost three thousand years old. Like Sin, he had jet-black hair and dark olive skin, only his hair, unlike Sin's, hung just past his shoulders.

Kish froze in place as he saw the woman on the couch. "Uh, boss, whatcha doing?"

"What does it look like I'm doing?"

Kish made a face as he scratched at the area right above his left ear. "It's looking pretty kinky. And here's where I should remind you that kidnapping a woman in this day and age, and in this country in particular, is a federal offense."

Sin wasn't amused. "Yes, and in your original time period it was a capital offense that resulted in the man's testicles being cut off before he was beheaded."

Kish jerked at the mention of castration and cupped himself. "Yeah, and so why are you kidnapping her?"

"Who says I kidnapped her?"

"The fact she's unconscious and tied up . . . fully clothed. I figure if it was really kinky and she was cooperating, she'd be awake and naked."

Kish did have a point.

He moved forward and looked more closely at her before he glanced back to Sin. "So who is she?"

"Artemis."

"Artemis who?"

Sin gave him a hard stare. "You know. Greek goddess bitch who stole my powers."

Kish let out a nervous laugh. "That's *the* goddess trussed up like a turkey on your couch. Are you insane?"

"No," Sin said as righteous fury drove him on. "I had an advantage and I took it."

Kish's face turned ashen. "And when she wakes up, we're both toast. Burnt toast. Charred toast. Whatever the hell is beyond charred, that's us." He moved his index finger back and forth between them to emphasize their coming doom. "She's going to kick both our asses. And no offense, I don't want my ass kicked by a goddess . . . well, Angelina Jolie in a black teddy and spiked heels notwithstanding. Angie-baby could drive those spiked heels all over me, but this . . ." He gestured toward Artemis. "This will get me painfully disemboweled, and that I'd like to avoid at all costs."

Sin shook his head at the man's hysteria. "Calm down before you wet my rug and I take a newspaper to you. She's not going to kick our asses. This net negates her powers. It's how she sucked me dry and left me humiliated."

Kish cocked his head as if he wanted to believe that but wasn't sure he should. "Are you sure about that, boss?"

"Positive. The *diktyon* was designed as a trap for gods and immortals. So long as she's held by it, we're fine."

Kish was still cringing. "I don't think 'fine' is the word I'd use in this situation. More like 'screwed' or 'dead' even. She's not going to be happy about this."

As if Sin gave a shit what she was or wasn't happy about. "Once I have my powers back, it won't matter. She'll be in no position to hurt either of us."

"And how are you going to do that?"

Sin had no idea. He honestly wasn't sure how she'd gotten them to begin with. After she'd given him nectar to drink in her temple, things had gotten fuzzy and he wasn't completely sure what all she'd done to him. His belief was that Artemis had sucked his powers out of him by drinking his blood. Personally, he didn't want to drink her blood—there was no telling what diseases the bitch might carry: rabies, distemper, parvo . . . But if it would reinstate him, he'd do it.

First he had to find out from her if a blood exchange would work.

He glared at his servant. "Don't you have something to do?"

"If not for the fact it would result in your breaking every bone in my body and making me cry for Mommy, I'd be calling some cops. As it stands, I think my neck is best served by trying to talk sense into you."

Sin clenched his teeth. "Kish, if you value your life, get out of here and stay out of here."

But the instant Kish took a step back, a feeling of dread consumed Sin. Kish was too panicked, and when panicked people always did incredibly stupid things—like call the cops on an immortal who didn't want to even begin to try to explain why he was holding a woman on his couch in a net.

Or worse, call Acheron, who would freak on Sin if he ever learned about this.

So Sin froze him in place.

Sin stared at Kish's statue with satisfaction. "Yeah, you chill and let me worry about this."

It was for the best and it would keep him from having to kill Kish later. And while Sin was at it, he sealed his door so that no one else could disturb him.

K*at came awake* with her arm aching. She tried to shift her weight off it, only to learn that she couldn't. A feather-light netting covered her. Unfortunately, it was a netting she knew all too well.

Artemis's *diktyon.*

Disgust consumed Kat over a prank that had grown old centuries ago when another of Artemis's handmaidens had thought trapping her like this was entertaining. Wouldn't the woman ever learn that Kat didn't find this funny?

"All right, Satara, stop with the stupid games and let me up."

But as Kat focused her eyes, she realized that she wasn't at home and Satara wasn't there, laughing at her.

Rather, there was a man, glaring his hatred at her. Again.

She let out a sound of deep aggravation. "What is your damage?"

"Simple. I want my powers back."

Of course he did. What god wouldn't want his powers back? But Lucifer's hell would freeze solid before she *ever* allowed a psycho like this to have even an inkling of power. "Yeah, well, tough shit."

He curled his lip. "Don't fuck with me, Artemis. I'm not in the mood."

"And neither am I, dumb-ass. In case you haven't noticed, I'm not Artemis."

Sin paused at her words and took a closer look at her. There were small things about her that were different. But the woman held the same green eyes. The same facial features. She was Artemis. He could feel the power emanating from her. "Don't lie, bitch."

She kicked at him, but he sidestepped it. "Don't you dare call me that, dickhead. I don't take that from anyone, least of all someone like you."

"Give me my powers and I'll gladly free you." And he meant that. Once he got his powers returned, he'd kill her and then she'd be free.

"Look, Brick Wall, I can't give you what I don't have. I. Am. *Not.* Artemis." She clipped each word as she spoke it.

He leaned over her so that she could see just how much contempt he held for her and her feigned conviction. "Yeah, right. Do you think I could ever forget the face that has haunted me for three thousand years? The face of the woman whose throat I want to cut?"

She literally snarled at him like a wild beast, "Get it through your head. I'm not Artemis."

"Then who are you?"

"My name is Kat Agrotera."

It was his turn to scoff. "Agrotera, huh?" He grabbed the netting over her chest and pulled her up so that they were eye to eye. "Nice try, Artemis. Agrotera means 'huntress'. Did you think I'd forget it was one of the names your followers applied to you?"

She struggled against his hold. "It's also the epitaph that's used by Artemis's *kori*—that would be me, you moron."

He laughed in her face. "You're one of Artemis's servants? How stupid do you think me? You fooled me once, but not twice."

Kat let out a long breath as frustration consumed her. She actually had the powers to break out of the netting. But if she did that, she'd give him a really big tip on how much power she had and who she really was. That was knowledge a creature like this didn't need to have.

No, it was better to make him think she was powerless and without consequence. "Believe it or not, I am."

He released her to fall back on the sofa before he gave her a repugnant glare. "Uh-huh. Artemis would never allow a *kori* near her who was her height. Nor one who had her eye color. She's too vain for that. *You're* too vain."

"If you want to be technical, I'm taller than she is. Didn't you remember that part?"

Sin hesitated. Honestly, he couldn't recall Artemis's exact height—it'd been too long since he'd last seen her. All he remembered was that she'd been over six feet tall. "I stand by what I said. Artemis would never allow a *kori* in her temple taller than her."

"News flash: She's mellowed with age."

Yeah, right. "Sure you have . . . just like me."

The woman leaned her head back and let out an irritated growl. "Look, you seem to have issues I don't want to even begin to know about. Let me go and we'll both forget this ever happened. If you don't, you're going to be real sorry."

He scoffed. "Not this time, Artemis. You're the one who's going to regret this. I want my powers back that you stole from me. You tricked my ass and then you stripped everything from me except my life, and you damn near took that."

Kat went rigid as his words pricked a deeply buried memory inside her. But it was fuzzy and fleeting, and she couldn't get a good handle on it, so she defaulted to what she remembered of the event.

"You were going to kill Artemis. She said you hated her . . . that you'd broken into her temple and tried to rape her and—" The words stopped as she realized the lie Artemis had told. How could a god from another pantheon have gotten into Artemis's temple on Olympus without an invitation?

It was something that hadn't dawned on Kat back then. She'd been too young and too afraid that he would hurt or kill Artemis. Back then, many of the gods had been at war with one another and those who policed them had been on hiatus. There had been many threats made against Artemis and several close calls.

But one thing would have been impossible. An outside god couldn't enter the domain of another without invitation.

Oh gods, it was another half-truth . . .

He screwed his face up at her. "What are you talking about? Have you lost your mind?"

"No," Kat said as a wave of guilt consumed her. "I'm not Artemis. Let me go."

"Not until I have my powers back."

This was getting annoying . . . "And for the last time, I can't give you what I don't have."

"Then you're going to stay in that net until eternity comes to pass."

She growled at him, "Well, that's really intelligent, isn't it? What are you going to do? Put drinks on me or just use me as a conversation piece whenever friends come over? And let's not even think about what's going to happen when I need to use the restroom, shall we? I hope you have a standing order at Sofa Express."

Sin wasn't sure if he should be entertained or appalled by her outburst. He had to give her credit, though, she certainly had a way with imagery. "Well, aren't you a wealth of sarcasm?"

"Oh, just wait. I haven't even started." She winced as she jostled her arm and pain must have shot through her shoulder.

Sin felt a prick of conscience over that and he hated himself for it. Let her suffer. What was it to him? Yet the part of himself that he despised most—the part that was still compassionate—begged him to help her.

But she was right. Her staying in that netting wasn't going to do either one of them any good. "Look, Artemis, or, assuming this isn't another of your lies and tricks, Kat, I have to have my powers back. It's imperative."

"Sure it is. You just want them back so that you can kill Artemis and take revenge on her."

"I'm not going to lie and say that's not true. It is. I want her dead in a way unimaginable. But I have bigger problems right now. And you just met one of them on that backstreet in New York."

Kat paused as she thought back to the creature she'd been fighting. It'd been scary all right. "I assume you mean that . . . thing that attacked me."

"Yes. The gallu demons are running rampant now and the Dimme are about to go free and I'm the only person alive who can push them back. If I don't have my powers to fight them, the world is going to end. You remember what happened to Atlantis? This is going to make that look like fun and games."

"No offense, old man, Atlantis was destroyed before I was born, so I don't remember squat about it."

But she did know the stories of how the continent sank.

She sat still for a moment, thinking. She knew Artemis wasn't trustworthy. But she didn't know if the same was true of Sin. Was he feeding her a line or was there truth to what he said? "What about those people last night? Why did you behead them and then burn them?"

She realized that was the wrong thing to ask as his eyes flared murderous rage at her. "You spied on me?"

"Artemis told me to, so yeah." His rage was so potent, she could honestly feel it filling up the air between them. "Don't look at me like that. I can spy if I want."

"And why did you spy on me?"

Kat squirmed a bit. Telling him that what Artemis had really wanted—his death—would most likely only piss him off more. So she opted for a more delicate explanation. "Artemis wanted to know what you were up to. She thought you were trying to kill her."

"Yeah, and as much as I want that bitch dead, right now I have bigger problems." He paused before he spoke again. "The reason I cut the heads off the gallu and burn them is that if I don't, they come back like a bad horror movie reject."

That at least explained part of it, but it didn't explain why he desecrated their victim. "Why did you do that to the human?"

"Why do you think? One bite from the gallu and their victim becomes a mindless demon they can control. Desecration is far kinder than what they do to humans like her. Whenever a human dies by their hands, they have to be slain and dusted or they'll be back, too."

Oh . . . No wonder he'd been frantically searching her for a bite wound before he'd knocked her out. "Is that why you burned your arm last night?"

He nodded. "If you can catch it early enough, you can cauterize the wound and stop the poison from spreading through your body."

Yeah, but that had to hurt and it made her wonder how many times he'd done that in the past. "Out of curiosity . . . does Artemis know about the gallu?"

"I don't know, Artemis. Do you?"

She sighed at his insistence that she was her boss. "I thought we'd gotten past this."

"Until I see conclusive proof, no. I stand by what I know about you, you bitch. Now give me my powers back."

Fury snapped through her veins at his denseness and insult. What was it going to take to make the man realize that she wasn't Artemis?

Break the net and then break his head . . .

That urge was so strong that it was all she could do not to yield to it.

"Katra?"

Kat jerked at the sound of Artemis's voice in her head.

"What's going on? Why are you so angry? Is Apollymi bothering you?"

Kat rolled her eyes. "Stop spying on me."

Sin curled his lip. "It's hard not to look at you sprawled out on my couch. Not to mention how funny that is coming from you given what you did last night."

She grimaced at Sin as she realized she'd spoken out loud.

"Katra? Tell me what's wrong or I'm coming to check on you. It's not like you to get this riled."

Now she's concerned about me? Kat didn't know what aggravated her more, being trussed up by a Sumerian ex-god or patronized by a Greek one.

Oh wait, the trussing definitely won this one out. It ranked right up there with eye gouging.

"It's all right, Matisera," she said silently to Artemis. *"I have it."*

"And why is it I find that hard to believe?" Artemis popped into the room right in front of Kat, hands on hips. Dressed in a long white sheath gown, Artemis wore her vibrant red hair down so that it flowed around her body.

Kat cringed as she realized what the goddess had just done.

Sin spun around. His jaw went slack as he took in Artemis's presence and realized that Kat hadn't been lying to him. Obviously, she wasn't the goddess after all.

To her credit, Artemis didn't panic. Instead she merely eyed him as if he were a mild annoyance. "Wow, look what the cow dragged in." She cast a penetrating glare at Kat. "Why is he here?"

Sin cursed as he realized he'd just been played by both of them. The handmaiden forgotten, he went for Artemis, but before he could reach her, the handmaiden somehow appeared before him.

How the hell had she gotten out of the net? He knew firsthand that it didn't give that easily. But that wasn't here or there.

What mattered was getting his hands on Artemis.

"Calm down," Kat said, cradling her arm.

He shook his head. "Move out of my way, girl. I won't be kept from what I want."

Artemis rolled her eyes. "And what do you want? Your mewling powers back?"

He lunged at her, but Kat caught him about the waist and slung him to the ground with a strength he'd never imagined a woman could have—especially considering the fact that she had a broken arm.

She landed on top of him.

Pushing her away, he growled, "I don't want to hurt you, but it doesn't mean I won't."

Kat glared at him. "Ditto."

He tried to move past her, but the woman was like Velcro. Kat attached herself to his body and kept him from reaching Artemis.

Artemis scoffed at their struggle. "Get out of the way, Katra, so I can zap him."

Sin paused as he finally calmed enough to realize something highly significant. He looked back and forth between Katra and Artemis.

And as he did so, he knew exactly how to get his upper hand back.

He pulled the long, ornate dagger out of its sheath in his boot before he grabbed Katra and held the blade to her throat. He cut a gimlet glare at Artemis. "Give me my powers back, Artemis, or I'll take your daughter's life."

CHAPTER FOUR

Kat cringed as Sin spoke a truth that only the bravest of souls would even dare whisper. And never within Artemis's hearing range.

Kat leaned back against him, away from the knife. "Damn, boy, you have an unholy gift for pissing off people." As was evidenced by Artemis's shriek of outrage. "Why don't you tell her that dress makes her look fat while you're at it?"

He answered by pressing the blade closer to Kat's throat. "I'm not playing, Artemis."

Artemis's face turned to stone. "And neither am I."

Before Kat could even blink, the dagger left her throat. She was pulled from Sin's arms by an unseen force an instant before the knife was ripped from his hand and plunged into his chest, three times. On the third time, it was left buried to the hilt where it slowly rotated in his chest.

Sin cursed foully before he jerked it out.

Kat held her hand up toward Artemis, trying to defuse the situation. "Matisera—"

"Stay out of this, Katra. Go home."

By the tone of Artemis's voice, Kat knew she should obey. But she couldn't stand by and let Sin die if what he'd said about the gallu was true. They couldn't be left without someone who knew how to fight them.

Artemis stalked toward him. "It's time I finish what we started."

Sin pushed himself up from the floor and ran at Artemis, but he didn't come close before he was slammed into a far wall. He growled, then slung his arm out.

Artemis went flying.

Kat took a step toward her mother to protect her. But before Kat could take two, Artemis's voice rang out. "Deimos!"

Kat came to a halt at the same time a large, fierce man appeared by Artemis's side. Dressed all in black, Deimos had short jet-black hair that was streaked with wide white stripes—a much different hairstyle than he'd had the last time they met. He was terrifying in appearance, especially with the tattoo that started out as a light eyeliner around his electric blue eyes and then zigzagged from his tear ducts down his cheeks to his neck. Beautiful and deadly, he stood before them with his legs braced wide apart, his head tilted low like a predator and his arms held at his sides, close to his weapons—one sword and one gun—ready to fight.

"Suck his powers out and kill him," Artemis snarled.

Kat gaped at the order. Once issued, it couldn't be taken back. Deimos was one of the most dangerous of the Dolophoni. A son of the dreaded Furies, he was the one the gods called out when they needed a relentless Terminator and he wouldn't stop until Sin was dead.

Deimos ran at Sin and slammed him to the floor.

"What have you done, Matisera?"

"What I should have done in the beginning." Artemis tried to flash Kat out of the room, but since Artemis had traded Kat's service to her grandmother, she didn't have that power anymore.

Kat's mother snarled at her, "Leave us, Katra. Now."

But she couldn't. She was the reason Sin was in this mess, and though he was giving Deimos a good fight, in the end she knew who would win it.

And it wouldn't be Sin.

Sin was fighting with one hand tied behind his back and three nasty chest wounds while Deimos could draw from the power of the entire Greek pantheon to kill him—it was one of many benefits bestowed on the Furies and their children. And though Sin might deserve to die, he didn't deserve death like this.

Not after what they'd done to him and not if what he'd said was true. They would need him to fight the demons of his own pantheon.

"Sorry, Matisera." Kat barely registered the confusion on Artemis's face before she ran at Sin. He was against the wall, fighting, while Deimos was pulling out his sword to finish him off. Kat grabbed Sin from the side and flashed them from his apartment to her own place in Kalosis.

They landed in a pile of twisted limbs in the center of her dark living room. Sin hissed before he pushed her away. Kat didn't go far. He was bleeding profusely, but what concerned her was the gaping wound his dagger had left. If he were mortal, that would have been fatal to him, and it was probably causing him enough pain right now that he was wishing it was.

She scooted herself toward him. "You need to be tended."

He glared at her. "Where are we? What did you do?"

"I kept you from dying."

He pushed her hand away from his wound. "Oh, believe me, I could have held my own."

Kat sat back on her legs. "Yeah, you were doing a real bang-up job of it. I particularly liked the way you were bruising his fists with your face. A few minutes more and I'm sure your heart would have been on the attack . . . after it was ripped from your chest."

He grimaced at her. "What do you know?"

"More than I want to most days."

Sin frowned at the catch in her voice as she spoke. It was apparent that she was weary, no doubt of Artemis and her machinations. They were enough to wear down even the stoutest of immortals.

And as much as he hated to admit it, she was probably right about him getting his ass kicked. He should have known better than to go up against Artemis without his full powers. It'd been stupid, and he was lucky the Dolophonos hadn't torn his heart out.

But he'd wanted his revenge, and nothing else, especially something as trivial as common sense, had mattered.

Katra moved forward and ripped his shirt open to expose the jagged wounds in his chest from the dagger Artemis had repeatedly planted there. He started to shove Kat away, but before he could, she manifested a cool rag in her hand so that she could clean the wounds. Her kindness made no sense to him whatsoever given her genetic makeup. Not to mention, he wasn't used to anyone helping him for any reason. Everyone he'd ever known had turned their backs on him and left him to suffer.

People weren't kind and he knew it. Not unless the act of kindness could benefit them in some way.

"Why are you helping me?"

She gave him a withering glare. "Who said I'm helping you?"

He arched a brow at her as he looked pointedly at her hand that was wiping away his blood.

She cleared her throat before she answered. "I don't like to see people get screwed over, okay?"

"And why don't I believe that? Oh wait, I know. Because you're the daughter of the biggest bitch who has ever lived. One who makes her entire life an event of screwing over anyone she comes into contact with."

"Would you stop saying that?" Kat said from between clenched teeth.

Like that would ever stop him. "She is a bitch."

"Not that, the other part. And actually you better stop saying both or I'm going to tend this wound with a salt poultice."

"Why? Aren't you proud of Mommy dearest?"

Kat's green eyes met his and they were smoldering. "I love my mother with everything inside me and I would kill or die to protect her. That's why you need to stop talking like that about her because I *will* kill you."

Sin paused as a frightening thought went through him. If Katra was Artemis's daughter . . .

He could remember Artemis pulling him toward her bed as his head was fuzzy from drink. She'd torn his shirt from him and then thrown him down on her mattress.

Artemis was supposed to be a virgin . . .

An awful feeling went through him. "Oh shit, you're my daughter, aren't you?"

Kat screwed her face up as if that was the most repugnant thought she could imagine. "Don't flatter yourself. Your genes could never have created me."

Yeah, right. She was beautiful and tall—taller than Artemis, which could easily have come from him. Her skin was a darker hue . . . His stomach shrank in trepidation. "Then who's your father if it's not me?"

"That's hardly any of your business."

"It is me, isn't it?"

She rolled her eyes at him before she knitted his wounds closed with her fingers. "Men and their egos. Trust me. My mother wouldn't have you in her bed even if you were dipped in chocolate-coated caramel."

Oh, now that really offended him. "Excuse me? I'll have you know I happen to be damn good in bed. My skills are unsurpassed. I wasn't just a god of the moon. I was *the* Sumerian god of fertility. You know what that means, don't you?"

"You have a lot of penis envy over the other fertility gods?"

He shoved her hands off him, then started to get up only to wince and fall back.

"Don't worry. I won't tell the other gods about your small penis problem."

She appalled him. "You *are* your mother's daughter."

"And I told you to stop saying that."

"Why?"

"Because no one's supposed to know about me."

He scoffed at the anger in her tone. "What are they? Blind? You look just like her."

"No, I don't. I look mostly like my father. I only have my mother's eyes. How you guessed it is beyond me."

There was no surprise there, either. "You have the same voice."

Kat pulled back and frowned. "Do I?"

"Yes. The accents are different, but the tone of it isn't. You sound just like her."

Kat pushed herself to her feet and moved away from him, disturbed by his disclosure. He was highly perceptive. Something most men weren't. Then again, people in general weren't normally that perceptive, and it made her wonder if anyone else had ever picked up on the similarities in her and Artemis's voices. If they had, they'd been smart enough to keep it to themselves.

"Thanks for the help," Sin said, indicating his mended chest before he repaired his shirt with his powers. Then he tried to leave her house by flashing out only to learn that he couldn't. "What the . . . ?"

Kat shrugged at his angry glare. "You have to stay here."

"Bullshit," he growled.

"No, no shit here," she said, indicating her clean floors with her hand. Then she cupped her broken arm to her chest. "You leave this place and you're a dead man. Trust me. The moment you spoke that which will not be spoken and my mother called out the Terminator to destroy you, your death warrant was signed."

Every part of him bled fury. "I won't be held hostage. You understand?"

She laughed at his righteous indignation. "Oh yeah, right. This from the man who knocked me out and then bound me up like a mummy? What was that action?"

"That was different."

"Yeah, only 'cause I was the victim. Oh wait, you're right. I'm doing this to protect you and you did yours to kill me. Maybe I should let you leave. It would serve you right."

"Then why don't you?"

She took a breath to calm herself before she spoke. Anger accomplished nothing and she knew that. It was what had gotten her mother into more messes than an entire crew of Molly Maids could get her out of. "Because I want the truth about what happened the night you came to Olympus. Artemis said that you tried to rape her."

He made a choking noise as if touching Artemis was the worst thing he could imagine. "And what do you think?"

"I don't know. You haven't exactly shown me any high moral fiber here. Maybe she's right and you did."

He moved to stand in front of her. His eyes practically glowed gold in the light as he raked a disgusted look over her. "Trust me, baby. I've never had to force myself on any woman. But let's say, for argument's sake, that I did. Do you think me dumb enough to try it on Olympus under the noses of the other gods?"

He had a point, but she wasn't about to let him know that. "You're arrogant enough. You might."

"Yeah," he said in a low, feral tone, "arrogant but not stupid."

"Then why were you there?"

His features blank, he moved away from her, which made her wonder what he was hiding. There was something about that night that he didn't want to even think about—she could feel it.

"Answer my question."

"It's none of your business," he snapped. "Now if you'll excuse me." He started for the door.

Kat held her hand up and clenched her fist. The door immediately vanished. "I wasn't kidding. You can't leave."

The next thing she knew, she was lifted from her feet and pinned to the wall. "And neither am I. Let me out of here or you will regret it."

She shook her head slowly. "Kill me and you'll never get out." She felt the pressure holding her to the wall increase before it set her back on the floor with a gentleness that surprised her. "Thank you."

He narrowed his eyes on her. "I have to get out of here. There's less than three weeks to Armageddon and I have a lot to do to prepare for it."

"Yeah, and right now I have a broken arm that needs to be tended. So I tell you what. You sit here contemplating Artemis's murder and Armageddon, and I'll be back in a few. But don't break or touch my stuff . . . or I'll take it out of your hide."

He opened his mouth to speak, but before he did, she flashed herself out of her small house and into the main palace of Kalosis.

Kat manifested in the main foyer and had to take a moment to locate her grandmother with her thoughts. As was typical of her grandmother, Apollymi was outside, in her garden.

Out of respect, Kat walked the short distance through the throne room to the gilded doors that opened out onto the grounds. Her grandmother didn't like for people to pop in on her unexpectedly—Kat was the only one who knew why. Once as a child, she'd done that and caught her grandmother weeping hysterically in grief and pain—it was something Apollymi couldn't stand for other people to see.

As the Great Destroyer, she only wanted people to see her strong and ruthless. But Kat's grandmother was much more than just that. She had a heart and she ached, just like everyone else in the universe.

All Apollymi wanted was to have her son, Kat's father, returned to her. A son she'd loved more than anything and one she'd only held twice in her life. Once briefly when he'd been taken prematurely from her to be hidden in the womb of another woman and on the day the Greek god Apollo had killed him.

There wasn't a day Apollymi didn't mourn their separation and ache for her son to come home. And she reacted harshly to anyone who caught her weeping. She was a strong, proud woman who didn't believe in showing any weakness to anyone.

Not even her own granddaughter. But Kat could feel Apollymi's sadness and grief in all its harsh bitterness. Kat's father's empathy was one of many things she'd inherited from him. It was why she would never embarrass Apollymi or anyone else if she could help it.

So Kat approached slowly, just in case Apollymi needed time to compose herself. There was a light breeze whispering by. The garden itself was surrounded by high black marble walls that shone so much they reflected images like mirrors.

Apollymi sat on a black chaise with her back to Kat. Two Charonte demons, a male and a female, flanked the chaise. The male demon was dressed in a loincloth that left the whole of his lean, muscular body bare. His skin was a pale maroon that had yellow mingled with it. His eyes were as black as his hair and wings. The female was orange and red in skin tone and dressed in a black leather halter top and shorts. Her hair was a dark brown bob that only emphasized the sharpness of her features and the redness of her eyes. The demons were as still as statues, but Kat knew they were highly aware of her presence and watching her every move.

Dressed in a black flowing gown that left her shoulders bare, Apollymi cradled a small pillow in her lap. It had been a gift that Simi, Acheron's personal Charonte demon, had brought to her years ago. And because it held Acheron's scent Apollymi kept it ever near her so that she could feel closer to the son she could never touch.

Kat's grandmother was absolutely beautiful and appeared completely serene. With long white blond hair and swirling silver eyes, she didn't appear any older than her mid-twenties. Her pale skin was luminescent, and small drops of glitter sparkled in her hair.

She turned her head slightly to greet Kat, but Apollymi's welcoming smile turned to a frown as she saw Kat's broken arm. "Child," she breathed, moving from her chaise. She placed the pillow on her seat before she crossed the short distance to Kat so that she could inspect her arm. "What happened?"

"I got caught in the cross fire."

"If that bitch Artemis—"

"Please!" Kat said between clenched teeth. "Enough with everyone insulting my mother. Am I the only one in existence who loves her?"

Apollymi arched a brow. "Of course you are. Everyone else sees her for what she is."

Kat growled at her, "Be that as it may, if not for her you wouldn't have me. So could we please not insult her and just make my arm better, okay?"

Apollymi's features softened instantly. "Of course, my baby." Apollymi touched Kat's shoulder and immediately her arm was cured.

Kat took a breath in gratitude as the pain finally receded. She'd inherited her grandmother's healing powers, but unfortunately, they didn't work on herself. Only on other people. Which really sucked when she couldn't get to her grandmother for comfort. "Thank you."

Apollymi smiled, then kissed her lightly on the forehead before she fanned Kat's long blond hair around her shoulders affectionately. "I haven't seen you in a while, *agria*. I've missed you."

"I know and I'm sorry about that. Time tends to get away from me."

Sadness darkened Apollymi's eyes as she patted Kat on the shoulder before she stepped away. "I wish I could say the same."

Yeah, it was hard on Kat's grandmother to be trapped here in what had once been the Atlantean hell realm. Eleven thousand years ago, Apollymi's entire family had banded together to imprison her, and so long as Acheron lived, Apollymi could never be free.

Kat felt deeply for the solitude her grandmother suffered from even though Apollymi commanded an entire army of Daimons and Charontes. They still weren't her family and they didn't make her happy.

"How are things with Stryker?" Kat asked. Stryker was Apollo's son and he now led the Daimon army Apollymi controlled. When Apollo had cursed the Apollite race to die on their twenty-seventh birthday, he'd unknowingly cursed his own son and grandchildren to die as well. Since that day, Stryker had hated his father and had plotted his destruction.

The only reason Stryker was still alive was because Apollymi had seized the opportunity to make Stryker her adopted son so that she could use him against Apollo and Artemis. For centuries the two of them had been united in their hatred against the Greek gods.

Then three years ago, after a rough confrontation between the two of them, Stryker had begun turning against Apollymi. It appeared to be an unending battle of one-upmanship.

Kat's grandmother laughed angrily. "We are at war, *agria.* So he sits in the next building, plotting my death as if I'm too stupid to know it. What he forgets is that far better men than he have tried to kill me and while I may be in prison, they are dead—which will be his fate once he grows enough nerve to openly attack me. But that's not why you're here, is it?" She took Kat's hands in hers. "What has you troubled, precious one?"

There was no need to sugarcoat her inquiries and Kat was nothing if not blunt. "Have you ever heard of a gallu demon?"

The two Charontes hissed vehemently the instant the word "gallu" left her lips. Kat's eyes widened at their unexpected response. She'd never seen them do that before, or even anything similar to it.

"Relax," Apollymi said soothingly to her bodyguards. "There are no gallu here."

The male demon spat on the ground. "Death to the Sumerians and all their progeny."

Apollymi let out a deep breath before she released Kat's arms and walked her away from the Charontes. "The gallu were created by Enlil, the leader of the Sumerian gods, to fight and kill the Charonte demons back in the day when the Charontes roamed the earth freely." That explained the unexpected hostility. "Needless to say, the Charontes can't stand even the mention of those disgusting creatures. Now why do you ask of them?"

"Do you know what has become of them?"

Apollymi nodded. "After I destroyed Atlantis and the gallu no longer had the Charonte to fight, they turned on the humans and on their creators. Eventually, three of the Sumerian gods united and locked them away such as was done to me."

"And the Dimme? What are they?"

Apollymi gave her a suspicious frown. "Why do you ask of the Dimme?"

"I was told they're about to go free and destroy everything."

A peaceful, dreamy look appeared on Apollymi's face as if she was relishing the mere thought of the bloodbath to come. A slow smile curved her lips. "That would be a beautiful sight, truly."

"Grandma!"

"What?" she asked as if offended by Kat's tone. "I'm a goddess of destruction. Tell me honestly that you find nothing exciting about the idea of a billion people screaming out for mercy and help when there's no one left who cares what befalls them. Of the entire earth being rained on by all manner of demons bent on ultimate torture and sacrifice. Them ripping and shredding human flesh as they claw in a drunken frenzy fueled by their hatred of everything. Drinking blood in an orgy of terror . . . ahhh, the beauty of annihilation. There's nothing like it."

Kat would have been appalled had it not been a very typical thought for her grandmother. "And I'm, well, not technically a goddess since I don't belong to a single pantheon, but I follow after my father, who likes to protect mankind, and I really don't want to see a bunch of demons eating people. Call me sentimental."

Apollymi made a noise of extreme dissatisfaction. "That's the only thing I detest about your father. You two are, what is that human word you use . . . wimps."

"Hardly. Dad and I can more than hold our own."

Apollymi gave an uncharacteristic snort that Kat decided to ignore.

"And you still haven't answered my question," Kat pressed on in spite of her grandmother's ill mood. "What are the Dimme?"

Now the goddess was irritated, which was manifested in her grabbing one of the sweet black pears that grew on black-barked trees of her garden. She crushed it in her hand. "They're Anu and Enlil's final revenge on us all. While the gallu may be seen as the atom bomb that negated my Charontes, Anu created the Dimme as a nuclear holocaust."

Kat wasn't sure what she meant. "How so?"

"The Dimme are seven demons unlike anything you can imagine. They are uncontrollable, even for the gods. They're so dangerous that the Sumerians never even dared release them. From the moment they were created, they were put in a cell that has a time release. Every few millennia, whatever is holding them weakens. If the Sumerian gods are still alive, they reseal the seven demon sisters and life goes on as normal. But should something happen to the pantheon and there be no more Sumerian gods to reseal their tomb, the Dimme are unleashed on the world to destroy it and whatever pantheon is in charge. It's Anu's last laugh against whoever killed him and his children."

So Sin hadn't been lying . . .

It made Kat's stomach ache to think of what the seven demons could be capable of. She already knew what the typical monsters could do. And the Charonte. There was no telling what the Dimme would be like. "Don't you think that harsh?"

Apollymi gave her an arch look. "I only wish I'd thought of it myself."

Kat shook her head. She didn't know why Apollymi hated her mother so much, since the two of them were pretty darn close in personality—and thought similarly on most topics.

Apollymi licked the sweet juice from her fingertips. "But that doesn't explain why you're asking me all this, child. What about the Sumerians has you so curious when you've never asked about them before?"

"Well, right now, I have their last survivor locked in my house."

Apollymi went rigid. "You what?"

"Sin's in my house, down the street."

Apollymi's swirling eyes began to glow—something they only did when she was highly agitated. "Have you lost your mind?"

Before Kat could defend her decision, Apollymi vanished.

Kat cursed. There was no doubt in her mind where her grandmother had gone. Aggravated, too, Kat flashed herself back to her house.

Sure enough, Apollymi was there and Sin was pinned to the wall.

"Grandma."

"Back off," Apollymi snarled.

Kat was stunned by her response. Not once in all her life had Kat's grandmother ever raised her voice to her. The next thing she knew both Sin and Apollymi were gone.

What in the name of Zeus was going on? Kat closed her eyes but couldn't find any trace of them.

They had to be at the palace and there was no telling what Apollymi was doing to Sin. But whatever it was, it was sure to be bloody and painful.

And that was what Apollymi did for people she *liked.*

CHAPTER FIVE

Sin cursed as he landed on his side in the center of what appeared to be a Charonte feast. There had to be at least a hundred Charontes present . . . and they were all staring at him in silence as he lay on the cobblestone floor in front of them. There was no sound whatsoever except for the occasional whisper of a Charonte wing.

The room reminded him of a medieval great hall with arched rafters and exposed beams. The stone walls gave the place an eerie chill that didn't seem to faze the half-naked Charonte who were eating everything from roasted pig, to cows, to things he couldn't even begin to identify.

"Is he for us to eat?" one of the young male Charonte asked an older one.

Before Sin could stand or respond, Apollymi appeared on the other side of the main banquet table beside the adult male Charonte the boy had spoken to.

Her silver eyes swirled violently as she stared at him. "Tear his worthless Sumerian hide to shreds."

"Sumerian?" the adult male snarled.

Sin cursed. Yeah—his being Sumerian to this group would go over like an Ozzy Osbourne/Marilyn Manson duet at the Southern Baptist Convention's annual meeting. He might as well be wearing a shirt that said "Kibbles and Bits", with a heavy emphasis on the "bits" part.

Sin pushed himself to his feet in expectation of the death that was about to run him over. "Look. Can't we all just get along?"

"Ekeira danyaha," a female spat, which was the obscene version of "screw you" in Charonte.

Suddenly a male Charonte came at his back. Sin caught the demon and flipped him to the ground. But before he could punch him, another demon bit Sim in the shoulder. Hissing in pain, he head-butted the demon, knocking him back. Sim's shoulder was ripped open as the demon fell away.

A woman ran at Sim then. He picked her up and tossed her at the next two men who were coming for him. "Where's a damn can of Raid when you need it," he growled as another demon caught him from behind.

He dropped all of his weight, which didn't do a damn thing, since the demon was so strong. Changing strategies, Sin kicked his legs back against the demon's knees. The demon shrieked in pain before he released Sin. He swung around and caught the demon a blow to the rib cage.

"Stop!"

Sin staggered back as the demons actually obeyed the order. He saw Kat standing to his right, staring in horror at what had happened.

"Do not interfere in this," Apollymi snarled.

Kat shook her head. "I won't let him die. Not like this and not without an explanation."

"Explanation?" Apollymi pushed past the male demon before her to approach her granddaughter. "I went to his pantheon and asked them to help me hide your father so that my pantheon wouldn't kill him. Do you know what they did?"

"They laughed," Sin said, remembering the tales of that event clearly in his mind.

Apollymi turned on him with her nostrils flared. He was amazed she didn't use her powers to splinter him against the far wall. Obviously a quick death wasn't what she had in mind—she wanted long-term pain. "My son suffered as no one should *ever* suffer and I want to return that to you . . . tenfold."

He could understand that. Hell, he could even respect her sentiment, but it didn't change the fact that he was innocent in this. "I didn't turn you away, Apollymi. I wasn't there that day. I swear, I would have helped you had I known. By the time I heard about it, it was too late."

"Liar!"

"It's not a lie," he said calmly as another demon inched closer to him. He swallowed as he remembered his own bitter childhood. He'd been one of triplets. Within an hour of his birth, it'd been foretold that he and his brothers would cause the end of their pantheon.

The sad thing was, the prophecy had been correct. But it hadn't been what his father had feared. It'd been the jealousy and hatred of his own family that had ultimately killed them. Their own actions had caused Sin to be the weak link that had allowed Artemis in so that the Greek gods could turn the Sumerians against one another and defeat them.

His pantheon had fallen only after he'd ceased to be a god, and his surviving brother had gone into hiding.

And when Sin spoke, his voice was thick with that grief. "My father killed my own brother over prophecy and he damn near killed me. I would never have allowed another child to suffer for such stupidity. *That* is not in me."

Kat frowned at his words as she saw the pain on her grandmother's face and heard the sincere emotion in Sin's voice. He really meant what he said.

"And how do I know you're not lying to me now?" Apollymi demanded.

"Because I've lost my children, too, and I know the ache that lives inside the heart that no amount of solace or alcohol will squelch. I know what it's like to have the powers of a god and to not be able to hold the one thing that means the most to me. And if you think for one minute that I would *ever* serve that to another being, even Artemis, who I'd like to torture for eternity, then go ahead and call down your army on me. I would deserve whatever death they give."

Kat swallowed as she saw the utter agony in his eyes as he spoke of his children and their loss. This was a man who felt that tragedy to the depth of his soul. It was enough to bring tears to her eyes, and it made her heart soften toward him. No one should hurt like that.

Apollymi stood as still as a statue. Her gaze was haunted and her skin was pale.

Sin backed the approaching demon up with nothing more than an angry glare before he spoke again. "I consider Acheron one of my very few friends, Apollymi. I would never have seen such a decent man hurt for any reason."

Still Apollymi didn't speak, but she did finally move. She came down from the dais with a regal grace. She moved to stand just before Sin. Without a word, she reached out and touched his bleeding arm and shoulder, which were instantly healed.

When she finally spoke again, her voice was only a whisper, but it held enough power to be heard plainly by all. "My son has few friends and even fewer who know him for what he is. So long as you protect him, you live. Sumerian or not. But if you prove false in anything you've said here today, I will bring a wrath down on you so severe that you will spend eternity trying to dig out your own brains to alleviate the pain of it."

He glanced past her to Kat. "Now I know where you get your gift for imagery."

Kat stifled a smile. Only Sin and her father would be able to find humor at a moment like this.

Apollymi ignored Sin's comment. "Katra." She spoke without looking at her. "He is your guest in my world. Take him from here and make sure he doesn't wander into those who would kill him."

"But I thought we could eat him," the little boy Charonte whined.

Apollymi turned a gentle look to the child. "Another day, Parriton."

Parriton pouted as Kat came forward to take Sin. "Can I just have a little bite of him, *akra*?"

Kat laughed at his eagerness. "Another day, Parriton, I promise."

The boy gave an exaggerated sigh before he went back to his steak.

Kat paused before Sin and held her hand out to him. She half-expected him to refuse, but instead he wrapped his large hand around hers so that she could flash him back to her house. A strange thrill went though her at the sensation of his touch. There was an indescribable power that was innate to him. An inner peace.

At least until they were back in her living room.

He released her hand and gave her a droll look. "Wow," he said, his tone flat. "That was fun. Anyplace else you want to take me while we're here? Maybe there's a darker corner of hell than that hall of flesh-hungry demons, huh?"

Kat smiled at his sarcasm. "There is the Daimon hall. I'm sure Stryker would love to lay fangs on you."

He scoffed at her threat. "Stryker's a pussy. I'd have him wetting his pants three seconds after seeing me."

His bravado only amused her more. "Yeah, right. I heard he kicked your ass last time you met." Not true, but she felt the need to tease him.

"Bullshit."

"No," she taunted, moving closer to him with her hands on her hips, "serious shit. It's all over the Dark-Hunter bbs how he mopped the floor with you and then laughed while you bled."

"Says who?"

Kat froze as she realized she'd unknowingly walked right up to him during their mock fight. Now they were so close that she could feel his breath on her face.

He was tall and sexy. There was no denying it. And those eyes . . .

She could see to eternity in those sharp, golden eyes that were fringed with thick, dark lashes. What's more, she was suddenly enticed with the texture of his skin. There was something electrifying about a man's jawline. Something edible. And it beckoned her to want to touch him.

Sin stood completely still as his gaze focused on her parted lips. Kat had a beautiful mouth that complemented her pale features, and a sudden burst of desire pierced him. She really was beautiful all over. Her skin was so smooth and pale. Her eyes bright and intelligent.

The more he got to know her, the less like her mother Kat appeared.

And it'd been a long time since he'd been around a woman who dared to stand up to him, never mind openly taunt him. A long time since he'd felt such heat in his loins.

Before he knew what he was doing, he dipped his head down to kiss her.

Kat shivered at the sensation of his lips on hers. She'd never had a real kiss before. Between her mother and her grandmother, Kat had been guarded and watched to the point that no man had ever really been alone with her.

At least not for long.

She'd always wondered what a tender kiss would feel like. And she had to say that Sin's didn't disappoint. His lips were soft and demanding, his body hard against hers. She wrapped her arms around his neck, drawing him closer to her. Oh, it was heaven all right. Wonderful and warm. Hypnotizing. Oh yeah, she could stay here for a while.

Until he was suddenly ripped out of her arms and thrown against the far wall. Sin cursed as he was held six feet above the floor.

"Keep your lips and other body parts to yourself or you'll be headless."

Kat laughed at the sound of her grandmother's booming voice in the room an instant before Sin was slammed to the floor so hard, she could hear his bones rattle.

He let out a disgusted sigh. "I swear I'm getting my powers back if for no other reason than to—"

"Sh," Kat said, interrupting him. "Be careful, she can hear you."

He rolled himself over and leaned his head back to look at Kat from the floor. She didn't know how such a pose could be sexy, but somehow he managed it. "How do you have a social life?"

"I don't."

"Yeah," he said as he rose to his feet. "I imagine Ash is even tougher on you than they are."

Sadness filled her at the mention of the father she would give anything to know. But the truth was, her mother had kept them apart and while it hurt Kat, she understood the reason and complied even though the daughter in her didn't want to. Honestly, their separation was the thing she regretted most in life. "Not really. My father doesn't know about me."

Sin was stunned by the news. If he knew anything about Acheron, it was that the man would be furious to learn he had a grown daughter no one had told him about. "How the hell have you kept that from him? He knows everything."

Kat shrugged. "Most everything. He can't see those who are closest to him, and since I share a genetic link, I'm a ghost to his vision. My mother hid me from him first and then my grandmother joined in once she realized that giving him the knowledge of me would only hurt him more . . . and it would give my mother another tool to use against him. Believe me, it's much better for everyone if he never learns I exist."

That made sense, but still it wasn't right. Personally, he'd kill anyone who would keep such a thing from him. "And none of you thought about how wrong you were?"

"What do you mean?"

"Ash will die if he ever learns he has a child that he has never seen, especially since you're grown."

"That's why he can never know and why you have to stop referring to Artemis as my mother. As far as anyone is concerned, I, like all the other handmaidens, was a foundling that Artemis raised."

Sin shook his head. Damn, with the exception of losing a child, he couldn't imagine anything worse than to have a child he didn't know about. Acheron deserved so much better than this. "You three have really done a number on him. Does anyone else know?"

"Just you, Simi, and us. And I'm depending on you to not say anything."

"Don't worry about me. I don't want to be the messenger he kills in anger." He gave her a devilish smile as he relished an image of Ash blasting Artemis into oblivion. "You know, there is a bright side to this. Sooner or later he's going to find out about you, and when he does he'll kill Artemis for me. I just hope I'm there to see it."

She gave him a peeved look that somehow managed to make his groin jerk. "Very funny. He would never hurt her."

"Yeah, I know. Damn it to hell," he said in a low tone. "Bastard is still in love with her. There's something seriously wrong with him."

"No," she said softly. "He's not in love with her anymore. I would know it if he was. I'm not sure if he was ever anything more than infatuated by her. But he understands her and it's not in his nature to hurt anyone if he can help it."

Sin snorted in disagreement. He'd seen Ash break loose on a few people over the centuries, which was one of the reasons Sin didn't push the Atlantean god too far. And those were for minor encroachments. Sin couldn't imagine how much fury Ash would unleash over something this major. "You don't know him as well as you think you do."

"And what makes you the expert?"

"Let's just say I understand betrayal. And having been where he is, I know the explosion to come. Trust me. 'Duck' won't quite cover it."

She tensed at his warning. "Artemis didn't betray you."

"Who said I was talking about her?"

Kat paused as she tried to read him, but Sin was anything but an open book. Even his emotions were hidden from her. Normally she could tell what anyone near her was feeling, and though she got twinges from him, it was nothing like what she normally felt. It was baffling and strange to be so clueless. "Who betrayed you then?"

He folded his arms over his chest. "That's the thing about betrayal. You don't really want to talk about it, especially not with strangers who are related to your worst enemy." He looked around the room before he spoke again. "So where does all this leave us anyway? You plan on keeping me here until after the gallu unleash the Dimme or what?"

That seemed to be the question of the day. She truly wasn't sure what she should do with him. "You're not lying about the Dimme, are you?"

He pulled his shirt off, over his head, to show her a body that was riddled with scarred muscles. Some of the scars appeared to be claw marks, while others were clearly from bite wounds and burns. "Do I look like I'm joking?"

No. He looked more battle scarred than an ancient warrior. A tremor of sympathy went through her. It was obvious he'd been fighting a long time to keep humanity safe.

And he'd been doing it for the most part alone. No one at his back.

That hurt her most of all. No one should face such a nightmare alone. "What can I do to help?"

He cocked a brow at her question as if he couldn't believe her offer, before he put his shirt back on. But that look was quickly replaced with one that was hard and bitter. "Send me back to my place and stay out of my way."

Kat shook her head. How could she have forgotten the fact that he was a prehistoric macho god? "This is where I should probably remind you of a certain Greek blood hound who has your name and calling card. Remember him? Demon isn't exactly into making friends or showing mercy. But one thing he has to do is listen to me."

"And why is that?"

She gave him an amused grin. "Because I once kicked his butt so well that he remembers it to this day." She approached him with a determined stride. "You need someone at your back."

His look was cold and frightening. "No offense, but the last time I was dumb enough to let someone stand there, they stabbed me in it. I like to think I learn from my lessons."

"Not everyone is treacherous."

"My experience says otherwise, and given your genetic link to someone who did me seriously wrong, I think you'll forgive me if I don't put you on the list of trusted friends."

He was right about that, but she was nothing like her mother. "I'm my father's daughter, too."

"Yeah, and by your own admission you've had a lot less contact with him than with your mother. So I think you'll understand if I side with caution on this one."

She couldn't blame him for his suspicion. How could she when she didn't trust her mother, either?

His look sharpened. "I need to get out of here, Kat. I can't do my job while I'm stuck in a nether realm."

"And I can't let you out of here until I know what your plans are."

He let out a disgusted breath. "To stop the annihilation of mankind and the earth. It's a simple plan really, but an important one. Can I go now?"

Part of her was amused, but the other part wanted to choke him for his obstinacy and secrecy. "Why do you need the Tablet of Destiny?"

He closed the distance between them so that he could stare down at her with those golden eyes snapping fire at her. "Let me out of here, Katra. Now."

"I can't."

"Then I hope you can live with the death of humanity on your conscience." He indicated her sofa with his thumb. "I'll just sit myself over here until it's over. You got any good DVDs I can watch? It'll help drown out the screams for mercy. Especially from the kids. Those are always the hardest to ignore."

His words cut her on the most fundamental level of her humanity. The last thing she could stand was the thought of a child suffering. He was hitting below the belt and it hurt. "Damn you."

His features turned to stone. "You're too late. Your mother already did that."

Kat looked away as she struggled with what she should do. She couldn't keep him if what he said was true, but then how long could he last with Demon on his tail? He didn't have his god powers and Demon was a fierce SOB.

"Do you understand what you're up against?"

He gave her a duh-stare. "If something as pathetic as a Greek Dolophonos can take me down in a fight, I deserve to die."

"What will happen to mankind then?"

"Guess they're screwed, huh?"

How could he be so cocky and lackadaisical? He knew what he was up against. Did he really think he could win without someone fighting beside him?

She couldn't stand the thought of him going down in a fight without someone else there who knew how to combat the gallu. Mankind needed more than a single defender. "Teach me to fight the Dimme."

Sin couldn't have been more stunned had she stripped her clothes off and jumped him. "Sorry? I know I didn't hear what I think I did."

She didn't back down. "Teach me to fight them and the gallu."

He laughed at the mere thought of her going up against them and their cruelty. Yes, she was tall and not too thin, but she was no match for the strength of the gallu, never mind the Dimme. They'd eat her alive. Literally. "You don't have any Sumerian blood in you."

"There are ways to get around that."

He took a step back from her as one of them flashed in his mind. "Does blood-sucking run in your family?"

"No, but if we take a blood bond, I would have your strength and Sumerian blood."

That wasn't all it would give her, and he knew it. "And it would give you power over me. So screw you."

She took a step toward him, her green eyes pleading. "Sin . . ."

"Katra . . ." he mocked. "I will not allow you or anyone else to deplete me any more than what's already been done. Ever."

"Then let me train by your side. Show me—"

"All my best moves so that you can kill me?" What? Was she insane? "Fuck you."

She growled at him, "Do you not trust anyone?"

"Did we not already cover this? Hell no. Never. Why should I?"

"Because no one can stand alone all the time."

Sin scoffed. She actually looked like she believed the crap she was spewing, but he was anything but green and gullible. "And there you're wrong. I've been alone my whole life and I like it that way."

Still she wouldn't relent. She pursued him even across the room as he sought to put space between them. "Trust me, Sin. I only want to help."

"You want *me* to trust *you*?" He stopped so suddenly that she actually ran into him. The softness of her body made him flinch, but he wasn't about to let his libido interfere with his logic. He set her back on her feet, away from him, and gave her a hard stare. He knew one way to put a stop to her bullshit. "Fine. I'll trust you on one condition only. Tell me how to kill you."

Her eyes widened in confusion. "Excuse me?"

Sin smiled, knowing he had her now. She'd never give him the source of her powers. "All gods have a secret that can render them powerless and subject them to execution. What's yours?"

Now he saw the suspicion in her eyes. Good, she wasn't a trusting fool. "How do I know you won't kill me?"

"Yeah," he said, his voice thick, "it's not so easy to trust, is it?"

Still, she didn't back completely down. He had to admire her for that. "You have the Tablet of Destiny. That can render me powerless."

"But that doesn't show your *trust,* does it? Tell me how to kill you without it."

Kat stopped dead as she seriously considered the consequences of answering him. Given his hatred of her mother, it would be all kinds of stupid to give him that kind of power. He could kill her, any time, any place.

She remembered all the things that had been posted on the Dark-Hunter boards about him. He was without compassion or even sanity. But then a man such as that wouldn't be scarred from battling demons to help mankind.

Such a man wouldn't have come to her rescue. No, he wasn't the monster other people had painted him. But he wasn't a saint, either.

Trusting him could cost her her life. Not trusting him could destroy the world.

Was there really a choice here?

Don't do it . . .

It was terrifying even to contemplate, but she really had no other option. One of them was going to have to open up, and it dang sure wasn't him.

"I tell you the answer and you'll train me?" she asked point-blank.

"Yeah, what the hell?"

She took a deep breath for courage before she spoke again. "Very well. My powers are derived from the sun and the moon. The longer I go without one or the other, the weaker I become. It's why I can't stay here with my grandmother for too long or I'll be sick. If I were confined here without exposure to the sky, it would kill me."

Sin stared at her incredulously. He couldn't believe she'd told him that. Was she insane? "Do you know what you've just done?"

"Yes. I trusted you."

Yeah . . . She was nuts. No doubt about it. What kind of fool let loose something this important? "You know how much I hate your mother."

"And I know what you think of my father."

"Who doesn't even know you live."

"There is that," she conceded. "But I want to help you do the right thing, and if that means giving you power over me, then I'll do it."

She really was insane. He couldn't get past that. What kind of being would be so damn stupid and trusting? And for what? To help a race that didn't even know she existed? "I can destroy you now."

"Yes," she said, her eyes burning with intensity. "You can. But I'm trusting that you won't."

Sin shook his head in disbelief. No one had ever trusted him like this . . . not even his wife. Gods just didn't relinquish that kind of control to anyone under any circumstance. "You're not right, are you?"

"Could be. Other people have definitely thought so, and right now my inner monologue is going wild with worse insults than that."

He lifted his hand to touch her cheek. Her skin was as soft as silk against his fingertips. She was so delicate and yet he sensed within her a core made of steel. "Do you understand the danger you're going to face?"

"Seeing how my arm was broken earlier by one of them and your body is pretty torn up, I have a real good idea. But I've never been one to back down from anything. You need help and I intend to give it whether you want it or not."

Someone by his side. To fight. What a novel concept. No one had ever made such an offer before and he still wasn't sure if he should accept. But he had given her his word and he wasn't the kind of person to break an oath.

Still he was doubtful of her. "How do I know you won't take what I teach you and use it against me?"

She made a rude sound at him. "Hello? You have the knowledge to kill me. I think in this I'm the one who's most likely to get screwed."

He nodded in agreement before he dropped his hand from her face. "All right then. I need to get out of here. Back to my place so that we can prepare."

"Okay."

In a blink of an eye, they were back in his penthouse in Las Vegas. He looked around for Artemis, but she, along with her Dolophonos, was gone. Kish was still standing by the sofa as a life-sized statue.

Kat arched a brow as she saw Kish's frozen form for the first time. "Friend or foe?"

"Depends on the time and day." He snapped his fingers and Kish returned to his normal self.

Shaking his head, Kish frowned. "Did you freeze me again?"

Sin shrugged. "You were annoying me."

"I hate it when you do that." Kish did a double take as he realized Kat was standing beside him, watching him with a curious glimmer in her eye. Confusion marked his brow before he turned back to Sin. "You and Artemis made up? Damn, how long was I frozen?"

Kat laughed. "I'm not Artemis."

"I made a mistake," Sin said, not wanting to go into it.

"And you admit it?" Kish held his hands up. "Don't blast me, boss. I'm going to check on the casino. None of this is my business. None of it. Kish wants to live, so he's leaving. 'Bye." He barely opened the door before he rushed through it, out of their sight.

Kat gave Sin an amused smirk. "Interesting help. Is he your Squire?"

Sin shook his head before he picked his coat up and draped it over the back of a bar stool. "I'm not a Dark-Hunter. I don't do Squires."

"Interesting choice of words."

He gave her a droll stare. "Ha ha."

She moved to stand beside him so that she had him trapped

between her and the bar. "So why are you considered a Dark-Hunter then?"

"Acheron's idea. He thought adding me to the payroll was the least he could do given what Artemis had done to me."

"But you don't hunt Daimons."

"No. Acheron knew from the beginning that the gallu were out there. So the two of us have been keeping them under control."

Kat frowned at that. "Ash helps?"

"Why are you surprised?"

"I thought you said no one outside your pantheon could kill them."

"Yeah, well, your father's a little different from others. I'm sure you know that."

Kat couldn't agree more. There was a lot about her dad that was odd, to say the least. "Then what makes you think I can't do it?"

"You're not a Chthonian. If you were, you wouldn't have a weakness."

Kat arched a brow. The Chthonians were god-killers. Rather like a check and balance system provided by nature. They alone had the power to destroy anything indestructible. The only problem was no one knew how to destroy them. The only person who could kill a Chthonian was another Chthonian. "Is that their secret?"

"Not really. Most ancient gods know that one. It's why they're so afraid of Chthonian justice."

True. They alone made the ancient gods sit up and listen. Unfortunately for Sin at the time her mother's pantheon was attacking his, the Chthonians were turning on one another and there had been no one there to protect his pantheon.

Kat glanced out the tall windows to her left where she had a spectacular view of the Vegas strip. "So why are you out here in the desert anyway?"

"Logistical management. My father put the Dimme and gallu out here because at the time the population in America was scarce and he thought it would be a good way to control them. Unfortunately, he lacked the vision to see nuclear development in the twentieth century. With Nevada's testing, it began to shake out the gallu and free them dozens at a time. As they go free, I hunt them and their victims."

Kat took his hand in hers so that she could study all the scars that marred its beauty. She remembered when she was a young woman and her mother had summoned her to her bedroom.

"Help me, Katra. We have to take his powers from him or he'll kill me."

Kat flinched at the memory. Sin had been unconscious at the time. Too young and gullible, she'd done what her mother had requested.

And she had ruined the man before her.

He'd kill her if he ever learned that truth.

"What happened to your father?" she asked.

Sin stroked her fingers with his thumb before he pulled away from her. "Infighting and out-fighting. What's the old saying? 'Beware Greeks bearing gifts'? Apollo and your mother came in as friends to spread lies. They systematically turned each of us against the other until there was no trust left. Not that I'd ever had much to begin with. After I was drained and degodded, I tried to warn the others, but they didn't think it could happen to them. I was a fool after all and deserved what happened. They were all smarter than I was. Or so they thought."

"And yet here you are while they're all gone."

He nodded. "Survival is the best revenge. Me and the cockroach."

"And the gallu?"

He laughed at that. "Probably. It would serve me right to have to fight those bastards for the rest of eternity."

Kat smiled at his humor. He really was a smart, funny ex-god. There was something about him that was absolutely infectious, and it made her giddy just to be around him. It wasn't often that she liked someone so readily. But even in spite of everything she'd heard about him, she wanted to believe in him.

It made no sense.

And yet all she wanted to do was reach out and touch him. To kiss him again and see what would have happened had Apollymi not blasted them apart.

Instinctively she took a step toward him. And she would have probably made a move had a strange shiver not gone down her spine. It was a tingle she knew all too well.

Daimon.

Born of the cursed Apollite race that was forced to die painfully at the tender age of twenty-seven, Daimons could only survive if they began feeding on human souls. It was why they had to be hunted and killed. As soon as a soul was taken, it would begin to die in the foreign body. The only way to save that soul and send it to its proper place was to kill the Daimon before the soul died.

Now one of the Daimons was nearby.

A knock sounded on the door. It made her blood run cold. There was a Daimon outside. She knew it.

She tried to stop Sin as he went to answer the knock, but he didn't listen. He swung the door open, and sure enough, there was a tall blond Daimon standing there in a black suit.

Manifesting a knife in her hand, she ran for him.

CHAPTER SIX

Sin caught Kat against him before she could reach Damien Gatopoulos and stab him through the heart. “Whoa, Kat.”

As Damien jumped back in a way that was reminiscent of a pogo stick, his eyes widened. But he quickly caught his composure once he realized Sin wasn’t going to let go of Kat and allow her to kill him.

“He’s a Daimon!” she snarled.

Damien gave her an indignant stare.

“Yes,” Sin said slowly, tightening his hold on her, “and he’s my casino manager.”

Kat went limp against Sin as she looked up at his face. Total astonishment colored her pale features as she gaped at him. Even though her grip slackened on the knife, he still kept his hold on her wrist tight lest she go after Damien again and ruin both their nights.

“Excuse me?” she demanded.

“He’s my casino manager.”

Her anger returned as she started struggling again. Even though it shouldn't, the friction of her body rubbing against Sin's set him on fire. It was hard to concentrate on anything other than how kissable her lips were while her cheeks pinkened from her anger. "You have a Daimon working for you?"

Sin tilted his knee to keep her from colliding any more with his groin before he laughed at her rage. "A couple of them, actually."

"Don't worry," Damien said, straightening his jacket with a slight tug at the lapels. "I only eat humans who deserve it."

That really didn't help.

Kat screwed her face up in distaste as she turned from Damien to look again at Sin. "And to think I was actually beginning to like you. I can't believe you tolerate a Daimon to work for you."

He didn't really expect her to understand, but he had no problem with Damien or any of the others who worked for him. They were men and women whose lives had been ruined because of a Greek god's anger. To him, they were kindred sprits. Apollo had cursed the Apollite race because some distant ancestor had killed the Greek god's mistress and child. While tragic, it should never have led to Apollo's cursing anyone born of their race to die painfully at age twenty-seven. The god had also banned them from daylight and had forced them to live only on the blood of one another. It was harsh and unbecoming of a god who should have had more compassion for the race he'd created, then turned his back on.

Besides, what Damien said was true. Neither he nor any of the others who worked here preyed on the souls of decent humans. They only destroyed the souls of people who deserved to die. And the gods knew there were many humans in this world who needed annihilation and it was only fitting they become victims of a noble predator. That, for once, fate handed to them a just sentence.

Sin smiled at Kat. "Yeah, but he's incredibly honest. Since he took over, no one tries to cheat me anymore. If they do, he eats them."

She grimaced at Sin's words. "Oh, you're both disgusting."

Damien made a noise of deep aggravation. "You know, I really resent the fact that you judge me based on one unfortunate fact. Honestly, I'm not a bad guy."

She wasn't buying it. "You eat people's souls. How can you not be bad?"

"Trust me, these aren't people you want reincarnated. The guy I ate yesterday was a wife-abusing hit man. Good, strong soul . . . rotten human being."

Sin had to force himself not to laugh when it was obvious Kat wasn't amused. But he knew for a fact that Damien was right. He only took the lives of those who deserved to die, and so long as he did, Sin had no problem with him.

Kat shook her head. "And if you eat enough of those souls, they begin to corrupt *you* until you become one of them. Everyone knows that."

Damien scoffed. "Only if you're stupid. I'm two hundred years old and I haven't turned yet. You just have to learn to hum a lot so you don't hear their bullshit echoing in your head. It gets really loud and ugly the closer to final death they go. But then you eat a new soul and it usually finishes off the old one, so there's no real danger of turning evil yourself."

She tried again to shrug off Sin's hold. "You disgust me."

Damien took it in stride. "Like you don't have any revolting habits."

"I don't eat people."

"Technically, I don't, either. I only swallow their souls. Which, I might add, you should try someday . . . Finger-lickin' good."

She let out a shriek before she lunged again.

Sin wrapped his arms around her waist and lifted her up from the floor, which was a really stupid move, since she then proceeded to kick him in the legs. "Why don't you go back downstairs, Damien? I'll call you when I have a minute."

"Sure, boss."

Sin waited until the door was safely shut before he released Kat. She turned on him with her nostrils flared and her green eyes snapping fury. "Don't you ever keep me from teleporting again."

"Why not? You did it to me."

Kat calmed a degree as she realized he was right. She'd done that to him. Funny, it hadn't seemed like a personal invasion until it'd happened to her. No wonder he'd been so angry in Kalosis. But that didn't change the fact that he was in the wrong where the Daimon was concerned.

"How can you condone what that man does to stay alive?"

"Me? I'm not the one whose uncle went wild on an entire innocent race. If not for Apollo and his condemnation and curse, none of the Daimons would even exist."

"They killed his son and his mistress," she said as if that warranted the god's unreasonable anger.

"Three soldiers killed his son and mistress," Sin reminded her. "The rest of them were completely innocent. How many of the Apollites did Apollo kill as children the day he went wild on them? Does he even care? Oh, wait a second, I forgot. How many of the Apollites were his own flesh-and-blood children and grandchildren that he condemned to death? Did he care they were damned over something they had no part in? He killed more of his own blood family in anger than the three soldiers who killed that mistress and child. A lot more."

Kat cringed. Again, Sin was right. The Stryker who served Apollymi was Apollo's own son. Originally, Stryker had had ten children who had been cursed along with him. Out of that ten, all of them had gone Daimon and been killed.

All of them.

"Tell me something, Kat?" Sin said, his voice deep and tense. "If you were going to die at twenty-seven and someone showed you how to live another day, would you really choose the life of a complete stranger over your own?"

"Of course I would."

"Then you're a better person than I am. Or maybe you just haven't had to fight for survival so you can't truly understand what it's like to look death in the face and have him stare right back at you." The heat in his voice sent a shiver over her.

Still she wasn't swayed to his side. "You're immortal. What do you know of dying?"

A cold look descended on his features as pain glowed in those golden depths. "Immortals can and do die. Some of us more than once."

There was something there . . . something she needed to know the answer to.

"And have you ever taken the life of an innocent to live another day?"

His eyes were harsh and cold. "I've done many things in my

life that I didn't want to. I'm not proud of them, but I'm still here and I intend to be here for a long time to come. So don't you dare sit in judgment of people when you haven't been in their shoes."

Kat reached out to touch him even though she knew she shouldn't. The instant she did, she felt the rawness of his grief. But more than that, she saw him with his daughter, screaming out her name as she was killed by demons. His black hair was plastered by sweat against his dark skin. Blood ran down his rage-contorted face and body in thick, crimson rivulets.

She could see him cradling Ishtar against him and feel the searing ache that made her gasp.

Then Kat felt the sharp, crisp pain of something piercing her heart.

She looked down, choking on what seemed to be her own blood, expecting to see a wound. But it wasn't her body she saw. It was Sin's. There was a sword stuck through him and it burned like the very fires of hell. Every beat of her heart sent more agony pounding through her until she wanted to scream from it.

And it wasn't the only painful memory he kept buried. She was in a long, open hallway that was light and airy, with thin white curtains billowing in the breeze. Sunshine poured through it as Sin walked toward the back of his temple in Ur. There was a feeling of happiness in his heart until the sounds of grinding sex intruded on it. The joy turned to vengeful rage as he entered his bedroom. He approached the bed in the corner and parted the heavy red curtains.

What she saw there jolted her into releasing Sin's arm. Kat gasped as she stepped back in shock.

She couldn't breathe. Couldn't see or hear anything other than the unbelievable agony inside her. It hurt . . . it hurt . . . Over and over images continued to flash in her mind. Sin's memories. She saw his wife in the arms of another man. Saw his son, Utu, and his daughter, Ishtar, as they died fighting the demons Sin's own father had created.

The agony was unbearable . . .

How could Sin stand all that had happened to him? How? They had laughed at him and they had shamed him.

Then they had died and left him completely alone . . .

Kat wanted peace, but there was no comfort to be found. All she could see was bitter images that ate at her. Bitter images of guilt and betrayal.

"Help me," she whispered, her heart breaking.

Sin stood beside Kat, watching her shake. The sadistic part of himself enjoyed the sight of her there like that. It was what she deserved for intruding on his emotions and memories.

But he wasn't the bastard he wanted to be and the joy only lasted a millisecond of a heartbeat before he was gathering her into his arms. She was sobbing against him.

"Sh," he whispered as he rocked her. "Let it go. It's not yours to feel." Closing his eyes, he cradled her against his chest and reached out with his powers to ease the pain she'd taken from him.

Kat continued to tremble uncontrollably as the images receded. She felt the comfort of Sin's arms that warred against the residual emotions that continued to sting her.

There was so much pain inside him. So much betrayal. How could he stand it?

But then she knew. It was what fueled his fight against the gallu. He channeled all the anger and pain and used it to strengthen him.

It was also what kept him isolated from everyone around him. Even Kish and Damien. And she finally understood what he'd said to her earlier. "There is more than one kind of death," she whispered.

"Yes." His own voice was low and that single word carried more emotion than a lovesick poet. "Cowards aren't the only ones who die a thousand deaths. Sometimes heroes do, too."

It was true. She'd seen it firsthand and she now understood so much about him.

Kat leaned back so that she could touch his face. He was so handsome in the dim light. His dark features were perfection. Yet she could still see in her mind the blood on his skin, the anguish on his features . . .

And she wanted to soothe him more than anything.

Sin's breath caught as he saw the compassion in Kat's eyes. The sympathy. It'd been so long since anyone had looked at him like that. Hatred, anger, disgust, those he could handle. But this one look was enough to weaken him.

It touched a part of him he didn't even know. And it softened him. He'd never been so naked to anyone. She'd seen his past and she didn't mock him for it. It was refreshing and terrifying.

She fingered his lips, which ignited a spark deep inside his body. It'd been a long time since any woman had . . .

No, he'd never felt like this with a woman. Not even his wife had attracted him the way Kat did. There was something about her that was infectious and inviting. Her humor, her courage. All of it.

And he wanted a taste of her so badly that all he could think of was stripping them naked and making love to her until the end of time.

Or at least until the Dimme ate them . . .

Kat watched the emotions sweep across Sin's face. His desire was bold and hot in those golden eyes, and even without using her powers she knew what he felt.

She held her breath in expectation of his kiss.

His hold tightened an instant before he took possession of her mouth. She laid her hand against his cheek so that she could feel the muscle in his jaw working as his tongue danced with hers. He tasted of wine and man. Of comfort and warmth. She didn't know why, but she found a strange sense of peace with him. Desire overwhelmed her.

Sin growled at the sensation of her tongue sweeping against his. Part of him expected Apollymi to blast them apart again, but as each second passed and all he could feel was Kat's warm touch, he relaxed. There was no one here to break them apart. No one to come between them.

That made him a lot happier than it should.

Gods, she was so sweet. So soft. The warm scent of her skin intoxicated him. He'd almost forgotten how good it felt to hold a woman who knew who and what he was. Then again, she had seen into a part of him that no one else had ever seen. It was a part of himself that even he didn't want to know existed.

He cupped her face in his hands as his senses swirled. All he wanted was to feel her naked against him. To have her long, graceful fingers stroking him. Have her long legs wrapped around his hips as he lost himself deep inside her body.

But instead, she pulled back to stare at him. Her wet lashes glistened as she looked up through them. "I'm sorry for what you've suffered."

"Don't be. You didn't do it."

Kat swallowed at his empty tone. No, she hadn't done it all, but damned if her entire family hadn't had a hand in it.

It'd been her grandfather Archon she'd seen in bed with Sin's wife. Kat wondered if Apollymi had known her husband wasn't faithful. If Apollymi did, it explained another reason she hated the Sumerians so.

The politics of the gods was always complicated. And usually painful, but never as much as it was in this case.

Bowing her head, she took his hand into hers and stared at the burn and battle scars. His skin was so dark compared to hers. There was so much strength there. But it was the loneliness he suffered that hurt her most.

"Strength through adversity." That was what the Chthonian Savitar had once told her when she'd asked him why some people had to suffer such unbelievable strife. *"The strongest steel is forged by the fires of hell. It is pounded and struck repeatedly before it's plunged back into the molten fire. The fire gives it power and flexibility, and the blows give it strength. Those two things make the metal pliable and able to withstand every battle it's called upon to fight."*

It'd seemed so cruel to her as a child. Sometimes it still seemed cruel.

But Sin had withstood it with grace.

Lifting his hand, she kissed the worst of the burn scars on the back of his left wrist.

Sin trembled at the tenderness of Kat's actions. Honestly, he didn't know how to deal with it. Insults and attacks he could handle.

Gentleness . . .

That terrified him. "I thought you hated me."

She let out a short laugh that sent a rush of air over his skin. "I do." She looked up with an openness that seared him. "You know you shouldn't condone Daimons working for you."

"My handful of Daimons haven't wrecked nearly as many lives as your mother and uncle, but I notice you still love them."

He did have a point. "Only on most days." Kat cleared her throat and moved away from him. "You were going to train me to fight the gallu."

Even as she said the words, she saw the image of his daughter in her mind. Ishtar had been ripped open by the demons. Literally torn apart. And by the look on his face, Kat could tell he was having the same thought.

"Don't worry," she assured him. "I can handle them. I'm born of two gods."

He scoffed at her bravado. "So was Ishtar."

Yeah, but Ishtar wasn't her and didn't have the same genetic makeup. "My father is the harbinger of death and destruction. My grandmother the Great Destroyer. My mother is the goddess of the hunt. I think I'll be okay."

"Yeah," he breathed, stepping away from her. "You do have the history of absolute terror and cruelty in your veins."

She winked at him. "Remember that if you ever come between me and my chocolate bar."

"I'll try." His tone was less than convincing. He didn't think her much of a fighter, but he would learn. She'd show him exactly what she was made of.

"So how many Daimons do you have in your casino?" she asked.

He shrugged. "I'm not sure. Don't study them close enough to worry about it. Damien keeps them in line. If they eat the wrong tourist, he kills them."

"And you're totally okay with this?"

"I trust Damien more than I trust anyone else."

That made no sense to her whatsoever. Then again, her grandmother controlled an entire army of Daimons and said nothing of the lives and souls they took in order to stay alive. Of course their leader, Stryker, was now plotting her death, but that was another issue.

It took Kat a minute to realize why Sin's tolerance bothered her so. It was because they were here on the same plane as the humans. Stryker and his army had to come to this plane to feed and she'd never witnessed it. Somehow it seemed more wrong to harbor Daimons right in the heart of humanity.

"I thought you didn't trust anyone," she said.

"I never said I trusted Damien at my back or with my life. Only my money."

"And yet you're trusting me at your back?"

"Not completely. You are to stay by my side so I can watch

you. Don't think for one minute that I've forgotten you're the face and voice of the one woman I want to kill more than any other."

It really was too much to hope he could get past that. But then if someone had taken her godhood, she'd be a little upset herself. "Understood. So what's the game plan other than to avoid Demon and my mother?"

"We have to find the Hayar Bedr."

Kat frowned at the unfamiliar term. "That would be what?"

"The Forsaken Moon."

"And would it be animal, vegetable, or mineral?"

"Animal. Definitely animal."

Why did that surprise her? Oh wait, 'cause it was completely normal to refer to an animal as a forsaken moon. Yeah . . . "Really? What kind of animal would be called the Forsaken Moon?"

"My twin brother."

Kat was stunned by the revelation. That was something she hadn't seen inside him. "There are two of you?"

His features darkened. "In a manner of speaking. Originally, there were three of us born to a human mother. She was a peasant my father had taken a fancy to and impregnated. We were no more than children when the prophecy came down that said we would destroy the pantheon. In anger, my father killed the eldest triplet; then he came for me and Zakar. Even though I was only ten, I was the stronger, so I hid Zakar in the dream realm and fought my father for the right to live. I told him I'd already taken care of my brother and absorbed his powers."

"But you hadn't."

"No, but the idea that I had possessed the power to kill my own brother scared my father enough to give him pause. Even though he still wanted me dead, he decided that since the prophecy had foretold the three of us would cause the destruction, one of us should be all right to live. So I took my place in their pantheon and Zakar stayed hidden for the most part. The humans knew him, but any time they made mention of him I told my father I was the one in their dreams using my brother's name."

"And he believed you?"

He gave her a wicked grin. "You don't screw with a fertility god if you want to stay vigorous."

True. Fertility gods had a way with a whammy that could ruin most men's nights.

And their egos forever.

"So where's your brother now?" Kat asked.

Sin let out a tired breath as he left her to go to his bar and pour himself a drink of whisky. "I have no idea. The last time I saw him was after Artemis had drained my powers and left me for dead. Zakar helped free me from her net, but he didn't stay around long after that. He told me there was something he had to take care of and then he vanished."

"And you have no idea where he went?"

He knocked back the drink with one gulp and poured another glassful. "None. I've tried to summon him. Call him, you name it. Nothing. Not a postcard or whisper for thousands of years. Part of me wonders if he's not dead."

"If he is, where does that leave us?"

"Basically screwed over raw." He tossed back another drink. "It was his blood we used to bind the gallu the last time. Which means we need his blood to bind them again."

"If you're twins, why can't we just use your blood to rebind them?"

He offered her a drink, but she declined with a shake of her head.

Sin put her glass away before he answered her question. "I'm not a Dreamwalker. Zakar is. In dreams, he once battled the demon Asag, the genetic father that was used to create the gallu. During their fight, Zakar absorbed some of the demon's powers. It's why he can stand against them alone and I can't. He understands them and their weaknesses. It was through Zakar that I was able to control and fight the demons."

"Then how is it that Ishtar died by their hands?"

This time he didn't bother with the glass. He drank straight from the bottle before he responded. "Once I was negated and Zakar had vanished, she was alone in the fight against them. I heard her crying out for help one night and I rushed to her even though I knew I didn't have the power to fight them."

He swallowed as pain filled his eyes. "It was too late. You have no idea what it feels like to hold your child in your arms and watch her die. To know that if you still had your powers, you could have saved her." His look pierced her. "I could have forgiven Artemis what she did to me. It's the death of my daughter that I will never get over. If I ever have a chance to kill that bitch, believe me, I will take it. All consequences be damned."

A chill ran over her at his heartfelt words. Not that she blamed him. She'd seen the pain of Ishtar's death through his eyes and she'd felt his horror and rage.

No father deserved that memory.

Swallowing the lump in her throat, she took a step forward. "Sin . . ."

"Don't touch me. I don't need comfort, especially not from the daughter of the woman who took everything from me."

Kat nodded. She understood that and it made her ache for him. "What happened to Ishtar's powers when she died?"

He polished off the bottle with one last swig. "Before she died, she transferred enough of them to me to keep the universe from unraveling—it's also why I can now fight the gallu and defeat them. After her death, the rest were released, which resulted in one hell of a volcanic eruption. Then Aphrodite entered our pantheon as the goddess of love and beauty to replace Ishtar, and it wasn't long after that, that my pantheon was history. Literally."

Kat swallowed as she remembered the Greek gods talking about that. Aphrodite had used jealousy as a weapon to turn the Sumerians against one another until they no longer trusted anyone near them. Kat's aunt had been insidious as a manipulator. It still amazed Kat how people who'd known one another for so long were so willing to listen to the lies of a newcomer.

How willing they were to give in to such a negative emotion to the point they would do anything to go after one another just to see their innocent enemy fall.

In the end, they had all paid a steep price.

But that was the past and it wouldn't cure their current dilemma. What they needed was someone who could . . .

She paused as she remembered something Sin had said.

"I have a question. Why can't you do what Zakar did? If you're twins, can't you fight Asag in a dream and then get the same kind of demon powers?"

He wiped his mouth with the back of his hand. "If I had my own powers and not half of Ishtar's, there's a lot of things I could do . . . like kill your mother for instance."

She'd walked right into that one. Choosing to ignore his rancor, she tried another thought. "What about the Oneroi?" They were the dream gods for the Greek pantheon. "Could we get one of them to find Asag and fight him?"

"Could try. Of course we have no idea how Asag's venom might affect them since they're born to another pantheon. Could be very interesting. Either it'll work or they'll become a new type of demon we'd have to learn to kill. Who should we pick as a guinea pig?"

Kat screwed her face up at his sarcasm. He was right, though. There was no telling how such a thing could adversely affect one of her cousins. "Looks like Zakar is our best bet."

"Unless you can talk your bitch mother into releasing my powers, yeah."

She narrowed her gaze at him. "Well, that's just a little hard, since I can't even talk her into sparing your life, huh? You haven't exactly endeared yourself to her."

"Oh, excuse my utter lack of manners there. Should we call Mommy dearest and invite her over for tea? I promise to be on my best manners when I choke the life out of her."

"Whoa," Kish said with a laugh as he entered the room to their right, "what is this? Battle of the Sarcastic and Pissed? Should I make popcorn? Forget *American Idol,* man. This is much more entertaining."

Sin cast a murderous glare toward his servant. "Is there a point to your latest irritation, Kish?"

"Had a sudden death wish. Felt the deep need to come up here and have you freeze me again. I like being a statue . . . just so long as you don't stick me in a park somewhere and let pigeons shit all over me."

Kat had to stifle a laugh. Oh, if looks could mutilate, Kish would be a kish kebab.

"O-kay," Kish said, stretching the word out, "so the point of my visit is there's a man downstairs wanting to speak to you. He says it's urgent."

"I'm a little busy."

"I told him that."

"Then why are you disturbing me?"

Kish held his closed fist out. "He wanted me to give this to you."

Sin had to struggle not to roll his eyes at his servant. "I don't take bribes." But as Kish let fall a small medallion into Sin's hand, his agitation evaporated. It was an ancient Babylonian coin. "Did he happen to mention his name?"

"Kessar."

Kat frowned at the name she'd never heard before. "Kessar?" she repeated.

Sin didn't speak as cold dread and anger shrank his stomach. "He is to the gallu what Stryker is to the Daimons," he explained.

Without another word, he snatched a cane from the wall and headed for the elevator to take him down to the casino.

CHAPTER SEVEN

Kat exchanged a frown with Kish before she followed after Sin to the hallway where his elevator was located. Sin gave them an agitated glare as they shuffled him aside to get into the ornate paneled elevator with him.

"What?" Kat asked irritably, looking up at him.

His response was a low growl.

"I take it you know this guy, boss?" Kish asked.

Sin still didn't speak.

Kat didn't need her powers to feel the feral rage inside him—to sense the killer he'd become at the mere mention of Kessar's name. She didn't know what past they had with each other, but it was obviously not a happy one. Apparently Kessar rated right up there with her mother in Sin's estimation.

Sin was ramrod stiff beside her and clutched the cane with a white-knuckled grip. His features were even sharper now. His eyes brittle. How he managed to look attractive like that she didn't know, but there was something about him and his anger that set her hormones panting.

Suddenly the Hinder song "Get Stoned" started going through her head. Totally inappropriate, especially at this moment in time. Still, she couldn't help wondering if anger really did make sex better. Then again, she had no real idea of what sex felt like even calm.

They really need to let me out more.

Sin glanced down at her as if he could read her thoughts. *Oh, that's good.* Just what she needed—him inside her head, hearing the fact that she felt compelled by his angry looks. Groovy. Just groovy.

She might as well squeal like a thirteen-year-old while she was at it and tell him how hot he looked when ticked off. Her luck, he'd stay that way.

Diverting her gaze to the doors, she didn't speak or make any movements that might betray the line of her thoughts. How embarrassing would that be? Especially given the fact that the man hated her entire maternal lineage.

There were just some degradations a person didn't need. This was definitely one of them. So she tried to ignore him. Something that would have been a lot easier if his image weren't reflected in the steel of the doors. Damn, the man was good-looking, especially when he had that hard, determined look about him. He was all predator and all man.

It was a dangerous combination to her sanity.

As soon as the elevator doors opened, Sin stepped out and walked in front of them—something amazing given the fact that he didn't like people at his back. *I guess he trusts Kish to warn him if I move to the attack.*

What a pleasant thought . . .

The casino was dark, with lights glowing from the slot machines and tables. Bells and electronic tones fought each other for supremacy while winners laughed and others shouted over low-playing music. The casino looked like total anarchy, and at the same time it was inviting and fun. She didn't know what it was about places like this, but they were hypnotic.

Oblivious to it all, Sin walked through the area with purpose, heading toward the gaming tables as if he knew instinctively where to find his enemy.

Kat looked left and right, trying to locate anyone who might be against them or anyone who might be one of those things that had attacked her in New York. She saw numerous humans who were incognizant of the fact that they were in the center of a war zone. Several tall, blond waitresses in short black dresses paused to look at her with malice. They were Apollites, but the one circulating with change was a Daimon female. That one actually curled her lip at Kat, baring a hint of fang.

She ignored the Daimon as she continued to search for the gallu demon.

All of a sudden, something went through her. It was like ice gliding down her spine. A sixth sense that warned her of evil. She paused as movement to her left caught her attention.

There were five men there—all in black suits and all devastatingly handsome. Their skin was dark and tanned, which given their Persian ancestry made sense. Three had black, curly hair cut in a shaggy style. One had straight black hair pulled back into a short ponytail. Their eyes were every bit as black as their hair. Like glimmering obsidian.

But the one leading them . . .

He stood out even more than they did. His hair was a dark caramel-colored blond with lighter blond streaks. His features were sharp and fine. Aristocratic. And even though it was dark inside the casino, he wore a pair of dark brown sunglasses that hid his eyes. It wasn't until he moved closer that she realized why.

His eye color was blood-red.

A sinister half smile curved his lips as Sin stopped in front of him.

There was something insidiously evil about Kessar even though he was beautiful. No doubt he'd been the kind of kid who had pulled wings off . . . well, most likely Charontes and then laughed while they cried.

"Well, well. Nana," he said in a voice that was almost jovial. "How long has it been?"

Sin ignored his question and quipped with his own. "Who the hell let you out?"

Kessar laughed low and evil, and like Sin, he chose not to answer the question. "The Dimme are stirring. I know you know it." He closed his eyes as if savoring something delectable. "I can hear their wings unfurling even as we speak. Feel the blood beginning to pump through their veins. My sisters will be hungry when they wake up. We shall have to make sure they have a smorgasbord."

Sin scanned the demons behind Kessar before he gave the demon a pointed stare. "And I know just what to feed them."

Kessar tsked at him. "We're not a cannibalistic species, so you're out of luck there. Just consider this a friendly call to let you know you won't find what you're looking for . . . So don't waste your time. We found the Moon first and now it lives where you can't touch it. And when my sisters awaken, you shall join it in utter misery."

Sin's face went white as his features hardened. Kat could feel the concerned panic inside him swell. "What have you done with Zakar?"

Kessar ignored him as he focused that cold, lethal gaze on Kat. A slight frown darkened his brow before he moved to stand in front of her.

"What have we here?" he asked in a singsongy tone. "An Atlantean. I thought you were all dead."

"Surprise," Kat taunted.

He seemed to savor her rancor. He lifted his hand to trace the angle of her jaw with the back of one knuckle.

Sneering, Kat jerked her head away from his cold touch. She wanted to spit at him, but she was too dignified for such a thing.

Sin separated them with the cane, using it to force Kessar away from her.

Kessar looked down at the cane and his face paled a degree. "You can't use that in front of the humans. What will they say?"

Sin shrugged. "What happens in Vegas stays in Vegas. It is, after all, *Sin* City."

"Hmmm." Kessar raised his hand and snapped his fingers over his shoulder. The demon with the ponytail moved forward. Kessar opened his hand and the demon laid a small box in his palm. Kessar then handed it to Sin. "In that case, here's a small token to remember me by."

Sin opened it. Kat turned away as she saw a severed finger with a ring attached to it. It was disgusting.

Hissing, Sin moved toward Kessar, but Damien pulled him back. "Not here, Sin. Not now."

"You bastard," Sin snarled from between clenched teeth. "You better watch your ass. I'm coming for it."

"Funny, that's what Zakar said, too. But he hasn't spoken in quite some time. All he does now is whimper and cry." He smiled coldly. "Just like you will."

Damien kept his grip on Sin. But Kat had had enough. She might be too dignified to spit, but at the end of the day, she was her father's daughter. Without warning, she walked up to Kessar and kneed him as hard as she could in the groin.

He doubled over instantly, groaning. Nice to know the demons were as susceptible to that tactic as a human. When the ponytail came forward she punched him so hard, he spun around. The others didn't so much as blink.

Kat pulled Kessar up by the hair so that she could whisper in his ear. "Never underestimate an Atlantean. We're not your average pantheon."

His face changed at that. Large veins protruded from his forehead before his eyes glowed. His mouth grew larger as the double row of fangs appeared. He went to bite her, but Sin caught him by the throat.

Sin shoved him into Damien's arms. "Take out the trash, Damien. I don't want it stinking up my casino."

Kessar's face returned to normal so fast that it stunned Kat. He shoved Damien away from him. "Don't touch me, Daimon. You're not worthy."

Damien curled his lip. "Up yours, asshole. I don't want the Sumerian slime pit stench on me anyway. Take your girlfriends and get the hell out of our casino."

Kessar straightened his sleeves. "Oh, we're so going to come back here. In force."

Sin's features were hard and cold. "Looking forward to it."

"So am I." And with that, they turned and left, literally in a V formation.

"Wow," Kat said under her breath. "They remind me of geese with that action."

"Yeah, and much like geese, they usually shit all over your lawn." Damien pulled a small container of breath freshener from his pocket and started spraying it. "Too bad we don't have demon-be-gone."

"Or do we?" Kat looked at the two of them. "What's the one thing the gallu hate most?"

"You would be looking at him," Sin said dryly.

"Yeah, but the next would be a Charonte. Right?"

Sin gave her a droll stare. "And in case you haven't noticed, they're not exactly in supply in this realm any longer. I believe your grandmother has cornered the market on them."

Kat laughed. "Not entirely. I know one in particular who likes to visit here and who would love to have a chance to go on a feeding frenzy, especially here in Vegas where there are lots of pretty sparklies for her to see."

Damien and Sin exchanged a frown.

"Who is this demon?" Damien asked. "And more important, is she attractive?"

"Oh, she's attractive all right. But I would advise against making a move on her. The last man who did, sadly, ended up dead." Kat pulled the cell phone off Damien's belt and dialed the one and only number that would ring a dainty pink Razr cell phone that was covered with white and pink sparkles.

"Hello?"

Kat smiled at the light singsongy voice she knew and loved so well. "Simi? You got some free time?"

Simi made a disgusted sound on the other end. "Of course I do. You know *akri* on Olympus with that heifer-goddess I want to eat, but he won't let the Simi have no dinner. So why you calling me, little *akra*-kitty?"

"I'm in Vegas and I find myself in desperate need of a quality demon. Bring your barbecue sauce, hon." Kat smiled in triumph at Sin. "Lots of it."

"Ooo . . . buffet?"

"Yes, ma'am. As much as you want."

Simi let out an excited squeal. "The Simi is on her way. Lemme pack a few things and I'll be right there."

Kat hung up and handed the phone back to Damien. "One really hungry Charonte coming our way."

Sin nodded, but his face was still dark as he looked down at the box in his palm.

Kat put her hand on him to comfort him. "We'll find your brother, Sin."

His expression made her heart ache. "Yeah, but what exactly are we going to find?"

Her stomach shrank at the thought and she could feel the fury inside him growing. If not for her mother, Sin would have been able to protect his brother and keep him safe. He must be plotting new ways to torture Artemis even as they stood there, and Kat couldn't blame him for it one little bit.

Damien cleared his throat. "It's daylight right now, boss. But tonight we can help you search for him."

Sin shook his head. "You stay out of this. They'll cut through you like butter."

The look on Damien's face said he wasn't a bit afraid.

"What about Savitar?" Kat asked, thinking of someone they might be able to sway to their cause. "Or any of the Chthonians, for that matter? Won't they help?"

"They haven't yet. Since their civil war, all they want to do is guard their own territories and ignore the rest." Sin set the cane down on the floor.

Kat cocked her head, remembering the way Kessar had reacted to it. It alone had given the demon pause. "What is that you're holding? Demon kryptonite?"

"Sort of." He lifted the handle to show her a thin blade, which was exactly what she'd expected it to conceal. "It was created by Anu much like the Atlantean daggers that kill the Charonte. It's how we kept the gallu in line."

Ooo, she liked the sound of that. "You got any more of them?"

"No," he said with a sigh. "After all these centuries, they've become brittle. This is the last one I have, and since Anu isn't around to make any more . . ."

They were screwed. He didn't have to say the words her mind said them for him. "Would an Atlantean dagger work on them?"

"I don't know. You got one?"

"Not really. I was just thinking out loud. You weren't supposed to call my bluff."

"Sorry to spoil your thinking." Sin turned to Kish, who'd been unbelievably quiet through everything. "Uncover the mirrors throughout the casino. Make sure that we have mirror coating on all the entrances."

Kat frowned. "To keep out the Dark-Hunters?"

"To keep out the gallu. Mirrors show them for what they are. They won't go near one."

Damien snorted. "I like the idea of keeping the Dark-Hunters out better."

Kat gave him an arch look. "I'll bet you do. I'm surprised none of them have been in here cleaning house, so to speak."

"I'm not real friendly to them," Sin said. "The ones here know I own this place and they give it space. After all, unlike true Dark-Hunters, I'm not banned from hitting or killing them, and they know it."

She gave him a sarcastic doe-eyed, worshipful stare. She even folded her hands under her chin and spoke with a fake southern drawl. "You're just such a sweetie pie. I can't imagine why the other Dark-Hunters won't let you play their reindeer games. Shame on them all."

He ignored her except for a little eye rolling. "Damien, keep a watch out for any more gallu until Kish can get the mirrors in place."

"You got it."

Kish headed off toward the nearest wall.

Picking the cane up, Sin turned and headed back for the elevators so quickly that Kat had to practically run to catch up to him.

He didn't speak as he held the door for her. She was rather stunned at his uncharacteristic chivalry.

"Thanks."

He inclined his head before he stepped back and let out a long breath. She could sense that he wanted to say something, but at the same time he didn't want to say it. He wouldn't even look her in the eye. There was something so incredibly boyish about his actions. It wasn't like him to be uncertain about anything, and she found it oddly endearing.

While the take-charge Sin was sex on a stick, this one was lovable. Adorable and sweet. A strange dichotomy for the man she was learning.

After a few seconds, he gave her a sheepish glance. "Do you have the powers to locate my brother?"

So that was what had bothered him. Sin had asked for her help. It was something she was sure he didn't do often. Heck, from what she'd seen, this could very well be the first time in his life he'd done it. "I wish. Sorry."

He cursed.

"But . . ." she said, hoping to cheer him, "my grandmother has the *sfora*. It might be able to locate him."

Sin frowned. "Sfora?"

"It's like a crystal ball. You ask it to show you things and it does. Usually."

There was no missing the relief in those gold eyes. "Would you try for me . . . please."

The way he added that word said that "please" might be a first for him, too. She had to admit, she liked this side of him. She could actually be friends with this man. "Yes."

Sin offered her a smile he didn't feel. All he could think of was Zakar out there alone. Of him suffering the gods only knew what at the hands of his enemies.

Who knew how long they'd had him. The very thought made Sin's stomach queasy.

How had his brother been captured?

Was Zakar even alive? But as soon as that thought went through Sin, he knew the answer. Of course Zakar was alive. The gallu lived for torture and bloodshed. To have an ancient god under their thumbs would be the bonus round of all time.

Damn them. Sin could barely breathe from the anger that thought ignited.

When Artemis had dumped him in the desert, Zakar had been the one to find him and restore his health. When no one else would come near, Zakar had nourished him back to health and taken him to safety.

And how had he repaid his brother?

He'd let the gallu take him.

Sin deserved to die for the betrayal. If only he could make it up to Zakar, but he knew better. Nothing could make up for torture and pain.

Disgusted with himself, he left the elevator as soon as the doors opened and returned to his penthouse. He leaned the cane against the bar and set the box down before he raked his hands through his hair. He wanted to scream out in frustration.

"Don't worry, Sin. We'll get them." Kat placed a comforting hand on his shoulder.

He didn't know how that one touch could soothe him, but somehow it did. More than that, it sent an electric charge through his body that heated him instantly.

And even though his body reacted hungrily to her presence, his intelligence wasn't fooled. In spite of her kindness, there was only one reason for her to be with him right now. "Your mother sent you in to kill me last night, didn't she?"

Kat was shocked by his unexpected question. How had he figured that out? "Excuse me?"

He turned to level a menacing stare at her. "Don't lie to me, Kat. Artemis wants you to kill me. Admit it."

There was no need for dishonesty. Sin had been lied to enough and she wasn't about to continue that trend. "Yeah. She did."

He gave a bitter laugh before he pulled a dagger out of its hidden sheath at his waist.

She held her breath, expecting him to come for her, but he didn't. Instead, he handed it to her.

"If that's your intent then. Go for it. I'm not going to sit around, waiting for your attack when my back is turned. Be a man about it and let's get the fighting over with."

She didn't know why, but she was strangely amused by his demand that she man up and face him. It still didn't change the fact that she had no intention of killing him now.

Kat placed the dagger down on the bar. "I am not my mother, Sin. She doesn't control me."

That seemed to pacify him. At least for a few seconds. "And when I go to kill her? Where will you stand? At my back or in my way?"

She offered him a slight smile. "I don't think you will go after her."

His look was harsh and deadly. "You're going to bet her life on it?"

"Yes. Because you know her death would rupture the fabric of the earth and, unlike her, you're not that selfish." Any time a major god was killed, their powers were released back into the universe. If no one absorbed the powers, they could easily detonate like a nuclear bomb. Especially when the dying god was born of the sun or moon. Those gods had to be protected more than any other.

And since Artemis had absorbed Sin's powers on top of her own, it made her destruction twice as dangerous as that of any other god.

Sin's gaze narrowed. "Maybe I'll absorb her powers and replace her as she did me."

Kat still wasn't buying what he was trying to sell her. "If you knew how to do that, then you'd have done it before now."

Glancing away, he shook his head. "You trust way too easily."

"And you trust not at all."

His face grim, he moved away from her. "You're damned right."

Okay, she'd learned a trigger for the ex-god. Don't even tease about trust. He had issues there.

Wanting to restore the comradery they had almost found before it had veered off the road and careened down the hill where it exploded into flames, she sought to change the subject. "So are you going to show me how to fight those things so that the next time Kessar darkens your door I can make him limp *and* bleed?" Her words almost got a smile out of him.

Almost.

"What about the *sfora* and finding my brother?"

"Hold that thought a second." Kat closed her eyes and let her thoughts drift. She saw her grandmother in her garden and though she wasn't weeping, Kat could feel Apollymi's sadness. Her grandmother wasn't up to receiving visitors just yet and that meant even her alone. She was still angry over Sin's last visit and aching over what had happened to Acheron.

Opening her eyes, Kat gave Sin a pointed stare. "Can we wait a bit? I don't think Grandma wants to see you or me just yet. Give her a little more time . . . another hour or two, and hopefully this time when we go she won't try to feed you to her demons. Is that okay?"

"Not really. But since I know better than to rush an angry goddess, I'll strive for an ounce of patience."

This was true. "Besides," she added. "We have Simi coming and I think it best we be here when she arrives."

"Yeah," he said with a low laugh. "I definitely don't want a hungry Charonte around my workers and clientele."

It was true. Simi could be a bit ferocious when left on her own. "So are we up for the training?"

He looked at her clothes. "We'll need to get you something else to wear. I don't think that's going to work for training."

Well, it worked for fighting, but she wasn't going to point that out and risk alienating him when she really needed to know how to kill those things that made her skin crawl.

Kat snapped her fingers and her jeans and shirt turned into black workout pants and a black tank top, complete with tennis shoes. "This work?"

"That'll work." He duplicated her gesture of snapping his fingers and his own clothes changed to black sweatpants and a white tank top that only emphasized the dark, sculpted muscles of his body.

Oh yeah, baby . . . She had to stop herself from sucking her breath in as desire tore through her. Good grief, he was yummy when barely dressed. And it made her wonder how much more yummy he might be naked.

Not to mention, his actions proved that he was a lot more powerful than the average Dark-Hunter. He might not have all his god powers, but he had enough to make him extremely formidable.

Wondering what he was going to show her, she followed him down the hallway to a large exercise room.

Ash groaned in his sleep as his dreams twisted through a hazy mist. He truly hated dreaming. He always had. They never made sense and this one was no more helpful or lucid than any other.

There were two women tormenting him that he didn't know. One was tall and blond. Strangely, she reminded him of Artemis. But it wasn't her. This woman had compassion and gentle eyes. She stood over him with a sad look on her face.

"One day we will know each other . . ."

Then the other stepped forward, but her face was completely hidden by the mist. Even so, he knew she was angry at him. Furious even as her eyes glared at him through the shadows. "Who do you think you are? I hate you! Get out. I don't ever want to see you again. I hope you get hit by a car in the parking lot. If I'm lucky, it'll even back up over you. Now go!"

The venom of the tone tore through him. What had he done to her? Why would she hate him? All women loved him. They coveted his presence.

But not this one.

She wanted to cut his head off.

Ash woke up in a cold sweat. It took him a minute to realize he was in Artemis's bed, safe from the scalding tongue of his tormentor. Wiping his brow, he sat up slowly, letting the white silk sheets pool around his waist.

Gods, how he hated to sleep. He'd never had a good dream in his entire existence. But at least these weren't focused on his past. They were from somewhere else . . .

"Worthless!"

He scowled at Artemis's shriek from the other room. It was followed by the sound of something breaking.

"I did my best."

"You're worthless!"

Ash didn't hear anything else, but he felt like someone had just slammed him against the floor. Every part of his body ached and he had to know why. Getting out of bed, he manifested his clothes on his body before he stalked across the floor and flung the large gold doors open with his thoughts.

Deimos had Artemis pinned to the floor by her throat. "You ever—"

He didn't get a chance to finish his threat before Ash picked him up and tossed him wide. Deimos hit the wall, then the floor. He sprang to his feet, braced for attack until he realized who he was facing.

His lips and nose bleeding, Deimos wiped at his face.

Ash gave him a cold, emotionless stare. "You should leave now. Really."

Deimos spat blood on the white marble floor. His gaze went to Artemis, who was now sitting where Deimos had left her. For once she wasn't looking arrogant. "If you want the bastard dead, Artemis, you should send your pet after him."

Normally Ash would have let such a comment pass without issue. But today it just struck him the wrong way. He threw his hands out and brought Deimos straight into his grip.

"I'm so in the mood to kick someone's ass for no good reason. Glad you dropped by." He kneed Deimos in the stomach, and just when he was going to punch him, Deimos vanished.

"Oh c'mon," Ash said out loud. "Was it something I said?"

As expected, Deimos stayed quiet. One word would have allowed Ash to follow him to his haven and finish it.

Bastard.

Still not appeased, he went to Artemis, who hadn't moved from her spot on the floor. How very strange for her. He clenched his teeth as he saw her throat was red from Deimos's attack and her cheeks were pinkened by anger.

"You all right?" he asked.

"Like you care," she spat in a snit. "You'd just as soon hurt me, too."

He bit back a sarcastic comment of agreement as he saw the pain in her eyes. Even though they'd had a less than idyllic relationship, it wasn't in him to kick her when she was down and hurting. He'd been hurt enough in his life to never want to deal that to someone else.

He sat down beside her on the floor and pulled his knees up to his chest. "So what happened?"

Her sullen pout would have made a toddler proud. "Nothing."

He drew a ragged breath as he saw where this was heading. She wanted to talk, but she was going to make him drag every word out. Lovely. Just how he wanted to spend his time here. Then again, given what she normally did to pass time with him, this was an improvement. "C'mon, Artie. I know better. You sent Deimos after Sin, didn't you?"

Her pout increased before she sniffed. "What choice did I have? *You* wouldn't do anything."

Would she *never* grow up? Just once, he'd like to deal with an adult . . . "I can't while I'm here. You know that. You refused to give me a break to go talk to him."

"You wouldn't do anything even if you weren't here."

Probably true.

She sniffed again and gave him a sideways glare. "No one cares what happens to me."

"Don't, Artemis," he said between clenched teeth. "I don't play that pity game and you know it. If you want Daddy to baby you, he's in the big hall up the hill."

The anger returned to her eyes. "Why do you stay with me if you feel that way?"

Funny, he asked himself that every day. "You know why."

She sidestepped his comment. "You hate me, don't you?"

Sometimes. No, most times. But he felt her current vulnerability and for some reason he could never fathom, he had a need to soothe her. Yeah, he was one sick sonofabitch. "No, Artie, I don't."

"You're lying," she accused. "Don't you think I know the difference?" A single tear slid down her cheek as she stared at him. "You used to hold me like I mattered to you."

She was right, and the sad thing was, back then she'd mattered to him more than his own life. But that had been eleven thousand years ago and many, many things had changed between them. "You used to not beat me, too. Remember?"

Artemis shook her head. "You changed even before that. You were angry at me before you died."

Ash so didn't want to deal with this. His past had been painful enough the first time around. The last thing he wanted to do was relive it in any shape, form, or fashion.

Getting up, he headed back to the bedroom, but Artemis followed him.

"What happened to you?" she asked.

He laughed at the stupidity of that question before he turned around to face her again. She truly looked clueless. "How could you forget? It was the day you told me I was nothing more than a booty call for you. Oh wait . . . What were the exact words you used? 'If you ever tell anyone about us, I'll have you flayed in my temple until you're bleeding all over my floor.' That was kind of a buzz kill, huh? And then when you fulfilled that promise even when I hadn't breathed a word of us to anyone, it destroyed whatever part of me cared for you, Artemis."

"I apologized for the beating."

Ash winced at her words. Words. Mere words she thought could erase the pain and humiliation he'd suffered because of her. He could still feel the sting of the lash against his naked flesh.

Even now he heard his sister's shrill cry that afternoon when his human father had confronted him over his absence. *"Father, stop! He's innocent. He was with Artemis. Tell him, Acheron! For the sake of the gods, tell him the truth so he'll stop this beating."*

His human father had knocked him to the ground. He then kicked him onto his back and pressed his foot to Ash's throat to the point where bile had risen to choke him. "What lies have you told her, maggot?"

Ash had tried to push the foot away, but his father had only pressed it even harder against his windpipe. Speaking had been all but impossible. "Nothing, p-p-please . . ."

"Blasphemer." His father had stepped back then and left Ash to strangle as he tried so desperately to breathe through his bruised esophagus. "Strip him and drag him to Artemis's temple. Let the goddess witness his punishment and if he really was with her, then I'm sure she'll come to his defense." He'd turned a smug look at Ryssa. "Beat him at the altar until Artemis shows herself."

The humiliation of that day still stung him to the core of his soul. The people who'd cheered for the executioner to strike him harder. The priests who'd slapped him while the executioner had beat him.

The water that had been thrown in his face to revive him whenever he'd passed out from the pain . . .

Every bit of it was still fresh in his memory.

And Artemis had shown herself all right. But no one other than Ash had seen her there. She'd watched his beating with relish. *"I told you what would happen if you betrayed me."* Then she'd moved to the beefy executioner who was beating Ash and whispered for him to hit even harder, to make the lashes more severe.

Ash had only been twenty years old at the time.

When it was finally over, and then only because the executioner's arm had gone out, Ash had been left to hang for three days in her temple. No food, no water. No comfort. Naked and bleeding. Aching. Alone. And while he'd hung there, people had come up to spit on him and curse him. They'd pulled his hair and hit him.

Told him he was worth nothing and deserved nothing but what he'd received.

When the priests had finally cut him down, his head had been shaved and they had branded the back of his skull with the bow symbol of Artemis.

Then he'd been dragged in chains behind a horse back to the palace. The ground had reopened his wounds and added even more. By the time he was back in his room, he'd been unable to even speak for the pain. He'd lain on the cold stone floor for days, weeping for the fact that the woman he'd loved so dearly had forsaken him when he'd done nothing wrong. He'd guarded her name to the bitter end.

And she thought a mere apology would ease all of that . . .

The bitch was crazy.

To this day, Artemis wouldn't tell anyone anything about their relationship. Not that anyone with a brain hadn't guessed it at this point. It'd only been what? Eleven thousand years of her sneaking him into her temple. Eleven thousand years of her abusing him.

They all knew, but none of them let on. It was a stupid game they all played, and for what? For Artemis's vanity.

"Hold me, Acheron," she said with a tremor in her voice. "Hold me like you used to."

It was all he could do not to shove her away. But that would be cruel, and in spite of what he might wish, he wasn't as cruel as she was.

Instead, he pulled her against him even though his insides cringed.

She sighed dreamily before she wrapped her arms around his waist and snuggled against him.

Ash hated her tenderness most of all. It reminded him too much of the dream he'd once had. A dream of her taking his hand in public. Of her smiling at him openly.

As a human, he'd been dumb enough to think that she would cherish him. At least acknowledge his presence.

But instead, he was and had always been her dirty secret. Before his death at the hands of her own brother, Ash hadn't even been allowed to speak her name in public. Never to touch or look at her or walk past her temple. Only in private had she ever acknowledged him.

He'd been so desperate for even that modicum of kindness that he'd accepted it.

"I love you, Acheron."

He ground his teeth at words she didn't even understand. Love . . . yeah. If this was love, he could definitely do without it.

She kissed his lips before she pulled away with a smile. "You always taste like sunshine."

And she always tasted of cold darkness.

He let out a tired breath. "Feeling better?"

Rubbing his chest, she nodded. "You look tired, my Acheron. Go back to bed. I'll join you shortly."

Yee-flippin'-haw, he thought sarcastically. He couldn't wait for that. It rated right up there with an acid enema. "Where are you going?"

She stood up. "I have something to take care of. But I'll be right back. Trust me."

Like he had a choice?

"Take your time." If he were lucky, he might actually have a whole grope-free hour.

It was really sad when that was the best thing an all-powerful, immortal god could look forward to.

Artemis smiled at him, before she vanished.

She took herself to the Underworld where the Dolophoni made their home in the darkest part of Hades' domain.

It didn't take her long to find Deimos. He stood before a large bureau of weapons, examining the blade of a small hand axe.

"What are you doing?" she asked, wondering what thought was in his mind.

He looked up at her question. "Testing the blade."

"Shouldn't you be finding Sin?"

He set the blade down but didn't look at her as he brushed his hand over other weapons. "Depends. Is your daughter going to keep getting in my way?"

Her stomach shrank at his words. "Excuse me?"

He turned toward her with a cold, sinister look. "Your daughter. You know, the tall blonde with a body made for sin who has your eyes and her father's powers. You didn't really think I was so stupid that I never knew, did you?"

Artemis couldn't speak. She was only grateful Acheron wasn't here to hear that. He'd kill her.

Deimos narrowed his gaze. "That is why you called me in to kill Sin, isn't it? He learned the truth and now he must die."

She refused to give him anything he could use against her. "I don't know what you're talking about."

"Of course you don't." His tone was mocking. He closed the distance between them.

Artemis backed up until she was pressed against the wall.

Deimos gave her a twisted smirk. "So does that mean I have your permission to kill Katra if she gets in the way?"

CHAPTER EIGHT

Sin ducked as Kat's dagger narrowly missed his throat. He smiled at her skill, extremely impressed by it. It wasn't often he found anyone who could come close to striking him, and especially not someone who was put together like a brick house. Like Kish had said about Angelina, he wouldn't mind having his ass beat by Kat, so long as she did it in a black lace or leather teddy. Yeah, the thought of her naked in spiked red heels made him hard even as she slashed at his face.

He caught her wrist as she swung back, but he wasn't expecting her knee a heartbeat later. It landed straight in his ribs.

He grunted before he squeezed the dagger out of her hand. The next thing he knew, she'd head-butted him.

Pain splintered his skull as his head snapped back and blood trickled from his nose. Damn, the woman could hit hard . . .

"Omigod!" she said instantly. "I'm so sorry. I didn't mean to. I got carried away."

He shook his head to clear it even though his forehead and nose were still throbbing and his ears were ringing. "You always apologize to your enemies when you land a solid blow?"

"Never, but I do so whenever I accidentally whack my sparring partner."

Rubbing his head, he smiled as he noted the red spot on her sweaty forehead. The flush on her cheeks made her eyes practically glow. Daughter of Artemis or not, Kat was absolutely beautiful.

"What?" she said, stepping back.

"Nothing. I was just looking at the red place on your forehead where you 'whacked' me. I was wondering if mine looked the same way."

She let out a light laugh before she reached up and touched his head where it was throbbing. "Just a little, Uni."

"Uni?"

Her smile made his cock twitch. "Unicorn. You look like someone sliced the horn right off your forehead." She lifted up to kiss the spot she was eyeing.

That kiss did nothing to ease the serious hard-on that was now aching unmercifully. It'd been a long time since a woman had turned him on like this without being naked in his bed. Or down on her knees in front of him.

Then again, he didn't really converse with his lovers. Basically he'd spy them in the casino, pass a few strategically flattering words, and in no time they'd be in his room completely naked and sweating. Once he was finished with them, he'd send them packing.

Yeah, he was what gave men a bad name and he knew it. But he always made sure that the women knew before they left the casino that he wasn't going to be interested in anything more than casual sex. He didn't take their numbers and promise to call, only to leave them hanging. They knew exactly what his intentions were from the get-go.

As a rule, Dark-Hunters were forbidden from having relationships with humans. And even though he wasn't technically one of their breed, he'd accepted that part of his life. His wife had humiliated him enough with her infidelities. The last thing he wanted was to give another woman any kind of control over his emotions. They just weren't trustworthy enough for that.

But something about Kat was different and he didn't know what it was. Part of him enjoyed her teasing. Hell, he even enjoyed her barbs. That was something that had never happened before.

She bit her lip as she gave him a sympathetic pout. "I really am sorry I head-butted you."

"It's all right. Remember to keep that aim. Unlike a Daimon, the only way to temporarily stop a gallu is to hit it right between the eyes."

"Or sever the spine," she said, to his surprise. "Believe it or not, I was listening."

"Good. That knowledge will save your life." But he wasn't really concentrating on their conversation. His thoughts were on the sweat that was rolling down between her breasts, which swelled underneath her tank. His mouth actually watered for a taste.

She was only a couple inches shorter than him, and in four-inch heels she'd probably force him to look slightly up at her. He didn't know why, but he found that thought incredibly sexy.

Yeah, he could easily see himself in his bed with her on top of him, her body naked except for those heels as she ground herself against him. It was enough to make him crazy.

When he'd developed a shoe fetish he didn't know, but he couldn't get that image out of his head.

Thanks, Kish. He'd have to beat the man later for this torture.

Kat swallowed at the hot look in Sin's golden eyes. She'd had men stare at her lustfully before, but she wasn't used to being affected by it. For some reason she didn't understand, she wasn't immune to Sin. He turned her on in ways she'd never thought possible.

Closing her eyes, she could feel his lips on hers. The scent of his skin filled her head and made her want to bury her face against his neck so that she could bathe in that scent. She wanted to feel those muscles rippling under her palms. To have him lying against her . . .

He was so hypnotic. She barely heard the sound of him dropping the dagger to the floor before he placed his hand on the small of her back and pulled her closer to him.

Still he didn't kiss her. He stared down at her as if waiting for her to shove him away or turn her head. His lips hung over hers as his eyes burned voraciously.

Unable to stand it, she lifted her hand to sink her fingers in his soft black curls and pull his head down to hers. When their lips touched, she moaned in satisfaction. She couldn't imagine anyone tasting better. Couldn't imagine a sweeter place than in his arms.

Sin knew he should break away from her. She was her mother's daughter . . .

And yet her touch set him on fire. The taste of her lips, the feeling of her body against his . . . it was enough to make him forget everything else. There was no hate inside him when she held him. No past tormenting his thoughts. All he could see, taste, smell, or hear was her.

And he reveled in it.

Her hand in his hair sent chills down his spine. Unable to bear it, he lifted her up in his arms. She wrapped her long legs around his waist as he pinned her to the wall. "I want you, Katra," he growled an inch from her lips as he stared hungrily at her. "Right now."

Kat couldn't think straight from the sensation of his body between her legs. She was throbbing with need and every bit as hungry for him as he was for her. "My mother will kill you."

He let out a wicked laugh. "You'd be worth it."

She bit her lip as she felt the swell of him against her. No man had ever touched her—not like this. Truthfully, she'd never been this close to one unless they were fighting. It was actually kind of scary. She'd lived her entire life without the complication of a man.

And they were a complication. Everything about them. Because of a man, her grandmother was imprisoned for eternity. Her mother was forever tied to her father even though she wanted to let him go. Not even Cassandra was free anymore. Wulf meant everything to her and he had become her life. Her friend Geary had given up her life's quest so that she could stay with Arik . . .

Don't be silly, Kat. It's only sex . . . it doesn't have to be a lifetime commitment.

If only she were sure about that. Would being with him change her?

Then again, how could it? Simi hadn't changed. She was still the same exact demon she'd always been.

Kat felt him lifting the hem of her shirt. She had to decide before he went any further.

Yes or no.

In the end, it was her curiosity that won out. She wanted to know what it was like to be with a man, and no other one had ever attracted her like this. If a woman had to lose her virginity, who better than a fertility god to give it to? If there was one thing any of them knew, it was how to please a woman.

And Kat was anything but a coward.

Taking a deep breath, she removed their clothes with her thoughts.

Sin sucked his breath in sharply between his teeth as he felt her naked flesh on his. There was nothing between them now. Nothing. They were skin to skin. It took a full second for that to register in his mind.

He looked down in awe of her bared beauty. Her breasts were perfect and pale. Her nipples were pink and taut, begging him to taste them. He dipped his head down to draw the tip of one into his mouth.

Kat groaned at the foreign tickle that made her stomach contract wildly in response to his gentle licks. The sight of him nuzzling her breast warmed her through and through. Groaning, she ran her hand down his spine and over the scars that marred his darker skin. She laid her cheek against the top of his head as her heart pounded. She and her family had taken so much from him that it only seemed right she should give him what she'd never given to another.

But more than that, she wanted to know him like this. To feel the strength of him surrounding her, filling her. She wanted to share her body with his.

He pulled back from her breast to blow a stinging breath across it before he kissed her again. Mmmm, he was divinity and she couldn't wait to experience more.

Then he slowly lowered them to the floor.

Kat ached at the pleasure of him lying on top of her. It really was scrumptious. He slid his hot mouth slowly down her body, licking and teasing every part of her. She shivered every time his tongue touched her skin and it made her nerve endings dance.

Sin smiled at the little twitches and murmurs she made with every caress he gave her. She was exquisite and he wanted to know every inch of her body.

Her fingers and palms danced over his skin, but when she took him into her hand it was all he could do not to immediately come. He hadn't been with a woman who knew what he was in centuries. Then again, since the death of his wife he hadn't had any woman who'd known even the most basic thing about him. All of his lovers had been one-night stands. Fleeting faces that came and went only when he couldn't bear celibacy any longer.

Unlike the others, Kat would still be here when they were finished. She wasn't going to walk out and never return. It made her special and it made him want to make sure that she had the best time possible in his bed.

When she left his side, she'd never be able to say he'd been lacking in any way. Kissing her, he slid his hand over her thigh to the short curls between her legs.

Kat gasped as Sin slid his fingers between her legs to touch the most private part of her. Fire shot through her as his fingers stroked her tender folds and found the part of her that came alive at his touch. And when he sank one long finger inside her, she moaned out loud.

Sin froze as he felt the impossible. It couldn't be . . . His jaw dropping, he pulled back to stare up at Kat. "You're a virgin?"

"Yes."

That confused him even more. "How?"

She lifted her chin, and when she spoke her tone was heavy with sarcasm. "I've never been with a man before."

He rolled his eyes. "I know how you're a virgin, my question is how did you manage to stay one?"

"I told you, they keep watch on me."

Yeah, but for eleven thousand years? Damn. That was extreme. "They're not watching you now."

She traced the line of his eyebrow while a smile twitched at the edges of her lips. "No. Only you're watching me."

Sin still didn't understand it. "Why would you wait all these centuries and then throw it away on a whim? You barely even know me."

Her expression had to be the tenderest one any woman had ever given him, and it made him melt. "I know you, Sin. I've been inside you . . . and I want you inside me. Is that so hard to understand?"

Part of Sin wanted to curse her and the tender feelings she stirred inside him. He wanted to tell her she was nothing and that he didn't need anything from her.

The other part of him wanted only to hold her. To crawl into her arms and have her soothe him even more than she already had.

In the end, it was his anger he listened to. He couldn't afford to open himself up to her or anyone else. He'd been hurt enough in his life. The last thing he wanted was to bring any more pain into his life. He was through being used and through being manipulated. "This won't give you any hold over me."

"I don't expect it to."

"Then what are you hoping for by sleeping with me?"

"Nothing, Sin." Her gaze was so sincere and guileless it actually sent a wave of guilt through him that he'd been so suspicious of her. "Nothing more than a few moments of pleasure. I don't want anything else from you. Promise." She made a small x over her heart.

He shook his head. It couldn't be this simple. It couldn't. "I find that hard to believe. Nothing comes free in this world. Ever."

"Then get up and get dressed." She looked to the right. "There's the door. I'm sure you know how to use it. It's a really simple process. You put one foot in front of the other, turn the knob, and keep going."

He should do that. It was what he intended, but as she laid her hand against his cheek, he was lost by the tenderness. He just wanted to be held . . .

Damn him for it. He was so tired of being alone. Of coming home to an empty room where he tended his wounds and lived for no other reason than to fight. He didn't even know why he fought anymore.

Why should he care about a world that couldn't care less about him? But when he looked at her, he saw things he hadn't seen in a long time. Compassion. Humor.

Beauty. And that was one thing that was lethal more times than it wasn't.

His emotions were churning as she rolled him onto his back and laid her body against his. His senses reeled as she teased his jaw with her tongue and teeth. Her hair slid against his skin, tickling him. But it was the warmth of her body that seared him most. He was lost to her for now. Lost to her touch and her comfort.

With her holding him like this, he couldn't have gotten up if the room was on fire.

Kat had seen thousands of beautiful naked male bodies in her lifetime. Flawless and perfect, they had come and gone.

None of them could compare to the scarred beauty of Sin's. His body told the story of a man with no one there to keep him safe. In that aspect, he reminded her of her father. But Sin was nothing like Acheron.

There was a spiritual coldness to Sin. He was a man who'd been wounded so many times that he no longer believed in goodness. He couldn't even accept her kindness. What a frigid place to live in.

And all she wanted to do was warm him. To let him know that not everyone meant him harm. Some people could be trusted. Not everyone was out to hurt other people. There was still goodness and decency to be found.

But she wasn't sure he would ever believe that. He most definitely wouldn't if he ever learned the truth about the night Artemis had taken his godhood.

No, the night *she* had taken it and given his powers to her mother. It'd been so wrong, but she'd done it trying to protect her mother. She could kill herself for her stupidity. Back then, she'd believed everything her mother had told her.

She was such a fool.

If only she could go back and change it. Unfortunately, she couldn't. All she could do was try to comfort him now. To be here when he needed help in his fight.

And that she would.

Sin watched her with hooded eyes as she slid herself down his body, exploring every part of it. Now he recognized the innocence in her hesitant touch. The curiosity.

And when she got to the center of his body, she paused. Holding his breath, he watched as she combed the soft tangle of curls with her nails while she studied him intently. It was painful to have her look and not touch him, especially given how hard he was.

Her gaze met his. One corner of her mouth lifted in a tender smile before she touched him. Groaning in satisfaction, he arched his back. Her fingers probed the length of his cock from his sac to the tip, and all the while she watched him writhing in pleasure.

Her smile widened before she dipped her head down to replace her fingers with her mouth.

Sin was forced to bang his head against the floor to keep from coming as she gently sucked and licked. Damn. Damn, she was seriously talented with her tongue.

"Are you sure you haven't done this before?"

She laughed, tickling him. She pulled back to shake her head. "Never before."

Damn . . . it was all he could think.

"You didn't have to stop."

Kat arched a brow at him. "No?"

"Hell, no."

She teased his tip with her tongue before she blew a cool breath across him.

Yeah, okay, it was time to stop. If she didn't, they were both going to be disappointed. Sin sat up and pulled her close. Kat actually purred as he nuzzled her neck. His whiskers teased her skin, making her breasts swell and tingle. She cupped his head to her as her senses swirled. He braced his hands on each side of her hips before he guided her down on top of him so that he could impale her.

She tensed as pain interrupted her pleasure.

"Sh," he breathed in her ear. His breath was scorching as his tongue swirled around her lobe.

Her body ignited as it adjusted to take in his thickness.

Sin felt her relaxing again. He ran his hands over her smooth back and cupped her bottom. He lifted her up and showed her how to move against him. She was a quick learner. In no time, she'd settled into a sweet, slow rhythm that resonated through his entire body.

He leaned back on the floor so that he could watch her while she rode him. She was shameless in her strokes. Oh, the sight of her there, like that . . . it was enough to kill him. Good thing he was immortal.

Smiling, he dipped his hand down so that he could stroke her clit while she rode him. The instant he touched her, she let out a small squeak of pleasure.

"Like that, do you?"

"Mmmm-hmmm," she breathed.

It was torture for him to hold back, but he wouldn't do that to her. He wasn't an ex–fertility god without reason. There was no way he was going to finish before she did. Even if it killed him.

Kat felt molten as she stared down at Sin. She'd never dreamt how good it would feel to have a man inside her. There was something so filling and special about this. She was sharing with him what she'd never shared with anyone else. It was intimate and special. She stared at those golden eyes before she reached to take his hand in hers. Lifting it to her lips, she placed a kiss in his palm, then one on the backs of his fingers.

How could anyone have ever hurt him? It made her angry and protective. Most of all, it saddened her. People could be so cruel and the gods were even worse.

Kat's thoughts scattered as a strange pleasure started inside her. It was warm and wicked and spread through every part of her. Like a wave, it seemed to build and crest until she couldn't stand it anymore.

A second later, her body exploded into intense sensations that made her shake all over.

Sin laughed in triumph as he felt her body spasming around his. Taking her hips in his hands, he thrust harder against her, intensifying her orgasm. She actually cried out as she leaned over him.

Her hair tickled him, and in one heartbeat he joined her climax.

He growled as absolute pleasure tore through him. She was exquisite and she left him breathless and weak. So weak he doubted he could ever move again in this lifetime.

She fell against him, covering him with her body. An uncharacteristic giggle escaped her as she snuggled in his arms.

"Are you okay?" he asked, concerned about her.

"Fine," she said in a dreamy tone. "I feel as satisfied as a well-fed kitten."

He laughed at her. "Yeah, I know the feeling." He wrapped her in his arms before he rolled over with her and pinned her against the floor. "I was right. It was worth your mother killing me."

He dipped his head down and kissed her.

Kat sighed at the way his muscles flexed under her hands. He tasted so incredibly good . . . She never wanted to leave this spot. Ever.

"Ah, gawd, naked people! I'm going to be sick!"

Sin tensed at the deep, feminine voice that came from the doorway. Turning his head, he gaped at the sight of not one but two Charonte demons . . . At least he thought that's what they were. But their skin wasn't mottled with swirling colors—something that always marked their species. Rather, they looked like two women in their early twenties.

One was dressed in black, like a Goth college student, with a short black velvet dress and corset-laced boots. Her hair was black with streaks of red through it. The other one was blond, wearing a pair of jeans and a loose, flowing red top.

"Well, then don't look," the dark-haired demon said to the blond one, who looked strangely like Apollymi. "Why you looking if you don't want to see? Look, right there." She pointed to his Dalí painting on the wall. "They got nice walls with paintings here. You should look at them instead, then you won't be sick. See how it works?"

Kat was biting back a smile as she slid from under him and manifested her clothes on her body. "Hi, Simi."

Sin quickly clothed himself and waited for the demons to realize what he was and attack.

They didn't.

The dark-haired demon smiled, showing off a set of small fangs. "Hello, *akra*-kitty. Sorry it took so long to get here, but someone"—she stared angrily at the blond demon—"wouldn't let me come without her, 'cause she said that Vegas has lots of sparklies she wanted to see. The Simi told her she was wrong, but you see who won the fight, don't you?" She made a loud huffy noise. "You're so lucky you're an only child. The Simi misses her time before someone"—she glared at the blond demon again, but the tirade didn't seem to faze her companion—"that would be Xirena came along and moved into my house. The Simi is just lucky that *akri* didn't make her share her room."

Xirena made a sound of disgust in the back of her throat. "Oh, stop it, Xiamara. All you do is whine, whine, whine. You're a demon. Act like it."

"Demon?" Simi snorted. "I have you know that I am more demon than an army of them. I am the Simi and the Simi acts any way she wants to 'cause *akri* says I am the best demon ever born. You're just jealous your *akri* don't love you like mine does me."

Sin was stunned by their exchange. He'd never seen demons this . . . chatty. Simi was more like a spoiled teenaged girl than a flesh-eating demon. "Is this . . . What is . . . ?" He stopped because he was rambling as he tried to make sense of them. "I have to say that I've never witnessed this before. They do this a lot?"

Kat laughed. "Simi hasn't adjusted to her sister yet. They're having socialization issues."

Xirena curled her lip. "I'm not having an issue with anything other than the fact the cursed god has made my sister strange."

Sin frowned. "Cursed god would be Acheron?"

"Simi belongs to him," Kat explained.

Oh . . . that couldn't be good.

Simi beamed. "The Simi is *akri*'s daughter."

Xirena made a choking noise. "How many times do I have to tell you that you are not the daughter of the cursed god? You are the daughter of two demons! Stop calling your *akri* your daddy. It makes my wings droop."

Simi stuck her tongue out at Xirena. "My *akri* is my daddy. He said so and it is so, so your wings can droop all they want, 'cause it won't change anything."

Sin was still befuddled by the two of them. How were these two supposed to help them combat the gallu? Kessar would tear them apart. Rubbing the back of his neck uncomfortably, he looked at Kat. "Are you sure we shouldn't see about getting another set of demons? I don't see how they're going to help given the way they're arguing."

"Oh, trust me," Kat said with a short laugh, "the fighting stops as soon as food comes into the picture."

"Food?" Simi stopped her tirade instantly. "Where's some food?"

"Is it good food?" Xirena chimed in.

Simi rolled her eyes at her sister. "Is there such a thing as bad food?"

"Well, yeah, there's Daimon. They're kind of gamey tasting and they stick in my fangs."

"Oh, that's true," Simi agreed. "But I have this one kind of barbecue sauce from New Orleans that can kill that gamey taste. It makes them really good eats. Rank Daimon meat right up there with human and opossum."

Xirena looked thrilled. "Is that that sauce I saw in your room with the woman with a leather whip on it?"

"Oh no. That's Pain and Suffering, but that one's good, too. This one got a man who's breathing fire like a fat dragon, only he's not fat, he's—"

"Excuse me, demons?" Sin asked, interrupting them.

They looked at him as if he were about to be added to their menu.

And coming under their full attention was a *big* mistake. As soon as Xirena's gaze met his, recognition lit her black eyes. "You a Sumerian."

Her eyes flashed yellow as her skin mottled with red and black and black wings grew out of her back.

He braced for the fight, but before she could attack, Kat stepped in front of him. "Calm down, Xirena. Sin's on our side."

Xirena spat on his floor, which irritated the hell out of him, and he was sure housekeeping wouldn't appreciate it, either. "Death to all Sumerians."

"They're not all bad," Simi said, crossing her arms over her chest. "*Akri* knew this one Sumerian who was a fisherman for a long time. He's really nice to the Simi. He used to feed me these tasty balls of fish all soaked in olive oil and wrapped in grape leaves. Then he'd let the Simi eat fishcakes and the eyeballs. Fish eyes are very tasty, especially in olive oil."

Xirena growled at her, "Sumerians are all enemies to the Charonte."

Simi put her hand on her hip and cocked her head. "Well, that's just stupid. You can't hate an entire race 'cause one or two of them are mean. What you got against the Sumerians anyway?"

"They created the gallu demons to kill us."

"Oooo." Simi's face brightened. "I like them gallu demons. They so crispy when you burn them. *Akri* used to let me eat them by the dozen. And he never cared, neither—not like when I'd eat people. But then all them gallu went away and the Simi couldn't eat them anymore. I really miss them. They were so yummy."

"And now they're back," Kat said, gaining their attention again.

Xirena's expression looked as if she'd just stepped in a manure factory.

Simi just looked excited. "Can I eat them?"

Sin nodded. "Bon appétit."

Kat gave him a chastising glance over her shoulder. "Yes, Simi. But we need you and Xirena to help us fight them."

Xirena jerked her chin toward Sin. "I think we should feed the Sumerian to them. He would deserve it."

Kat tsked at her. "Xirena . . ."

"I told you, Katra," Simi said in a singsongy tone, "she all kinds of mean. You should have her eat your earrings when you're not looking. And they were the good ones, too. Covered with diamonds . . . they sparkle a lot."

Xirena glared at Simi. "Well, you would be mean, too, if you saw how them gallu killed us, and eating them won't be easy without your *akri* there to shield their powers. They are evil demons who can kill us." She looked at Katra. "Will the cursed god help?"

Kat hesitated. She wished, but that wasn't an option right now. "We're going to try and do this without his help."

Xirena's eyes widened. "Why would we do that?"

" 'Cause *akri* don't know about Katra," Simi explained. "If he learned about her, he would be really sad and the Simi don't want to make *akri* sad, so you can't say a word about Katra to him. He sad enough already because he has to deal with that bitch-goddess with the red hair."

"Simi," Kat said in a warning tone.

"Well, she is a bitch-goddess. I know you love her, *akra*-Kat, but facts is fact and she a mean heifer."

Xirena smacked her lips. "I haven't had a heifer in a while. Are there any heifers here?"

Simi cast a sideways look at her sister. "I know where a big red one is on Olympus."

Kat shook her head. "Simi!"

"What?" She batted her eyes with a wide, innocent expression. "If Xirena eats her, then how can I get in trouble for it?"

Sin snorted. "It's like dealing with children. Ye gods, how did the Atlanteans stand it?"

Kat pressed her hand to the throb in her temple as she wondered the same thing herself. "They're normally a bit more silent than this."

He looked less than convinced. "Really?"

"Apollymi keeps a tight rein on them."

At the mention of Apollymi's name, Xirena hissed. "Death to the bitch-goddess! May she die in a flaming pit of Charonte spit."

Sin laughed at Xirena's condemnation. "Damn, Kat, you can't win for losing. Is there anyone, other than you, who actually likes your family?"

She sighed in resignation. "Some days it seems not."

"You one to talk," Xirena said testily. "Nobody likes your family, either."

"Yeah!" Simi paused. She put her hand to her face to whisper at her sister, "Is that true?"

"Yes."

"Yeah!" Simi shook her fist in the air to prove her point.

Sin shook his head at her. "I think I'm getting a migraine from this."

"You can't get migraines," Kat reminded him.

"Then it's a tumor . . . one the size of two demons."

She laughed at his acerbic tone. "You wanted help. I give you the cavalry."

Well, she had done that. But Sin wasn't convinced the cure might not be a thousand times worse than the ailment. "Strange, I have this feeling our cavalry may yet run us both over . . . then eat us."

Kat gave him an agitated stare. "So where do they stay?"

Sin hesitated at the question. Leaving them alone didn't seem like a good idea to him. "Can they be left alone?"

She shrugged. "I don't see where they're any more dangerous than the Daimons you have downstairs patrolling tourists for dinner."

"They don't have wings and horns."

Xirena returned to looking human. "Neither do we. Unless we want them."

Simi lifted her hand like a student. "If the Daimons are eating tourists, can we?"

"No," Sin and Kat said simultaneously.

"Well, poo." Simi pouted. "Why them Daimons get special treatment?"

Xirena screwed her face up in a huff. "Maybe we ought to go back to Katoteros. At least there we got them dragon things to eat whenever we're hungry."

Simi's face paled. "You ate *akri*'s pets? Bad Xirena. He don't like it when they go away. Oooo, you better hide when he come home and finds them missing. He'll be very upset."

Kat cleared her throat and hoped to get them off this topic and back to the one that needed to be discussed. She looked at Sin. "You can put them in a room with QVC and they'll be as happy as clams."

"QVC?" the demons said in unison.

Simi looked at her watch. "It Diamonique time, too. Where's a TV?"

Sin rubbed his eyebrow before he went to call Kish and book the two demons a room down the hall from his suite.

They were still chattering about the yummy Diamonique flavor when Kish came to get them and show them to their room.

Sin stood in the doorway watching them leave. "Those are some demons you've got there."

"Yes," she said with a smile as she closed the distance between them, "they are. We just have to make sure nothing happens to Simi. Acheron would kill us both."

Sin's eyes softened as he looked down at her. "I somehow doubt he would kill you. But I, on the other hand, would most likely be short a couple of heads."

She frowned. "Couple?"

He pointed to the one on his shoulders, then dipped his hand down to his groin.

"Ah." Kat laughed. "You're awful."

"Yes, but while I know I can hold my own against most creatures, Ash is one I know for a fact can hand me my ass in a box. Therefore, I try to stay on his good side as much as possible."

She wasn't sure she bought that statement. "You're not really afraid of him, are you?"

"Definitely not afraid. Just highly respectful. I thank the Fates for what they did to him by making him live as a human being for a while. Had they not, can you imagine what the universe would be like? Think of the power he and Apollymi command. Now put the ego of a typical god on it."

Yeah, it was the stuff of nightmares.

But it also begged the question of whether or not that was what had made Acheron the way he was. It was a question Kat had pondered a lot. "Yet you have a conscience. I can't imagine you running over people to get what you want."

"I'm not the same creature now that I was when I had my godhood. When I was a young, I was angry and bitter over what my father had done to us and, as a god, I had a lot to prove. Not to mention living as a human has a very sobering way of altering your perspective on many things."

Kat's stomach shrank at the tone of his voice. Her gaze fell to the scar on his neck. She reached up to touch it and thought about how much pain that wound must have caused him. She had to bite her lip to keep from apologizing to him for taking his powers.

She'd been so young and stupid herself. Like most children, she'd been blind to her mother's faults. She'd only wanted to please Artemis and make her happy. How was she to know one mistake would hurt someone else so badly and alter the history of the world?

If only she could take his powers from her mother and return them to him, but Artemis would never allow her to do that. If she tried, she'd lose her mother forever, and even in spite of Artemis's faults, Kat loved her. She would never do anything to hurt her mother.

Sin took Kat's hand from his neck and placed a light kiss on her palm. Even so, there was a wild look in his eyes. He was allowing her near him, but he could turn on her any moment. It was scary and titillating.

"We still have to find my brother," he reminded her.

Kat nodded. "All right. I think it best if I go alone. I'll go see if my grandmother can help with the *sfora*." *And if she's in a receiving mood.* For something like this, they wanted Apollymi to be happy and helpful. Otherwise, it would be a waste of time to visit and would most likely result in her refusing to help them at all.

Kat stepped away from Sin, but before she could flash out of the room, he laid a hand on her arm.

"Thank you, Katra. I appreciate the help."

She didn't know why, but those few words made her heart soar. "You're welcome."

He inclined his head before he gave a tender squeeze. "And I haven't forgotten your gift to me. Thank you again."

She stepped forward and laid a gentle kiss to his cheek. "I'll be back soon."

Artemis hesitated as she neared her bedroom. She chewed her thumbnail in indecision. Maybe she should just go to Zeus's temple for a while and think of something on her own . . .

"What did you do?"

She jumped at the sound of Acheron's voice coming from behind her. "I thought you were in bed," she snapped.

"I had to go to the bathroom."

"Oh."

His swirling silver eyes were piercing as he glared at her. "What have you done, Artie? And don't say, 'Nothing.' I know by the way you're acting that it's going to seriously piss me off."

She hated when he could read her so easily. How did he do that?

But she refused to be the one on the defensive. So she did what she always did. She went on the offense. "Well, it's your own fault."

He rolled his eyes at her. "Of course it is. Everything's always my fault. So what did I do now?"

She narrowed her gaze at him in anger, but there was still a part of her that was terrified of him. Most of all she was terrified of what he was going to do when she told him what she needed . . . and mostly why she needed it.

"You have to promise me two things before I tell you."

A tic worked in his jaw. "What?"

She took a step back to put more distance between them. "First that you won't kill me. Ever. And the second that you'll stay here another week."

Ash hesitated. This had to be even worse than he suspected for her to want to make such a bargain with him. His gut knotted in anger. He could feel his eyes turning red and his cheeks growing warm. But she wouldn't care about that.

And he knew her well enough to know that if he didn't give her what she wanted, she'd never tell him whatever it was that had her so nervous.

"Okay. Fine."

"Say the words, Acheron. I want to know you are bound by them."

He cursed before he spoke between clenched teeth. "Fine. I promise I won't kill you, and—"

"Ever."

Ash took a deep breath before he said, "Ever." Gods, how he'd like to choke her.

"And you'll stay here for another week . . . unless I need you to do something for me."

That made his blood run cold. "Do what?"

"Say it, Acheron, and then I'll tell you."

Oh yeah, this was going to infuriate him. He only hoped he could keep his word. If not, he'd perish from it right alongside her. "All right. I won't leave here for another week, unless you need me to do something."

She let out a long, relieved breath. "Good. Now you stand right there."

Okay . . . He did and wondered what the hell was wrong with her . . . besides the fact that she was selfish and cold.

She, on the other hand, moved to the other side of the room, far away from him.

"What are you doing, Artemis?"

"I had something to tell you."

"Have," he corrected. "And yes, we've already ascertained this. What is it?"

"You're getting angry."

Disgust filled him that she was continuing to play this game. "You didn't make me promise not to."

"Only because I knew you would and then you'd die."

"Artemis!"

"Fine," she said in a huff. "Don't shout at me. I can't stand it when you do that."

"I'm about to do more than shout."

"Okay, be that way. Do you remember when you were first brought back from the dead?"

Remember it? It haunted him daily. It'd been one of the more painful moments in a life marked by agony. "What about it?"

"Well . . ." Biting her lip, she twisted her hand in her gown. "There were months where you wouldn't come to my temple even though I tried to summon you."

"Yes. I was just a little pissed at what you and your brother had done to me."

"But I want you to remember that I did do my best to summon you."

She was a little too eager about this for his tastes, but he sought to ease her stress in spite of the fact that what he really wanted to do was choke her. "I remember, Artemis. You damn near drove me insane with your insistent shrieking that I come to you."

"And when you finally came, do you remember what happened?"

Ash let out another frustrated breath. He could see that moment clearly. Artemis had met him outside her temple here in her forest. He'd stood in the center of a clearing, glaring at her. He'd been hungry and furious, and he'd wanted her blood in the worst sort of way.

She'd approached him cautiously that day as if terrified of him. "Please don't be angry at me, Acheron."

He'd laughed bitterly. "Oh, 'angry' doesn't even begin to describe what I am at you. How dare you bring me back."

She'd gulped. "I had no choice."

"We all have choices."

"No, Acheron. We don't."

As if he'd believed it. She'd always been selfish and vain and no doubt that was the only reason he'd been brought back when he should have been left dead. "Is this why you've been summoning me? You want to apologize?"

She'd shaken her head. "I'm not sorry for what I've done. I would do it over again in a heart pound."

"Beat," he'd snarled.

She'd waved the word away with her hand. "I want there to be peace between us."

Peace? Was she insane? She was lucky he didn't kill her right now. If it weren't for fear of what could happen to the innocent, he would have.

"There will never be peace between us. Ever. You shattered any hope of it when you watched your brother kill me and refused to speak up on my behalf."

"I was afraid."

"And I was butchered and gutted on the floor like an animal sacrifice. Excuse me if I don't feel your pain. I'm too busy with my own." He'd turned to leave her then, but she'd stopped him.

It was then he heard the muffled whimpering of a baby. Scowling, he'd watched in horror as Artemis withdrew an infant from the folds of her *peplos*.

"I have a baby for you, Acheron."

He'd jerked his arm away from her as fury singed every part of him. "You bitch! Do you honestly think that could *ever* replace my nephew you let die? I hate you. I will always hate you. For once in your life, do the right thing and return that to its mother. The last thing a babe needs is to be left with a heartless viper like you."

She'd slapped him then with enough strength to split his upper lip. "Go and rot, you worthless bastard."

Laughing, he'd wiped the blood away with the back of his hand while he stared venomously at her. "I may be a worthless bastard, but better that than a frigid whore who sacrificed the only man to ever love her because she was too self-absorbed to save him."

The look on her face had scorched him. "I'm not the whore here, Acheron. You are. Bought and sold to anyone who could pay your fee. How dare you think for one minute you were ever worthy of a goddess."

The pain of those words had seared a permanent place in his heart and soul. "You're right, my lady. I'm not worthy of you or anyone else. I'm just a piece of shit to be dumped naked in the street. Forgive me for ever sullying you."

And then he'd vanished from her, and for two thousand years

he'd avoided any and all contact with her. The only thing he'd accept from her was vials of her blood so that he could eat and live.

If he'd had his way, he'd have never seen her again. But then she'd used the powers she'd stolen from him to create the Dark-Hunters under the guise of using them to protect the humans from the Daimons Apollo had created. The reality was, she'd used the Dark-Hunters to tie Acheron to her forever and to force him to come and barter with her for their freedom.

They were the only reason he had anything to do with her. Them and the guilt he felt over their creation.

Damn them all for it.

But that was the ancient past and it was best left alone. "Why are you dredging up such bitter memories now, Artemis?"

And as soon as the words left his lips, he had sudden clarity.

"I have a baby for you, Acheron."

Ash stepped back as disbelief and pain slammed him hard in the stomach. "The baby . . ."

Artemis nodded. "She was your daughter."

CHAPTER NINE

Acheron staggered away from Artemis as his rage ripped through him with razor-sharp talons. He put his arm against the wall and watched as his skin turned blue. His breathing was ragged as his teeth grew to large fangs and his vision became cloudy.

He wanted Artemis's blood so badly, he could taste it. More than that, he wanted to rip her throat out.

"Damn you!" he snarled.

"I tried to tell you. I gave her to you and you rejected her."

He spun around to glare at her. "You said, 'I have a baby for you.' Not 'I *had* your baby,' Artemis. There's a big fucking difference. I thought the baby was nothing more than an offering to you from one of your worshipers that you were trying to pawn off on me to make amends for my dead nephew, and you knew that." All of her handmaidens had come into her service in such a manner. Back then, it was nothing for people to leave infants as offerings to the gods.

He raked his hands through his hair as more hated memories surged and tore through him.

He could see himself again as a young man on the cold stone slab, chained down and held in place by servants as the surgeon came forward with a scalpel.

Acheron hissed and flinched at the remembered pain.

His breathing ragged, he approached Artemis with his hands clenched into fists so that he didn't begin choking her. "They sterilized me. There's no way I could father a child. It's not possible."

Her face hardened. "As a human you were sterile. But on your twenty-first birthday . . ."

His godhood had been unlocked.

He wiped his hands over his face as he remembered that. All the scars on his body had been removed. Physically, he'd been restored.

Obviously it hadn't all been on the surface. That night must have undone their surgery, too. Dammit, how could he have been so stupid?

"Why didn't you tell me you were pregnant?"

She glared at him. "I tried. You wouldn't listen to me or speak to me. 'I hate you, Artemis. Go die.' That's all I heard from you for two thousand years."

Ash laughed as bitter grief assailed him. For once, she was right. He'd been the one who ignored her. Dear gods, who would have thought *this* was what she'd been trying to tell him?

Worse, she had held his daughter out to him and he'd cursed her for it. Now he cursed himself for being so damn blind and stupid. How could he not have known? How could he have allowed his anger at her to blind him to something so important?

He could kill himself for his own stupidity. He had denied his own child. Gods only knew what she must think of him and his rejection.

"It's been eleven thousand years, Artemis. You know, you could have mentioned this to me before now."

Her eyes were filled with tears. "I wanted to hurt you then. I held her out to you and you insulted me and refused what I loved more than anything else in this universe. You have no idea what I went through trying to prevent anyone from knowing I was pregnant. I suffered through her birth alone, with no attendants. No one to help me in any way. I didn't have to have her, you know."

Artemis was still trying to hurt him with that last remark, but he wasn't willing to let her get away with it. "Then why did you?"

"She was a part of you and she was mine. The only thing in my life that has ever been purely mine. There was no way I wouldn't have had her. By the time you started talking to me again, she was grown. I didn't see the point of losing you over something I couldn't help when I'd already done everything I knew to do to make you love me."

Ash gave a bitter laugh. "I'm happy for you, Artie. You got to love my daughter and I'm nothing but a stranger to her. Thank you."

"Don't be so surly. I didn't have her long to myself before she went behind my back to find your mother. She's just like her father—ever out to punish me when all I want to do is hold her."

He went cold at her words. *You've got to be kidding me . . .* "My mother knows about her?"

"Of course the bitch does. I had to give up my protection of my daughter to your mother to save you that night in New Orleans when Stryker was about to kill you."

Ash seethed in anger even though he didn't know why. He'd been screwed over by his mother and Artemis more times than he could count. There had never been a woman in his life who hadn't lied and betrayed him.

Not a one.

Simi had been the only pure thing he'd ever known. And even she had gone behind his back to seduce his best friend. She'd lost her innocence and he'd gained an enemy who now had no intention of stopping until Ash was dead.

Or until Ash killed him.

Yeah, women were the very bane of Ash's entire existence. He wished he'd been born gay so that he would have spared himself centuries of pain at their hands.

But there was nothing he could do to change the past. Letting out a long, angry breath, he glared at Artemis. "And where is my daughter now?"

"That's why I'm here. I sent her to kill Sin."

"You what!"

Artemis squeaked and put more distance between them. "Don't

worry. She's too much like you and wouldn't do it. So I had to call out Deimos to do it."

Oh, this was going to be good. "Let me guess. Deimos is on the loose now after both of them?"

She nodded. "I told him not to hurt Katra, but he doesn't listen. And somehow he knows she's my daughter."

Now it all made sense. "You want me to stop Deimos."

"I want you to kill him."

He laughed in disbelief.

"Don't shake your head at me," she snapped. "I know you can do it. You're a god-killer. His powers are nothing compared to yours."

He cut a lethal glare at her. "Oh, you have no idea, Artie. Not really. In fact, you're lucky I don't cut you down right now where you stand."

"You can't. You swore you wouldn't."

"Yeah, but I'm thinking right now your death might be worth mine."

"You wouldn't dare."

He growled, knowing she was right. If he died, it would unleash his mother on the world and mankind would go up in a fiery blaze. Damn him for caring about that.

He released a slow breath before he asked Queen Dense the obvious. "So how can I protect my daughter if you won't let me out of here for two more weeks?"

"If Katra needs you, you can go to her. But she has to be in danger first."

Ash paused at hearing his daughter's name for the first time. "Katra"? In Greek, it meant "pure".

Artemis nodded. "She looks just like you." Holding her hand up, she summoned an image of Katra's face so that he could see her.

Tears gathered in his eyes as he saw the beauty of his daughter, but he refused to let them fall. And as he looked at her image, he was stunned to realize that he did know her. It was the face he'd seen in his dreams. The blond woman he couldn't identify. Somehow his mind must have known she was out there and it'd been struggling to tell him.

"Have I ever seen her?" he asked, his voice barely more than a whisper.

"Just once that I know. She was rushing out with the other *koris* when you showed up unexpectedly. You glanced at her before I made you look at me."

He remembered that. He'd been struck by the fact that one of the *koris* was obviously taller than Artemis when he knew that Artemis couldn't stand having a woman taller than her around her. "The tall blonde . . ."

"Yes."

Ash swallowed the pain that swelled inside of him. To think he'd been that close to her . . . it cut him deep. "Does she know about me?"

"I never kept the identity of her father from her. It was why she went to visit your mother."

A sick feeling settled deep in his stomach. "What did you tell her, Artie? That I rejected her?"

Her eyes snapped fire at him. "You know, Acheron, I get tired of you hurting me, too. Really tired. Had you been decent to me, you would have known all about her. So don't you dare take that hostile tone with me. I did the right thing. You were the one who walked out on her. I was there for her, raising her, while you were off pouting."

Pouting. Yeah. That was so him. He'd been learning to use his powers and had been trying to control a very young Simi who had never been in the human world before. Those early years after Artemis had brought him back had been hard and frightening.

And he'd had no one to turn to. His mother had been bitter and irrational every time he tried to speak to her. Artemis had nagged without cessation. If Savitar hadn't appeared to him to show him how to channel and use his powers, he'd have been completely lost.

But that was the past and he couldn't change it. All he could do was make sure that no one hurt his daughter from this point forward. "Simi!"

He'd barely finished the call before Simi appeared before him. "Akri!" She beamed in delight. "Can you come home now?"

He cast a malevolent stare at Artemis. "Not right now. But I have an assignment for you."

She looked a bit confused. "You do?"

"Yeah. I apparently have someone I need you to watch over. I want you to make sure nothing at all happens to her. Do you understand?"

Simi paled. "You don't want the Simi to watch over the bitch-goddess, do you? 'Cause no offense, *akri,* that would just be wrong, and I love you, but that's more love than the Simi has for anything. Even Diamonique."

He smiled at her honesty. "Not Artemis, Sim. I need you to watch over a woman named Katra."

She scowled at his request. "*Akra*-Kat?"

A bad feeling went through him. "You know her?"

She became antsy, which was never a good thing.

Artemis made a sound of disgust. "He knows she's his daughter, twit."

Simi turned on her with an arch look. "Twit? Moi? The Simi? Why, I do believe the bitch-goddess has done gone and gotten herself confused. She thinks she's me, not that I blame her. All women want to be me because of my beautoneousness and the fact that I have such stylish clothing and sparklies. But believe me, I ain't no heifer-goddess."

"Oh, please, you stupid demon. Like I would ever want to be you."

Simi's eyes flashed dark so fast that Ash barely had time to grab her and hold her back from eating the bitch-goddess. "No, Sim. Leave her alone." Then he looked at Artemis. "Insult her again and she's the least of your concerns."

Artemis scoffed. "You can't hurt me."

"You're right. *I* can't. But you never said I couldn't give you over to my girl here."

Simi laughed happily. "Oooo, I finally get to eat the bitch goddess? Oh, goodie!"

Artemis vanished instantly.

Ash would have taken satisfaction in that if he wasn't so upset. He released Simi and turned her to face him. "You knew about my daughter?"

She lowered her chin like a child afraid of a spanking—something he'd never done to her. "Is *akri* angry at his Simi?"

He pulled her to him and held her against his chest. "How could I be angry at you?" She was the only thing in his life that had ever loved him without conditions or embarrassment. But it still didn't stop him from being hurt that she'd kept this secret. "I just wish you'd told me."

"But the queen goddess said it would make you cry to know. She said it would hurt you so much—like she hurts 'cause she can't have you with her. I didn't want you to sit and cry like *akra* does."

He tightened his hold on her. "I know, Sim. It's okay."

She pulled back to look up at him. "Are you sad, *akri?*"

"A little."

She took his hand into hers. "The Simi didn't mean to hurt you, *akri*."

"Oh, baby, you didn't hurt me. I'll be all right."

"Okay," she said gently, " 'cause if you're not all right, I'll eat the heifer-goddess for you and make it all better."

He smiled at her. "You can't do that."

She pouted. "Just a little nip? Maybe her heel or a finger. She'd never miss it . . . unless she went to pick something up and then, well, who cares. Well maybe you, but no one else would."

"No, Sim. Your little nips are the size of a shark bite. I need you to find Katra for me and guard her."

"Oh, the Simi knows right where she is. I just left her."

His jaw went slack. Though to be honest, at this point he didn't know why anything shocked him. "You what?"

"She with that ex-god who hates the heifer-goddess like I do. They asked for me and Xirena to help them fight those gallu demons you used to let me eat. Apparently, there's a bunch of them out now." She reached into her purse and pulled out a bottle of barbecue sauce. "I'm all prepared."

Ash shook his head, trying to understand. "The gallu are loose now?"

She nodded. "Sin said they're coming out by the dozen—just enough to make a good appetizer for us."

Yeah, and enough to do serious damage to the human race. "Go, Simi. Watch over Katra for me."

"Okay, *akri*. But don't be sad." She blew him a kiss before she vanished.

He let out a tired breath as he surveyed the empty room. Everything on earth was falling apart and he was trapped here because of Artemis's insatiable libido. Where was the justice in that?

"What the hell's going on?" He had to know.

Closing his eyes, he tried to locate Sin and the gallu, but all he saw was a haze with no real form or substance. That didn't surprise him, though. He usually had a hard time seeing anything below while he was in Artemis's temple. She didn't want him to know since it would make him even more restless to leave than he already was.

But there was one person who could tell him what he needed to know . . .

He returned to the balcony outside Artemis's main room and leaned against the railing. Closing his eyes again, he let his *ensyneiditos* travel out of his body, through the cosmos until he was in his mother's garden. It was the only break he was allowed while here. Because the *ensyneiditos* was simply the conscious part of himself and not his body, he could use it to visit others while trapped on Olympus.

It was also the *only* way he could ever visit with his mother. If he ever appeared to her in the flesh, it would release her from her prison and allow her to destroy the world—which was her one goal in life.

His goal was to prevent that.

Floating into Kalosis, he found her sitting near the pool in the back. The obsidian rocks were as iridescent as her pale skin as she scrythed by using the black water to make a *sfora*. His mother had lifted a portion of the water up to form a dark swirling ball in the air.

But what stunned him was the woman who stood beside her. It was a face he'd seen before, but only in his dreams. Her features were similar to his, only there was enough of her mother in that face to mark her for what she was.

His daughter.

"Katra?"

The ball splintered and fell in droplets back to the water as the two of them turned to face him. And when those green eyes looked into his, he wanted to cry. But pain was nothing new to him. He was so used to hiding it that it didn't even require any real effort on his part.

"Apostolos," his mother said breathlessly before she rose to her feet. She looked back and forth between them. "Are you angry?"

Kat couldn't move as she waited for an answer. By the way he'd said her name, she knew someone had told him about her. And she couldn't believe her father was here . . . with them. But she knew he wasn't really here. He was only an apparition. He couldn't have any real contact with his mother without it freeing her.

Still, he was looking at Kat with a stern expression.

She'd dreamt of this moment where he knew her for what she was millions of times in her life. Only in her dreams she was filled with happiness, not trepidation. She'd tried to imagine every possible scenario for their meeting, but none of them had come close to this.

Now she wanted to run to him and hug him. If only she could. His cold demeanor was such that she was afraid to even move.

"Dad?" she asked hesitantly.

He looked away as a single tear fled down his cheek and he faded away from them. It made Kat's own eyes swim as her emotions gathered in her throat to bitterly choke her.

Her grandmother placed a tender hand on her shoulder. "Go to him, Katra. He needs you."

She nodded before she flashed herself from Kalosis to Olympus. She was on the balcony where she'd frolicked and played as a child.

And her father was only a few feet from her.

Kat wasn't sure what to say or do. She wanted to run to him. Or, better yet, say something. But nothing came to mind while she felt his pain and sorrow.

He stood as still as a statue, gazing out on the garden below.

Suddenly he gasped as his consciousness returned to his body. Her heart stopped the instant he turned toward her and met her gaze.

Her tears flowed down her cheeks as her emotions overwhelmed her. She wiped angrily at them. "I don't normally do this. I'm really not that emotional."

Still he didn't speak. He merely walked toward her as if he couldn't believe what he was seeing. He stopped just before her and stared at her as if she were a wraith.

Up close, he seemed so much larger. Much more powerful. She supposed it was normal for a daughter to be intimidated to a degree by her father. But she was honestly scared.

"Have you had a good life?" he asked in a gentle tone.

That single question only made her cry harder as she nodded. "I only wanted for one thing."

"And that was?"

"You."

Ash couldn't breathe as his own tears fell from his eyes. It infuriated him. He didn't cry. Ever.

Yet the thought of having missed so much of her life, the knowledge that he was a complete stranger to his own daughter, tore him apart.

How many children had he coddled and protected over the centuries? How many had he held, wishing he had his own, but convinced that he was incapable of it? Now to learn that he'd had a daughter all this time . . .

It was so unfair.

He swallowed as he ached to reach out to touch her but was afraid she'd shove him away like everyone else in his past. Surely she must hate him for his neglect. He wouldn't blame her if she did. God knows, he'd felt that way when he learned about his real parents. He'd despised them for never telling him who they were, for never being there when he needed comfort or love.

Until now, he hadn't realized how hard his first meeting with his mother must have been for her.

"I don't even know what to say to you," he whispered.

"Me, either. I guess we'll just stand here and cry at each other, huh?"

He laughed at her unexpected humor.

Kat wiped at her eyes again. "Can I hug you?"

Ash held his arms out, and before he could move she ran to him. The feel of her there as he wrapped his arms around her rattled him to the depths of his soul. This was his daughter. *His* true flesh and blood. A wave of possessive pride ripped through him, but the love he felt for her was enough to almost drown him.

Now he fully understood his mother and her anger on the night she'd learned about his past. He wanted to hurt anyone who'd ever hurt Kat.

The guilt over not being there . . .

Not once in Kat's life had he held her. Never had she cried and felt his comforting touch. She'd lived knowing nothing about him other than the fact that he had donated DNA to make her. His only comfort was that he'd never known about her existence.

How much worse had it been for his mother to know he was out there but to not be able to go to him?

"I'm so sorry," he breathed against Kat's hair as he cradled her head in his palm. "I didn't know."

"I know you didn't."

Still he wanted her to understand just how sorry he felt. "Why didn't you ever come to me?"

"When I was young I was afraid you'd be mad at me. Every time I saw you come here, you were always so angry. You hated Artemis and I was afraid you'd hate me for tying you to her."

He pulled back and cupped her face in his hands. "I could never hate you."

Kat had waited her whole life to hear those words, as more tears gathered in her eyes. To feel the touch of her father. It was so much sweeter than she'd ever imagined. "I love you, Dad."

Ash let out a sob as pain wracked him. Those words tore through every fiber of his being. "I'm so sorry, Katra."

"Me, too. I should have told you. I know that. But I really didn't know what you'd do to Mom. I was afraid you'd kill her."

He gave a bitter laugh. "I probably would have." He shook his head as he looked her up and down. "You're so beautiful. I wish I'd seen you as a child."

She gave him a coy grin. "You didn't miss much. I had buck teeth and stringy hair."

He laughed. "I seriously doubt that."

"It's true, and I was really hideous as a preteen. Tall and gawky. I used to bump my head into everything. Still do sometimes."

He shook his head at her. "You *are* my daughter."

"Sure I am," she scoffed. "I can't imagine you ever being uncoordinated."

"Oh, I assure you I've nailed quite a few signs with my forehead.

It's a wonder 'Exit' isn't permanently imprinted right between my eyes."

Her melodic laugh filled his ears and made his heart ache.

Ash couldn't get over how similar her mannerisms were to his. It was like looking into a mirror and seeing someone else's face in your stead.

But his joy was cut short by another fear as he realized just how similar the two of them were and what that might have meant for Katra growing up. "Has your mother been good to you?"

A slow smile spread across her face. "For her, yeah. I mean other than the fact I could never call her Matisera unless we were alone, she really was good."

How awful to never be able to acknowledge Artemis as her mother in public. He knew that pain well and it made him even angrier that Artemis, having done that to him, would also do it to his child.

How selfish could one person be?

"Is she loving to you?"

Kat swallowed at his question and she knew exactly what he meant by it. He was afraid her mother had been cold to her. But in spite of Artemis's shortcomings, that had never been the case.

Wanting to set his mind at ease, Kat took his hand into hers and closed her eyes so that she could show him.

Ash jerked as he saw Katra's memories in his mind. She was no more than seven and she was alone with her mother in Artemis's bedchamber. They were curled up together in Artemis's bed.

Katra frowned as she laid a tiny hand to Artemis's moist cheek. "Why do you cry, Matisera?"

"You're too young to understand, my little one."

"Then you can tell me why you cry and I won't understand it. Then you'll feel better and be happy again."

Artemis smiled through her tears as she lifted the blanket higher around Kat's shoulders. "I made a horrible mistake."

Her young brow was furrowed in puzzlement. "But you're a goddess. You can't make mistakes."

Artemis took Kat's small hand into hers and placed a tender kiss on it. "Trust me, little one. Everyone makes mistakes. Even the gods, and ours are much worse than those of humans. Unlike humans, we don't suffer alone. Rather, we share the pain with thousands. That's why you must learn to be like your father. To hold in your tears and anger. Try not to punish what you love."

"But you don't punish me, Matisera."

Artemis kissed her on the forehead. "No, Katra, I don't. I love my little treasure."

Still Katra looked confused by her mother's tears. "Am I your mistake, Matisera?"

"Oh, great Olympus, no! Why ever would you think that, child?"

" 'Cause no one can know about me. Aren't you supposed to hide your mistakes?"

"Oh, baby, no. That's not why I have to hide you. I just don't want to share you with anyone. You are mine alone. You will always be my little girl and I don't want to share you with anyone else."

Kat scratched her tiny head. "Do you think my father would love me?"

Artemis rubbed her nose against Kat's before she answered. "Your father would love you even more than I do. He would wake you with tickles and kisses, and send you to bed with a warm hug."

"Then why don't we find him?"

The sadness returned to Artemis's face. "Because he hates me and he wants nothing to do with me."

"Why would anyone hate you, Matisera? You are wonderful and kind. Loving. I can't imagine why someone wouldn't see that about you."

Artemis smoothed her blond curls. "I wronged him, Katra. Greatly." She sighed regretfully. "I had the entire world in my hand at one time and I didn't know it. I let stupidity blind me and I lost him because of that."

"Then tell him you're sorry."

"As your father would say, there are some things 'sorry' can't repair. Some pains run too deep to ever be healed by something as simple as words, no matter how much you mean them."

Katra sat up in bed. "But I can heal anything. I will put my hand over his heart and make it all better. Then he will love you again."

Artemis pulled her close and held her tight. "My little treasure.

How I wish that you could. But it's all right. He gave me you, and you I can love without regret."

Kat released Ash and pulled her thoughts away from that memory. "She wasn't always a perfect mother, but I couldn't have had much better. And even when she was less than perfect, I always knew that she loved me."

Ash couldn't speak as the image of them haunted him. It was a side of Artemis that he'd forgotten existed. Since the day Artemis had brought him back from the dead, she'd punished him for the fact that she loved him.

She would pull him into her bed to use his body and then kick him away once they were finished. Even when he'd loved her, her love had been selfish.

She'd blamed him for everything.

But in the beginning, she'd been kind to him. She'd once held him and laughed with him over nothing at all. Now he couldn't remember the last time they'd laughed at anything. The last time she'd just touched him for no other reason than he was near her.

The loss of the friendship still made him ache.

He took Kat's hand in his. "I'm glad her anger at me never spilled over onto you."

She gave him a teasing smile. "Me, too." She reached up and brushed a strand of hair away from his face. "I can't believe this is real. That you're here, seeing me."

Neither could he. It was surreal.

But for a quirk of fate, they wouldn't be here now.

Which brought another question to him. "Why were you with my mother in her garden?"

"I was trying to help Sin fight the gallu and Dimme. He has a brother—"

"Zakar."

She didn't know why, but she was surprised he knew about Zakar. "You know him?"

Ash nodded. "I've met him a few times. He's a decent enough guy."

That was nice to know. The last thing she wanted to do was unleash another enemy into the world. "Well, he's missing. One of the gallu says that they have him held prisoner. Sin needs to know if that's true."

"Did my mother help you find him?"

"We saw something, but I don't know if that was him or not. It was blurry."

"Yeah, the *sfora* has its moments." He reached under his hair and removed his necklace. It was a small red glass ball, and it wasn't until he put it around her neck that she realized it was a tiny *sfora*. "This is a bit stronger than the pond. It has a part of me in it."

Her heart hammering, she closed her hand around it, unable to believe he'd give her something so valuable. With his DNA in it, she could use it not only to see what she needed, but to destroy him.

Given how little he trusted anyone, she understood the total significance of his gift.

He stepped back. "Tell it what you need and it'll guide you to it."

"Thank you."

He inclined his head to her.

Smiling up at him, Kat lifted herself on her tiptoes and placed a kiss to his cheek.

Ash couldn't breathe as he felt her gentle kiss. His daughter's kiss. It was tender and sweet and it made a wave of love well up inside him that he'd only ever known whenever Simi was near him.

He wanted to crush Kat to him, but she was too old to be held like a little girl. His daughter was grown and he'd have to respect her as a woman.

"Be careful," he whispered in her ear.

"You, too."

Ash took another step back and did the hardest thing he'd ever done. He let go of his daughter's hand. "If you need me, call and I will come no matter the cost."

"I know . . . Thanks, Daddy."

With tears in his eyes, he watched as she vanished and left him alone again in Artemis's room. He wiped at his eyes with the back of his hand.

I have a daughter . . .

It seemed so unbelievable.

"Are you angry at me, Apostolos?"

He clenched his teeth at the sound of his mother's voice in his head. "No, Metera. I'm just hurt that you kept her from me."

"I would rather you be angry at me. Your hurt makes me ache."

"I'm sorry."

"Why do you apologize when I'm the one in the wrong?"

"Because I would never hurt you for anything."

His mother appeared to him then as a pale Shade. "Come home, Apostolos. Free me and I will make sure you never hurt again."

He shook his head. "I can't, Metera. You know that."

She let out a tired breath. "One day, my child, you will seize the destiny you were born to."

Ash hoped not. If he did, the world would end.

Kat manifested back in Sin's penthouse. He was right where she'd left him by his bar, looking just as gorgeous.

He stood up from the bar stool and crossed the short distance between them. She could see the worry in his eyes. "Did you find him?" he asked anxiously.

She shook her head at the irony. She'd gone to find his brother and instead had found her father.

"Not exactly. But my father gave me this." She lifted the tiny red ball on her chest up so that Sin could see it. "He said it would lead us to Zakar."

A deep scowl marred his brow. "You met your father?"

She nodded.

"Are you all right?"

His concern warmed her a lot more than it should have. It was so touching. "Yeah. In a weird way, I think I am."

He approached her slowly and placed his hands on her shoulders. "Are you sure?"

"Yeah. I really am."

There was a tenderness on his face that she couldn't even begin to fathom. But it only lasted until his next question.

"So did he kill Artemis?"

Well, that was certainly an "ah" mood killer that wasn't helped by the eagerness of his tone. "Sin!"

"What?" he asked, his face a mask of innocence. "It's a legitimate question. I hope he cut her head off and stuck on a pike."

Men! Or more to the point, Sin! He was terrible. "Sorry to disappoint you, but she's still breathing."

"Damn," he said in a low tone. "Just once couldn't he give that—"

She arched a warning brow at him before he used the noun she despised.

"Woman," he said with an expression that let her know he really resented using that word, "what she deserves?"

"Would you punish the mother of *your* daughter?" No sooner were those words out of her mouth than she realized she'd hit a hard chord in his heart. She could feel his pain and it stung her deep.

Honestly, he looked as if she'd struck him.

"Sin . . ." She took a step toward him, but he quickly stepped back.

"We need to find Zakar," he said from between clenched teeth.

"Sin, don't change the subject. I want to know what's wrong. Why did my comment hurt you?"

"Let's just say you gave me clarity with one comment and leave it at that."

But she didn't want to leave it at that. She wanted to understand him. "I know your wife cheated on you. I saw it."

"And now you know why I never killed her over it. She was the mother of my children. Any other sore spots you wish to salt? I was once humiliated when I first tried to use my powers of flight as a kid. Instead of soaring over the mountain, I fell down and busted my chin. Why don't we call me incompetent all the way around? I assure you it was much less embarrassing than being a fertility god who couldn't satisfy his own wife."

So that was the source of it . . .

His shame made her ache for him. She cupped his face in her hands and stared at him so that he could see her sincerity. "And having been in your bed, I can honestly say that there had to have been something profoundly wrong with a woman who wasn't satisfied by you. Maybe it was a birth defect."

He looked at her with hooded eyes. Even so, she could feel the comfort her words had given him. He reached up and covered her hands with his. "I can't believe you're related to . . . what was the term Simi used? 'Bitch-goddess'?"

She rolled her eyes at him. "I know. I'm the watered-down version and you're lucky for that."

He took her right hand and placed a gentle kiss on her knuckles. "Thank you, Kat."

"Hey, I never say anything I don't mean. It's a curse I inherited from my father."

Sin grinned at her. "I don't think it's a curse so much as refreshing."

Her heart pounded at the light in his dark golden eyes. She had a bad feeling where he was concerned. There was something about him that she found so comforting and she didn't even know why. Something about him that just called out to her. She wanted to ease the pain in his gaze, and at the same time he gave her so much by doing nothing more than looking at her like he was doing right now.

It made her uncomfortable. She brushed her thumb over his fingers before she took a step back. Looking down, she picked up the small *sfora*. "I don't know if this will work, but are you ready to try?"

"More than ready."

Kat closed her eyes and summoned Simi and Xirena to her side. Sin stiffened as they appeared in the room looking a bit peeved.

Kat smiled at him and his reservations. "We're having to go into who knows what. While I know you can kick serious demon ass and I can kick most demon ass, I still like the idea of having a little cavalry standing at our backs. Especially since they're probably hungry."

He shook his head but didn't say anything.

"Where are we going, *akra*-Kat?" Simi asked.

"Food?" Xirena asked hopefully. "Watching all that Diamonique made me hungry."

Kat wrinkled her nose at Xirena. "Knowing my luck, there will be many gallu for your dining pleasure tonight."

Xirena and Simi rubbed their hands together in delight.

Kat laughed before she covered the *sfora* with her hand. "Okay, folks. Fasten your seat belts. This could very well be a bumpy ride." She concentrated and waited with bated breath.

Nothing happened.

"You're not doing it right," Simi said petulantly. "*Akra*-Kat has to take it off, put it in her palm, and think of who you're trying to find."

"Oh." She glanced to Sin. "Your brother looks like you?"

"Since we're twins . . . yeah."

"Okay. One sexy Sumerian coming up." Kat took the necklace off and closed her hand around the orb. As soon as she began to imagine Sin in her mind with Zakar's name, the orb began to glow. The rays spread out from between her fingers and danced along the walls like a strobe.

Then the red light slowly encompassed them. Two seconds later, they were in a damp cave. By the heavy earthen smell, it seemed to be deep underground. The *sfora*'s light faded and left them encased in the darkness.

In fact, it was so dark that the only way she could see Simi and Xirena was by their glowing eyes. The silence was only broken by the sound of heavy, angry breathing. Kat tried to peer through the darkness to the source of the sound, but her eyes couldn't focus on it at all.

She reached out and felt Sin's biceps under her hand.

Sin lifted his hand and a small flame appeared from his palm so that they could see in the darkness.

At first all she could see was the earthen walls of the cave. Then the breathing stopped.

And so did hers.

There on the other side of the cave was the body of a man lying on a stone slab. But that wasn't what horrified her. It was how he'd been laid out. His left shoulder was pinned to the slab by a sword that had been buried through his body to the hilt in the stone. His right arm had been lifted and a smaller sword driven through his wrist to pin it down. His legs had been done in a similar fashion, only the swords had been planted through the fleshy parts of his calves.

Bile rose in her throat as they moved toward him.

Sin was silent, but she could feel the anger roiling through him. And once they were close enough, she saw the blood that was running from the wounds and the scars that marred every inch of the man's naked body. His hair was matted and long, as if it'd been years since anyone had washed or combed it. He was clean shaven, but it was easy to see why that one bit of hygiene had been observed.

There were bite marks all over his neck. Some of them were long and jagged, as if the gallu had torn themselves away from his flesh in an effort to cause him as much pain as possible after their feedings.

But the worst was his eyes. Someone or something had seared them shut.

Xirena accidentally touched his leg as she neared him.

The man jerked his head toward her. "Fuck you, gallu," he snarled in Sumerian before spitting in Xirena's direction. He tried to fight.

Kat winced as the swords tore into his flesh.

"Stop it, Zakar," Sin said, moving closer to his brother so that he could hold his brother in place.

Zakar tried to bite him.

Sin cupped his brother's head in his hands. "Stop it. It's me. Sin. I'm here to free you."

"Fuck you," Zakar spat again.

Sin wiped the spittle off his face with the back of his hand. "Stop fighting. You're only hurting yourself more."

Kat cringed as Zakar pulled his wrist up and the sword made a slight scraping noise against the stone. The pain of that action had to be killing him.

Sin held his brother's arm in place before Sin jerked the sword free. Instead of being grateful, Zakar tried to punch him. When that failed, Zakar grabbed Sin by his hair and slammed his head into the stone by his side.

Sin cursed before he twisted out of Zakar's grasp. "Dammit, boy, you better be glad I love you."

As Zakar continued to fight, he ignored Sin.

Kat stepped forward to help Sin. "I'll get the ones in his legs."

"Let us," Simi said as she pushed her back. "Charontes are stronger. We can pull them out in one clean motion and it'll hurt him less."

Kat was grateful for their help—anything to spare the poor man more pain.

Moving to the side, she watched as Simi, Xirena, and Sin pulled the remaining swords free of the stone and Zakar's body. Zakar let out an echoing scream that sent a chill all the way to Kat's soul as he thrashed about in utter misery.

And as soon as he was free, he rolled to the floor and crouched to attack.

"Zakar!" Sin snapped, trying to make him understand. "It's Sin."

Zakar lunged at Sin and wrapped his arms about him before tackling him to the floor.

Kat wanted to help but wasn't sure what would be the best course of action. More than that, she didn't want to hurt Zakar any more.

By Sin's face as he tried to keep his brother from hitting him, she could tell he felt the same way.

"Can we eat him?" Xirena asked.

"No," Simi said quickly. "Eating people is wrong . . ." She made a face. "The Simi sounds like *akri* now. But *akri*'s right. Besides, it would make *akra* Kitty-Kat mad."

Suddenly bright light filled the cavern. Sin and Kat froze as they realized they were no longer alone with Zakar.

"Well, well, looks like more food has arrived."

CHAPTER TEN

Kat turned at the growling tone that was similar to Kessar's voice. The demon looked a lot like him, but his hair was darker and his eyes were coal black. If that weren't enough to warm her day, there were six more demons behind him. Five men and one female.

"How cute," the female said as she came around the men to stand in the front. "The blood slave has friends."

Before Kat could even blink, the demons vanished only to reappear directly in front of each of them.

Except for Sin. The leader and two of the male demons surrounded him.

She tried to watch Simi and Xirena as their wings came out of their backs and they attacked the demons in front of them, but her vision was blocked by the female in front of her. *Gah*, in demon form, the gallu were really an unattractive race. The female's eyes were sharp and beady, and her lower jaw was distorted by the double row of fangs. Curling up with one of the gallu would be like getting close to Stephen Sommers's Mummy after only two kills.

Ew . . .

The female tilted her head and smiled, showing off her fangs. "How wonderful. An Atlantean to eat."

Kat snorted. "How wonderful. A bitch to declaw."

The female ran at Kat, who quickly sidestepped, grabbed her arm, and slammed her into the cavern wall. That really had to hurt. Good. It was almost enough to make Kat smile.

Shrieking, the female gallu turned back to face her. Kat kicked her back and slugged her hard. She then stabbed the gallu straight in the heart and waited for her to explode.

She didn't.

"Between the eyes," Sin snarled at her. "You can't take them out like a Daimon."

Duh, how could she have forgotten that so soon? So much for her training.

The demon lunged at the same time Kat recovered her dagger and shoved it straight between the demon's eyes. The demon let out a piercing sound before she exploded all over Kat.

Ugh, gross . . . Give her a Daimon any day over one of these. At least Daimons didn't smell when they exploded.

Disgusted, Kat shook it off and turned to see Simi and Xirena "eating" their gallu demons. Oh yeah, she'd never order pizza again after seeing that.

Note to self. In the future tell Simi to bring a bib along with the barbecue sauce.

Trying not to watch them as they feasted on body parts she could no longer even identify, Kat went to help Zakar, who was blindly stabbing at the demon who was tormenting him like a cat with a stray ball. Sin had two of his attackers dead at his feet and was working on the third as she ran across the room.

Zakar narrowly missed her with his slash.

The demon laughed. "That's right, slave. Kill your rescuer." The demon came at her, but she twisted in his arms and lifted him up. Instead of her crashing into Zakar as the demon intended, it was the demon who did. Zakar slashed the demon's throat. He screamed out.

Kat caught Zakar's wrist and pulled the knife from his hand before she used it to finish off the demon. She'd just killed him when Zakar grabbed her from behind and sank his teeth into her shoulder. Yelping, she barely caught herself before she struck him.

Suddenly Sin was there, pulling him away. Zakar fought like a man possessed by unreasoning fury. He grabbed handfuls of Sin's hair and pulled with all his strength.

"Stop it!" Sin shouted in his ear. "It's your brother."

"Fuck you, gallu, fuck you!"

Realizing there was nothing else to do, Kat held her hands out and blasted Zakar with a kind, but no less stunning, god-bolt. He instantly collapsed into Sin's arms.

Her and Sin's gazes met and she saw the gratitude in his eyes as he swung his brother up into his arms. "Let's get out of here before more of them come."

She nodded in agreement. "Simi? Fry all the other demons and let's get out of here."

Simi pouted. "But I'm still hungry."

"We'll order Diamonique as soon as we get back."

Simi's bloody face lit up immediately. "Ooo, that's so much better than gallu." She and Xirena quickly set fire to the demons before Kat and Sin flashed them back to his penthouse.

Kat used her powers to conjure a large bag of Diamonique, which she handed over to Simi and Xirena once they joined them. Squealing, the demons ran to their hotel room to gobble up the stones and left Kat alone with Sin and his brother.

Thank the gods for Diamonique. That should keep the demons occupied for a little while.

His face sad and bitter, Sin carried his brother toward the sofa, which unfolded itself to make a queen-sized bed. The covers pulled back an instant before he laid Zakar on top of the white sheets.

"Is he going to be okay?"

Sin couldn't speak as he looked at the vicious scars on his brother's body. What had they done to him? He looked as if they'd been feeding from him for centuries.

Sin wanted blood for this. Kessar's . . . the gallu's.

But most of all, Sin wanted Artemis. If not for her, he'd have been there to stop this. He'd have had the power to protect Zakar from their brutality.

No, he took that back. It wasn't Artemis's fault. It was his own and he knew it. If only he hadn't wanted acceptance. Wanted companionship. None of this would have happened. It was his own weakness that had wounded his brother. There was no one else to blame but him.

His stomach shrank from the weight of pain and guilt that gnawed at him.

He felt Kat gently pulling him back. He started to snap at her, but the intent look on her face kept him silent. Rubbing her hands together, she neared Zakar. She placed the palms of her hands against his eyes as she whispered in Atlantean.

A translucent yellow glow spread out from her hands to cover his body. As the glow moved over Zakar, it knitted his wounds closed and healed the deep scars that marred his skin . . . even his missing finger was repaired.

Relief and gratitude poured through Sin's body as he watched her heal Zakar.

That she would do this without Sin's asking . . . it meant the world to him.

When she pulled back, he saw that Zakar's eyes were no longer seared closed. His eyelids and lashes lay against his cheeks in perfect repose. With the exception of the long, gnarled hair, this was the brother Sin remembered.

"Thank you," he breathed, grateful for what she'd done.

She inclined her head before she moved away from the bed. "They'd punctured his eardrums. I think that's why he didn't respond when you told him who you were. He was deaf."

Sin cursed as more rage filled him. "I want them dead. *All* of them."

Her face said she agreed completely. "I hate to say this, but I give Stryker credit. At least he has a code of ethics, screwy though it is at times, that he follows. I can't imagine him doing something like this."

"It's why we can't let the gallu loose on humanity. They are completely without compassion, mercy, or decency."

"I agree. But I'm not sure Zakar will be able to help us now. He looks pretty battered, and there's no telling what's been done to him mentally that I can't fix with a simple healing spell."

Sin hated to admit it, but she might be right. The man on the bed wasn't in any kind of fighting shape. He looked gaunt and weak. They'd be lucky if Zakar could even stand without help. "I wonder how long they've had him."

"I don't know. But by the looks of it, it's been a while." Kat brushed at Sin's hair before she rubbed the small of his back. "Are you all right?"

He glanced down at her, his heart heavy. "If he were your brother, how would you answer?"

She didn't hesitate with her answer. "I'd be out for blood."

"Then you understand me."

She nodded before she gave a comforting squeeze to his arm. "And I'll be right here, helping you collect it."

Emotions and tenderness for her choked him at her words. At the fact that she'd been by his side through all this. That she'd healed Zakar . . .

In a weird way, it'd been like a dream.

Unable to cope with it, Sin pulled her against him and kissed her with everything he had.

Kat sighed at the taste of Sin. She could feel his turmoil even while he held her like she was the most important thing in the world to him, and she wished she could ease it. He'd had a rotten day. But even so, he tasted of heaven and man. How she wished things had turned out better for him and Zakar. They still had the gallu to deal with and Deimos. None of whom would rest until Sin was dead.

It felt as if the whole world was against them. But right now, in his arms, she felt strong enough to take them all on.

Sin growled as he pulled away from her lips to bury his face against her neck. He loved the scent of her skin and breath, the feel of her body against his. For once he didn't have to practically double over to kiss a woman. She was a perfect height for him, and her strength amazed him.

"I think I'm becoming addicted to you."

She laughed. "You barely know me."

"Yes," he said with a wicked grin, "but I know parts of you better than anyone ever has."

She blushed at that. "You're incorrigible."

"Not true, I'm highly encourageable. I take very little prodding most days."

She kissed his cheek before she moved away. "I can't believe you're this playful considering what's going on."

He let out a tired breath before he raked his hands through his dark hair. "I'm trying to distract myself from the utter misery of guilt and doubt that's plaguing me. There, for a second, it was actually working."

Kat went immediately to his side to put one hand on his hard stomach and the other on his back. She looked at him with a pained expression. "Oh, hon, I'm sorry. Should we get naked now?"

He rolled his eyes at her sarcasm. "Forget it. Too much of a cock-kill."

She stepped back, laughing. "Cock-kill, huh? What an interesting expression you've developed." She gave him a devilish smile. "Perhaps a little mouth-to-mouth resuscitation could bring it back?"

He took his earlier comment back; she was her mother's daughter. She could torment a man with the best of them. "You are evil taunting me like this."

"I know. I'd apologize, but the agonized look on your face makes it all worth it."

He lifted his hand to touch her hair. It was like silk on his skin. Rubbing it between his forefinger and thumb, he remembered the feel of her on top of him. "I still don't understand you. Why you're here with me. Helping me. It doesn't make sense."

"Maybe it's your compelling personality that draws me to you like a moth to a flame."

Sin snorted. "Repellent, you mean."

She arched a brow as if surprised by his words. "Is that self-deprecation from a god?"

"Ex-god."

"Even so, it's not something one usually finds in your breed."

He rubbed her cheek with the backs of his fingers, savoring the soft texture of her skin. "Neither is a heart or a soul. Yet you seem to have both."

Kat shivered at the tender look on his face. Warmth spread

through her at the sensation of his hand on her flesh. He was delectable. "I keep telling you I'm not a god."

"Yeah . . . but you would have been had your mother not been afraid of the other gods finding out she was sleeping with your father."

Perhaps, but Kat wasn't into titles or power trips. Pantheon politics had worn her down eons ago. She truly wanted no part of that. She just wanted . . .

Honestly she didn't know. She'd spent most of her life serving her mother's whims. Kat hadn't been born to a world where dreams or ambitions turned out well. Usually those two things resulted in someone's ultimate humiliation or a grand disembowelment.

It'd been her life's ambition to save herself the pain of both. Truly, she'd never even dreamt of knowing a man at all. It seemed inconceivable to her now. But she had been living her life blindly, with no thoughts of a future. The world, her world, just was.

Sin had changed that.

For the first time she did want something, and that actually scared her, because she knew he would never share himself with her that way. It wasn't in him to settle down and have a family. He was a warrior who wanted nothing to do with her mother's pantheon, and though Kat wasn't a goddess in it, she was still a part of it.

Trying to force the issue would only lead to her humiliation. She was sure of it.

"So what were you like as a god?" she asked, trying to imagine him all those centuries ago. He didn't seem like he'd be any better at their politics than she was.

He shrugged. "Like all the others, I suppose."

She couldn't believe that. "No. I don't think you were ever like them. I know from my glimpse into your life that you never cheated on your wife even though she cheated on you. Why is that?"

A veil fell over his face, obscuring his thoughts and emotions from her. She felt nothing but emptiness.

"I went to Artemis, intending to cheat."

Kat looked away as she summoned what she'd felt while in his past. He was lying. "No, you didn't."

"How do you know?"

Not wanting him to know what she was doing, she met his gaze. "I don't believe you'd be faithful all that time and then toss it to the wind on a whim. There was another reason you went to Artemis."

Anger darkened his brow, before he moved away.

"Sin?"

There was no mistaking the wrath in his gaze as he looked at her. "What?"

An intelligent person wanting to live would have dropped the subject, but Kat was more suicidal than most. "Why were you on Olympus?"

His eyes were hollow. "Do you really want the truth?"

"I wouldn't have asked if I didn't."

He left her then and went to the bar to pour himself a double shot of whisky—it appeared that was always his answer when something truly disturbed him.

He tossed the drink back and grimaced before he glared at her and answered, "I was lonely." The pain on his face actually stole her breath. "I didn't sleep around for one simple reason. I was tainted. Half human, half god, I didn't fit in anywhere, and believe me, the Sumerian gods were quick to point that out. Ningal, my wife, had abandoned our bed centuries before. She only married me because I was exotic and different. But once the others started in on her for being with a mongrel, she banned me from her bed. After all, what kind of children would she breed with someone who wasn't a full-blooded god?"

He clenched his teeth as if the pain were more than he could bear before he spoke again. "I thought something had to be wrong with me. Whoever heard of a fertility god not sleeping around? A fertility god whose wife was never in his bed? But I wasn't about to become my father and prey on a human woman who wouldn't be able to resist me. It's wrong to use people that way, and I knew how much pain my father's lust had caused my mother. Then Artemis appeared one day while I was out riding in Ur. She was surrounded by deer, looking peaceful and, don't laugh, sweet. I'd never seen a more beautiful woman, so I stopped to chat with her, and then next thing I knew, we were laughing. And in no time, we were friends."

It made sense to Kat. They were both gods of the moon. They probably had a lot in common. "What made you go to her that night on Olympus? Really?"

He looked away. "Anger. Ningal had humiliated me and I was tired of being laughed at. I was a powerful god, but not the most powerful of my pantheon. I knew there was no way I could confront them and win. They would have united against me. So I went to Artemis, wanting her to help me weaken my own pantheon. I thought that if she really loved me as she claimed, we could join forces against them."

He laughed bitterly. "Be careful what you wish for you, you just might get it. I wanted all of them destroyed for what they'd done to me, and they were. I just didn't see my own downfall as part of that plan."

Guilt tore through her at the agony she heard in his voice, the self-loathing she saw in his gaze. She'd never meant to hurt him or anyone else. "Artemis is incapable of giving what you sought."

He scoffed. "Thanks, but I'll let you in on a secret. I learned that three thousand years ago when she bound me up and sucked me dry."

Wanting to soothe him, Kat crossed the room to take his hand before he poured himself another shot. "You do realize what you've just done, don't you?"

"Insulted your intellect?"

"No." She took his hand into hers. "You've opened yourself up to me. Trusted me."

Sin grew silent as he realized she was right. He'd told her things he'd never told anyone else. But it was so easy to talk to her. Unlike others, she didn't seem to judge him for his past or his mistakes.

She made him forget to be guarded.

"I guess you and your mother will have a good laugh at me then when you talk later."

Her expression changed instantly to one of indignation. "I would *never* tell someone what you've told me here. Ever. What kind of person do you think I am?"

He didn't answer. "Perhaps we should go back to insulting each other. I think that was easier."

She shook her head at him. "Not easier. Just safer."

Damn, she was intelligent. Sometimes more so than was good for his peace of mind. "I like safety."

Kat laughed out loud. "This from a man who fights demons single-handedly? Are you really that afraid of me?"

"Unlike you, demons are easy." They didn't make him want to hold them.

"How so?"

"They only take your life."

She arched a single brow. "And me?"

You could easily take my heart. The truth of that seared him right where he stood. He hadn't felt like this in thousands of years.

Thousands.

Then again, he wasn't sure if he'd ever felt this way about a woman. He could barely remember courting his wife. If he'd ever had any feelings for her, they had been killed by her callousness.

But Kat . . .

She was honest and caring. Two things his wife had never been. When Kat touched him, his body reacted viciously. A single smile from her could make his entire being burn. One touch from her hand and he was undone. It was terrifying to think of how much power this one person had over him. How one single gesture from her could affect him so profoundly.

Still, she held that playful look on her beautiful face. "You didn't answer me, Sin."

He stepped away from her. "Answer you about what?"

"Why you're afraid of me?"

Could she be more relentless? Unwilling to confess his feelings, he gave her a flippant response. "You command two demons with barbecue sauce. Who in their right mind wouldn't be afraid of you?"

She tsked at him. "Why are you hiding?"

"Who says I'm hiding?"

"That nervous look you keep casting to the door like you're wanting someone to come through it and rescue you." She made *bock-bock* animal noises at him as she bent her arms and flapped them like wings.

Sin was aghast by her actions. "You're not seriously calling me chicken?"

The playful look on her face was extremely attractive. "If the beak fits . . ."

He should be angry, but a foreign part of him was amused by her audacity. "You live to taunt me, don't you?"

"We have to live for something, and I have to say it's quite amusing to watch the confusion in those gorgeous eyes of yours. They just sparkle whenever I nettle you."

He was stunned by her unexpected compliment. "My eyes are gorgeous?"

"Yes. Very striking."

That should have no effect on him whatsoever and yet her words set him on fire. He didn't know why the thought of her finding him attractive should even register. Millions of women, literally, had found him attractive all throughout history. They used to worship him by the thousands.

But her words made his heart speed up. Made his palms sweat. Made him so hard that he could barely stand being around her.

She took his hand in hers.

"C'mon." She tugged him toward the bedroom.

"What are you doing?"

"You need to rest. It's been a long day and I intend to tuck you into bed."

A smile quirked up the right side of his mouth as he hardened even more. "Really? Can I tuck myself into you?"

"If you play your cards right and stop with the cheesy lines it might be possible."

Kessar blinked twice at Nabium, who'd interrupted his feeding. He raised up from the dead showgirl on the floor and wiped the blood from his lips with a linen napkin. "What do you mean the Hayar Bedr is missing?"

The demon who was tall and dark haired gulped audibly as he noted the fury in Kessar's tone. "The god Nana went to the cavern and—"

"Ex-god," he corrected Nabium.

Nabium cleared his throat. "Ex-god, and he took him."

Kessar cursed at the timing. It pissed him off that Sin had

found some way into their hole and found one of his favorite toys. Not that it mattered. They could still free the Dimme, but owning the Moon had made their succession as the dominant life force on the planet a little easier.

"Where's my brother?"

Nabium grew quiet.

Kessar let out a sound of disgust at his younger brother and his libido. He had never learned a sense of timing. "Tell him to get off whatever female he's found and come here. Now."

"I-I can't, my lord."

"Why not?"

Nabium took a step away from him before he gulped again, and then spoke. "They killed him."

Kessar couldn't breathe as that news registered. It couldn't be. "What?"

"He died fighting them, my lord. I am so sorry."

Kessar felt his fangs come out as rage filled him. He wanted blood for this.

As he walked toward the closet, Nabium practically bolted in fear. Not that Kessar would ever hurt his second in command. No, Kessar needed someone weak to torture.

Opening the closet, he pulled the college student out he'd captured earlier after they'd left Sin's casino. She was short, with long mousy brown hair and beady blue eyes that were rimmed with small, round glasses. Her mouth was taped so that she couldn't scream, and her hands and feet were tied. She was dressed in a pair of faded jeans, black boots, and a black Boondock Saints T-shirt that showed off her beefy upper arms.

But what he found fascinating, and the main reason he'd captured her, was that she had a small bow and arrow tattoo on her wrist. Before he'd taken her, she'd told him the bow and arrow was to protect her from nightmares. Strange, really, since it was also the mark of Artemis and as such made the student a prime target for them.

Using his powers, he muffled the room so that no one in the hotel could hear her scream. Then he ripped the tape from her mouth.

She cried out. He shoved her into Nabium's arms. "Hold her still."

"P-p-please," she begged as her gaze fell to the body of the other woman. "I'm pregnant."

"Like we care?" Kessar felt his face shifting over to that of his real demon form.

She screamed even louder, exciting him even more.

Kessar picked her up and latched onto her neck, tearing through the flesh so that her blood would fill his mouth. As soon as she stopped fighting, Nabium joined him by tearing into the other side.

When she was dead and drained, they threw her to the ground. Kessar frowned as he saw a small leather bracelet on her right arm. Jerking it off, he read her name.

Scoffing, he tossed it on top of her body and wiped his mouth.

His good humor restored, he pulled his shirt off over his head and tossed it over her body before he manifested another one.

Nabium duplicated the gesture before he returned to their previous topic. "At least the good news is we have negated Zakar. He will be worthless to them now."

Possibly, but Kessar wasn't the kind of demon who counted on things going as planned. "Never underestimate Nana. He travels with an Atlantean."

"Are you sure?"

"Of course. How else would he be able to destroy my brother?" Kessar's grief was gone now. The kill had placated him. If his brother was stupid enough to die at the hands of them, then he deserved it.

"What do we do now?" Nabium asked.

"We have to find some way to negate Sin's powers."

"He's already stripped of them."

"Not enough. He is the only thing standing in the way of the Kerir. We must get Zakar back and get that Atlantean bitch and convert her."

"How?"

Kessar smiled. "The same way we captured Zakar. We infect her. Then we'll have both Zakar and Nana, and there will be no one to stand in our way."

Nabium laughed until he realized the humans were starting to stir. "Speaking of infection . . ."

Kessar looked at the women. "They're too ugly to keep, especially the short bitch. Cut their heads off and throw them in a ditch somewhere."

He watched as Nabium covered the women with a jacket to disguise the blood on their clothes before he led them out of the room and to wherever he'd finish them off.

Humans. They disgusted him.

Soon, though, they would all be under the thumb of their masters. But first, he had to get Sin and Zakar . . .

CHAPTER ELEVEN

Kat sighed in contentment as Sin's body relaxed behind hers, letting her know he'd finally gone to sleep. She was actually surprised that she'd won the argument for him to go to sleep and not get frisky with her.

But even though she wanted to be with him, she still needed a little space. Their relationship was going way too fast for her. She'd just met him, literally, and though they'd shared so much already, she still needed time to breathe. To think. To adjust.

So he'd given her a playful pout, then wrapped his arms around her and settled down to sleep. In some ways this was even more intimate than having sex with him. It at least took more trust, since it required his having to close his eyes and relax around her. She could do anything to him right now and he'd be powerless to stop her.

She could shave his head, paint his fingernails pink . . . put makeup on his face.

Biting her lip, she had to stifle a laugh at the thought of him in such a girlie way.

"What are you doing?" His deep voice was a sleepy rumble.

"I thought you were asleep."

"I was until your hip touched my groin." Those piercing gold eyes opened to stare at her. "Kind of hard to stay asleep with the smell of you so close and your body rubbing against mine." He rolled over, onto his back. "It's actually cruel."

"I'm sorry." She moved to snuggle up to his side. She laid her head on his chest and just inhaled the masculine scent of his body. She stared at her hand, which was incredibly pale on top of his dark skin. Kissing him just above his nipple, she closed her eyes.

Sin's body jerked at the sweetness of her actions. He still couldn't believe he was sharing his bed with her and they weren't doing anything other than sleeping in it.

What the hell was wrong with him? He'd never done this with a woman before.

"We're adults. You'll live." Her glib words rang in his head now. And he wasn't so sure he'd survive this.

And yet at the same time, it was wonderful to feel her lying against him. He ran his hand through her pale hair. He didn't know why, but he'd always been fascinated by blond hair. Hers was like spun gold whispering against his skin. He fanned it over her shoulders and smiled at the sight of her pink flannel pajamas.

Pajamas . . . in his bed. Would the indignities never cease? The least she could have done was wear a negligee.

"Those aren't comfortable. They crawl up your nether regions while you sleep."

But who cares? *You would have and you wouldn't have been able to keep your hands off her in that case.*

Yeah, she'd pegged him on that.

Sin sighed as he pulled at the flannel sleeve. Personally, he wanted to go back in time, find whoever had created pajamas for sleepwear, and beat the hell out of him. Surely he wasn't the only man who'd ever felt that way.

Of course it wouldn't be nearly so bad if Kat couldn't conjure her own clothes. Then he could have insisted she sleep naked or at the very least in one of his T-shirts.

Flannel sucked.

Sleep, Sin . . .

That was easier said than done. Honestly, this felt like a whole new kind of torture. His body was white-hot and aching, with no relief in sight. No wonder some men begged for castration.

But before long, his exhaustion overtook him and he found himself falling asleep again. His dreams drifted through his battles, then back further in time . . .

He could see Anu, looking proud as the first of the gallu were born—not of a mother's loins but of eggs so that they could survive and be born even if the mother was killed.

After sex, one female could lay two dozen fertilized eggs. Eggs that would survive heat or cold. They were virtually indestructible.

Anu had stood on a precipice high above the nest as the first hatchlings began cracking open their shells. "Look at them, Sin. This is the ultimate weapon. Let any pantheon try to defeat us now."

"They are beautiful," Anatum had said, her perfect smile beaming on her patrician face. Not only Anu's wife, she was the goddess of creation. Tall and graceful, she'd been a vision standing by her husband's side.

She'd also been the first victim of the gallu. As soon as they'd broken free of their eggs, they had rushed up the cavern walls to the three of them.

Sin had killed two while six had attacked Anatum. They'd gotten her free, but not before she'd been bitten. At first they'd thought nothing about it. At the time, no one knew the gallu bites could create others of their kind.

Because the demons were young and their venom weak, Anatum hadn't turned right away. She'd merely been ill. It wasn't until nightfall that they'd learned the true horror of what had been created.

Anatum had gone after Anu in his sleep. He'd barely been able to keep her from biting him and converting him. After a brief fight, he'd confined her to a cage.

Even though they were gods, there was no way to save her. And because of her god powers, she was even more dangerous than the others.

With no choice, Sin had taken his daughter, Ishtar, and they had destroyed Anatum and allowed Ishtar to absorb her powers and replace her in the pantheon. Anu had been sick over the loss. Sick with guilt over what he'd unleashed.

At least until Enlil had come forward.

Because of his powers over demon kind, Enlil was able to weaken the demons enough so that they could gain control of them.

Sin had begged them all to destroy them.

"Why would you kill something so valuable?" Enlil was emphatic that the gallu be saved. "They are the only thing we have to fight the Atlanteans with. Imagine if they were to ever come after us."

"They're not a warring pantheon," Sin had argued.

"Tell that to the Greeks who are locked in war with them even as we speak."

Still, Sin had tried to talk sense into his father. "The Greeks gods were the aggressors."

"Mark my words, one day the Atlanteans will come for us and we need to strike the first blow. Let our gallu destroy their Charonte demons before their gods unleash the Charonte on us."

But Sin had known the future. He'd sensed it, and no one would believe him. "There's only so long you can hold a jackal by its ears before it turns on you, Father. We can't let these creatures live. Sooner or later, they will destroy us."

Enlil had scoffed at him. "You are a fool, Nana. We need them. You've seen the Atlanteans. This will keep them out of our beds . . . if you know what I mean." He'd looked past Sin to where Sin's wife sat with Ishtar. "And I know that you do."

Shamed to the depth of his soul, Sin had to catch himself before he attacked his father. So long as Enlil had possession of the Tablet, there was no way to defeat him. "My manhood doesn't need the backing of a demon army to secure it. You are sowing the seed of our own destruction."

"I am securing our future survival."

Disgusted with his father's unreasonableness, Sin had walked off. There was no convincing those who refused to see what they were shown.

On his way out, he'd passed by his wife. Ningal's gaze had met his aloofly until he'd glanced to her chest where she wore an

Atlantean sun symbol. The seal of their pantheon. One corner of her mouth had turned up in a mocking smile.

He'd felt slapped to the core of his soul. How dare she flaunt her affairs so openly. But then Archon was a full god and he was not.

So be it.

"Ignore them."

Sin had continued on his way with Zakar, invisible to the others, by his side. It was a trick that Zakar had learned as a child. Even though it was dangerous, Sin was grateful for his brother's support. "Easier said than done."

"Ningal is a faithless bitch. Don't worry about her. I'll make her dream of snakes and gorgons every night when she tries to sleep."

Sin had smiled at the thought. But it didn't distract him from what troubled him most. "I'm right about this, Zakar. I know it."

"I'm sure you are. But none of them are going to listen to you. They're so afraid of the enemy outside that they are blind to the one they're creating in their own house. It's never the invader from outside who destroys the kingdom. It's always the one from within. That one person trusted who didn't deserve it. The one liar who smiles in your face and then spits on your charity because they think they deserve more for no other reason than they want it."

Zakar was right. But it changed nothing.

Sin had paused in the garden to look at him. "What can I do to stop this?"

"Be the last one standing, Brother. Let them play their games and spew their venom. In the end, they are the ones their poison will destroy. Nothing negative survives for long. They will turn on each other because they know no other way."

"And the world outside? What of it? The humans who look to us for protection? What will happen to them once the gallu are released?"

"They will have their champions. We will be there, you and I. We won't let the demons hurt them."

Only Zakar wasn't standing anymore and neither were the warriors they had once trained to fight the gallu. The humans were all dead and the demons had torn Zakar down and tortured him until there was nothing left but a shell of a man who had once walked with the powers of a god.

It was sobering and horrifying.

Suddenly Sin felt a warm hand on his shoulder. He turned with his lip curled, expecting to see his wife.

Instead, it was Kat. She looked like an angel standing there, and it made his entire body burn. He'd never been happier to see anyone.

"What are you doing here?" he asked her.

"I brought her to you."

Sin turned back to his brother, who was now circling them. "I don't understand."

"This isn't a dream, Sin. It's a war." Zakar shot a blast of fire at him.

Even though it was a dream, it knocked him off his feet and burned his chest. Gasping, Sin rolled until the fire was out. He looked up at Zakar. "What are you doing?"

Zakar threw out his hand and a barbed whip coiled around Sin's forearm. He hissed in pain as Zakar jerked the whip and wrenched his arm out of joint.

Kat turned on Zakar.

"No! Don't hurt him."

Zakar moved to blast Kat. She ducked and shot back a blast that sent him reeling.

"You got any more tricks? How about this?" She blasted him with ice.

Sin pushed himself to his feet and ran to her. "Kat, stop. You're hurting him."

"He doesn't care about hurting you or me. I say let him have it."

To his surprise, Zakar started laughing. Rising up from the ground, he floated toward Kat, who tensed, ready to fight.

"Listen to her, Sin. She's right. How do you even know this is me?" He changed into the form of Kessar. "Maybe I'm here to destroy you." The apparition ran at him.

Sin caught him by the throat and threw him to the ground. "What are you?"

"I'm fractured, Brother. I've come here because this is the only realm where I'm what I want to be. I'm no longer in control of myself when I'm in my body. I can't trust me when I'm awake, and neither can you."

Sin sat back on his haunches. "You're infected?"

"Not exactly." Zakar pushed himself up so that he could sit in front of Sin. "Because of my immunity, the gallu don't have full control of me, but then neither do I. It's something else . . . something dark and deadly, and it lives inside me. I don't know who I am anymore and I can't control it. The only place you can trust me is here." Zakar hung his head. "I'm sorry I ended up being the coward Father always suspected me to be."

Kat scowled at him. "Coward? Are you serious? My God, we saw how cruel and vicious these things are. You fought them alone, even when you were held down. How could you ever consider yourself a coward?"

"I failed." He returned his gaze to Sin. "The gallu are worse than even you know. They can weaken you in this realm and learn how to attack you here. It's here they'll find your weaknesses."

Sin found that hard to believe. "Why have you never come for me in my sleep to tell me what was going on with you?"

"I couldn't. Because of them I'm weak even here. You were dreaming of me just now and summoned me. It's the only reason I'm here. I couldn't have come on my own. I don't have those powers anymore."

Kat stepped forward to stand in front of them as his words haunted her. "You have to explain to me how this works. I know the Greek sleep gods, the Oneroi, can enter anyone's dreams at any time. They have potions they can use to seduce a waking person to sleep. Are the gallu the same?"

Zakar shook his head. "Unlike your gods, they can't infiltrate the dreams of someone they haven't met. They must have physical contact first."

Sin winced as he remembered Kessar earlier. So that was what had brought him into the building. "The casino today. I knew there was something more to that bastard's visit."

Zakar nodded. "They touch you and then they can find you when you sleep."

Kat cursed. "And I let him touch me. Smooth move."

Sin patted her on the arm. "Don't feel bad. You're not the only one who screwed this up." He clenched his teeth as rage washed through him. "I could kill Enlil for this."

"You warned them," Zakar said. "But he thought he was too smart to be victimized. At least you didn't see what the gallu did to him when they killed him."

Sin could just imagine the horror and he was grateful he'd missed it. "What became of his powers?"

"Most were locked in the Tablet."

Thank the gods that Sin had been able to recover that from the museum. With those powers inside the Tablet, there was no telling what the gallu could do with it. "And the rest?"

"Kessar took them. He sent his agents out to take Enlil and then bring him to the caverns. Enlil had long enough to hide the Tablet before he was captured, and once he was in Kessar's presence Kessar bled him dry . . . in more ways than one. Kessar is even more dangerous than you think. And now that he's been freed . . ."

"What freed him?" Sin asked.

"The locks on their prison are weakening along with the Dimme.

Kat frowned. "But why hasn't Kessar come out before this?"

"He was being held in a different part of the cavern that had a separate locking system. Now that system has weakened to the point he and his worst disciples are able to be free. He wants total mayhem and bloodshed. Most of all, he wants Sin to suffer for helping to lock him in there."

Kat made an exaggerated happy shake. "Oh, this just gives you the warm and fuzzies, doesn't it?" She sobered. "I vote we unleash my grandmother and let her eat the whole lot of them."

"Your grandmother?" Zakar asked.

Sin laughed in a low tone. "Apollymi."

Zakar paled. "How well imprisoned is she?"

"Well enough we're basically safe from her wrath."

Kat's eyes lightened. "But I can invoke her powers if I need to."

The men gaped at her.

"You can do what?" Sin asked. This was the first time he'd heard this part of her powers.

"Invoke her powers," she repeated. "Sweet sixteen birthday present. Anyone who messes with me gets a taste of Atlantean destruction. It's why I said Deimos is no problem for me. I can take his ass out, blindfolded, and beat him."

Sin was glad to have that knowledge. However there was one drawback to it. "But we have to keep you charged."

She nodded. "It helps."

"Good," Zakar said. "We have at least one surprise they don't know about. But both of you have to remember that in dreams nothing is what it seems. They may attack you as demons, but they may not. They could come at you as your best friend." He looked at Kat. "Your mother. Your brother. Anyone or anything that you're close to. They are masters at this and they've had a lot of practice. They can't really hurt you, but they can disturb your sleep enough to impair you while you're awake."

Sin rubbed his hand over his face as he considered that. Damn.

"Kytara?" Kat shouted out suddenly. Her voice echoed around them.

Sin scowled at her. "What are you doing?"

She folded her arms over her chest. "I want to sleep in peace at night. Be damned if I'm going to let some two-bit piece of demon like Kessar keep me from resting. He thinks he's a badass? Well I know a few myself." She paused before she shouted again. "Kytara!"

"Stop yelling at me." A woman almost as tall as Kat appeared behind her. She had wavy black hair, porcelain skin, and large eyes so blue they didn't look real. She was dressed in a black leather pantsuit with a silver loop belt and four-inch-heeled boots.

Kat smiled as she turned to face her. "There you are, my evil friend."

Sin was wary over Kat's greeting. "Evil?"

"To the core of her rotten soul."

"It's true," Kytara agreed. "There's nothing like a bitch in heels, of which I'm the biggest." She turned back to Kat. "I know there has to be a point to this, since you're in a dream with gorgeous twins and nobody's naked. I could have sworn I taught you better, Katra."

Sin crossed his arms over his chest as he narrowed his gaze on Kat.

Kat held her hands up in mock surrender. "She didn't mean it like that. I *never* did such a thing."

"Umm-hmmm," he said, not believing her for a minute. No wonder she'd been so skilled.

"It's true. Kytara, tell him."

"Tell him what?" she asked innocently. "Kat's a raging nymphomaniac."

"Tara!"

"Oh, all right," Kytara finally conceded. "She's so bland she makes plain toast look spicy."

Kat's look of agitation only increased. "Thanks a lot."

Kytara laughed. "Well, you are. You're too much of a goody two-shoes. I've been nagging at you for years to loosen up. Now why am I here if not to help you strip these two naked and have some adult fun?"

Zakar stepped forward. "I think I like her suggestion."

Sin stared him down.

At least to a degree. "Look, I've been trapped in that cave with those bastards gnawing on me for centuries. It'd be a really nice change to have a goddess nibble on me."

Feeling sorry for him, Sin ignored his outburst. "We have demons who are going to try and attack us in our sleep."

"Skoti?" Kytara asked.

"No," Kat said. "Gallu demons."

"Ooo." Kytara looked like the mere thought gave her an orgasm. "They're a bloody lot. I like it."

Sin was confused by her eagerness. "I thought the Greek Oneroi were devoid of emotions."

"They are," Kat explained. "Kytara is a Skotos. She sucks emotions from dreamers and uses them for her own."

Kytara smiled. "It's the only way to live. Really. The Oneroi are just too stodgy for words."

Sin had no comment to that.

But Kat gestured to the three of them. "We don't want the gallu attacking us at night. Can you watch our backs while we sleep?"

Kytara bit her lip and wiggled her hips as if she enjoyed the thought way too much. "Voyeurism . . . kinky. I like it even better."

Kat shook her head. "You are the worst."

"Of course I am. Isn't that why you called me?"

Suddenly the idea of having her here didn't seem so bright to Sin. Having a Greek Oneroi in his dreams just seemed like asking for trouble. "Curious . . . Can you wander over to the gallu and spy on them while they sleep?"

She brushed a finger along the edge of his chin and gave him a sexy smile. "In a dream, baby, I can do anything I want."

Kat pushed her back, away from Sin. "And keep your hands off that one, Kytara, or lose them to some big mean hand-eating dream monster."

She gave Kat a knowing look. "Yes, ma'am."

Sin found Kat's jealousy amusing and flattering. But right now they had more important things to focus on. He cleared his throat to get their attention back on the matter at hand. "Will you watch them then?"

"Depends." Kytara paused for effect before asking, "Is he a good-looking demon?"

Kat nodded. "Very."

"Ooo, gotta go check it. Later." Kytara vanished instantly.

Sin crossed his arms over his chest, grateful to have some space away from the Skotos. "You have interesting friends, Kat."

"True, and sometimes they're very helpful."

Zakar sucked his breath in sharply as if something had just struck him in the chest.

Concerned for him, Sin put a hand on his brother's back. "Zakar?"

"They're trying to find me." He shoved Sin away from him and staggered to his left. "Run."

"I won't leave you here to face them."

Zakar gave him a furious glare. "It's only a dream. Go."

"Then what's the harm in my staying if it's only a dream?"

Zakar shook his head. "You don't know what you're doing."

"Yes, I do," Sin said emphatically. "I'm protecting my brother."

"One quick question?" Kat asked, distracting the two of them. "Can you kill the gallu in this realm?"

"No," Zakar said. "Why?"

Kat pointed behind the men. " 'Cause they're here."

CHAPTER TWELVE

Sin braced himself for the coming fight, but strangely, Kessar didn't make any moves toward him.

Instead, he stared at Zakar with a twisted half smile. "I see you found my pet, Nana." He returned his gaze to Sin and his face turned to stone. "And my brother."

Sin shrugged in feigned sympathy. "He attacked us," he said sarcastically. "What was I supposed to do? Invite him to dinner?"

"You were supposed to die." Kessar narrowed his eyes on him. "It would have been a good start."

Sin shook his head. "I don't know. I die, you get bored. World ends. Doesn't really fit, does it? Besides, I can't make things too easy on you. What's life without pain?"

Kessar's gaze went back to Zakar. "That's a question best answered by the pet, isn't it?"

Fury darkened Sin's gaze as he saw the shame on Zakar's face, but before he could move to retaliate, Zakar blasted the demon.

Kessar turned it away with a wave of his hand. "Don't you ever learn, dog?"

Zakar glared at him. "I will fight you till I die."

Kessar laughed. "Oh, you're going to die all right. All of you. And for what you've done to my brother you will suffer unimaginably."

"Yada yada yada." Kat slowly enunciated each word before she looked at Sin as if bored by their exchange. "Am I the only one who gets sick of the bad-guy monologue?" She held her arms out like a zombie and mocked Kessar's accent. " 'Ooo, I'm the big evil. I'm going to kill you all. Just wait while I bore you to tears with my egomaniacal bullshit. I'm just a demon windbag who likes to hear himself speak and I'm trying to intimidate you.' "

She looked back at Kessar and put her arms down. "Really, if that's the case, you need to stop letting your mother dress you funny. It's hard to take anyone serious as a killer when he looks likes an investment banker. The only part of me that's nervous is my checkbook."

Kessar ran his tongue over his fangs as he eyed her as if she were a tender niblet. "Your girlfriend has quite a mouth, Nana. I'm going to enjoy shoving her words down her throat."

Sin glared at him. "Not nearly as much as I'm going to enjoy killing you."

Kat rolled her eyes. "What is this? A hen party? For a couple of guys, you're talking more than an episode of *Oprah*. If we're going to fight, let's fight."

Zakar frowned at her. "So eager to die are you?"

Kat shrugged. "Not particularly, but I'd rather go down clubbing Kessar than from boredom."

Suddenly there were four dozen Kessars all around them.

Kat cursed as she realized she might have spoken too soon. This could get ugly—and given the number of Kessars present, that was putting it mildly—fast.

"Yo, Toto," she said to Sin, "I'm having a bad *Matrix II* flashback and hearing Mr. Anderson in my head from that guy who was the elf in *Lord of the Rings*."

Sin arched a brow. "Orlando Bloom?"

"No, the other one."

Without warning, Kessar started for her. Kat moved to attack him, but before he reached her, she was jerked out of the way.

All of a sudden, someone was shaking her. Hard.

"Ow!" Kat blinked open her eyes to find Kytara standing over her while she lay in bed beside Sin. "What the . . . ?"

"Wake up your boyfriend. I'm going to get the one in the other room before Kessar tears him apart." Kytara vanished.

Yawning, Kat rolled over and did what Kytara had told her. Sin came awake, ready to fight.

"Whoa," Kat said, ducking his grip. "It's me. Kat."

It took him a second to focus on her face and to realize he was awake. "Where's Kessar?"

"Not here. He's only in our dreams." She scooted toward the edge of the bed. "Kytara just woke me, then headed out toward your brother. Let's go see if she can explain all this."

They left the bedroom to find Kytara in the main room, which was so dark, they could barely see. Sin turned on a small lamp on the bar that cast a dull yellow glow around them.

The Dream-Huntress was kneeling on the floor beside Zakar, staring at him while he continued to sleep.

Sin went to wake him, but Kytara grabbed his arm to stop him. Her eyes were vibrant and blue in the low light. "He's not what you think."

"He's my brother."

"Yes," she breathed as she met his gaze, "but ask yourself why they let him live."

"To torture him."

Kytara shook her head. "To ruin him, Sin. He's no longer a god of dreams. He's become one of *them*."

Sin shook his head in denial. "He fought against them. I saw it for myself."

Kat stepped forward, agreeing completely with Sin. There was no way Zakar could be on the side of the gallu after all he'd gone through. Not after all Kessar and his minions had done to him. It wasn't possible.

But her friend knew something . . . had seen something that had her panicked. Kytara was hiding a truth she didn't think Sin could handle.

Kat knelt on the floor next to Kytara. "He told us he'd been fractured. What did he mean?"

Kytara sat back on her feet before she rose to tower over Kat.

"They have infected him and he can't control it. He's as likely to kill you as he is them."

Kat rose immediately as those words haunted her. Surely not . . .

By Sin's face, she could tell he refused to believe it. "Kat fixed his injuries."

"On the outside. It's what's inside him that's deadly. He now has the same blood hunger they have."

"No. He battled Asag and survived. It gave him immunity to the gallu."

"It gave him resistance, not immunity. They have been feeding on him for centuries with no letup. The gallu is inside him and it's trying to gnaw its way out even as we speak. He is a danger to all of us. Why do you think they had him tied down? He has their strength, the powers of a god, and the demon inside him that will kill anything without remorse."

Kat was sick at the news. It wasn't fair for Zakar to have suffered so much only to die now that he was free. "There has to be something we can do."

"Kill him," Kytara said simply.

"I can't." Sin's voice broke with the weight of his emotions. "He's my brother." His eyes betrayed the agony inside him. "My twin."

Kytara was merciless as she approached him. "Then he will kill you when he awakens." She met Kat's gaze. "You have no idea what you're up against. I've been in the dreams of every kind of evil. But these . . ." She visibly shivered. "They make Stryker look like a pussycat. And now they're in your dreams. You're going to need an army to guard your rest."

"What army?" Kat asked.

"A strong one."

Well, that was helpful, not at all. Kat stepped around the pulled-out bed to stand beside Kytara. "I don't understand."

Kytara took a deep breath before she spoke again. "I was only in contact with Kessar for a brief time. You weren't kidding about his powers—they are unbelievable. We need some serious muscle in the dream realm for you two whenever you sleep. They know how to find you now and they will weaken you there, then swoop in here for the kill."

Her face paling, Kytara placed the heel of her hand over her eyes. "I wish I could burn the images I've seen tonight out of my memory. It's enough to make me want to be Oneroi again." She lowered her hand so that they could see the tears in her eyes. "I wish to Zeus that I could go back to feeling nothing. It was the most horrific thing I've ever seen and now I'm scarred by it. You have to kill him, Sin. Trust me."

"No," he said emphatically.

"Then I'll do it for you." Kytara pulled out a knife and headed for Zakar.

Sin grabbed her and pushed her back, away from the bed. "Hell, no. You want to hurt him, you'll have to come through me. I'll be damned if I ever let anyone hurt him again."

The cold look on her face as she raked him with a sneer could have made glaciers. "Fine then, I'll make sure and mark that on your grave." She moved to stand beside Kat. "Do yourself a favor. Get out of here before that one"—she indicated Zakar—"wakes up. Trust me. You'll thank me for it later."

Kat ignored her words. She wasn't about to leave Sin alone in this. "Can you speak to the Oneroi and see what can be done about the gallu in our dreams?"

"I can try. I'm sure M'Adoc, M'Ordant, and D'Alerian would love a chance to be able to keep someone else in line."

Kat thought about the three Oneroi leaders Kytara had mentioned. She was speaking out of turn and had no idea how right her prediction was. Kat was one of the few people who knew that the Oneroi's emotions were coming back to them. Because of that, it meant they had emotional outbursts that were sometimes hard to disguise. A mission like this could very well help the Oneroi leaders maintain control of themselves. It would definitely be something they'd relish.

"Tell D'Alerian he owes me and I need to collect my favor."

Kytara cocked her head at that. "D'Alerian owes you a favor?"

Kat nodded. "From years ago, and I know he hasn't forgotten it."

A mischievous glint entered Kytara's pale eyes. "What did you do?"

"It's between us. Now go."

Curling her lip in response, Kytara dissolved.

Feeling Sin's concern and sadness, Kat went to Sin's side as he pulled the blanket up higher on his brother's body.

As soon as Sin's hand neared Zakar's neck, Zakar came awake with a curse. He reached for Sin's throat, but he caught Zakar's wrist in his hand.

Time seemed suspended as their identical gazes met. Neither moved, and like them, Kat was held transfixed by the tenseness of the moment. The only difference between them was their hair. Sin's was well-groomed and fell just to his collar, while Zakar's was long and gnarled.

But other than that, it was like watching someone stare at himself in a mirror.

How extremely unnerving.

"Zakar?" Sin whispered, finally breaking the tense silence. "It's me. Sin."

Zakar let go and leaned back. He looked around as if dazed by his surroundings. "Where am I?"

"My place. We rescued you from the cavern."

Even though he'd been with them in their dreams, Zakar seemed unable to believe what he heard, what he saw.

An odd twinge went through Kat as she watched him. She sensed something inside him . . . something cold and evil. Something powerful. She wanted to warn Sin, but by the look of affection on his face as he watched his brother, she knew he wouldn't listen to her any more than he had to Kytara. And why should he? This was his family.

All Kat could do was stand by and be ready should Zakar attack.

Zakar's golden gaze met hers. "You're the Atlantean."

"Half Atlantean," she corrected, wondering why that was important to him.

His gaze went back to Sin. "How did you heal me?"

"I didn't." He indicated her with a tilt of his head. "Kat did."

Zakar turned back toward her. "Thank you."

She inclined her head to him. "Anytime. How do you feel?"

He gave a short laugh, but the smile on his face didn't reach his eyes. "Free."

That could be a good thing or a really bad thing. If Kytara was to be believed, it was really, really bad.

"Are you hungry?" Sin asked.

"No, but I'd kill for something to drink."

That wasn't exactly something Kat wanted to hear coming out of his mouth given the nature of the gallu and the warnings of Kytara.

"Wine?" Sin asked as if unfazed by his brother's words.

Zakar nodded.

Kat stepped forward as Sin went to the bar to get his brother a glass. Not moving from his bed, Zakar turned toward her with a taunting grin. "You have a problem with me?"

"Nope. I'm just thinking."

"About?"

She narrowed her eyes on his neck, which, courtesy of her, no longer held a single trace of the bite marks that had once marred the tanned flesh. "Blood exchanges."

"And what do you know about them?" His tone couldn't have been more patronizing had the man been a militant kindergarten teacher asking a student to define the Hobbesian State of Nature.

"A lot more than I care to," she said, duplicating his snotty tone. "For one thing, they usually link the participants together."

"What are you saying, Kat?" Sin asked as he rejoined them.

She didn't know why, but she took comfort in his presence. "It's never the enemy without that destroys. It's the one from within."

She expected Sin to argue, but he didn't. He simply handed the glass to Zakar and remained uncharacteristically quiet. There was something in his demeanor that made her think he might have used that phrase himself a time or two.

Zakar sat up and downed all the contents in a single gulp. He wiped his mouth with the back of his hand before returning the glass to Sin.

Zakar then cast that gimlet glare back at her. "You don't trust me."

"I don't know you."

He smiled a smile that was so familiar and at the same time alien. Looking at him, he was identical to Sin, except for the scars that marred Sin's body. Yet she didn't react to Zakar's presence at all. There was no heart racing, no clammy hands. No desire to jump on top of him . . . nothing. It was just like looking at any handsome naked man. It left her cold and reminded her why the other handmaidens had often called her frigid.

Zakar tilted his head to look around her to where Sin was standing. "I don't believe your woman thinks much of me, Brother."

Sin gave her a devilish wink that managed to warm her. "Don't feel bad, she doesn't think much of anyone including me most days."

"True," she agreed. "People are basically irritating. Myself included."

Sin's cell phone started ringing. He excused himself and went to answer it.

Zakar leaned back against the back of the sofa and draped an arm along the top. His gaze stayed focused on Kat, who didn't flinch under his intense scrutiny. Rather, she duplicated it, letting him know that she wasn't the least bit intimidated by him.

Finally he broke the silence. "You want to say something to me, don't you?"

"Not really. Just chillin'." She glanced over to where Sin was moving to stand outside on the balcony while he talked. What was going on?

No doubt, she'd find out soon enough. So she turned her attention back to Zakar. "You must be relieved to be away from the gallu."

"You've no idea."

"Seeing how you were pinned down, I wouldn't go that far. I imagine it was pretty gruesome for you."

That succeeded in making him look away from her. "I need clothes."

She frowned at the odd note in his voice. "You going somewhere?"

He didn't answer. He merely got up, completely bare assed, and headed for the bedroom like there was nothing wrong with streaking through his brother's penthouse in front of her. Kat would have gaped, but then she knew ancient men hadn't been modest . . .

Then again, there weren't many modern men afflicted with modesty, either.

Sin stepped back in from the balcony and swept the room with his dark gaze. "Where's Zakar?"

"Said he needed clothes."

Sin frowned. "My bedroom?"

"That's where he went, so that would be my best guess."

Sin headed toward the room with her right behind him. When they got there, the room was completely empty. Dumbfounded, she kept waiting for Zakar to reappear before them.

He didn't.

Sin went to the closet and opened it, but there was no sign of Zakar anywhere. They even checked the bathroom. The man had flashed himself out of the room and gone . . . who knew where.

"Where do you think he went?"

Sin shrugged. "I have no idea. But something with him wasn't right."

"I thought it was just me."

"No, I felt it, too." He slammed the bathroom door shut. "Damn it. What have we unleashed?"

She sighed. "Doom, destruction . . . at least he's not nuclear, right?"

A smile toyed at the edges of Sin's lips. "At this point, who knows?"

Kat beamed. "Oh look, Mr. Positive has come out to play again. Welcome back, Mr. Positive. All the boys and girls have missed you so."

Sin smiled in spite of himself. Her humor should irritate him, but instead he found it a refreshing relief from the seriousness of the situation. Honestly, he couldn't remember any time in his life he'd enjoyed more than this time with her. And all things considered, this had to be the worst part of his existence, since they were only days away from Armageddon.

The only thing that made any of this bearable was her wit and courage. "You're really not right, are you?"

She scoffed. "With my background and genetic makeup, buddy, you're lucky I'm as normal as I am."

"Point well taken." He let out a tired breath as he tried to locate

Zakar, but nothing would come to him. It was as if his brother had vanished into a black hole. "Can you locate him?"

"Not even a buzz. What about you?"

He shook his head. "As much as I hate to say this, I guess we'll have to wait for him to return."

By her face he could tell the idea appealed as much to her as it did to him. But what choice did they have? Without a bearing, they had no idea where to even begin searching for Zakar. Sin could kill his brother for this.

Kat moved over to him and rubbed his back. "Who was on the phone?"

"Damien. He said a gallu tried to get in, but the mirrors repelled him."

Her smile warmed him before she rested her chin on his shoulder and wrapped her arm around his waist. Yeah, a man could get used to this. There was something not only comforting but highly unsettling about the way her innocent touch set him on fire.

"Maybe we ought to get mirrored armor," she said. "You know, like they had in the Brothers Grimm movie?"

"That was just metal they wore."

"But we could make it out of mirrors. Then they'd be repelled any time they came near us . . . you know, we could start like a whole fashion line of mirrored clothing. One that could save humanity. Just think about it."

He laughed at her train of thought. Oddly enough, he appreciated it, but it was highly impractical. "And when we broke one of the mirrors while trying to fight them off we'd have seven years' bad luck."

She didn't miss a bit before she retorted, "Ah, we're immortal. What's seven years to us?"

"An eternity when it's bad."

She stuck her tongue out at him in a playful gesture that somehow managed to be adorable on her.

What was wrong with him?

"Just be a spoilsport, why don't you?"

He supposed he was. He wanted to be playful like her, but he wasn't. At the end of the day, he was all about doom and gloom and he couldn't help wondering what his brother was up to. Where Zakar had gone . . .

Sin raked his hands through his hair as guilt gnawed at him. "What have I done?"

Kat tightened her grip around him. "You saved your brother."

He leaned his head against hers and inhaled the sweet scent of her hair and skin. "What if I haven't? What if Kytara is right and we should have killed him while we had the chance?"

"Is that really what you think?"

"At this point, I don't know."

Kat laid a gentle kiss to his shoulder blade that seared him. "I do know, Sin. I believe in you and your judgment. I know you've done the right thing."

Sin was stunned by her conviction, and it meant more to him than he could even begin to put into words. "Thanks. I just wish I shared your faith."

"Don't worry, I've got enough for both of us."

Sin smiled even though he was worried about what Zakar was doing. He felt like he should be searching for Zakar. But he didn't know where to begin. Like Kat, he wasn't picking up anything from his brother. Not even a small trace.

And Zakar wasn't answering Sin's summons. There was no telling what his brother was into.

A bad feeling went through Sin. Had he been blinded by loyalty and love? Gods, what if he'd unleashed something unholy onto mankind?

"Stop fretting." Kat smoothed his frown with her fingers.

"Yeah, but we don't know what he's doing or who he's doing it to."

"I know." She pulled the small *sfora* from around her neck and held it in her hand. "Let's try finding him this way, shall we?"

Sin stepped back as she used the stone to summon Zakar. But after a few minutes, she looked up with a grimace. "It's not working."

"What do you mean?"

"It's like he's not on the earth. Anywhere. You think he went back to the cavern?"

"Hardly believable, given what they'd done to him. But for argument's sake, even if he did, the *sfora* found him there last time. Wouldn't it be able to find him there again?"

"One would think." Kat looked up to meet his gaze. "You ever feel like the world no longer makes sense?"

"Every day of my life."

"Yeah, well, I'm not used to that feeling and I find it highly disturbing."

He rubbed her arms and kissed her lightly on the forehead. "We'll find him."

Kat wanted to believe that, but she wasn't sure. What had they brought back? Was Zakar the demon Kytara had warned them about or was there enough of his decency left to combat it?

"If he's fighting for the gallu . . ."

Sin's face hardened. "He won't. I have to believe that."

"But if they converted him?"

"I will kill him," he said with a conviction so sincere, it was almost believable.

But Kat knew how much he loved his brother. "Do you really think you can do that?"

He hesitated as if he was considering his answer. When he met her gaze, there was no denying his intent. "I won't have a choice. I can't let the Dimme out and I can't allow Kessar to win in this. Whatever it takes. Whoever I have to sacrifice. I will do what I have to to keep them away from the innocent."

She couldn't imagine the strength inside him that would allow him to carry out such a thing. She laid her head on his chest and held him close as she tried to fathom the source of his courage. To kill family was hard . . . to kill a twin brother you'd spent your life protecting to save the world . . .

He was incredible.

"You're a good man, Sin."

He laid his cheek against her head. "No, I'm not. I'm just trying to make right something I should have never let go wrong."

Kat leaned back to kiss him. She couldn't believe how she'd misjudged him when her mother had sent her out to kill him. In all her life, she'd never met anyone who came close to the compassion and altruism of her father.

Until now.

Sin was everything a woman could hope for.

It gave her hope for the world and she wanted to touch him. To give him something of his own to hold on to. Pulling his T-shirt over his head, she threw it to the floor.

He frowned at her. "What are you doing?"

"Seducing you."

"Shouldn't we be looking for my brother?"

"Will twenty minutes really matter?"

He laughed low in his throat. "Twenty? You seriously underestimate my fortitude."

Spoken like a true fertility god. "Then let's make it an appetizer for later."

His smile warmed every part of her as he slowly unbuttoned her pajama top. Kat groaned as he ran his hands over her breasts after he parted the soft material. And when he dipped his head down to take her nipple in his mouth, she swore she saw stars from it.

Sin couldn't breathe as he felt her hands in his hair. He slid her pants down her long legs until they pooled at her feet. He'd never seen a more beautiful woman. Never.

Unable to stand it, he slid to his knees so that he could taste her better.

Kat leaned back against the bar while Sin gently tongued her. Waves of pleasure pierced her until she could barely stand. How could any man be so talented with his tongue? She gripped the wood behind her with her hands as she rose to her tiptoes.

Unable to stand it, she came in a searing moment of ecstasy. Leaning her head back, she cried out.

Sin growled at the taste of her climax. Rising to his feet, he pushed his pants down and separated her legs.

She bit her lip as he entered her, then wrapped her legs around his waist. Sin sucked his breath in sharply at the pleasure that went through him. Using the bar as leverage, she took control.

He'd never seen or felt anything hotter. She was absolutely shameless, taking what she needed from him.

The moonlight cut across her body, highlighting her breasts as he held her hips to his.

Kat licked her lips as Sin thrust against her. Each stroke felt deeper than the last . . . more fulfilling. No wonder people were willing to risk death for this.

When she came again, Sin joined her.

Sin held her close as his body withdrew from hers. "I think you just killed me."

She laughed. "No, I do believe you're made of sterner stuff than that."

"I'm not so sure." He kissed her tenderly before he pulled back. "We'll shower, then head out after Zakar."

"If we can find him, you mean."

"Yeah."

He took her by the hand and led her back through his bedroom to the bathroom so that he could turn on the water and let it heat. Kat dropped her shirt to the floor and watched as Sin leaned into the shower to test the temperature.

The lean muscles on his back were a symphony of movement. Dang, he was gorgeous. From the broad shoulders, to his muscular legs, to his rump, which was absolutely prime.

He was so beautiful, she could barely stand it. "I swear, you have the best-looking butt on the planet."

He shook his head as he came out of the shower to face her. "One of two of them, anyway."

"Huh?"

"I have a twin, remember? His butt would look just like mine."

Actually, she didn't remember that. Zakar's butt hadn't turned her on when he'd left the room earlier. Not the way Sin's did. Honestly, she wanted a bite of it so badly that she could think of little else.

"Like I would know. I'm not interested in checking his assets."

Sin rolled his eyes at her bad pun. He didn't believe her for a minute. In his experience, women were very quick to check out some other guy's parts. "Sure you're not."

She pulled him by the arm until he turned to face her. The look on her face made his heart stop beating. "I'm not Ningal, Sin. I have no interest in anyone but you."

Those words touched him a lot more than they should.

He cupped her face in his hands before he kissed her with everything he had. He wanted desperately to believe her. But could he? There was so much left to do, so many other men who might turn her head and her heart. He was the only one she'd ever known. What on earth made her believe that she'd be content with him?

He was grateful she at least made the effort. But in the back of his mind was the image of her with someone else, and it cut him so deep that he swore he could taste the blood from it.

She pulled back and stared up at him. "What's wrong?"

"Nothing."

"Don't tell me, 'Nothing'. I can feel it. There's something inside you that's eating a sore place in your heart."

"There's nothing there. Believe me. I don't have a heart left."

Kat didn't know why he was lying, but it was obvious he didn't want to discuss it. Sighing, she stepped into the shower, and Sin followed her.

She wet herself first while he watched with a guarded expression. "I won't bite you, Sin."

"Seems I've heard that before." He looked down at his arm where there was a huge scar in the shape of a fanged bite.

She picked up his arm and placed her hand over the scar. "My bites don't wound and they don't leave scars."

"We'll see about that, won't we?"

She kissed his hand before she released it and soaped her hair. Was there any way to get through to him?

Then again, did she really blame him for his skepticism? How much could one person be hurt in his lifetime and continue to believe that not everyone was out to screw him? Sin was allowed to mistrust. The gods knew he'd earned it.

Sin forced himself to move away from Kat. Trying not to stay focused on the way the water cascaded over her body, he turned on the second showerhead, then yelped as he was pelted by ice-cold water.

Kat laughed before she stepped aside. "I will share, sweetie."

He paused at her endearment and the way it pierced him straight through his heart. "Sweetie?"

"Yeah?"

He didn't know why something that stupid touched him, but it did. "You are the first person in history to apply that term to me."

"Yeah, well, the others must not have known you all that well." She reached out and put a dab of soap on the tip of his nose.

Laughing, he pulled her against him and pinned her to the wall before he nipped her chin. And in that one moment, he realized he was in paradise. The feel of her soft, slick skin on his with the hot water pelting down his back and the sound of her laughter in his ears . . .

There couldn't be a better moment than this to be had. And he wanted to savor it. If he still had his powers, he'd stop time and make this last for eternity.

But instead of eternity, he heard someone banging on the bathroom door.

"Yo, boss!"

Releasing Kat, Sin stepped back at the intrusion of Kish's voice on his happiness. "There better be something going on worth your life, Kish. Because if there isn't, I'm going to kill you."

"We need you downstairs, right now. There's a demon eating a tourist!"

CHAPTER THIRTEEN

Sin flashed himself out of the shower and into clothes before he snatched open the door to find Kish standing in the hallway. "What?"

"Downstairs, boss, now. Gallu eating people."

It wasn't in Sin to follow anyone's orders, but for once he didn't question it. He did just what Kish said—he went straight downstairs.

As soon as he was in the casino, it was easy to find the gallu. Even though the gallu looked human, his true demon form was reflected in the mirrors around them. There was chaos everywhere. People were screaming and running for the doors. Stools were overturned and the human employees were joining the patrons while the Daimons and Apollites were trying to cover those who fled.

And that was why he used them in his casino. Unlike human help, they could be relied on to stay calm in a crisis and to assist in the event something "unnatural" happened. Credit had to be given to the Apollites and Daimons. They seldom panicked.

Sin turned away from the doors to the back corner.

It appeared Damien and his guards had the gallu trapped by one of the roulette wheels—although "trapped" might be more hopeful than true. Sin reached the demon just as he grabbed one of the guards and bit into him. Luckily he was a Daimon and not human—at least that was the thought until the Daimon turned instantly into a gallu.

Holy shit. Their metabolism sped up the change. Whereas a human took about a day to complete their conversion. Daimons were virtually instantaneous.

Oh, the things you learned when you ran a casino . . .

Now they had two gallu to fight.

Damien took his suit jacket off. "Cover their heads so they can't bite you, and beat the shit out of them."

"Screw you!" one of the Daimon guards shouted before he ran toward the door.

So much for not panicking . . .

Damien curled his lip at the fleeing coward. "Yeah, run home to Mama, little girl, and don't come back." He paused as he saw Sin.

Sin didn't speak. He kept walking toward his targets. He held his arms out to his sides as he manifested his weapons on his biceps and hips.

The gallu Daimon was the first to come at him. Sin flipped him over, onto his back, and held him in place with his knee. He jerked the knife from his belt and plunged it between the Daimon's eyes and then buried a second knife in his heart, just to be sure.

The Daimon didn't burst apart, which let Sin know that when a Daimon crossed with a gallu, they were serious shit.

But Sin would deal with this one later. The knives would keep him dead until they could burn him. Right now, Sin had the gallu to finish.

"Come to Papa," Sin said, rising slowly to his feet.

The demon did, but he was smarter than the gallu Daimon. He didn't run at Sin, he approached him slowly. And when the demon was within striking distance, he punched. Sin blocked the strike and delivered a fist of his own straight to the demon's solar plexus. It didn't even faze him. The demon moved forward to bite Sin, but he stepped right, out of range.

"Who taught you to fight? Your sister?" Sin struck the demon's back.

Spinning, the demon caught him with a solid punch so hard that it knocked him up, off his feet. He hit the ground flat on his back.

Sin flipped himself back to his feet, ready to battle. But before he could move, a steel spike appeared between the demon's eyes.

It was jerked free as the demon slid to the floor to show him Deimos.

"Nasty little bastards your family created. Now it's time to finish the fight we started earlier."

"Looking forward to it."

Deimos swung at him. Sin blocked and the next attack came so fast he barely had time to counter it. He jerked his head back just before Deimos would have hit him. His fist came so close, Sin could feel the windburn of its passing on his cheek. He swung at Deimos's chin, but the Dolophonos jerked his head to the side. Sin missed him by only scant millimeters.

In spite of that, Sin smiled. It'd been a long time since he faced someone he considered an equal.

Kat popped in just as Sin landed a staggering blow to Deimos's chest. The Dolophonos reeled back.

She paused beside Damien. "What did I miss?"

"Not much," he said dryly. "Killer Daimon that was eaten by a gallu. Sin killed the gallu Daimon on the floor over there. Then numb-nuts popped in, killed the gallu, and attacked Sin." He glanced askance at her. "Want to wager on the winner?"

She was appalled by his suggestion. "Damien!"

"What?" he asked, his face a mask of confused innocence. "I manage a casino. Gambling is my life. If I were smart, I'd start running odds and bets right now. Trust me, Sin would not only appreciate it, he'd approve."

The sad thing was, Damien was probably right about that. "You are so amoral."

"No. I'm a Daimon. Morals don't become us."

Kat made a feigned sound of disgust at him before she turned her attention back toward the men who were fighting. She had to give Sin credit, unwounded, he was more than holding his own against Deimos. She truthfully couldn't say who would win.

At least not until Sin kicked Deimos back so hard, Deimos went flying into one of the mirrors, shattering it. She cringed in sympathetic pain as Deimos slammed to the floor.

Deimos paused as he saw Kat. A sinister smile curved his lips as he started for her.

Kat braced herself for his attack.

But he never reached her.

His face filled with the wrath of hell, Sin went for Deimos and pulled a barbed cord from around his wrist. Just as Kat moved to strike him, Sin wrapped the cord around Deimos's throat and snatched him back from her.

"That was your fatal mistake," Sin snarled in Deimos's ear as he tightened his grip.

Deimos's eyes bulged as he tried desperately to pull the cord from his throat. But Sin gave him no quarter.

"Don't kill him," she said.

Sin scowled at her. "Are you insane? He won't stop otherwise."

Maybe, but Deimos was still family, psycho though he was, and she didn't want to see him killed. "Deimos, swear you'll leave us alone."

"Never."

Sin's biceps bulged as he tightened the cord even more. Deimos was dead. She knew it and it broke her heart.

Suddenly a woman's voice echoed from the open doorway "Damien! A gallu just dragged off a young woman on the street. Her mother's screaming for help."

Sin's face went white as he heard those words. Kat saw the indecision in his eyes. He looked down at Deimos, cursed, then let go of the cord and ran for the door.

Deimos fell forward, onto his hands and knees, coughing and gagging as he unwound the cord from around his neck.

Kat cringed as she saw the blood from where the cord had cut into skin. No doubt Deimos would carry that scar for the rest of eternity. Shaking her head in pity, she ran after Sin, who was on the street now, chasing after the gallu.

The demon ran into a side street, dragging a young woman behind it.

All of a sudden, the demon stopped as if it'd ran into something invisible. Sin pulled the woman from the demon's arms and kicked it back. He handed the woman off to Kat, then turned to fight the demon as the woman collapsed against her.

Just as the demon reached Sin, it burst into flames.

Kat gasped.

Deimos stepped out from the shadows. "They are filthy bastards, aren't they?"

Sin tensed, waiting for Deimos to attack him. Honestly, he was getting a little sick of it. But to his utter consternation, the Dolophonos looked past him to the woman who was sobbing hysterically against Kat.

"Is she all right?" Deimos asked.

"Shaken, but she doesn't appear to have been hurt. I think Sin got to her in time."

Deimos stepped around Sin and placed his hand on the woman's head. She fell back, unconscious. He caught her against him, then gently laid her down on the sidewalk as her mother came running over to them.

"Crystal?"

"She's fine," Deimos said quietly. He looked over at Sin. "He saved her."

Tears of gratitude were flowing down the mother's face as she looked at Sin. "Thank you. Thank you both. I don't know what he would have done to her had you not helped us."

Deimos nodded, then he placed his hand on her head to erase her memories of them. Like her daughter, she collapsed, and Deimos placed her carefully on the ground.

He looked at them over his shoulder. "We have exactly one minute before they come to again. They'll think it was a mugger who left them and ran."

Sin eyed him suspiciously. "We're not going to finish our fight?"

Deimos shook his head. "Contrary to public opinion, neither the Erinyes nor the Dolophoni are the lapdogs of the Greek pantheon. I don't follow orders unless I see a reason to. I was willing to kill you only because you desecrated human remains and didn't appear rational. Now I'm willing to spare you because you chose the welfare of an innocent human over your own . . ." He glanced to Kat before he spoke again. "And over that of someone you care for. In my book, that makes you worth forgiving."

Sin was still stunned by his turnaround. It didn't seem logical. "So you're bowing out of this?"

Deimos scoffed. " 'Bowing out' implies a chivalry I lack. Let's just say, lucky for you, I didn't find what I needed to. The Dolophoni only kill for a reason, and that reason has to be justified to Themis or we're executed." He wiped at the blood on his neck that was left by the cord Sin had used to choke him. "Killing you isn't worth my life. But you still have an enemy who wants you dead. Watch your back."

Kat smiled at him. "Thank you, Demon."

"Don't thank me, Katra. I didn't do a favor here. I just did my job." He faded into the darkness.

Sin gave her an arch look as the mother and daughter began stirring.

Kat held her hand to her lips to silence him before she flashed them back to his casino where they'd left the gallu bodies.

Damien was there with a questioning look. "You're still alive. Good. Any chance you want to help clean up the mess?"

Sin gave him a wry glare. "That's why I pay you the big bucks, Damien."

"Thought so, boss. Just checking." Damien's smile faded as he turned away from them and started mumbling under his breath.

Kat had a feeling it wasn't complimentary to Sin. "I can't believe Deimos is off your tail. I have to say I've found a new respect for him. I really, truly thought you were dead when he appeared."

"As I recall, he was the one about to die. Maybe I scared him off."

She laughed. "There is that. Seriously, though, he doesn't scare that easily and I wouldn't be surprised if he hadn't allowed you to pin him as a test to see what you'd do. It's not like him to give up a death hunt."

"You think he was lying then?"

"No," she answered honestly. "He's the son of Alecto. She's the Erinys in charge of unceasing anger, and his mother's fury, pardon the pun, runs thick in his veins. But in addition to that, the Furies are also called the Eumenides—the kind ones. They are vindictive but fair. Like Deimos said, I think you proved yourself to him."

"Good," he breathed. "That's one noose off my neck. How many are left?"

She thought about that for a minute. "Counting your brother . . . couple of dozen. At least."

He looked less than amused. "Thanks for the reminder." But even though his response was sarcastic, she still had a feeling he wasn't as irritated as he pretended.

"Sorry."

He rubbed at his eyes as if he were exhausted. At least for a couple of seconds. Then he suddenly paused. "Where are the demons?"

"I think you killed them all."

"Not mine. Yours. The Charontes. Where have they vanished?"

Oh, that was a good question. In all the chaos, she'd forgotten them. "Hopefully not eating someone."

Terrified, they both flashed up to the room where Simi and Xirena were staying. It took a second for Kat's eyes to adjust to the darkness.

When they did, Kat had to stifle a laugh as she saw the two of them lying asleep, looking like spontaneous crash victims. Simi's legs were propped up on the wall and her body twisted while her head and one arm were draped over the side of the bed, toward the floor. Xirena was facedown with the top of her head on the floor while her body was spread diagonally across the bed. Her wings covered her like a blanket.

Scowling, Sin angled his head as if trying to match their twisted positions. "How do they sleep upside down like that? Wouldn't all the blood rush to your head and hurt?"

"I have no idea," she whispered, pushing him back toward the door. "But let's let them sleep."

He walked through the door, literally, without opening it and pulled her through behind him. A shiver went over her at his actions. "That was eerie."

"Yeah, but you have to admit it's kind of fun. I used to do it on Halloween to scare kids."

Kat laughed at the devilish look on his handsome face. "You're awful."

"Never claimed to be otherwise." He opened the door to his penthouse and allowed her to enter first.

She could sense his exhaustion and his concern for his brother as Sin joined her inside and closed the door behind them. "He'll turn up."

"Yeah, but how? I have a really bad feeling about this, Katra. Did I make a mistake by freeing him?"

She reached up to cup his face in her head so that she could soothe some of the guilt she felt from him. "Oh, Sin, you know better. There was no way you could have left him there, like that."

Those beautiful golden eyes were tormented. "I know. But . . ."

"Don't think about it," she whispered, giving him a light kiss on his whiskered cheek.

Sin nodded as she withdrew from him. He still felt terrible. A feeling that wasn't helped as he saw Kat put her hand to her head as if there was a sharp pain behind her left eye. "You all right?"

"Mmm, my head really hurts all of a sudden."

"You want some aspirin?"

With only her right eye open, she gave him a winsome smile. "Wish that would work. No. I think I just need to lie down for a sec."

Wondering what could be wrong with her, he took her to his bedroom and helped her into bed. "Is it any better?"

"No. I feel really sick."

He grabbed the plastic trash can from the floor and held it up for her.

Kat groaned as she saw it. "You know nothing says love like a man holding a bucket, waiting for you to hurl into it."

"No offense, you start hurling and I'm going to be needed immediately downstairs in the casino . . . I guarantee it."

She glared at him with only her one open eye. "That's not very romantic."

He scoffed at her aggravated tone. "Excuse me? Did I miss something? What has *ever* been romantic about vomit?"

"A man standing by your side when you're sick. Holding your hair back from your face . . . that's romantic."

"In what alternate universe do you live? Here in a place I like to call reality, that's disgusting. Who in their right mind would find that romantic?"

She managed to open both eyes to pin him with a less than complimentary snarl. "So you'd just leave me here alone to be ill?"

"I didn't say that," he said, trying to defend himself. "I'd have Damien come check on you."

She curled her lip at him and pushed him away from her. "Just go. Get out of here."

Sin didn't budge from the bed. "I can stay. You're not regurgitating at the moment."

She dry heaved and he actually inched toward the door. "You're just messing with me, aren't you? That wasn't real."

She leaned back on the bed and closed her eyes again. "I can't believe what a baby you are."

"Me? Like you'd stand over me if I were hurling? Give me a break."

"I might."

He didn't believe that for an instant. "Yeah, uh-huh. Let me go get ripped and put that theory to the test."

She pulled a pillow to her stomach. "You're awful."

"I'm honest. Trust me, no one ever comes to check on someone when they're ill."

"It doesn't matter anyway. You're a Dark-Hunter. You can't get sick or drunk."

That wasn't true by a long shot, and he'd had the hangovers to prove it. "I'm an ex-god your father gave a job to. I can, and have, been both many times."

Kat opened her eyes again to frown at him. "You've been ill?"

"Yes. Apparently, I lost whatever common cold and flu immunity I had when your mother sucked my powers out of me."

"And Damien or Kish didn't come help?"

"They'll bring food. That's about it."

Her heart ached for him. "I'm sorry, Sin. No one should be sick alone."

"Yeah, well, we all muddle through, don't we?"

Kat supposed. But it seemed terribly harsh and a wave of guilt went through her. No one should suffer without having someone to take care of them. It broke her heart to think of Sin in this bed with no one to bring him food and check his temperature.

She tried to reach for him, but suddenly the entire room spun and she started to fall from the bed.

Sin caught her against him and cursed as he felt the heat coming off her body. She was on fire. "Kat?"

She didn't answer him. Instead, she made a strange gurgling noise.

"Kat? Are you all right? Speak to me!"

"She can't."

He looked to see Zakar in the doorway. "Where the hell have you been?"

"Out," he said with a hostile note in his voice.

"Out where?"

He shrugged nonchalantly. "You've got bigger things to worry over than my previous whereabouts."

"Such as?"

Zakar jerked his chin toward Kat. "Your girlfriend must have been bitten by one of the gallu. What she's doing right now is converting into one of them."

CHAPTER FOURTEEN

Sin couldn't breathe as his brother's harsh words rang in his ears. He looked down at Kat on his bed, and while she might be burning with a fever, there was no sign of her changing over into a demon. "What do you mean, she's converting? She wasn't bitten."

Zakar indicated her with his hand. "Trust me. I know the symptoms. She's becoming one of them."

Sin cradled her against his chest. Even though she was unconscious, her eyes were half-open. Her body was completely limp. Her features were as beautiful as ever. Calm. Serene.

She wasn't becoming a demon. He refused to believe it. There was no sign of her teeth changing. Of her hands deforming. She looked as she always did.

His brother was wrong. "She's just sick."

Zakar laughed at him. "An immortal goddess, sick? Have you lost your mind?"

"I get sick," he said defensively. "It's possible she gets sick, too."

"Do you really believe that?"

No, but he wanted to, desperately. He honestly couldn't cope with the thought of her becoming a demon he'd have to kill.

Sin tightened his grip on her, afraid Zakar might be right. "What can I do?"

"Kill her."

"Bullshit!"

There was no mercy in Zakar's eyes as he watched Sin. "You know what I know. There's no cure for this. There's no way back. Once the conversion starts, it's over for the victim. All you can do is put her out of her misery."

Still, he denied it. The thought of killing Kat . . .

He couldn't bear it. In only a short time, she'd come to mean way too much to him. "You're immune to the demon venom."

"Am I?"

A cold chill went down Sin's spine. "Zakar . . ."

Zakar laughed. "You were a fool to come for me, Nana." He leapt across the bed at him.

Releasing Kat to fall back on the mattress, Sin caught him, and they slammed into the wall. Zakar looked normal, except for the single set of fangs in his mouth. A tremor of anger went through Sin. "Who the hell are you?"

"I'm your brother."

"No, you're not." He slugged his fist into Zakar's jaw, knocking him to the floor. This wasn't Zakar, this was something else entirely.

"Kytara!" Sin shouted. "If you can hear me, get your ass here now."

As Zakar stood up slowly and wiped the blood from his lips he tsked at Sin. "How pathetically weak you've grown that you now have to call for backup from a woman."

Sin raked his brother with a sneer. "She's not my backup. She's your babysitter." He blasted Zakar with a god-bolt.

And he didn't let up.

Zakar tried to run, but he couldn't. Every time he tried to stand, the blast would knock him back to the floor. With Zakar squirming in a corner, Sin kept him pinned until Kytara showed herself in the room.

She actually looked excited as she saw him frying his brother. "Good man. Kill the bastard."

But Sin didn't kill him. He couldn't do that to his own brother—he could only beat the shit out of him, and that only when Zakar deserved it.

As soon as Zakar was unconscious, Sin stopped pounding him with the bolts. He knelt by Zakar, who was slumped on the floor, and double-checked his pulse. It was strong and frantic against Sin's fingertips.

Satisfied that his brother would live, Sin laid him down more comfortably on the floor and covered him with a blanket. Sin looked up at Kytara, who was standing next to his bed. "What do you know about gallu conversions?"

She shrugged. "Not much really. I'm the other pantheon, remember? Why?"

"Because I think Kat was bitten by them." He went back to her on the bed. She was shaking now so badly that her teeth were chattering. And she still didn't wake or respond to him. "I need you to stay here while I get her help."

Kytara's face paled as she realized what was wrong with Kat. "There's no help for this. You know that."

He shook his head. There was no way in hell he was going to let Kat die. Not like this.

Or worse, kill her for it. There had to be something they could do. Anything, and he was willing to move the heavens and earth to save her. "I refuse to believe that." He picked Kat up from the bed and faced Kytara. "Watch Zakar for me. Don't let him out of your sight, and whatever you do, don't kill him."

She made an indignant squawk. "Are you kidding me? I'm not a babysitter."

He gave her the most hostile glare he could muster. "No, I'm not kidding. I don't want my brother dead. You said he's fractured. If that's the case, then we can fix him. But first I have to save Kat."

"It's impossible, Sin, and you know it. You're insane and you're wasting your time."

"We'll see." He paused before he left. "And Kytara, if my brother isn't still breathing when I return, the Oneroi are going to be the least of your concerns."

She gave him an indignant huff.

Ignoring her, Sin closed his eyes and flashed him and Kat to the last place he needed to visit . . .

Kalosis.

And he naturally manifested right in front of a Charonte who eyeballed him as if he were a prime steak on a plate. But Sin wasn't in the mood to deal with it. He ignored the beast.

"Apollymi!" Sin shouted as he walked down the long, narrow hallway with no idea where to go to find her. "I need you."

She appeared in front of him with her hands on her hips and her face flaming angry.

Until she saw Kat in his arms.

Apollymi's countenance instantly changed to one of concern as she rushed forward to place her hand on Kat's brow. "What happened?"

For some reason, that one single question coming from Kat's grandmother hit a raw nerve in him and all the repressed emotions he'd been holding back came rushing forward. His throat tightened as fear for Kat overwhelmed him.

But there was more to it than that. The thought of her dead . . .

Sin hadn't hurt like this in so long that it was all he could do to draw a breath. He couldn't lose her. He couldn't.

Swallowing against the lump in his throat, he spoke in a hushed tone. "I think she was bitten by a gallu demon and she's becoming one of them. I need you to heal her . . . please."

Tears filled Apollymi's eyes as she met his gaze, and he saw a hopelessness there that tore through him like fire. "I can't heal something like this."

Anger singed him. "I saw you mend her when she was hurt. You can heal this. I know it."

She shook her head. "I can heal wounds, but this . . . this is in her blood. It's spreading through her. I can't fix this. It's beyond me."

He felt as if someone had just sucker punched him. He shifted Kat in his arms so that he could press his lips against her feverish temple. Every laugh she'd ever given him . . . every touch burned through him now.

The thought of never hearing another sarcasm-laden quip . . .

It couldn't be over. He couldn't lose her over something so stupid as a bite they'd failed to cauterize. If not for helping him, she wouldn't even be in this.

No, there had to be something else he could do.

He glared at Apollymi as he felt his own tears pricking his eyes. "I won't let her die like this, Apollymi. Do you hear me? There has to be something. Anything. Don't tell me that out of two pantheons we don't have a solution."

She brushed a loving hand through Kat's pale hair. "Maybe her father can do something. He understands demons a lot better than I do."

A chill went over Sin at her words—the last known address for Ash was Artemis's bed. "What?"

Apollymi locked gazes with him. "You have to take her to Olympus. Apostolos is the only one I know who might have a solution or cure for this."

Personally, he'd rather have both eyes gouged out than ever step foot on Olympus again. The last time he'd ventured there, it'd cost him everything he had, including his dignity.

But one glance at Kat's beautiful face and the obvious pain she was in and he knew he was willing to walk through the fires of hell to make her better.

"Where is he on Olympus?"

"Artemis's temple."

Of course he was. Where else would Acheron be when Sin needed him?

How unfair was this? But his past didn't matter right now. Only Kat did.

"All right," he breathed, "but I can't go there on my own. Artemis stripped that power from me to keep me from killing her."

"Oh, we can only hope." Apollymi touched him on the shoulder. "Do me proud," she whispered. Then, louder, she called out to her son, "Apostolos?"

Ash's answer was almost instantaneous. "Yes, Matera?"

"I have Sin here with Katra. She's ill and she needs you, but I can't send them there without your help."

Sin barely had time to blink before he found himself on the balcony of Artemis's temple.

The large doors to his left opened to show Acheron in a pair of black leather pants and a long, heavy silk Atlantean robelike *formesta* that billowed out around his boots as he walked. "What's wrong?"

Sin met him halfway across the balcony. "A gallu bit her."

Ash's face paled. "Where?"

"I don't know and I'm really not sure. We went to a cavern to free my brother and several of them showed up and attacked us. It's the only time I think it could have happened, but she didn't tell me she'd been bitten." He looked down at her, wondering why she'd kept that secret from him. "She was fine until a short time ago. She told me she had a headache and then she started burning a fever. I thought she was sick until Zakar told me she was converting."

Acheron took her from his arms and carried her inside to a white chaise where he laid her down. Sin's heart sank at how pale she appeared. Her eyes were rolled completely back in her head, but at least her teeth were no longer chattering.

Then again, he wasn't sure if that was a good or bad thing.

"Katra?" Ash asked, kneeling down by her side. When she didn't respond, he laid his hand on her cheek.

She screamed the instant Ash touched her face, then tried to bite him.

Ash jumped back, out of her reach.

Sin cursed at the sight of her double set of fangs. She really was converting . . . Agony welled up inside of him at the thought of losing her. He was nauseated and wanted to kill Kessar for this.

"It's too late, isn't it?"

Ash looked up at the pain he heard in Sin's voice. And in that one moment, he had a realization about their relationship that made his insides shrink. Why else would Sin have come here and not be after Artemis to kill her?

He could have just left Katra with Apollymi and returned home. Instead, he'd come here with her and now watched over her with fear in his eyes and agony in his voice.

There was only one conclusion to be drawn.

Sin was Katra's lover.

Ash wanted to curse in anger, but it was too late for that.

They'd already been together. He could feel it. Besides, he barely knew his daughter—who was he to parent her now and tell her that she shouldn't have slept with Sin? She was a grown woman.

One who was in deep trouble.

And unfortunately, Ash couldn't get her out of this alone. To cure her, he needed help. Standing up, he pinned Sin with a gimlet stare. Ash had to know the truth of what existed between them.

Katra's life depended on it.

"What does Katra mean to you?"

A wall came up inside Sin over that question. Ash could almost hear it closing, but he couldn't tell if it was motivated by suspicion, fear, or guilt.

"Why do you ask me that?"

Ash ground his teeth as he glanced back to his daughter, who was thrashing about on the chaise. There was only one way to save her, and it broke his heart. It was the last thing he wanted to do to anyone. But it was the only way to get the demon out of her.

"I have to bond her to someone."

Sin was confused by Ash's strange behavior and his words. Ash was reticent about helping his daughter, and Sin couldn't understand that. He would have brought down the heavens to protect his own. Why was Ash so upset now?

"Okay. What's the problem with that?"

Ash seared him with that swirling silver gaze that seemed to be able to see straight to his soul. When Ash spoke, his voice was thick with emotion. "Listen to me, Sin. I'm going to have to summon the demon out of her . . . by draining her blood. If I know the demon within, it won't let go of her until I've taken so much blood that she's going to die from it. The only way to save her will be to bond her to someone else by using their blood. When I do this, she will need that person for the rest of her life to feed from. She'll be a vampire."

Sin hesitated. He wanted to make sure he understood exactly what Ash was saying. "But not a gallu."

"No. She'll be just as she was . . . unless she goes too long without feeding. Then she'll turn cold and will feed from anyone who's capable of sustaining her."

"Then what are you waiting for?"

Still Ash was hesitant. It was obvious he didn't like the thought of bonding them together, and Sin couldn't understand why until Ash continued. "Blood bonds like this are very sexual. She's my daughter. For an obvious reason, I don't want to bond her to me . . . That leaves"—he hesitated—"you."

Could he have growled that last word and spoken it with any more distaste?

But Sin could understand what had put a burr up Ash's saddle. As a father he'd have felt the same way. "You're offering your daughter to me?"

A muscle worked in Ash's jaw as he averted his gaze from Sin. "I condemned my best friend to death for taking the innocence of the only daughter I've ever known." His eyes misting, he looked at Katra, and the love he had for his daughter actually choked Sin up and it gave him a new respect for Ash.

Ash cleared his throat before he spoke again. "I try to always learn from my mistakes. I don't like what you've done, but I'm not going to see either of you die for it. I've let my emotions do enough damage to people I care about. But before I intrust her life to you, I have to know how much she means to you."

Sin held his arms out like a supplicant as he admitted something to Ash he didn't even want to admit to himself. But it was the truth. "I'm standing before you in the temple of my worst enemy and I'm not trying to kill Artemis. What do you think Katra means to me?"

Ash inclined his head to Sin. "This isn't a typical blood bond I'm doing. Once this is done, there will be no way to undo it. You understand?"

Yes, he did. "Whatever it takes, Acheron, save her."

Ash actually looked relieved, but it passed by his face so quickly that Sin wasn't sure if he saw it or imagined it. "Hold her legs."

Sin went to her feet and held her ankles while Ash took her hands into his. Then, in the blink of an eye, Ash changed forms. No longer human, he had mottled blue skin and black lips and horns. His eyes were a monstrous red that swirled with yellow. And while Sin watched, Ash's incisors grew to long, razor-sharp fangs.

Gaping, Sin had never seen anything like this. "What are you?"

Ash gave a bitter laugh. "I am death and sorrow." And then he leaned over Kat and bit into her neck.

Kat screamed and tried to fight, but Ash didn't stop. Sin held her feet as tight as he could without hurting her while Ash drew back and spat her blood onto the floor. Only it didn't hit the marble. Instead, it splashed into what appeared to be an invisible jar of some kind. Her blood swirled around before it slid to pool in the bottom.

Sin curled his lip as Ash repeated the gesture again and again like someone siphoning gas from a car. And as Ash continued to spit the blood into the jar, the blood congealed. Before long, it was forming a small, angry demon. It tried to run at Ash, but it couldn't. It seemed to be stuck to the jar's bottom like an insect on flypaper. Even though it was headless, it managed to shout in a language Sin had never heard before as it raised a fist, then slapped against the side of the jar, wanting release.

Ash ignored it.

Sin focused his gaze on the mottled blue skin of Ash's hand as he held Kat's hands in place. Ash's long black hair was draped over both of them while Ash's red eyes glowed.

"Kat doesn't turn blue like you, does she?"

Ash cut Sin a harsh glare with those spooky fire eyes that made his weird-ass silver eyes suddenly attractive by comparison. "I have no idea," he said before he returned to suck more blood from her.

As Ash continued to drain her Sin cringed and hoped it wasn't causing her pain. He couldn't stand the thought of her being hurt because of him.

Once the demon was completely formed in the jar, Ash released Kat and sat back on his haunches. Kat had long since stopped fighting them. Now she lay quietly against the white cushions, serene and unmoving.

Sin held his breath in fear. She was so pale . . . her skin was no longer healthy looking. It held a grayish cast, and her lips appeared to be turning bluish.

She was dying.

"Acheron?" He hated the note of panic in his voice.

Ash grabbed Sin's arm and pulled it across Kat's body. "She'll most likely attack you. Don't let her take too much blood or she could kill you."

"You sound like you're going somewhere."

"I have to take care of the gallu spirit."

Sin sucked his breath in sharply as Acheron used a long black claw to slash open his wrist. He hissed in pain. Acheron held Sin's arm over Kat's lips to let the blood drip into her mouth. As soon as the first drop touched her teeth, her eyes opened.

Frantically she grabbed Sin's wrist and held it to her mouth so that she could drink. Her breath scorched him as her tongue tickled his skin while she sought to get as much of his blood as she could.

Without looking at them, Acheron picked up the invisible jar with the demon who kept screaming at them, and vanished.

Sin was so relieved by Kat's recovery that all he could do was watch her. He should be disgusted by what she was doing, but his gratitude was such that it didn't faze him at all. If bleeding for her would save her, then he'd gladly open a vein anytime.

At least that was his thought until she released his wrist and pulled him against her. He saw the hunger in her eyes an instant before she sank her teeth into his neck. The pain was only brief before a deeply erotic pleasure tore through him.

And when it did, a million images began filling his mind. He saw all kinds of moments from Kat's past. Her as a child, an adolescent . . . as a woman.

It took him a minute to realize they were her memories.

Suddenly the images slowed and he could hear actual sound bites while they danced through his mind.

He saw her in her mother's garden, laughing with other handmaidens. Saw her in Greece on a boat with a woman named Geary as they discussed Atlantis. Then the memories changed to a club in Minnesota where Kat was dancing with a blond woman . . .

It was so strange to be inside Kat like this and it gave him insight into what it must have been like for her when she'd viewed his dreams. Surreal and dizzying, he had a hard time sorting through the memories.

Cradling her head in his hands while she fed, he saw her as a young woman in a girl's white and light blue bedroom, sitting at a white table, reading a small leather-bound scroll.

"Katra!"

She jumped at the sound of Artemis's frantic call. "What now?" she muttered under her breath.

"Katra, please. I need your help."

Kat flashed herself from her room to Artemis's bedroom. She drew up short as she saw . . .

Sin lying on the bed, half-dressed.

He flinched at the image that hit him through his own memories and through hers, but curiosity kept him from banishing it. He wanted to know what had happened that night.

Artemis was panicked as she pulled Kat into the room, her eyes damp from tears. "You must help me, Katra. He . . . he broke into my chambers and tried to rape me."

Artemis was covered in blood, her gown torn. And for the first time in centuries, Sin remembered the past that his mind had buried.

He remembered Artemis smiling at him and handing him a goblet. "Yes, it is a shame about Ningal. I saw her earlier tonight sleeping with my brother in his temple. She is a faithless whore, isn't she?"

Sin had refused to answer. His and Ningal's relationship wasn't any of Artemis's business, and it was something that never failed to cut him to the bone. "I don't want to discuss it, Artemis."

Part of him had suspected she'd mentioned it hoping he'd kill his wife in anger and unleash the Chthonians on him.

But Artemis surprised him with her reason. "I have a proposition for you, Sin. You solve my problem and I solve yours."

"And what problem do I have?"

She'd wrinkled her nose in distaste. "Don't be stupid, Sin. Everyone knows your wife cheats with anyone she can drag to her bed . . . that the children you claim as yours aren't. That your own pantheon looks down on you even though you control the moon, the calendar, and their fertility. I can't imagine how terrible it must feel to be laughed at by everyone, especially given how much power you have."

It was much more complicated than that. As much power as he held, he knew it could be negated in an instant by the Tablet of Destiny. Without power, he'd be an easy kill. Not to mention, he was kept at bay by loyalty to Zakar. If Sin died, they'd soon learn Zakar was still alive and in no time they'd kill him, too.

Artemis had leaned against Sin and breathed in his ear. "Haven't you ever wanted to get back at them?"

More than she could imagine.

However, his hands were tied and he knew it—better he be unhappy than his brother be dead. And as that thought went through Sin, he realized he didn't want to be here tonight . . . with her.

This all felt wrong and he needed to leave.

Sin had set the goblet aside. "I made a mistake coming here."

Artemis had pulled him to a stop and smiled prettily at him in a way no goddess had done in centuries. "No, love, you didn't. You belong here with me." She'd pulled him toward her room. "Like you, I'm tired of being alone all the time." She'd raised his hand and placed a tender kiss on his knuckles as her eyes seduced him. "Stay with me, Sin, and I will make you the next reigning king of the gods."

"I don't need to be king."

She'd left him to get more wine. "Of course you don't. But think of the others bowing down before you. Imagine them all doing any- and everything they can to please you . . . wouldn't it be fantastic?" Returning to his side, she held the goblet to his lips. "Drink, my sweet. It's good for you."

Sin had downed it all. But no sooner had he finished it than the room began to swim. Too late, he'd realized that she had drugged him.

He'd tried to walk but stumbled to his knees. "What have you done to me?"

Her face had hardened. "I want your powers, Sin. I need them."

"You lying bitch," Sin had growled, and lunged at her.

She'd slapped him hard. Sin had grabbed her and thrown her to the bed, intending to kill her. But no sooner had he wrapped his hands around her throat than he'd passed out.

Now he saw himself on the bed through Kat's eyes. Artemis's throat was bruised from his attack. Her dress torn, but he hadn't done it.

Artemis gestured toward him. "You have to strip his powers

from him, Katra. If you don't . . ." She started crying. "He'll return and may Zeus have mercy on me then. He'll kill me when he wakes. I know it."

"Matisera, I . . ."

"You what?" she asked angrily, "Don't tell me you won't protect your own mother from an attacker? Look at him, spread out on my bed, sleeping peacefully as if this was nothing to him. Look at me! If I hadn't blasted him, he'd have violated me and taken my powers and left me as weak as a babe. Who do you think would protect you from the other gods then?" She'd begun sobbing hysterically.

He could feel the pain inside Kat at seeing her mother hurt, at hearing her tears. Artemis never cried, and it broke Kat's heart. She wanted to soothe her mother.

"Please, Matisera, don't cry."

"How can I not? My own child doesn't love me."

"I do love you."

"Then prove it! Give me his powers!"

He could see the indecision in Kat's eyes and feel it inside her as she walked to the bed and touched his arm. The minute she touched him, his wrath and anger had seared her. She'd dropped his arm instantly. "He wants you dead."

"I told you that! If he's still a god when he wakes, I won't be here to protect you anymore."

Kat was terrified. Her mother meant everything to her. The thought of losing her . . . she couldn't deal with it. "I won't let anyone hurt you, Matisera. I promise." Cringing, Kat had reached for him again and then held her hand out for her mother.

Artemis joined her by the bed and took her hand into hers. Kat covered the center of his chest with her palm, then closed her eyes.

Sin gasped as he felt his powers traveling from his body, through Kat to Artemis. And with every beat of his heart, he grew weaker while Artemis grew stronger . . .

Anger and betrayal tore through him as he realized the truth. Artemis hadn't taken his powers from him.

Kat had.

She had been the one to cover him in the *diktyon* so that her mother could dump his body . . .

He couldn't even go there. Even after all these centuries that pain was too raw. The humiliation too severe. Damn them both for it!

Unable to breathe, he opened his eyes and saw Kat still drinking from him. He cursed before he shoved her away.

Kat was dazed as she looked up at Sin and saw the fury on his face. It didn't matter. The bloodlust was turning into something more.

Her entire body was on fire and she needed him. It was more than she could deny. She had to have him.

Now!

Rising from the chaise, she stalked toward him.

"Don't touch me," he growled, holding her back.

She was baffled by his anger as she wrapped her arms around him, trying to pull him back toward her lips. "I need you, Sin."

He extracted himself from her hold and put two feet between them. "You betrayed me."

She moved even closer to him so that she could bury her face against his neck and inhale the scent of him . . . and his blood. "Sin," she breathed against his skin as she tongued the area she wanted to bite.

He pushed her away. "You betrayed me. Why didn't you tell me it was you who took my powers?"

She was trying to follow his words, but it was useless. She could smell the blood . . . taste it, and that desire was all-consuming.

Sin tried to leave, then cursed as he realized he didn't have to powers to leave Olympus. "Release me, Katra. Now."

Still she pursued him.

He held her by the shoulders to keep her away from him. He'd trusted her in ways he hadn't trusted anyone in centuries. Around her he'd dropped his guard, and for what? To learn that she'd kept this from him? That she'd duped him and allowed him to blame her mother for something Artemis hadn't done?

God, how many times had Kat told him she couldn't give him his powers back when she could?

Damn her to hell!

He felt like such a fool. "I don't want you touching me right now. Do you understand? You ruined my entire life and then you didn't even have the decency to tell me it was you when you knew I was blaming Artemis for it."

"I'm sorry."

"Sorry?" He couldn't believe that was her comeback. "Is that all you have to say? 'Sorry' doesn't even begin to fix what you've broken. Because of you, my entire family is dead except for my twin brother, who has spent centuries at the mercy of demons who've tortured him. And now he's one of them. I put my faith in you . . . came to the home of my enemy to save your life, and for what? To find out that you're the same lying sack of shit that everyone else is? That the one person I put at my back is the one person who has hurt me most in my life? I hate you for what you've done. You made me believe in someone again, and then, the moment I did, you screwed me over."

Kat let go as those words cut through the haze in her mind. "I never meant to hurt you."

"What? Did you think I was going to wake up powerless and thank you for it? And what about when you came after me in New York to kill me? What about that? It seems to me all you've ever tried to do is hurt me." He raked her with a cold, hard look. "Congratulations, Kat. You hit the mark with this one."

She reached for him, but he moved away.

"Acheron!" he shouted.

Ash appeared instantly in front of him. Sin was thankful that he looked like a man again and was no longer blue.

"Send me back to my penthouse."

Scowling, Ash looked back and forth between them. "She hasn't finished feeding."

Sin glared at him. "And I really don't care."

Ash stiffened. "That's not what you told me."

"Yeah, well, I've learned a few new things about her."

"Such as?"

Sin shot a heated glare toward Kat, who was standing there with tears in her eyes. A few hours ago, that would have mattered to him, too. But right now, he never wanted to see her again as long as he lived and if she were hurting . . . good. "She stole my godhood from me and gave it to her mother."

Ash snapped his head toward Kat, who was looking down at the floor in front of her. "She what?"

"You heard me, and you have no idea what that kind of betrayal feels like."

Ash laughed bitterly. "Man up, Sin. Trust me, when it comes to betrayal, you're a neophyte, and what she did to you doesn't even register on my scale of pain." He walked slowly toward Kat, who practically cringed at his approach. "You're a conduit?"

She nodded. "I thought he was out to hurt her. I was only trying to protect my mother."

Sin could respect the reasoning, but it didn't change the facts of what she'd taken from him. "I was innocent."

She looked up, her green eyes swimming from her unshed tears. "I know that now. How do you think I feel when I look at you, knowing what I cost you? Do you think any of this has been easy for me?"

"Then give me my powers back."

A single tear sped down her cheek, and in spite of himself it hurt to see her cry. But how many tears had she caused him? No, he would not let his sympathy for her negate his anger in this.

"Don't you think I would return those powers if I could? My mother knows how to block me. The only powers I could possibly give you are mine."

He arched an expectant brow at that.

"No," she said adamantly. "Acheron, tell him I can't do it."

"I'm pretty sure he heard you."

Sin shook his head as his anger continued to build. "I want to go home, Ash. It's the least you can do."

Ash was torn between loyalty to a friend and to the daughter he didn't really know. But in the end, he knew the best thing to do would be to get Sin away from Katra for a while. They both needed to calm down.

But first, Ash wanted to remind Sin what he was about to walk away from. "You told me you were willing to do anything to save her. That her life was the only thing in the world that mattered to you."

"That was before I knew she was the one who'd betrayed me. That is the one thing I'm incapable of forgiving."

Pride goeth before the fall . . .

"Send him home," Kat whispered.

Confused by her request, Ash looked at her. "Are you sure?"

She nodded. "I don't want him here."

Well, that settled it. If she wanted him gone . . .

Before Ash approached Katra he flashed Sin back to his penthouse. "You're not fully fed."

"I'll live."

"Yeah, but the longer you go without feeding, the more amoral you'll become. In time, you'll be like a gallu . . . only worse."

She looked up at him with those eyes that were both innocent and all-knowing. "Is that why you tolerate Artemis?"

He nodded. There was no need to hide that fact from Katra when it was so obvious.

But his relationship with her mother wasn't the one that was important right now. "Sin loves you, Katra. You should have seen the look on his face when he brought you here. He was terrified of losing you."

She wiped at the tear on her face. "That really doesn't make me feel any better, since I'm the one who ruined it."

Ash pulled her against him so that he could hold her and soothe some of the pain she felt over this. "You know the incredible thing about hearts is their unbelievable capacity for forgiveness. You'd be amazed what people will overlook when they love someone."

She wrapped her arms around his waist and tucked her head under his chin. "Do you forgive Nick for sleeping with Simi?"

Ash ignored the razor-sharp pain that one question evoked. He still didn't like it, but he'd put the matter behind him. "I have."

"But he hasn't forgiven you."

No. He wasn't sure if Nick would ever get over the death of his mother. But honestly, Ash would rather Nick blame him than try to live with the guilt of his own part in her death. God help the man if Nick ever took that responsibility on his own shoulders. It would kill him.

"I can't control Nick's feelings."

She swallowed before she spoke again. Her voice was scarcely more than a whisper. "And what about Mom? Have you forgiven her for what she's done to you?"

Ash drew his breath in sharply at that one. That question hit him in an extremely raw spot. "That's a little more complicated,

Katra. We're not talking one single mistake to forgive. Every time I think we're past one betrayal, I learn of another she's committed . . . like hiding you from me."

She pulled back to look up at him. "But you do love her, don't you?"

Ash didn't answer. He couldn't.

"Dad?"

He offered her a smile he didn't feel. "I can't answer a question I don't know the answer to. You can't hate to the extreme I do without having loved someone first. When all that hatred is shoved aside, is there any love left? I honestly don't know."

He brushed the hair back from her face and cupped her cheeks in his hands. He wanted to give her the gift he wished someone had given to her mother. Katra needed to understand the crossroad where she was standing right now.

"But I do know this, Katra, the first betrayal, even as severe as it was, could have been forgiven had your mother just apologized and meant it. Had she come to me and promised that she'd never hurt me again, I would have laid my life down for her. Instead she let her pride get in the way. She was more focused on punishing me for her imagined embarrassment than she was on the future we could have had together."

Kat frowned at him. "What are you saying?"

"I saw Sin, Katra, when he came to me, begging for your life. People don't do that when they don't care. It's not too late yet. He can forgive you this."

"But his past—"

"Is one that hurts and that's why this cut him so deeply. But because of that hurt, he needs you even more."

Kat held her breath as her father told her what she needed to hear. But she wasn't sure she could believe it. "Are you sure?"

"Trust me, baby. Everyone wants someone they can hold and love. Someone who will be there to help pick up the pieces when everything falls apart. Sin is no different from anyone else."

Tears stung her eyes as she realized he spoke from the depth of his own pain. He was trying to help her, to spare her the centuries of agony that he'd known. "I love you, Dad."

He took her hand in his and laid a tender kiss to her cheek. "If you have any care for Sin at all, don't leave him in darkness. It's not fair to show someone the sun and then to banish him from it. Even the devil may cry when he looks around hell and realizes that he's there alone."

She nodded and squeezed his hand. "I hear you, Dad. I just hope Sin will listen."

One corner of his mouth lifted. "If he doesn't, you know where Artemis keeps her nets."

Kat sucked her breath in sharply. "I don't think that would endear me to him."

"No, but it would keep him in place."

Laughing, she let go and stepped back. "I'm going to try this."

"No, baby. Trying is for fools." His gaze bore into hers. "You're going to succeed."

She smiled at his confidence and his wisdom. "Wish me luck."

"Better than that. I wish you happiness."

Love for him warmed her as she nodded and flashed herself from Olympus back to Sin's penthouse.

The minute she popped in, something slammed into her. Kat gasped as she hit the floor. She shifted, trying to move the weight off her.

It was then she realized what the weight was.

Sin, and he was bleeding profusely.

CHAPTER FIFTEEN

Kat tried to crawl out from under Sin, but he wouldn't let her. "Stay down," he growled in her ear before he rolled away and stood up to confront whatever had knocked him into her.

I should probably listen . . .

But that just wasn't who she was. So she pushed herself up, then wished she'd listened to him after all.

Kessar was in the room with six other demons. That alone made her blood run cold. Yet it wasn't the only bad news. They had Zakar in chains again, and the worst was Kytara, who lay dead a few feet from her.

Her eyes misting, Kat stared in horror at her friend's lifeless body. It looked as if they'd tried to literally tear Kytara apart. The sight and grief made Kat sick to her stomach. How could they have done such a thing?

Sin was on his feet, trying to fight the demons—"trying" being the operative word. It was obvious something was wrong with his powers.

Infuriated over what they'd done, Kat tried to blast Kessar and then realized exactly what had happened to Sin. She had no powers, either. Something was negating them.

"He has the Tablet," Sin said from between clenched teeth as he slung one demon into another.

Well, that explained it, but it didn't help. The Tablet was sucking their powers out of them. Oh, fabulous. No wonder they demons had been able to take Zakar and kill Kytara.

Kessar laughed before he headed toward Kat with a deadly intent.

To her shock, Sin put himself between them. Kessar swung at Sin, who jumped back and struck him a fierce blow in the chest. It didn't faze Kessar as he kicked Sin so hard, it lifted him off his feet.

"Simi!" Kat shouted at the top of her lungs. It was time to put a stop to this.

Simi and Xirena instantly appeared. "What?" Simi asked until she saw the demons.

Both she and Xirena exploded into demon form. Kat stumbled back . . . it was the first time she'd ever seen the whole of Simi's true form. Her skin was a deep bloody red with black lips, hair, wings, and claws. She wrapped herself around the nearest demon and ripped his throat out.

Kat turned away from the awful sight.

Kessar pointed the Tablet at Simi before he spoke in Sumerian.

Xirena laughed. "We're not gods, you moron. We're demons, and that has no effect on us." She flew at him.

He dodged, grabbed the chains holding Zakar, and vanished with him.

"No!" Sin shouted, trying to catch them before they vanished, but he was too late.

And he had no powers to follow.

Kat felt the grief she saw on his face as he turned to look at her while Simi and Xirena finished off the demons they were "eating." She'd never seen any man look more stricken.

"I'm sorry," she whispered.

There was no forgiveness in his expression at all as he stalked toward her. His eyes were filled with utter agony. "You keep saying that."

"But I'm sincere."

He raked her with a sneer. "Sincerity doesn't fix any of this, now does it?"

No, it didn't, and it didn't bring back Kytara's life. How the hell had they managed to kill her? It didn't make sense. "What happened?"

He let out a tired breath as he wiped the blood from a cut over his left eye. "When I came back, Kessar had Zakar in chains and was holding the Tablet in his hand." He gestured toward Kytara. "He must have used the Tablet to drain her. She was already dead when I arrived."

"How did he get his hands on the Tablet?"

"Damned if I know. I had it locked in the safe in my bedroom."

This was awful. Kat covered her eyes as guilt and pain settled deep in her soul. This was all her fault. All of it.

If not for her, Sin would still have his god powers and there would be no danger to the world.

Kytara would still be alive . . .

How could she even begin to make this right? Everything was falling apart because she'd made a really bad decision centuries ago. Her heart sank to her stomach as she tried to imagine the coming attack from the Dimme. "We're doomed, aren't we?"

"Yeah," he said, his voice thick. "We are. If you have any last wishes to accomplish before total annihilation hits, I suggest you get started."

Still in demon form, Simi approached them with an ecstatic gleam in her eyes. "Can I eat the bitch-goddess?"

Kat sighed in resignation. "I'm afraid the only bitch-goddess around right now would be me."

Simi shook her head. "*Akra*-Kat isn't a bitch. You're always nice to the Simi."

"But I wasn't nice to Sin." She walked slowly toward him, wanting him to understand the depth of her sorrow and guilt. "I know you don't believe me, but I am sorry about all this. More than you'll ever know."

His expression was cold. "I appreciate the thought, but it doesn't really change anything, does it?" He walked over to Kytara and closed her eyes, then he covered her with a blanket. "You should probably take her body home to Olympus. It's the least we can do."

Kat was confused. "We don't have to burn her?"

He shook his head. "No. They just killed her. There's no bite marks on her that I could see. Guess they didn't want to convert her over."

Kat couldn't imagine that, since Kessar and crew seemed intent on converting as many people as they could. Surely a dream god would have been a big boon for them. But then nothing the demon did made sense.

How had all this gotten so out of hand?

Sighing, she frowned as she saw Simi and Xirena changing back into their more human forms. "Why didn't you call for Simi and Xirena when you saw them?"

He gave her a cold glare. "Well gee, since I popped in here in the middle of a fight and I was trying to save my brother and had hoped Kytara was only wounded and not dead, I really didn't think about them. Sorry I was so self-absorbed in staying alive that I forgot about the demons down the hall."

Kat had to bite back an equally caustic retort. He was hurting and she knew it. This wasn't easy on either one of them, and more sarcasm wouldn't accomplish anything more than to further alienate him from her. "Are our powers gone for good?"

"No. Not unless they have a conduit"—he gave her a meaningful sneer—"to drain you. Our powers will be back. Personally I think the prick is just playing with us."

Kat didn't believe that. "No, he was honestly afraid of Simi and Xirena."

"That's because they can rip his heart out and, as we learned, they're immune to the Tablet."

"Which gives us an advantage."

"As long as their numbers are small, yes. But the minute they open the doorway and let the whole demon clan out to party, our demons are dead."

Xirena's eyes widened. "Um, I don't like dead. Dead is bad."

Simi nodded in agreement. "*Akri* would be really sad if his Simi died. The Simi wouldn't be happy about it, either."

"And neither would I," Kat assured them. "Don't worry. We won't let them eat you."

Sin folded up the couch. By his demeanor, she could tell he was trying to think of a solution. Finally, he met her gaze. "Any chance Grandma will let more demons out of her sight?"

"I don't know. Too many Charontes out of Kalosis without Apollymi here to rein them in would be like too many gallu set free. I think we'd just be changing the face of human annihilation."

"Of course it would," Sin growled. "Now they have the Moon, they have the Tablet that I found for them, and we have no powers so long as they hold it. If we attack, they drain us. I should just shoot myself and end my suffering before they turn me into one of them."

Kat rolled her eyes at his melodramatic tirade. "Don't go Socrates yet. It's not over until they let loose the Dimme, right?"

He snorted. "Excuse me if I'm not feeling really upbeat and hopeful at the moment. After all, the one person I thought I could trust is the one who fucked me the hardest."

Kat had to clench her hand to keep from slapping him. Her first instinct was to give tit for tat. But as she opened her mouth to let him have it, she remembered Acheron's words.

"But I do know this, Katra. The first betrayal, even as severe as it was, could have been forgiven had your mother just apologized and meant it. Had she come to me and promised that she'd never hurt me again, I would have laid my life down for her. Instead she let her pride get in the way. She was more focused on punishing me for her imagined embarrassment than she was on the future we could have had together."

Those words quelled her tongue. She didn't want to make the same mistake her mother had made. She'd wronged Sin and they both knew it.

Taking a deep breath for patience, she turned toward Simi. "Simi?" she said quietly. "Will you please take Kytara's body home to Olympus? Give her to M'Adoc."

Simi nodded as she came forward to hug her. "Don't be so sad, *akra*-Kat. We'll eat all them gallu demons and make it all right. You'll see."

Kat smiled at the two demons. "I know you will, Simi. Thank you."

As Simi went to pick up Kytara from the floor, Xirena looked a bit awkward, as if she wasn't sure what she should do. "I'll wait in our room." Xirena vanished an instant before Simi did.

Sin headed for the bar to pour himself a drink. "You might as well join them. No need in staying around here."

Kat followed him behind the counter. "You're not getting rid of me that easily."

He slammed a glass down on the counter so hard she was surprised it didn't shatter. "Don't push me, Kat. My anger at you right now is only surpassed by my desire to kill Kessar. Since I can't lay hands on him, you might prove a worthy substitution." He poured the glass full.

"And I want you to understand the depth of my sorrow over what I did to you and your family. If I could put a hair shirt on to make amends, I would. I wish by all the gods I've ever met or even heard of that I could go back and return your powers to you. You deserve them. But I can't do that."

He turned to leave.

But she wasn't willing to let him go that easily. Angry over his dismissal, she spun him around and kissed him. "I love you, Sin. I just wanted you to know that."

Sin was stunned by both her actions and her declaration. He couldn't move. All he could see was the tender look on her face. The sincerity. But even so, he heard the laughter of his wife echoing in his head. *"You're incompetent as a god, a lover, and a man . . ."*

The only thing he'd ever been good at had been killing. But Kat made him feel as if he had more skills than that. She made him feel as if he mattered. As if he had value.

And that shredded his resistance to her.

She laid her soft hand to his cheek. "We will win this and we will save your brother. I promise. I won't ever let you down or hurt you again. I swear it by all that I am and all I hope to be. You *can* trust me, Sin."

He swallowed as his emotions choked him. He wanted to turn and walk away from her, but he couldn't. It was too late for that.

"Don't disappoint me, Kat. I don't think I could recover from it if you did."

Kat's eyes teared as she heard those words from him. He didn't say that he loved her, but it was a start. He hadn't laughed at her or thrown her out.

He'd given her the promise of a relationship. A chance to rebuild the trust that had been broken. She couldn't expect more than that.

"You have my word, Sin."

He dipped his head down and gave her the lightest whisper of a kiss. Even so, it sent shivers over her and it fired her blood.

She buried her hand in his hair and held him close so that she could nuzzle her cheek against his. The scent of his skin made her hot and shivery. Her entire life had been spent wanting this kind of contact. He felt so good in her arms.

She didn't want to be her mother. She didn't want to miss him. To live her life with a memory of what they'd had and then to know she'd lost it all because of stupidity.

For the first time in her life, she had total clarity on Artemis's relationship with her father. It was a tragedy she didn't want to duplicate.

She rubbed a lock of Sin's hair between her fingers as she realized just how much she really did love him. Not just his body, which was hot, but the man inside it. "We're going to win this."

"I can almost believe it when you say that."

Stepping back, she smiled. "So what do we need to do?"

He took a deep breath before he answered. "One. Don't die. Two. Don't get bitten."

She really hoped there was more to it than that. "And?"

"Kick their ass," he said simply.

"Good plan. Little vague on the details."

He gave her a wicked grin. "Isn't it though?"

She laughed at his mischievous demeanor. It would be infectious if their lives didn't hang in the balance. "I've found that specifics aren't necessarily a bad thing at times like this. Plans can actually be your friend."

"Really? I've found a game plan usually gets in the way. Better to hang loose and improvise."

She took his glass and drained it. "Hang loose, huh? Is that really want you're going to do?"

Sighing, he stepped away from her, and his face fell to complete sobriety. "No. We have a time bomb in our hands and a lot to do. Step one—"

"Get your brother."

He shook his head. "We have to get the Tablet first."

"You're willing to leave Zakar in their hands?"

He winced as if the mere thought cut him. "It's not my first choice, but now that they know we can get to him, they'll be guarding him a lot closer than before. And if they have the Tablet when we go for him . . ."

"They'll kick *our* asses."

"Exactly. We have to get the Tablet back. The question is how."

Kat considered that for a minute. They couldn't exactly waltz in there and demand it. They didn't even know where it was. What they needed was an insider.

"Does Kessar have a weakness?" she asked.

"None that I know of."

Why didn't that surprise her? Simple. If he'd known of one before now, he no doubt would have used it. "Well, I might know someone who can find it. Hold that thought."

He scowled at her. "Where are you going?"

"The Vanishing Isle. You stay here and rest and I'll be right back."

He actually appeared to be afraid for her. "You sure you don't want me to come with you?"

"Yeah. This I'll need to do alone."

"Be careful."

Warmed by his concern, Kat nodded before she tried to flash. She didn't get far.

"It's the Tablet," Sin said as she let out a frustrated growl. "You're still drained."

She let out a fierce growl. "This is just a little inconvenient."

Sin moved to stand behind her. She closed her eyes as she felt the heat of him radiate through her. There was something about him that never failed to warm her body. His scent, his presence, it filled her with desire and strength.

He placed his hands on her hips and bent his head so that he could whisper in her ear. As soon as the melodic Sumerian words started, she felt power radiating from his hands to her body. It sent a warm fissure up her spine to her scalp, where it tingled.

"What are you doing, Sin?"

"I'm loaning you what powers I can."

His whispered words brought tears to her eyes and choked her. "You're trusting me?"

His lips were so close to her cheek that they tickled her skin. "You asked for another chance. I'm trying my best to give it to you."

Don't fail me.

Even though he didn't say those words, she could feel them in her heart. "I won't fail you, Sin," she whispered back to him an instant before their weakened powers united enough to flash her to the hall where Simi had taken Kytara. But Simi must have returned to Las Vegas, since she was nowhere to be seen.

Her raw emotions still churning, Kat paused in the corner to give herself a moment for composure. D'Alerian, M'Adoc, and M'Ordant stood with their backs to her. From this angle, the dream gods were almost identical in appearance. D'Alerian had long, straight black hair that hung just past his shoulders. M'Ordant's black hair hung to his collar and was straight, while M'Adoc's was the same length, only wavy. All three were dressed in black and speaking in a low tone.

M'Ordant lifted his hand and covered Kytara's body with a light silk sheet. "It's disturbing to imagine a gallu with this kind of power. I thought we'd seen the last of those bastards centuries ago."

D'Alerian shook his head. "Only on the human plane. Their gods were smart and hid them well from the rest of us."

Kat cleared her throat to let them know they weren't here alone. The three of them turned toward her with stern frowns that melted as soon as they realized it was her and not one of the other gods.

She closed the distance between them. "I'm sorry to eavesdrop."

M'Adoc didn't appear very forgiving of her actions. "Been there long?"

"No. I came in on the disturbing comment and concur with it."

Unlike M'Adoc, D'Alerian's expression was completely stoic. "So what brings you here, Katra? Does Artemis want us to haunt someone?"

That was normally her reason for disturbing them. "No. Not this time. I need to know if any of you have ever been in a gallu's dreams? More important, has any Dream-Hunter been in Kessar's?"

Still D'Alerian's face showed no emotions whatsoever. "Why would an Oneroi—"

"Not Oneroi," she said, interrupting him. "I'm not looking for someone who'd have been helpful or healing toward the gallu. I need a vicious Skotos. Someone who would know what Kessar is truly afraid of."

They exchanged puzzled looks.

M'Adoc folded his arms over his chest. "There are only two who would fit that. Solin or Xypher."

"Xypher," the other two said in unison.

M'Ordant folded his arms over his chest. "Even though he's vicious, Solin is too into women and sex. He doesn't stir fear unless it's to kick an Oneroi out of a dream."

D'Alerian concurred. "Xypher is the one who thrives most on fear and always has. But he's a complete renegade that not even we can rope in."

Xypher sounded exactly like what Kat needed. "Great. Where is he?"

"Tartarus," M'Adoc said coldly. "We were forced to kill him and now he's spending eternity being punished for his crimes."

Yeah, this was getting better by the minute. "You killed him?"

M'Adoc nodded. "Let me reiterate the part about him being a complete renegade. He is what made people afraid to go to sleep. But if there's someone who's going to know a way to scare a demon, he's your god."

"Sweet." Kat put as much sarcasm into that single word as was possible. "Can't wait to meet him. Would one of you care to send me over to Hades' place?"

M'Adoc scowled. "Can't you go yourself?"

"I'm a little low on juice at the moment and would deeply appreciate a small hand."

D'Alerian snapped his fingers and an instant later she found herself in one of the last places she wanted to be. The Underworld. It was a special kind of spooky. The kind that went down your spine like an ice cube and left you wanting to look over your shoulder to see what might be stalking you for dinner. There were all kinds of unsavory beings who called this place home.

But it wasn't all bad. The Elysian Fields were actually nice. They were the paradise where decent souls were sent to live out eternity in total happiness. If only Xypher were there. Instead, he was in the worst place of all. Tartarus. It was where the evil were sent to be punished. There was no light here. No laughter. Nothing pretty or nice.

It was dark and pain filled. The entire area was lined with caverns and holding cells where screams of agony echoed, begging for mercy. The occupants were seldom in a state to be recognized by even their own mothers, and the caverns were laid out like an intricate labyrinth.

Without help, Kat would never be able to find Xypher.

"Eris!" she called, summoning the goddess of discord—her less than favorite friend. The last time the two of them had been together, they'd ended up in a bolt war that had ended only when Zeus had intervened and sent them both to their rooms for a solid decade.

Eris appeared before her in a pique. Dressed in a sheer black gown, Eris was as pale as a ghost. Her black hair was swept up toward the crown of her head, where curls cascaded down to fall all the way to her hips. As beautiful as Aphrodite, Eris was the most evil of any god. "You rang, bitchtress?"

Kat took a deep breath to keep from answering that insult. As a goddess of discord, it was always Eris' nature to pick a fight. "I need to find an inmate here and you're the one I'm sure who can lead me straight to him."

She arched a brow. "Really? What makes you think that?"

Kat looked around the dismal place. "The fact that I know how much you love to torture people. Any time Ares is bedding someone, I know you come here to play."

Lifting her chin defiantly, Eris narrowed her gaze. "And who told you that? Persephone?"

"It doesn't matter who told me. The point is I need your help."

"And what will you give me for that?"

I won't kick your ass. If only she could say that out loud. "Hmm . . . I guess what I'll do is continue to keep the secret that you're the one who told Zeus about Hera's affair with that cover model in New York last fall."

Eris's face paled as all smugness left her features. "How do you know that?"

"Unlike you, I have friends all over the place who love to gossip. Now are you going to help me?"

Eris's nostrils flared. "You know—"

Kat put her hand up. "Don't even waste your time threatening me. You do anything to irritate me and I'll make you eat that golden apple you love to throw at people. Now show me where the former Skotos Xypher is kept."

A mischievous glint came to her dark eyes. "You do like to live dangerously, don't you? But to be fair, I should warn you that he's an animal."

"Goody . . . now lead me to him."

Eris smirked before they vanished. When Kat could see again, she was inside a small cavern. She couldn't see anything, but she could hear the constant sound of something in motion. She wasn't sure what exactly it was.

At least not until Eris snapped her fingers and light appeared.

Kat cringed as she saw a man on the floor whose entire back was covered with bloody welts. The noise she'd heard was of a whip that was wielded by a skeleton who stood over him beating him constantly.

Growling, he rolled over and grabbed the whip only to have it disintegrate in his hand. Another one appeared in the hand of the skeleton, who continued with the lashes.

Eris made a clicking noise with her teeth. "Here, little Xypher . . . want to play with Cousin Eris?"

"Fuck you, bitch."

"Oooo," Eris said, wrinkling her nose, "feeling spry this morning, are we? Should I join the fun?"

"Eris," Kat said quickly. "Leave us alone."

Eris gave her a pout that any spoiled toddler would envy before she vanished.

Kat stepped forward as Xypher tried to grab the whip again, only to have the same thing happen. She could see and feel the frustration from him, the pain. Every lash cut through his body. But he didn't cry out.

Closing her eyes, she summoned as much of her powers as she could. The *sfora* heated on her chest as she wished the skeleton out of the chambers.

To her amazement, it worked.

Dressed only in a pair of black leather pants, Xypher lifted his head to look over his shoulder. He turned to her with an angry glare. That glare lacerated her with its hatred as he rose slowly to his feet. "Bring it on, bitch."

His anger baffled her. "Bring on what?"

"Whatever torture you've got planned. I'm ready."

She felt bad for him that he would expect nothing else from a visitor. "I'm not here to punish you."

"Sure you're not . . ."

"Really. I'm not."

"Then what are you here for? Fun and games?"

"Information."

He laughed cruelly. "Since I've been stuck for centuries in this hole, I find that hard to believe. I don't even know what year it is, so what information could I possibly have that would be of any use to you?"

"I was told that you're a Phobotory Skotos. I need to know if you've ever been inside the dreams of demons."

He hesitated before he answered. "What of it?"

"I need information about what scares one of them."

No sooner had she spoken than two more skeletons appeared—both holding barbed whips.

Kat cringed while Xypher backed up, eyeing the two of them warily. She would tell them to go away, but she held no authority here to order them, and what little power she had left she needed to conserve until the Tablet's effects wore off.

When the first skeleton swung the whip, Xypher dodged it. But it didn't do him any good. Vines grew out of the earthen ceiling to wrap themselves around his arms. He fought as best he could, but in the end, they dragged him up and held him for his beating.

Cursing in frustration, Xypher leaned his head back and tensed an instant before they both lashed him with the whips. He tried to kick at the skeletons, but it did no good.

Finally, he lifted his head to stare at her. "You want my help. Get me out of here."

"I can't do that."

"Then I don't know anything." He hissed as they lashed him again.

Kat turned away, sickened by what was going on. He was right, she couldn't leave him like this. It was cruel beyond cruel. She didn't know what he'd done, but surely it didn't warrant this amount of abuse.

Very well, she could hope for the best and try to negotiate. "Hades?"

The dark god appeared before her. Tall and lean, Hades was gorgeous. His black hair curled becomingly around his shoulders as he eyed her with an amused gleam in his eyes. "You again? Don't you have anything better to do than chafe my tolerance?"

She frowned at him. "I haven't seen you in more than a decade."

"Really? It seems like yesterday. Oh well." He stepped around her to grimace at the skeletons. "What are you? Girls? Learn to hit like you mean it. Damn, my wife could beat him harder than that."

Kat winced as the skeletons picked up speed and vigor. "Could you please stop with the beating?"

Hades scoffed. "He's being punished. Hello? This is Tartarus, remember the purpose of this part of the Underworld? We're not really warm and fluffy over here."

"And I need a favor from him, which he will not do so long as you're beating him."

Hades looked less than pleased. "What favor could you possibly need from something like him?"

"Information about a dream."

He dismissed her request. "Get it from one of the other Oneroi."

"I tried, but they sent me to Xypher. They said he was the only one who could help me."

"Poor you, then."

"No, Hades," she said sternly, wanting him to understand

what was at stake. "Poor all of us. The Sumerian gallu demons are breaking out and they're about to unleash the Dimme. We are currently powerless to stop them, and I need someone who can get me inside their heads and tell me how to stop them."

Hades held his hand up. The skeletons stopped moving. "Do you know what happened the last time one of the Dimme went free?"

"No, but given what I've seen of the gallu, I imagine it was rather rough."

"You have no idea." He left her to approach Xypher. The only way anyone could tell he was hurt other than his wounds was by his ragged breathing. "Do you know about the gallu?"

Xypher didn't answer.

Hades punched him fiercely in the side.

"Hey!" Kat said, closing the distance between them. "I think he's had enough."

"No, he hasn't."

Xypher spat at Hades, only the spittle didn't make it to the god. It reversed course and went straight to Xypher.

Hades smirked at him. "Nice try, dick. Think you're the first one to attempt that? Now answer my question."

She couldn't believe the angry look on Xypher's face. He was practically goading Hades. "Why should I tell you shit?"

"Because I can make your stay here even worse than it already is."

"I look forward to it."

Hades drew back, but Kat grabbed his hand. "Please, Hades, can we try this my way?"

"You're a fool, Katra. He only respects violence. It's why he's here. Did you know it took eleven Oneroi to kill him? Eleven and they barely survived it."

"Yeah," she breathed, "and the last Dream-Hunter I sent in after the gallu was killed by them."

By his face she could tell it wasn't news to him. "Kytara. She's in the Elysian Fields now."

Kat was grateful for that at least. She couldn't stand the thought of Kytara being punished like this. "I need someone who can go into the demons' sleep and not be taken out by them."

Hades cut a glare at Xypher. "He is already dead."

"Yes." Kat stepped around Hades so that she could speak directly to Xypher. "If we give you back your life, will you help us?"

"No!" Hades growled. "I will not allow something as monstrous as him to walk free again."

"What did he do that was so awful?"

"He tortured people, Katra. He drove them mad with nightmares and didn't care who he hurt. He is without conscience or morals."

"I don't want my life back," Xypher snarled, interrupting them. "You can shove that up both your asses."

Kat was baffled by his anger. "Then what do you want?"

"My freedom."

Hades snorted. "Freedom for you? Never."

"Hades, please," Kat begged. "I know you're able to negotiate. Do I need to get Persephone in on this?"

At the mention of his wife, Hades tensed. Since Kat and Persephone were longtime friends, Seph always sided with her and it never boded well for Hades.

Luckily, he knew that. "Fine, what do you want?"

Kat took a deep breath in relief that she was going to win this. She looked up at the Skotos. It was a gamble she was taking here, but with any luck it might work out. "Xypher, if you will help me, Hades will set you free and make you human." With him a human, they could always kill him again if he went back to being Rogue.

There was doubt in his eyes, but it was mixed with a tiny amount of hope. "You swear to free me from here?"

She nodded. "By the river Styx."

"Then it's a deal."

Smiling, Kat turned toward the god. "Hades?"

He hesitated as if debating whether or not he should agree. When he spoke, his voice was stern. "If he helps you, I will grant his freedom. But he will only be human for a month. If at the end of the month he hasn't shown himself worthy of humanity, he comes right back here."

By Xypher's expression it was obvious he wanted to tell Hades where to shove his pact. But in the end Xypher knew this was the best he could hope for.

"Fine. Let me go and I'll help."

The vines released him so suddenly that he fell against the floor. He rose slowly to tower over Kat. Even wounded, he made a formidable sight. "What do you need?"

"I need to know where the Tablet of Destiny is and I need a weakness for the demon Kessar . . . and I need it yesterday."

Xypher nodded before he looked at Hades. "I need all my powers returned to me."

He curled his lip. "You're dead."

"And I need my Oneroi powers back if I'm to help her."

Hades narrowed his eyes. "Don't think you can escape me even with them. You made a bargain and you are bound by it."

"And I will abide by it."

Hades snapped his fingers.

Relief flashed across Xypher's brow before he dressed himself. When his gaze met Kat's, she saw sincerity and gratitude there. "I'll be in touch." He vanished.

Kat smiled in contentment until Hades shook his head. "I hope you know what you're doing."

"I think I do."

"No, Kat, you don't. Did you even bother to ask anyone why he was served with a death sentence?"

"You said it yourself. He was a Skotos who refused to be reined in."

"Yes, he was. He would also hunt down humans and terrorize them until they went mad from it. Not a few people, Kat. We're talking more than a hundred. His last victim set himself on fire, trying to escape the nightmares Xypher had caused."

Kat covered her mouth as horror filled her. "Why didn't you tell me that?"

"Because you said you knew what you were doing. Nice to know you lie like everyone else."

That stung on more levels than she wanted to acknowledge. She hadn't meant to lie to anyone, and she hated the fact that Hades knew just where to attack someone.

But she wouldn't let him know that he'd struck a nerve. "Thanks for your help, Hades."

He inclined his head before he left her alone with her own fear over what she'd done. By trying to make things better she had a bad feeling she'd just unleashed another menace into the world.

At the rate she was going, who needed to fear the gallu? It appeared she was the biggest threat to humanity.

Her guilt churning, she left to go tell Sin the latest good news.

CHAPTER SIXTEEN

Kat flashed back to Simi's room first to make sure the two of them were fine, especially Simi. She didn't know if the demon was friendly with Kytara or not, but experience had taught her that Simi took the death of her friends extremely hard—it was something Kat should have thought of before she'd sent her to Olympus with Kytara's body.

But as soon as Kat entered the room, she realized that she'd worried over nothing. Xirena had ordered room service, and the two of them were steadily eating their way through it.

"Fighting makes a Charonte really hungry," Xirena explained as she paused while eating a hamburger.

That worked for Kat, who wasn't going to pursue the matter any further than the fact that the demons were occupied and she hadn't scarred Simi.

Kat left them and went to Sin's penthouse. She found him lying sprawled across the bed, fully dressed. It looked as if he'd just laid down for a second, only to succumb to exhaustion. Her heart broke for him. He'd been through so much in the last couple of days.

Poor baby.

Using her limited powers, she stripped his clothes so that he could lie more comfortably. She bit her lip at the choice sight he made naked. He really did have one of the best bodies she'd ever seen on a man. From the broadness of his battle-scarred shoulders to the deep indentation of his abs, he was yummy. And it took all her willpower not to nip at that bronzed skin with her teeth. Really, he was as tempting as sin.

She stifled a laugh at her bad pun before she brushed her hand through his silken curls.

"How did it go?"

The deep rumble of his voice made her jump. "I thought you were asleep."

"I was until you touched me." Yawning, he rolled over onto his back.

Kat arched a brow at the sight of another part of his body that had also awakened. "You sure you're not Priapus?"

He snorted at that but made no move to cover himself. "Last I heard, that fool was trapped in a book to be a sex slave to women. Definitely not me—I can only seem to satisfy one woman." He gave her a meaningful look.

His expression made her weak with hope. "Does this mean I'm forgiven?"

Sin caught himself an instant before he said what he thought—*I can only wish that I could stay mad at you.* The words were on the tip of his tongue, but he didn't dare speak them. The last thing he needed was for her to know exactly how much control she had over him. That knowledge could only come back to bite him, most likely on the ass.

"Maybe," he whispered as she leaned over him to place a gentle kiss to his lips.

"I meant what I said earlier. I'll never hurt you again, Sin."

"And I want to believe you . . . I know you mean it when you say it, but my experience hasn't taught me that people can be trusted."

Shaking her head, she began kissing her way down his chest.

Sin sucked his breath in as his head swam from the heat of her lips on his skin. There was truly no better feeling than to have her with him, touching him like this. It was what made her so dangerous to him. He craved her, and when people craved something this badly it made them incredibly stupid.

And even knowing that, he was mesmerized by her as he watched her working her way over his chest. Her soft hand cupped him gently. He knew he was lost to her. Lost to the feelings she evoked as she made love to him.

He arched his back as she took him in her mouth. His heart racing, he cupped her head in his hand. He was in heaven at the moment, but he couldn't help wondering how long before it turned into hell.

Every woman in his life had taught him some vital lesson. His mother had taught him hatred. His wife scorn. His daughter love and Artemis betrayal.

What would Katra teach him when all was said and done? That was what he was terrified of. He'd let her into a place in his heart that he'd never allowed another being.

And she had the power to destroy him.

Kat groaned at the taste of Sin, at the hooded look of pleasure on his face as he watched her. She wasn't really sure what she was doing, but he seemed to be enjoying it and that was all that mattered to her. She wanted him to trust her even though she didn't deserve it, and she wanted to make amends for what she'd done to him.

If she ever could.

She'd always been so afraid of giving herself over to a man, of allowing one to hold any part of her, that she couldn't believe how easily Sin had wormed his way into her heart. What was it about him that touched her so deeply? That made her want to do anything to please him?

It was insane, but there was no denying what she felt. No denying the joy that something as minuscule as a smile from him could evoke.

His eyes were on fire as he pulled her up his body to kiss her. He rolled with her until she was beneath him. She sensed a desperation within him, an unnamed need.

But when he entered her, all she could feel from him was what she felt inside herself—the love she had for him. It was incredible.

Sin made love to her furiously as she ran her hands over his back and lifted her hips to drive him in even deeper. She was as hungry for him as he was for her, and that stunned him. Sure, he'd had other lovers more skilled and those who practically raped him in their fervor. But that wasn't the same as what he had with Kat. This wasn't two people scratching a mutual itch. This was two people who cared for each other.

And she loved him—that was what she'd said. No woman had ever told him that before. None. It was an impossible thing for him to accept, but still he wanted to believe it desperately.

Tenderness for her overwhelmed him as long-buried dreams rushed from some part of his heart he didn't even recognize. He wanted to have a future with her.

A family.

That thought jolted him so hard that he actually slid out of her for a moment. A family? What was he thinking? That would be all kinds of stupid.

Yet he wondered what a child with her would be like. Fair like its mother or dark like him? Would the baby be powerful? But the most important thing was that it would be a part of him and a part of her.

Ah jeez, I'm turning into an old woman.

Next thing, he'd be crocheting tea cozies and clipping coupons.

Or worse, wearing a pink bathrobe with fuzzy slippers.

Kat felt a strange shift in Sin's touch. He cradled her body tenderly against his and it melted it. She kissed him heatedly as he thrust against her. This was what she wanted. What she needed. Until him, she'd never known love, and she couldn't imagine ever feeling like this toward anyone else.

She wanted to hold him forever. To keep him close to her and to protect him from anyone who would hurt him.

Her body tingled as all her senses swirled together. In a bolt of white-hot pleasure, her orgasm came. Throwing her head back, Kat screamed in ecstasy.

Sin continued to thrust until he joined her there in paradise.

He collapsed against her, holding her tight while she listened to his heart pounding against her breast and his breath tickled her neck.

"I think," she whispered in his ear, "you've broken me."

"How so?"

"I can't feel my legs and I have no desire to ever leave this bed again."

He laughed. "Can I sleep up here?"

"Um, no. I want on top. You're heavy."

He faked an indignant gape. "Heavy? I'll have you know—"

"You're six feet, seven inches. Your bones alone weigh a ton."

"And what about you?"

"I'm heavy, too, but I want on top."

He nibbled at her lips. "Fine. I'll make a deal with you then . . . feel free to climb on top of me any time you want to." He rolled over then and pulled her across his body.

Smiling, Kat settled down by his side. "Oh yeah, this is perfect." She splayed her hand over his chest and merely took delight in the feel of his skin under her palm.

Sin couldn't breathe as he felt the heat of her body pressed up against his as she told him about Xypher and what she'd accomplished in Hades. While she talked, the scent of her body hung heavy in Sin's head and, to his surprise, he could feel his cock starting to harden again.

How could that be? And yet he couldn't deny what he felt. Some alien part of himself needed her more than his body needed to breathe.

Katra had a hold on him that he couldn't even begin to understand. But that same alien part of himself wouldn't change that hold for anything. And when she slid herself over him to feed, he felt an inexplicable closeness to her. It was like they were sharing more than blood with each other. They were sharing souls.

And as he lay there, lost in the scent and sensation that was Katra, he drifted off to sleep.

Well fed and sated, Kat smiled as she heard Sin's light snore. It was a sweet sound that quickly lulled her to sleep. But unlike the wonderful sharing that had zapped her strength, her dreams were fraught with nightmares.

All she could see was the gallu coming after her. Hear Kessar calling down the Dimme to kill them.

If only she knew it was a dream and not a premonition . . .

Kat *woke up* to an empty bed. She actually felt like pouting at the missing sight and warmth of Sin.

At least until she heard someone moving around outside. Smiling, she grabbed Sin's button-down shirt from the bed and shrugged it over her shoulders, leaving it unbuttoned to hopefully entice him back to bed before she went to sneak up on him.

She opened the door and smiled as she saw him bent over behind the bar. Biting her lip, she snuck up to him, but before she reached him he straightened.

Kat squeaked in alarm as she realized he wasn't tall enough or wide enough at this angle to be Sin. Kish turned around with a frown that turned to a gasp as he saw her nearly naked state.

Embarrassed to the depth of her soul, she ran toward the safety of the bedroom and slammed the door.

"Kat," he said from the other side. "It's okay. I didn't see anything. Really."

"Yeah, right."

"Okay, look. I will never *admit* to seeing anything. Please don't tell Sin or he'll gouge out my eyes. Okay? It's our secret. I swear."

Kat growled as she snatched up her clothes and dressed, only to remember that she could have done it without touching them. But at this point, she was so rattled, she didn't know what she was doing. "Why are you here?"

"I was cleaning up. Sin won't let housekeeping in. He doesn't trust them."

Kat snatched open the door. "He doesn't trust anyone."

"True. And I was keeping breakfast warm for you. Sin told me he'd have my balls if I didn't take care of you. Personally, I like my balls attached to my body, so I intend to take really good care of you in a purely platonic way."

He was an odd yet strangely amusing man. "Where is Sin?"

"Downstairs plotting gallu destruction with Damien. He said that you needed to rest and that I wasn't to disturb you. I didn't, did I?"

"Not until a second ago."

He gave her a really pained expression. "You're going to get me killed, aren't you?"

She thought about it . . . hard. But in the end, she wasn't that mean. "No."

He let out a relieved breath as he backed up toward the bar. "I didn't know what you liked so I ordered some of everything. Cheese blintz, French toast, eggs nine different ways, bagels . . . you name it and it's here or I'll get it here ASAP. I figure whatever you don't eat we can feed to the demons."

Kat smiled in spite of herself. "I'm sure they'd appreciate it."

"You have no idea. The kitchen staff is going wild about the orders they're placing. We've had to import extra cooks from other casinos and restaurants for the two of them alone."

Laughing, Kat stepped around him to grab a piece of toast. "I'll just take some scrambled eggs, bacon, and toast with juice."

"Great. Sit right there"—he indicated a bar stool at the counter—"and I'll take care of it." He pointed toward the toast in her hand. "Jelly, jam, or butter?"

"None of that, thank you. I like it plain."

He held up two thumbs. "Works for me."

Kat took another bite as she watched him prepare a plate for her and she wondered what had brought such a quirky person into Sin's service. "So have you been with Sin long?"

Kish shrugged. "A few thousand years, give or take a decade or two."

She choked at his unexpected response. She'd assumed he was human, but obviously she was wrong. "Get out. Really?"

"That's why he trusts me." He set the plate down in front of her, then added the silverware and a linen napkin.

"But you're human, aren't you?"

He nodded. "I'm human, except when I first wake up in the morning. Even I don't want to be around myself then."

Normally that would have amused her. However, she now had a mystery to solve. "But if you're human—"

"How am I still alive?" He grinned and winked at her. "I'm a mind reader, too."

Yeah . . .

He cleaned up some of the eggs he'd spilled while filling her plate before he answered. "Back in the day, I made a really bad bargain with a demon for my soul in exchange for immortality and wealth." He met her gaze and she saw and felt his admiration and gratitude. "Sin saved me."

"How?"

He shrugged. "I never asked for the details. I was too afraid to find out what it had cost him. All I know is he bartered to free me and I've been with him ever since. There's nothing I wouldn't do for that man."

She could understand that and had to admire Kish for his loyalty. She'd been around enough centuries to know that most people, even when bailed out by someone, tended to turn on them for no apparent reason as soon as they had the chance. It said a lot for Kish's character that he was still here and still acknowledged the debt he owed Sin. "How did you meet?"

A wry light came into Kish's eyes as he covered up the leftover food. "Same as Damien—I was trying to kill him."

She choked on her eggs. That wasn't what she expected Kish to say. "And he let you live?"

"Freaky, huh?" Kish laughed before he continued. "Sin lives his entire life up to his eyeballs in death. Believe it or not, he saves everyone he can, when he can. I hadn't been bitten by my demon yet and so he was able to pull me out. Most of the people, and I use that term loosely, who work below owe Sin their lives in one way or another."

Wow. She was amazed by Sin's compassion even though he tried to keep his distance from others . . . especially after all the betrayal in his life. The fact that he would still reach out to help another . . .

He was incredible and it made her love him all the more.

She took a drink of juice before she spoke again. "But how can you still be alive?"

"Sin was the god of the calendar year. Even though Artemis took most of his powers, she didn't get them all, and that was one he semi-maintained. He's able to stop the aging cycle. Not as effectively as he could when he was a Sumerian god, but enough to keep me alive and not aging."

That was a neat power to have. "Couldn't he do that for Damien?"

"No. They tried it once and it almost killed him. Damien's cursed—that's a whole other animal to skin, and Sin's powers don't extend to it."

"But he saved you," she said, her heart melting at the thought. "You must have been a good man."

He scoffed at her. "I was the worst sort of trash. A liar, a thief. For pocket change I would have cut the throat of anyone, man, woman . . . child. It didn't matter. I'm not proud of what I was. Had Sin cut my throat and left me for dead, I would have deserved it." He looked up, his eyes filled with turmoil. "I've never been able to understand why he saved me. God knows I didn't deserve it. I had no concept of compassion until he spared my life."

The more Kat learned about Sin, the more she was amazed by him. And she wanted to fully understand what had made Sin spare Kish. She reached out and touched Kish's arm. In an instant, she was there in that moment.

Kish was on the ground, bleeding while Sin stood over him fingering the knife he'd taken from Kish's hand while Kish had tried his best to kill him.

"Do it," Kish had snarled.

Sin had pulled the smaller man up from the street by his tunic front. He held Kish by his fist as he stared into Kish's dark eyes. And it was then Sin saw the life Kish had lived. The terror, the pain. A runaway slave, he'd lived his life wanting freedom and comfort.

Wanting something he didn't have to fight for, and it resonated in Sin's own soul. He understood just how much something so inconsequential could mean.

Sin had set Kish on his feet. "Life only has the value a person gives it. If I killed you here and now, yours would be worthless and no one would mourn you. Is that truly what you want?"

Kish had curled his lip at Sin. "I don't own my life. It means nothing to me."

"Then it means nothing to anyone." Sin had narrowed his gaze on Kish. "But if you had your life again, would it still be worthless?"

"I don't understand riddles. I'm only a servant."

"Servant or master, you're not stupid. The question is simple . . . if I give you back your life, will you throw it away again or will you make it worth something?"

Kish hadn't spoken, but the hopeful glimmer in his eyes had said it all. And so Sin had spared him.

Kat let go of Kish's arm and smiled at the warmth that filled her.

He made a noise of disgust. "You know that's kind of rude to spy on someone like that and not to ask. Not to mention really intrusive."

"I'm sorry. I just wanted to know."

And still he looked less than placated. "So that's supposed to excuse you just traipsing into my past and my emotions?"

"Okay, sorry. I get it. Damn, you are a lot like Sin. I promise I will never do that to you again."

"Good, 'cause I didn't like it. How would you feel if I went frolicking through your past without your permission?"

"Kish . . ."

He moved away from her, his face sullen. "I'm just saying you should put a leash on that power. That's all."

She held her hands up in surrender. "It is leashed. Now drop the subject or I'll tell Sin you've seen me naked."

That instantly cleared the sullen look. "I will never bring this topic up again. Oh wait. What topic? I have Alzheimer's. I know nothing at all." He ran to the food and held up one of the silver domes, then changed the subject, "Do you want the rest of this or can I take it to the demons now?"

"Have at it."

If a man could leave skid marks, Kish would have as he whisked the cart out of the room to Simi's.

Laughing at his haste, Kat finished her breakfast, showered, then dressed before she headed downstairs to find Sin, who was supposed to be in Damien's office. Instead she found Damien sitting at his desk, talking on his cell phone.

He hung up the instant she appeared.

"I didn't mean to interrupt," she said sheepishly.

He shrugged it off. "You didn't. I was only bitching."

"About?"

"Sin's family, who thought they could contain and control demons."

Ah, that explained it. "I have that same rant about my family some days. Only mine usually involves their tempers."

Damien put his hands behind his head and leaned back in his office chair as he watched her with an odd half smile. "You really sent a Skotos in to spy on the gallu?"

"You have a better idea?"

"Not really. Seems my bright idea only served in getting my ass handed to me on a platter. I don't want to repeat that humiliation, if you know what I mean."

At least he had a sense of humor about it. She looked around his office that was decorated with cult movie figurines and posters. He looked so normal and nice . . . like anyone you'd meet on the street, and yet at the same time he was lethal. And he lived on people's souls. "Do you know how disturbing it is for me to be having a conversation with a Daimon?"

"About as disturbing as it is for me to work for a Dark-Hunter. But you do get used to it eventually."

"You do seem to have adapted."

He straightened up in his chair. "We all do what we have to, to survive."

"I suppose, and speaking of survival, have you seen Sin?"

Damien straightened a stack of folders on his desk. "He left a short while back, why?"

"I was just wondering. Any idea where he went?"

He shrugged. "We were talking about next week's schedule when he got that weird demon-sensation he gets whenever they've busted loose. Told me to stay here and that he'd be back."

She was surprised by that. "You let him go alone?"

He gave her a duh-stare. "Well, given the fact that it was in this time zone and there's a little thing outside called the sun . . . yeah. Burnt-up Daimon wouldn't be helpful to nobody, least of all me and my tailor."

She narrowed her gaze on him. "Damien . . ."

"Kat." He dragged her name out the same way she'd done his. "What?"

"Why didn't you come tell me he was heading out alone?"

"'Cause he does it all the time. Didn't think anything about it. But now that you're here I'll make sure and keep you updated on everything he does. That way you can cut his meat up for dinner and help him tie his shoes and use the potty, too."

She wasn't sure if she should be irritated or entertained. "You know, I never thought I'd ever meet my sarcastic match. Still haven't, but you come dangerously close."

He smiled. "I will take that as a compliment." Damien got up and pulled his jacket from the back of his chair. "Now if you'll excuse me, I need to go make rounds on the floor. See you later."

Kat shook her head as he left her alone in his office. She had a childish urge to boot up his computer and start deleting files, but she was above that . . .

At least for the moment.

Besides, she had an ex-god to locate. Closing her eyes, she used her powers to find him. She honed in and flashed herself to his side. Or rather, a few feet from his back as he held a man down on the street and was beating him for everything he was worth.

It wasn't until she took a step closer that she realized the man on the ground was a gallu. Even so, Sin was relentless as he rained blow after blow on him.

This was the madman she'd met that night in Central Park.

"Sin!" she snapped, trying to get him to focus. "Just kill him already."

Sin got in one last blow before he did as she asked. When he turned to face her, his expression was hell born and honestly scared her. He set fire to the demon with relish.

When they'd first met she would have thought Sin an animal for doing such a thing as this, but she'd learned enough about him to know he would never do such a thing without a good reason. "What happened?"

"He was trolling a day care."

She felt sick at the news. No wonder Sin had been so angry. "But you got him in time, right?"

"Barely. Had I been even a second later . . ." He shook his head. "It was too close. My attention was on you and your comfort. It wasn't on what it needs to be. I can't allow my attention to falter for even a second. Good gods, can you imagine what it would have done to a child?"

Kat went cold with dread. "What are you saying?"

His golden gaze froze her to the spot. "I need you to go back to Olympus and stay there until this is over."

The mere thought of what he was asking set her temper on fire. How dare he even suggest such a thing. "Like hell."

But there was no backing down in his determined gaze. "Don't you understand?" he said between clenched teeth. "This isn't a game. We are playing with people's lives . . . children's lives. It's not worth it."

She more than understood that. But for him to go up against the gallu by himself was suicide. "You can't stand alone."

"Bullshit. I've been alone since the dawn of time. I've been fighting the gallu single-handedly and doing a pretty damn good job. Believe me, this has to be done."

No, she didn't believe that. Not for a second. "Sin . . . you can't throw *us* away because of what could have happened. You got here in time. You have to trust in that."

"And what if I hadn't? What would you have told that kid's parents then, huh? 'Sorry I missed saving your daughter, but I was too busy having a nooner'?"

She was appalled at his crudity and deep down she knew there was more to this than just the close call. "What is really bothering you?"

All emotion fled his face. "I don't know what you mean."

"Yes, you do. You know exactly what I mean. Something much deeper than a near miss is hurting you. What is it?"

Sin didn't want to feel the pain that was building up inside him. He wanted to stay angry. Rage was something he could deal with . . .

Guilt, fear, regret, anguish, loneliness—those were emotions he'd gladly banished. They were the ones that weakened a man.

But when he looked at Kat, he felt all of them and he didn't know how to rid himself of them without getting rid of her, too. "They got to my brother because I was tending to you, Katra. I was more worried over your welfare than his. And now I almost let one of them get to a kid. I can't live like this. I can't. I need my thoughts uncluttered. I don't need a weakness of any kind in my life."

"Weakness?" He heard the pain in her voice and it tore him apart. "I can kick your ass any day of the week and six times on Sunday."

A part of him wanted to pull her close, but the sane, rational part knew he couldn't. She was a danger to him, and he couldn't lose her. He'd held his daughter in his arms as her life had drained out of her. He refused to relive that pain with Kat. Her death would shatter him. "You were bitten in a fight that I wasn't even scratched in. Remember? You almost became one of them."

"Okay," she snapped, holding up her hands, "so I made a mistake. I forgot about the bite in the ensuing chaos of getting Zakar back. My bad. I own it. I named it. Sue me."

"You make it sound so simple, but it isn't. I can't afford any mistakes here, and worrying over whether or not they're going to kill you makes me sloppy. It leaves them an opening to kill us both."

She gave him a knowing look as she calmed a degree. "I'm not Ishtar, Sin. I won't fall victim to them."

He wanted to trust her, but he couldn't. "You already did."

"It was a simple learning experience. I got it. It won't happen again."

She was right about that. Sin wanted to reach out and touch her. But he knew he couldn't. If he did, she would destroy his resolve. "And now you understand my point of view. I won't bury you or burn you and I won't jeopardize anyone else. It's over, Katra. I want you to take your demons and leave."

Kat curled her lip as she contemplated the dismemberment of a stubborn man. Why wouldn't he see reason? "Leave and let you be overrun by the gallu? What kind of a stupid plan is that? If you don't want me, fine. I'm a big girl, I can handle that. But keep Simi and Xirena. They're the one thing the gallu can't take from you. Let them stand at your back and protect you . . . please."

"Fine. If that will make you happy, they can stay. Now I want you out of this."

Infuriated, Kat held her hands up in defeat. She could tell by his demeanor and tone of voice that he had no intention of allowing her to stay.

Maybe if she gave him some space, he might see reason. But knowing him, she doubted it.

"Whatever. Play all macho if that's what makes you happy. I'm out of this."

Sin watched as she faded before him. His throat burned as every part of him screamed out for him to call her back. But he wouldn't.

No, he couldn't.

She was a distraction. But most of all, she was a weakness he couldn't allow himself. He'd buried everyone in his life who ever meant anything to him.

He refused to lose her, too. Better to hurt a little bit now and know that she was alive and well than to be here and see her dead.

She would get over this and so would he.

Kat was livid as she shoved open the doors to her mother's throne room. "Matisera?" she called, wanting her mom. She didn't even really know why. Her mother wasn't the most sympathetic or affectionate of women. Still, Kat needed to feel the comfort of her mother's presence.

But Artemis didn't come.

Acheron stepped out of the bedroom to look at her with a quizzical stare. "Is something wrong?"

Part of her wanted to run to him for comfort, but the other part wanted to keep her distance. Right now, he reminded her too much of Sin. "Where's Artemis?"

Acheron pointed over his shoulder with his thumb. "Big house on the hill. It's the one you really can't miss. Gaudy as hell and seriously overcompensating for a complex of some sort. Zeus is apparently throwing a party and Artemis wanted to stop in and visit."

Of course she did. She'd probably be gone for hours—it was just Kat's luck.

Acheron crossed the distance between them. "Is there something I can help with?"

"No," Kat said petulantly. "You're a man and I hate all of you right now."

He took two steps back. "Fair enough. Since my presence is obviously causing you pain, I'll take my manhood outside to the terrace, where you can join me if you can overlook my obvious birth defect."

Kat glared at him. It was just like a man to try to make light of this when it hurt so badly. It was why she hated all of their dreaded species at the moment.

Her father went outside to sit on the railing, with his back against a column. The angry part of her wanted to run outside and shove him over it and let him go sprawling to the ground below. And even though the thought gave her a moment's amusement, she knew the truth. She wasn't really angry at her father.

She wanted to crush Sin.

Unable to stand it, she went outside.

Acheron turned toward her with an arch stare.

"Why do all men have to suck?" she asked, folding her arms over her chest. "I knew you all sucked and still I stupidly fell in love with one of you. Why? Why would I be such a masochist? You pour your heart out to a man and what does he do? 'Could you change the channel, babe?' " she mocked in a faked masculine tone. "You're all pathetically cold. You don't care about anyone but yourselves."

Acheron duplicated her pose, folding his arms over his chest. "Do you want my input or is this just an angry tirade you need to vent?"

"Both!"

"Okay, you rant and I'll add my comments at the end."

Why did he have to be so damned reasonable? It actually snapped her out of her anger enough so that she was moderately accommodating. "No, by all means, go ahead. You have something to say, say it."

"For the record, this isn't a male/female thing. It's a people thing. You talk about men being cold . . . you should see women from my standpoint. We're talking Arctic tundra would be warmer. Believe me, you don't want to know my vantage point on your gender. As a man, if I grabbed your breasts, I'd be arrested. Any idea how many women have felt free to grab my crotch at will?"

"Dad!"

"Sorry, but it's true. Women are just as quick to use a man as a man is to use a woman. It's not right to judge an entire gender or group by the actions of a few assholes . . . Now what has Sin done to cause you to hate all the rest of malekind?"

"It's not just Sin," she said defensively. "Look at what Grandpa did to Grandma. What—" She caught herself before she let her next thought slip.

"I've done to your mother."

Damn, he'd guessed it. She bowed her head down, feeling sheepish and churlish. "I didn't mean it like that."

"Don't apologize. You thought it and I heard it loud and clear."

Oof, she'd forgotten about his ability to do that. "I'm sorry."

"No, you're not," he said with an understanding smile. "It's something you've thought about a lot. Don't forget, you get that ability to read people and their emotions from me."

She was really squirming now. No wonder poor Kish had taken her head off. "Am I this obnoxious with it?"

"Probably."

"No wonder people get so irritated with me."

"I'm sure they forgive you quickly enough."

Not really, but she didn't want to argue with him.

He leaned forward to pin her with an earnest look. "For the record, I haven't done anything to your mother."

"You seduced her."

"I kissed her, and believe me when I say my intent was never to make her crave me. I was actually hoping she'd kill me for it."

His confession startled her—it was so extremely different from the way Artemis had portrayed the event. "What?"

He nodded and she could feel his sincerity. "There has never been a woman born I wanted to seduce, and that's the truth. I have spent my entire lifetime trying to get people to keep their hands off me. So before you blame me for seducing your mother and then scorning her, get the facts. I kissed her once, hoping for death, and then she came after me."

It was hard for Kat to wrap her mind around that, but then again, it made a lot of sense.

"As for my parents . . ." he continued, "they were totally screwed up from the beginning, but that has nothing to do with you or me. And it definitely has no bearing on your relationship with Sin unless you make it so. Don't. Your problems with Sin are simple. He's scared and you're pushing him to take a step he's not ready to take."

"You told me to go to him. I did."

"And did you apologize?"

"Yes."

"Then give him time, Katra. When you've spent a lifetime being betrayed by everyone around you, it's really hard to let that go. Sin is afraid of love."

She didn't understand that. "How can anyone be afraid of love?"

"How can they not?" His face was completely aghast. "When you love someone . . . *truly* love them, friend or lover, you lay your heart open to them. You give them a part of yourself that you give to no one else, and you let them inside a part of you that only they can hurt—you literally hand them the razor with a map of where to cut deepest and most painfully on your heart and soul. And when they do strike, it's crippling—like having your heart carved out. It leaves you naked and exposed, wondering what you did to make them want to hurt you so badly when all you did was love them. What is so wrong with you that no one can keep faith with you? That no one can love you? To have it happen once is bad enough . . . but to have it repeated? Who in their right mind would not be terrified of that?"

Kat swallowed against the lump in her throat as she heard the pain inside him. Her eyes tearing, she walked forward, into his arms, and hugged him.

Ash couldn't breathe as he felt his daughter's arms around him. Only Simi had ever held him like this. There were no demands or payment expected for the embrace. It was meant for comfort only.

And it meant everything to him.

"I love you, Dad, and I would never hurt you."

He closed his eyes as those words touched him deeply. "I know, baby. Just give Sin a little space and let him come to grips with himself and his past."

"And if he doesn't?"

"I'll take him outside and beat him for making my girl cry."

She laughed through her tears as she backed away from him. "Really?"

"Absolutely. Forget medieval, I'll break Atlantean on his ass, and you've seen what a ticked-off Atlantean god can do. Makes Hannibal Lecter look like a crybaby."

Smiling, Kat sniffed back her tears. "I'm going to hold you to that, you know?"

"Feel free. I live to kick the snot out of people."

Kat really liked that thought. She could just see Ash doing that, too.

She wiped her eyes before she had a weird off-topic question. "What do you do when Mom leaves you alone like this?"

He shrugged. "I write romance novels."

His response was so quick, deadpan, and unexpected that she was stunned. "Really?"

"Nah." He winked at her. "I'm not that talented, and I know absolutely nothing about romance. I only wanted to see your reaction."

Ha ha. She wasn't sure if she'd ever get used to his humor. "So what do you do? Really?"

"Nothing. Really. It's boring as hell. Artemis won't allow me to bring anything here with me. No guitar. No Cartoon Network. Occasionally, I sneak a book in just to watch her wig out when she finds it."

That didn't make any sense to Kat. Why would her mother be so cruel? "Why doesn't she allow you to have anything here?"

"It's a distraction and she won't tolerate it. My part of the bargain is to be at her beck and call. So here I wait. It's another power trip . . . a small victory she can claim over me."

"Why do you tolerate it?"

The look in his swirling silver eyes sent a shiver down her spine. "The same reason Sin hasn't resigned himself to death. There are six billion people on earth who need someone to protect them from things that are scarier than the tax man or the knife-wielding stranger. Things that a gun won't stop. As long as their lives hang in the balance, what's a little humiliation for me? Besides, I'm used to it."

Maybe, but she wondered if she'd be so altruistic in his place. "Yeah, but you're a god of fate. Can't you change that?"

"You're thinking like a child, Katra. Things that appear simple very seldom are. It's like the mechanic who goes to fix the carburetor and in doing so accidentally puts a hole in the radiator and causes even more damage. Every person on this planet is connected. Sometimes those lines are easy to see, and others are more complex. You change one insignificant thing and you change the very core of humanity. Case in point, had I stopped you from taking Sin's powers he wouldn't have become what he is now. He'd have been just as cold as your mother."

"But his pantheon would have survived."

"Would it? Fate is never that simple. It doesn't go in a straight line, and the more you try to circumvent it, the worse you make it on yourself. Fate will not be denied. Sin would have lost his powers by another means, at another time and place. And whoever took them then might have killed him. Had he died, the world would have ended a long time ago or the gallu would have run free and taken over. There are infinite possibilities."

"But if fate won't be denied . . . if it's set, how could there be infinite possibilities?" That was a question she'd never fully understood.

"Only certain aspects are fated. The outcome isn't. It was fated that Sin would lose his godhood, the means and what followed were determined by free will. Free will is that one scary variable that sets so much into motion that no one, not even I, have control over."

"I don't understand."

He took a deep breath as he rubbed her arm comfortingly. "Here's an example. When I first met Nick Gautier it was fated that he was to get married at age thirty and have a dozen kids. As our friendship grew, I lost the ability to see how his future would play out. Then in one moment of anger, I changed his destiny by telling him he should kill himself. I didn't mean it, but as a god of fate, such proclamations when made by me are law. Fate realigned the circumstances around him that would lead him to make a decision to take his own life. The woman he was to marry ended up dead in her store. His mother's life was taken by a Daimon and Nick shot himself at her feet. *My* free will would have been to not lash out at him. Instead, I did. His free will would have been to seek revenge as a human against a Daimon and not kill himself. But because of who I am, my proclamation that he kill himself outweighed his will and he didn't really have any choice. I took his free will and I cost him everyone who was close to him. Do you understand?"

She was beginning to see, but there was still the matter of the original plan for Nick. "If fate won't be denied, then Nick could still find someone to marry and have a dozen kids, right?"

"That might have been true, but the moment I forced my will onto his life I altered that. His fate is no longer set and it's his free will now that leads him toward a destiny I can't see. But I know his future actions will touch the lives of people I love and whatever happens to them is ultimately my fault for being stupid. Don't be stupid, Katra. Never speak in anger and never try to force your will onto someone else. You'll never find peace in that."

Kat paused as she realized exactly what he meant. For centuries her mother had been trying to force her will on Kat's father. Her grandfather had tried to force his will onto her grandmother. And in each case the outcome had been disastrous for everyone involved. As much as Kat wanted to have Sin, unless he was willing, there would never be any happiness between them. "I understand."

"Good. That's the first step."

She supposed. But honestly, doing the right thing really hurt when all she wanted to do was go force Sin to take her back.

Kat looked at Acheron and shook her head. "You are incredibly wise."

He laughed. "Only when it comes to other people. It's easy to see how to fix their lives. It's much harder to see the cracks in your own house."

"Well, I appreciate it. Thank you." She kissed him on the cheek before she left him alone and headed for her room. She had to leave the temple to walk across to the dormitory that belonged to all of the *koris* who served Artemis. Kat's room was the last on the left.

She would give Sin the space he needed to see what he wanted out of his life. She wouldn't seek him out. Let him be the one to call. It was the only way.

As she went to open her bedroom curtains to let daylight in, she heard something behind her. Turning, she watched as Xypher appeared in the center of her room.

His expression was cold and brutal as he dragged a male demon, in true demon form across her floor. He held the demon by the scruff of his neck as he kicked and screamed, demanding release. Xypher was covered in blood. Scratches marred the left side of his face.

But he didn't seem to notice as he walked calmly toward Kat.

As soon as he reached her, he dumped the demon at her feet. The demon tried to rise, but Xypher kicked him back down. "I found this piece of shit trying to eat a woman outside a deli. Thought it might prove a good snitch and I was right."

He grabbed the demon by the hair and pulled him up so that Kat could see his face. "Now tell the good lady where Kessar put the Tablet of Destiny."

"It's around his neck. He won't let anyone near it."

"And Zakar?"

"He's pinned to the side of the master's throne."

Xypher let the demon fall back to the floor. "Good enough? Now, can I kill it?"

She looked at Xypher's bleeding wounds. "What about you? Are you converting?"

He laughed bitterly. "I'm dead. Can't convert me when I don't have a pulse."

That made her feel better . . . in an odd way.

"Can I kill it now?"

Kat hesitated and she didn't even know why. Looking at the demon, helpless on the floor . . .

It was one thing to kill in a fight but another to kill after the person, or demon in this case, had been defeated. It just seemed wrong somehow.

"What are you? Weak?" Xypher snarled when she didn't respond. "Don't tell me you want me to spare this pathetic animal when it wouldn't show you any such mercy. Believe me, it's better to take the head off a cobra before the cobra strikes you."

"A cobra can't help what it is. Why should you punish it because it's doing what the gods created it to do?"

He rolled his eyes at her. "Are we going to debate philosophy or should I just kiss and make up with the demon now? Let it get a good shot at your throat so it can rip it out?"

Xypher was right. This was no time to be merciful, especially since she'd seen what demons were capable of firsthand. They didn't show mercy or compassion. But that didn't mean she had to be just like them. "Put him down mercifully."

"Yes, Queenie," Xypher said, his tone full of venom and sarcasm. "I'll make sure and use a cushioned blade."

"I could do without your sarcasm."

"And I could do without your bleeding heart."

She narrowed her eyes on him. "Just remember, my bleeding heart is what gained you a shot at freedom."

His face turned to stone. "Queenie, it was a bleeding heart that put me in that position to begin with. The person I was trying to protect when I was taken didn't return the favor. The bitch was only using me. So take my advice, whatever compassion you have, kill it off. You'll thank me for it later." And with that he vanished.

Kat stood there for a full second as his words rang in her ears. It made her wonder if maybe Xypher wasn't right. Betrayal seemed to be the worst part of humanity.

At least with the gallu, they didn't pretend. They merely were what they were. Demons. You knew where you stood. They didn't pretend to like you and then try to stab you in the back. They came at your throat from the beginning.

She could almost respect them for that. Maybe they were a higher life-form after all. Betrayal wasn't in their nature.

With that thought, another terrifying one went through her mind. Sin knew how to kill her. She'd given him a secret that no one, not even her mother, knew.

Was his kindness toward her only a facade meant to blind her until he betrayed her?

Surely not . . .

I took his powers. He'd been after her mother for centuries to kill her for that. Now he knew Artemis was innocent and Kat was the one who'd done it.

Maybe I'm being stupid and paranoid. It was more than possible.

"Stop it, Kat. Sin wouldn't hurt you." He wouldn't and she refused to let herself continue on with such nonsense. Right now Sin was hurting and confused. Just like her.

She wouldn't let unfounded fears destroy what they had built together.

And what do you have? He told you to get lost.

Ugh, how she hated that voice in her head. "I won't listen to you. I love Sin and I'm not giving up on him yet."

She only hoped he shared that sentiment about her. If not, he was going to kill her.

CHAPTER SEVENTEEN

"You know, you could just kill Kat off."

"Kish!" Sin snapped, wanting to splinter his servant across the wall behind him.

"What? It's been a full week since she left and all you've done is sulk like a dying cow."

"Dying cows don't sulk."

"How do you know? Do you make it a habit to hang around dying cows?"

Sin glared at the man who was busy trying to clean up his penthouse. For over a week he hadn't left his couch except to kill demons and hunt for Kessar and his brother. He'd slept on it, eaten on it, and sulked on it. And all in a useless effort to push Kat out of his life.

But the truth was, he missed her. He missed the scent of her skin and hair. Missed the way her forehead crinkled whenever she thought he was nuts. He missed the sound of her voice, the touch of her hand.

Most of all, he missed the laughter they'd shared. Her razor-sharp sarcasm.

His stomach ached from the emptiness left by her absence. It was a pain so profound that it permeated everything about him. He didn't want to talk to anyone. He had no energy.

All he wanted was Kat back.

Damn her to hell for that.

Kish picked up the pizza box, which still held an untouched pizza, and added it to the garbage. "I'm just saying a dying cow could sulk."

"The least you could do is call him a dying bull," Damien said as he entered the room behind Kish. "Man his ass up a bit. At least that would be an improvement to the whiny little girl we've had to deal with these last seven days."

Sin shot his hand out and sent a jolt to each of them. They yelped before they went flying. "Anything else you girls want to complain about?"

"Ow," Kish whined. "I think he broke my body."

"What part?"

"My whole body. It all hurts."

Damien pushed himself up on one of the bar stools to glare at him. "Do you even own a mirror?"

Sin scowled at him. "What are you talking about?"

"You. Man, no wonder Kat left you. You smell, your hair is knotted, and you haven't shaved in how many days? Forget fighting the gallu. One whiff of you would kill them." He looked at Kish as he stood up. "Don't strike a match. The alcohol fumes alone would send him up like a Roman candle."

"Shut up," Sin snarled as he got up and grabbed the half-empty bottle of Jack Daniel's off the coffee table. He headed for his bedroom so that he wouldn't have to put up with their nagging anymore.

At least that was the plan, but the walls were so thin, he couldn't help but overhear them.

"When was the last time he changed those clothes?" Damien asked.

"I think it was the last time he bathed . . . the day Kat left."

Sin heard the sound of glasses clinking together.

Damien cursed. "How much shit is he drinking?"

"Let me put it to you this way . . . I restock the cabinet twice a day now."

"Damn, how can he fight the demons and be that wasted?"

"I think you were right earlier. He strikes a match and breathes at them. Like a human blowtorch."

"If it wasn't so sad and probably true, I'd laugh."

"Yeah. I hear ya. Personally, I stopped laughing when I found this under his pillow."

Sin cursed as he realized what Kish had found and he went to his bed to quickly verify exactly what was in his hands. Just as he feared . . . Katra's heinous flannel pajamas.

What a pathetic fool he was. He'd been keeping them near so that he could smell her whenever he slept. Her scent had comforted him on a level that was unimaginable.

And right now, he felt like a jackass at having been found out. But that feeling vanished behind the realization that another man was holding Kat's clothes . . .

Infuriated, Sin stormed back into the main room and snatched them from Kish's hand. "Do you mind? These don't belong to you."

"Sorry."

He turned to catch Damien's smirk.

"What are you looking at?"

"Nothing. I'm just trying to imagine you in flannel pink sock monkey pajamas. I'm sure you look stunning in pink."

Kish burst out laughing. "Actually, with his skin tone, he probably does look really good in it. I would definitely say he's an autumn."

"That's summer, you dweeb."

Sin gave them a cold look. "I find it fascinating that you two women know that color palettes for clothes have a name." He turned to Damien. "The fact you corrected him *really* scares me."

"Hey, I'm not the one sleeping in pink pajamas. I don't want to hear it from you."

Sin glared at him. "It's a good thing you don't embezzle from my casino or I'd kill you where you stand." And with that he returned to his room.

Sin closed the door and leaned against it. Before he could stop himself, he lifted the pajamas to his nose and smelled the gentle scent that was unique to Kat. How something so stupid could both soothe and crush him he didn't understand. But there was no denying what he felt.

He wanted her here with him. And it killed him to be here alone.

"What have I done?"

But he knew. He had to keep her away from him. It was for her own good. If Ishtar had fallen to the gallu, what chance did Kat stand? He would never jeopardize her safety for his selfishness.

Disgusted with his own weakness, he forced himself to toss the pajamas to his bed and head for the bathroom. As soon as he caught himself in the mirror, he understood Damien and Kish. He did look like hell.

His eyes were sunken from lack of sleep . . . he couldn't remember the last time he'd shaved. His hair was shaggy and unkempt. Kat would kick him sideways for looking like this, and he probably did smell as bad as he looked.

Disheartened, Sin went to the shower to bathe and prove to all of them that he could function without her.

He just didn't want to.

As he waited for the water to heat, he balled his fist and placed it against the cool wall outside the shower before he pressed his forehead to the tile. Closing his eyes, he could see her so clearly in his mind . . . feel her.

"Sin?"

He tensed at the sound of her voice saying his name. It sounded like she was right behind him. But he knew better.

Then he felt it. The soft whisper of a hand on his shoulder. Afraid it was nothing more than torture invented by his mind, he didn't want to open his eyes.

"Are you all right?" she asked.

"That depends."

"On what?"

"Whether or not you're still there when I turn around."

"Do you want me to leave then?"

The word "no" hung in his throat. *Dammit, man, shake your*

head and tell her to leave. It's for her own good. It's for your *own good.*

Still her touch was on his skin.

Forcing himself to turn around, he opened his eyes and saw the most beautiful thing he'd ever seen in his life. Kat's face. Unable to stand it, he pulled her to him and kissed her.

Kat couldn't breathe at the ferocity of Sin's embrace. She tried to bury her hands in his hair, but her fingers became stuck in tangles. She had to be hurting him and yet he didn't seem to notice as his tongue danced with hers and his thick whiskers scraped against her face.

The scent of Sin and whisky filled her head, and her heart raced. She'd been so afraid of his reception that this was a startling surprise for her.

"Does this mean you're happy to see me?"

"More than happy." He pinned her against the shower door, and before she could blink her clothes were gone.

Kat couldn't breathe as he dipped his head down to tease her right breast. His whiskers scraped her skin and sent chills all over her while his tongue tormented her with pleasure. He was ferocious as his hands and lips sought out every part of her body.

Ecstasy assailed her. When she'd come here, this reception was the last thing she'd expected. Truthfully, she'd thought he was going to throw her out and tell her never to come back. Or at the very least to turn and walk away without hearing a word she spoke.

Not in her wildest dreams had she expected him to be as hungry for her as she was for him. He was desperate to touch her, and it made her smile to know just how much he'd missed her. It felt so good to be in his arms again. To have his breath scorching her skin. Just the feel of his strong arms was enough to make her wet and needy.

"I want you, Sin," she breathed in his ear. "I don't want to wait."

She reached over her head to grab onto the shower bar as he entered her.

Sin growled at the feel of being inside her again. Every part of him shouted in relief. He looked up to see the precious smile on her face as she watched him thrust against her. His entire body was shaking from the pleasure of this. From the heat of her body welcoming his.

Waiting for her was the hardest thing he'd ever done in his life, and it seemed to take forever before she finally sank her nails into his arm and threw her head back to cry out. The minute he felt her climax, he joined her.

Kat's head was swimming as she released the shower rod and realized the metal groove had cut into her palm. Still, she didn't care as she wrapped herself around him and just listened to his breathing in her ear.

"That was an unexpected treat," she said with a laugh.

Sin wanted to laugh with her, but he didn't find this funny. He'd jeopardized her and recanted everything he'd tried to accomplish this last week.

And for what?

For the touch of her hand on his face . . .

The truth tore through him. He'd sell his soul for one moment with her. But he couldn't tell her that.

"Why are you here?" he asked, his voice thick and strange sounding even to himself.

"Xypher told me Kessar's weakness and I thought you should know it."

That was *it*? That was the only reason she'd come here? Part of him had wanted her to tell him that she'd missed him. That she'd been unable to function without him. But now that he looked at her, he realized that she looked great. Unlike him, she hadn't lost sleep. There was no sign of her having moped around or grieved.

And that seriously pissed him off.

She frowned at him. "Are you okay?"

"Fine," he snapped.

"You don't look fine. You look . . . kind of pissed. I thought this would make you happy."

"I'm ecstatic." Oh yeah, there was no sarcasm in that tone . . .

She slapped lightly at him. "You're such an asshole."

"Asshole?" he growled. "Is that all you have to say to me after a week?"

She folded her arms over her chest as she met that golden gaze levelly. "Yeah, that and you need a bath."

"I was about to do that when you showed up."

She scoffed. "By the looks of you, I'd say you're a couple of days late."

He grabbed a washcloth from the stack of them in the wall cupboard. "Are you simply here to insult me? Because if you are, I have two others who beat you to it. They're better at it, too."

"Oh, I seriously doubt that."

He ignored her as he checked the water temperature. "Just tell me what you found out and go."

"No. Not until you tell me what's wrong with you."

"Nothing is wrong with me."

"Right. C'mon, Sin, stop sulking and answer me."

"I don't sulk."

Yeah, right. "You're pouting like a two-year-old."

"I am not."

She put her hands on her hips and imitated a small child. Then she answered in the most juvenile tone she could muster, "Are, too."

Sin glared at her. Even though he wanted to be angry, he couldn't stop a small laugh that betrayed him. "I hate you." But there was no emotion in his voice to back those words.

She popped him on his butt cheek. "Fine. Be that way. I'll go find me someone else to love."

As she stepped away from him, he grabbed her arm.

Kat paused as she saw the angry look in his eyes. It was absolutely furious and it chilled her to the bone.

"Who?" he growled.

What the hell was he talking about? "Who what?"

"Who are you going to?"

Suddenly everything was clear to her. His demeanor, his anger. Everything. "Oh, good grief, Sin, you couldn't possibly think I was really going to find someone else. I didn't remain chaste for eleven thousand years to start sleeping around now. Believe me, if there's one thing I am, it's capable of controlling myself. So put that jealousy back in its box and cover it with a stainless-steel lid. Nail it shut and stick it where the sun never shines. I don't ever want to see this side of you again."

He stepped back. "Well, what am I supposed to think? You don't look any worse for the wear."

"Wear of what?"

He looked away from her. "Never mind."

She stopped him before he entered the shower. "Do you think this week was easy on me?"

He raked her with a sneer. "You look pretty unscarred."

She growled at him. "Boy, you better be glad you're stunning when you're naked or I'd skin you for that. I've been through utter hell this week because of you. Do you think I wanted to come crawling back here only to have you tell me to get lost again? I know it's hard for you to believe, but I do have my pride, and you've kicked it for the last time."

His face brightened. "You missed me?"

And that just irritated her more. "Is that all you got out of what I just said?"

"No, but it's what I need to know the answer to."

She let out a frustrated breath. "Yes, Sin. I missed you. I've mourned for you. I've hated you. I've wanted to sic Simi on you with barbecue sauce and I've done nothing but think about how much I just want to hold you . . . and yes, I've missed every part of you, from that annoying little sound you make when you're irritated to the way you hold on to me when we sleep. Now are you happy?"

His golden eyes sparkled. "I'm delirious." He kissed her again.

Kat pulled back and shook her head. "You know, I'm starting to feel like a yo-yo here. Either you want me or you don't. You have to stop playing with me, because I can't take it."

"I want you here with me, Katra. I do. I've barely been able to function this week."

She cocked her head. "Are you sure?"

"Yes," he breathed. "You're twice the distraction when you're gone as you are when you're here."

She wasn't sure if that was a good thing or a bad thing, but she was willing to take it. Pleased by his rancor, she wrinkled her nose at him. "Well, in that case, get a bath. You're kind of smelly."

"No, I'm not."

She held her hand up with her forefinger and thumb about an inch apart. "Just a little."

He snorted. "Fine." He opened the shower and stepped in. To

his delight, Kat followed him inside and took the cloth from his hand before she began washing his back.

"So what did you find out about Kessar?" he asked over his shoulder.

"The only thing he fears is a woman named Ravanah."

Sin gave her a duh-stare. "She's not a woman. She's another demon."

"Is she a living demon?"

"There's some speculation that she is alive and well, but no one has heard from her for centuries."

"Is she gallu?"

"Oh no. She's unique to herself."

"How so?"

"She eats the flesh of other demons. Hence Kessar's fear of her."

"Ooo, nice. She could come in handy."

"If we could find her. But I wouldn't hold my breath. Not to mention, when there aren't any demons around, she eats the flesh of infants and pregnant women. She's a vicious one."

"She sounds lovely. Maybe we should invite her for dinner one night?" Kat turned him around so that she could soap the front of him. It was actually hard to concentrate while she was touching his naked body. She'd forgotten how breathless he made her. He was so large and powerful . . . so incredibly sexy. It was hard to think about anything other than the fact that she really wanted another go-round that ended with her bending him like a pretzel. "By the way, I also found out that Zakar is being kept—"

"Chained to Kessar's throne and the Tablet is around his neck."

She looked up to catch the heated glint in his eyes as she ran the cloth over his cock and under his sac. "You knew that?"

"I made sure I got that information from a few of my recent kills."

"Sweet. All my information was useless. Nice to know."

He cupped her hand with his and rubbed it gently against him. Kat swallowed at the silken feel of him sliding against her soapy fingers. If he wasn't covered in soap, she'd be tonguing his nipples.

"At least you tried." He dipped his head to kiss her lightly on the neck. "That's more than most."

"I only wish it were more useful."

"It was useful."

He took the cloth from her hand and added more soap.

Kat almost moaned when he started washing her breasts. "Well, there is more."

"Such as?"

She had to put her hands on his shoulders to steady herself as he tenderly bathed her. "You probably know that the Dimme aren't really friendly to the gallu. So Kessar is stockpiling his demons around their tomb."

He paused. "Do you know where the tomb is?"

"Yes."

Sin laughed before he picked her up and kissed her. "Thank you."

"Aha! So I am useful."

"Yes, you are. Now all we need is a plan."

Kat nodded. "One that doesn't end up with all of us dead."

"That would be a good start."

She widened her legs as he dipped his hand to stroke her between her thighs. Then he let the cloth fall to the floor so that he could stroke her with his long fingers. Kat sucked her breath in sharply as he slid his index finger deep inside her.

"I was in such a hurry before that I didn't even get to taste you."

Kat couldn't speak as he toyed with her. All she could do was watch as he dropped to his knees and nudged her legs farther apart until he could replace his fingers with his tongue. Her breasts tightened in response while his gruff whiskers rubbed her tender flesh, adding even more chills to her.

Sin growled as he tasted her body. He wanted her scent all over him. Wanted to taste her pleasure. Her thighs were wet from the water, and her soft moans were precious to his ears. He'd never wanted to please a woman the way he wanted to her. There was nothing more gratifying than the sight of her orgasm. The sound of her calling out his name as she came for him.

The hot water pounded against his back while he tongued her. He slid his fingers deep inside her, wringing another cry of pleasure.

And in one hot moment, she gripped his hair and shuddered above him. Sin laughed in triumph as he continued to lick and torment until he'd wrung every last bit of her orgasm from her.

When she was finished, he rose up to pull her close against his chest.

Kat couldn't breathe as Sin entered her again. He held her pinned to the wall as he thrust against her. Her entire body burned and his last made her hungry. Holding him close, she sank her fangs into his neck. She was so weak, it was all she could do to stand. How he had any energy left, she didn't know. But it didn't take him long until he was growling in her ear as his own release took him.

"You are insatiable," she panted as she released him.

"I was a fertility god, remember? We tend to be that way."

She laughed. "I can certainly see why women would worship you." She laid a gentle kiss to his cheek. "But don't let that go to your head."

"Don't worry. I know you better than that. I'm sure you'll be cutting me down to size any moment now."

Kat gave him a squeeze before she withdrew and finished her bath.

As soon as they were finished with the shower, Sin called Damien, Kish, and the two Charonte into his room.

Simi squealed the instant she saw Kat. "Ooo Akra-Kat you're back!"

"I am, Simi, how have you been?"

"Really good. We've been doing lots of shopping." She held out her hands to show Kat that each finger held a new ring. "Did you know there were stores here in the casino? Xirena and the Simi had been shopping like the demons that we are."

Kish scoffed. "Yeah. Their room looks like a warehouse."

Simi tossed her hair over her shoulder. "And I like warehouses. They have lots of good stuff in them."

"Which is why I introduced them to the Container Store's Web site." Kish winked.

"Ooo," Simi cooed, "we loves that too. They have lots of boxes to hold the Simi's QVC and sparklies."

Sin cleared his throat. "Yeah and I hate to interrupt but we're facing an even bigger crisis than stockpiling demon wear." He turned to Kat. "Show them the underground layout."

Kat used her powers to draw the cavern diagram in the air. "According to Xypher, Kessar sleeps here." She marked an X down one corridor. "He holds court and plans strategy with the other demons here." It was the corridor furthest from his sleeping chamber. "The Dimme are back here." Which looked like a round chamber quite a ways from where Kessar slept.

"Now the problem is he's intending to move all the gallu to the Dimme area and have forty humans there as sacrifice to them. While the Dimme are chowing down on the humans, he intends to propose an alliance between them. If the Dimme agree to the alliance, they and the gallu are coming for us as a united force."

Damien frowned. "If they refuse?"

"He plans to let them bust a large hole to the surface for all the gallu to run out and then kill the Dimme before they can leave the cavern."

Kish duplicated Damien's scowl. "Can Kessar do that?"

"Don't know," Kat said with a sigh. "The Tablet doesn't work on Simi or Xirena." She looked at Sin. "Would it work on a Sumerian demon?"

He shrugged. "The only people to know that would be Anu or Enlil and they're dead."

"Which is not useful to us," Damien said sarcastically.

Kish let out an aggravated breath. "Can't we just nuke these bastards in the ground?"

Sin scoffed. "Nuclear testing is what started freeing them. It's mother's milk to their kind."

"But if you can burn them . . . ?"

"Burning is a separate process. It's not the same as the bomb. Different molecular something or other. I'm an ex-fertility god, not a scientist. All I know is nuclear bombs don't work, but fire does."

"Then someone get some napalm," Kish said.

Kat ignored him. "Question? Why haven't they established themselves on earth? Seriously. If they can get out in small groups, why haven't they nested on the surface before now?"

"They have." Sin stepped closer to her diagram to study it while he talked. "Acheron and I have been going after them whenever we find them. Kessar has stayed underground because he has protection there. They're stronger on their home soil which is what the caverns have become for them."

"Plus there's safety in numbers," Damien added. "Out here they're controlled since they are killed within no time of leaving their territory. In the caverns . . ."

"There are thousands of them to fight," Sin added. "Even going after the Dimme in there is suicide."

Kat laughed. "Who wants to live forever?"

Kish put his hand up. "For the record, I do."

Sin scowled at him. "Then why do you irritate me so often?"

"Suicidal tendencies are inherent in my species?"

Kat ignored their banter as she stared on the opposite side of Sin. "It's like Kytara said, isn't it? We need an army."

Sin shook his head. "Yeah, well, we're a little short-handed. The Dark-Hunters can't unite to fight without weakening each other. The Greek gods could care less and those who care are dead. Except for us."

Damien nodded. "And we will most likely die in a good cause."

"Yeah," Sin said slowly. "Kessar has been battering me all week in my dreams and I'm exhausted from it. What we need is a miracle."

Kish quickly added, "Or at the very least a plan that doesn't end with my death."

K*essar growled as* he dragged Xypher away from his throne in chains.

Xypher fought against his restraints. He wasn't in corporeal form. How the demon had managed to capture him, he had no idea. But he didn't like it and if he got free, he was going to tear the bastard limb from limb. He looked at Zakar who refused to meet his gaze.

Had the dream god managed to sell him out? It was what he deserved for trying to free him. How many times was he going to let someone betray him before he learned? People were always assholes only out for themselves. Damned be everyone else.

Zakar was the only way Kessar could have found him. Zakar was the only one he'd allowed to see him. So much for trying to help him.

A demon female grabbed him and sank her fangs into his thigh. Xypher hissed in pain. He tried to knock her away, but Kessar jerked the chain on his hands back so that he couldn't reach her.

She pulled back in confusion as she spat his blood on the ground. "He doesn't taste right."

"I'm not alive, bitch. My blood is thicker because it doesn't pump through my body like a human's."

Kessar kicked him in the ribs. "Thank you for the science lesson."

The female wiped her hand across her bloodied lips. "What good is he to us? Kill him."

Kessar studied him as if he were an insect. "If he's dead, I don't think we can."

Xypher tipped his finger to him. "Score one for the genius."

This time, Kessar kicked him hard in the back. Xypher grunted, wishing pain was banned after death. But what the hell? He was used to it.

"So what are you doing here?" Kessar demanded. "Spying for Sin?"

"Who the hell is Sin?"

Kessar kicked him again—oh he was going to enjoy ripping that bastard's throat out. "Don't be coy. You're here to spy and the only one with a vested interest in this place is Sin."

"Not true," Xypher said slowly. "I was just skimming through when I noticed there's a lot of angry people here. A Skotos could live a long time on say, you, alone."

Kessar bent over him and when he did, Xypher saw what he needed. The Tablet medallion.

Gold, round and shining, it was a beautiful thing.

Before Kessar could guess his intent, he grabbed it and ripped it free of the demon's throat and kicked him back. Xypher rolled away from him.

Kessar screamed out, his face changing as he grabbed for the chain.

Xypher was sure Kessar had him. But as the demon reached for him, he was knocked back.

Zakar grabbed him and pulled him toward the throne. "Tell Sin the Rod is in the house. He'll understand."

The next thing Xypher knew, he was back on Olympus, in the quad between the temples of Zeus, Apollo, Artemis, and Ares. "What the . . ."

He didn't move as he ran through the last few seconds in his mind and came up with the only plausible outcome.

To save his life and get a message to Sin, Zakar had just condemned himself to death.

CHAPTER EIGHTEEN

Sin leaned against the bar, studying the map in silence while Kat and Damien made notes on a pad across from him. There had to be some way to settle this without everyone dying.

But damned if he could think of it.

No matter how he looked at the situation, it was going to be a bloodbath. He could feel it. Every scenario, every plan he devised ended up with them being eaten.

There had to be something he was missing . . .

Sin cocked his head as a new thought entered his mind. Scowling at the map, he moved closer to it as he realized what he'd over looked.

"Where's the lock?"

Kat glanced up from her pad. "What lock?"

"The one I have to reset to keep the Dimme in their cage. Zakar was the one who reset it last time. It should be somewhere near them on a chain, but I don't see it."

She got up to study the diagram with him. "What would it look like?"

"Sumerian."

She gave him an unamused stare. "I don't see it."

"That is a really bad thing," he said. "If there's no lock, there's no stopping them."

Her eyes widened.

The hair on the back of Sin's neck stood up as he felt a new presence behind him. He spun around, ready to battle, only to find the Dream-Hunter Xypher there, looking a lot worse for wear. "What happened to you?"

Xypher snorted. "Was mistaken for a punching bag again." He wiped the blood from his lips as he joined them by the diagram. "Your brother just resigned himself to death to get me out of danger."

Sin's stomach sank. "What?"

He nodded. "We have to get him out of there immediately. Kessar is planning on using him as a sacrifice to the Dimme—if Kessar doesn't kill him over the fact he freed me."

As bad as Sin felt about that, a tiny part of himself was relieved to know that his brother wasn't completely converted. He was still trying to do the right thing.

"Zakar also wanted me to tell you that the Rod is in the house. I really hope that makes sense to you because I have no idea what he means by it."

Sin frowned as he shook his head. He had no idea either.

At least not at first. "Wait a sec . . . The Rod." He spun around and headed for his bedroom. He could feel Kat behind him, but he ignored her as he went into his closet and opened the safe.

He pulled several old scrolls out of their clay containers, then headed to his bed to spread them out.

Kat grimaced. "What are you doing?"

"Can you read Sumerian?"

"It's been awhile, but I used to."

He handed her a scroll. "We're looking for anything to do with the Rod of Time."

She snorted. "Rod of Time, Forsaken Moon, Tablet of Destiny . . . you Sumerians really liked your hokey terms, huh?"

He gave her a droll stare. "They didn't exactly ask my opinion before they named them."

"Good, cause my estimation of your intellect would be seriously scarred if they had." She leaned playfully into him and nudged him sideways.

Hiding his amusement, he jerked his chin toward his desk. "Get your butt over there and start reading before I beat you with my Rod of Time."

She tossed him a playful look. "I can think of much better things to do with your rod than beat me, baby."

Sin made a painful noise. "Aww, gawd, we've degenerated into really bad punage. I yield. Save me before my IQ points are damaged."

"Fine, you fun-vampire. I'll take my scroll over here and play by myself."

"Fun-vampire? What is that?"

"That would be you sucking all the fun out of life."

Sin shook his head. "You have the most interesting terms for things."

"Yes, but notice mine are creative unlike the so stellarly named *Rod* of Time."

Ignoring her, he spread the first scroll out and started reading.

Xypher came in and joined the search. Time seemed to drag as they read line after line with no clues. Sin had forgotten just how long-winded and boring his people could be.

Damn, imagine what a good editor could have done with the story of Gilgamesh . . .

He was about ready to give up when Xypher stepped back from his side of the bed. "Found it." He held up the scroll to show them an image of the Rod. It looked like a dagger with a crooked blade.

Sin took the scroll and studied it. He only vaguely remembered seeing this centuries before. "Now the question is, what house did he put it in?"

Xypher shrugged. "He said you would know."

And in that instant he did. It was genius really and it was the only place Zakar could have meant. "Ishtar's tomb."

Kat's face paled. "What?"

Sin set the scroll aside, feeling ill at the thought of having to go there again. "It's the only safe place. No gallu would think to go there and it's hidden—not even the nosiest of archeologists would be able to find it. Zakar must have stashed the Rod there after he locked the Dimme down last time. It's the only place that makes sense." He took a step back, intending to leave.

"Wait," Kat said, taking his hand. "I'm going with you."

He shook his head. "Kat . . ."

The stern, determined look she gave him both touched and warmed him. "You don't need to be alone there."

He would have argued had she not been completely right. It was the last place he wanted to be without her and he knew it. "Thank you." He laced his fingers with hers.

She inclined her head to him before he flashed them out into the remotest area of the Sahara, into a hidden cave that was concealed by ever-changing sands and guarded by a spell that would never allow mortal eyes to see what it contained.

It was here that Sin had laid his daughter to rest and here Ishtar slept in a peaceful repose he had never been able to find for himself. At least not until Kat had come crashing into his life.

Kat hesitated as they appeared in a deep, dark cavern. She could hear the sounds of rodents and insects scurrying out of their way. Cringing in dread, she hoped they didn't come any closer to her.

Sin held his hand above his head and a torch appeared to light their way. Kat was instantly relieved as she looked about and didn't see any icky things running toward them or even away from them—she hated bugs and rodents.

But as she looked around, she was struck by the beauty of this place. The walls surrounding them were covered with inlaid art of children playing in fountains and of deer running through a forest. An eternal fountain made of solid gold splashed in one corner. It had a bird and raven perched on one side and a small girl on the other who was looking into the pool to catch her own reflection.

"How beautiful."

Sin swallowed and she could feel the awful wave of grief inside him. "Ishtar used to love to play in fountains and with animals when she was a child." He paused by one scene of a little girl who had a butterfly sitting on her shoulder while she fed a fawn out of one hand and a jackal out of the other. He splayed his hand over the image and she saw the tears in his eyes. "I found her like that one day when she was four. She looked up at me with her deep blue eyes and said, 'Don't worry, Daddy. I won't hurt them.' "

Kat wrapped her arms around him and held him close as his grief reached out and brought tears to her own eyes. "She wasn't really your daughter?"

"It didn't matter to me. She was always my daughter in my heart."

"I know."

He cleared his throat as he laid one arm over hers. "I was never sure who her real father was. Ningal wouldn't say and she had lovers by the handful. It could have been anyone."

But he'd never held that against Ishtar. He'd loved her regardless and that made Kat love him all the more.

"I don't know why Ningal hated me as much as she did. I tried so hard to make it work, but there was never any pleasing her. It was as if she just wanted to hurt me."

Kat tensed as a bad feeling went through her and she had to bite her lip to keep from speaking. Given what he'd just confided, she wondered if Ishtar wasn't his daughter after all. How cruel to lie to him and tell him his own daughter belonged to someone else . . .

Surely Ningal hadn't been that mean. But as she stood there, she felt the truth in her heart. It would be the deepest blow and it was one Kat was sure Ningal had taken.

Sin stepped away from her and headed down the narrow corridor to a chamber at the end of it. As soon as he entered, the torches lit themselves all around the room. The fire made dancing shadows that formed the images of children playing and deer running.

Kat gaped at the splendor. Every part of the room was covered in gold. Emeralds and diamonds were encrusted along the wall to make the grass where the children danced and there in the center was a sarcophagus in the shape of an ancient temple. It was exquisite.

On the top of it was carved the likeness of Ishtar whose eyes were two perfect sapphires. In her features, Kat saw the likeness to Sin. She'd been right about Ningal and it amazed her that anyone could be so cruel. How could Ningal have lashed out so viciously at the one person who should have meant the most to her? It defied logic.

Sin paused before the image to place his hand on Ishtar's face. The agony of his features tore through her. The thought of opening Ishtar's tomb was ripping him apart.

Kat wanted to spare him any more pain. "You want me to look for it?"

"No," he said, his voice thick. "She never liked strangers to touch her. She was actually very shy." His expression guarded, he closed his eyes and pushed at the lid. It shook slightly before it moved. The sound of scraping stone echoed through the cavern.

Kat moved forward and then gasped as she saw Ishtar. Because she was a goddess, her body hadn't decomposed. She was as perfect as the day she'd died. Her eyes closed, she appeared to be sleeping and a part of Kat kept waiting for her to wake up and look at them. She wondered if Sin was having the same thought.

Ishtar had been laid to rest in a crimson gown, the hem was encrusted with rubies that set off her dark complexion perfectly. Her hands, covered in gloves made of gold, were crossed over her breasts and beneath them she held the Rod of Time. In the shape of a raven, it, too, was gold and encrusted with gems.

Kat looked up at Sin. "She's beautiful."

"I know." He reached in to pull the Rod out from under Ishtar's hands. As soon as he touched her skin, a single tear slid from the corner of his eyes. "I miss her so much," he breathed. He glanced up. "I don't want to see you like this, Katra. Do you understand?"

She nodded as her emotions choked her. She didn't want to bury him either. "Ditto, bud. If anything happened to you, it would definitely ruin my best day."

Sin didn't speak again as he closed the sarcophagus and gripped the Rod tightly in his hand. "We have the key."

"Now we need the lock."

"And a miracle."

K*essar stood before* the lock with Neti behind him. Tall and slender and dressed in dark brown, Neti had been one of their better conversions. The former chief gatekeeper to the Sumerian Underworld, he now worked for Kessar who kept him in deep seclusion.

"You are devious, master."

It was true. He was the master and he was devious. Kessar laughed as he stroked his chin. He'd embedded the lock that would hold back the Dimme inside Zakar's chest. The only way for Sin to save the world would be to kill his own twin.

He relished the image of Sin ripping Zakar's heart out to save mankind.

The only thing better would have been to have taken his woman and have her hold the lock in her chest. But that would have been suicide since her death could very well unleash a Charonte army to hunt for them.

No. This was much better. It would be like Sin killing himself, only worse.

Stepping forward, Kessar cocked his head as he looked down at Zakar who was weeping from the pain of his chest having been ripped open. The chain that led to the Dimme tomb flowed out of his back.

He smirked at the man's pain. "What is that quaint human expression I learned last night? Sometimes you're the dog and sometimes you're the hydrant?" He tsked at Zakar. "Guess you're the hydrant today, eh?"

Zakar's entire body was shaking as he bravely lifted his head to pin Kessar with a lethal glare. "Fuck you."

"No, thank you. I prefer women." He ducked as Zakar tried to spit on him. "And you gods think you're so superior. You cry and spit and beg for mercy, just like everyone else. You have no more dignity than the lowest beggar." He balled his fist in Zakar's hair and pulled it hard. "I can't wait to see you die."

Zakar panted as more pain assaulted him and that thought actually made Kessar hard.

Kessar stepped back. He needed to find a female for a few minutes. "Neti. Guard him well. I'll be back to play with him shortly."

S*in had just* returned to his penthouse with Kat when the Rod started glowing. Two seconds later, something that felt like an earthquake shook the entire casino.

"What the . . . ?" Damien asked as several pictures fell to the floor and shattered. "Is that more bomb testing?"

Sin shook his head as a bad feeling went through him. "No. It's something else." He looked at Kat to see if she felt what he did.

"I don't know what that is," she said her voice tone filled with apprehension. "But I don't like it."

Kish pushed himself up on the wall. "Maybe it was the quake they're always saying is going to hit Vegas."

"Maybe . . ." But the Rod was still glowing and now a low-level hum had started emanating from it. "Something's not right."

All of a sudden, a light shot from the Rod, illuminating the area in front of Sin. A tall, black-haired woman appeared in a dark brown ancient gown. He had no idea who she was . . .

"The seal has weakened," she said in Sumerian. "The Dimme will be freed in six marks. Whoever holds this tool, you must reseal their tomb . . ."

"Six marks?" Damien asked. "What the hell does that mean?"

"Two hours," Kat and Sin said simultaneously.

Kat looked at Sin. "I thought we had a couple of weeks?"

"So did I," he said gruffly. "Something else must have happened to accelerate the clock."

Damien made a face of exaggerated happiness. "That's just beautiful. Zippity-doo-da! What a wonderful day."

Kat sighed heavily. "So much for planning an attack, huh?"

Sin walked through the diagram as he went to retrieve his last sword that would easily kill the gallu. "We need to gather everyone we can."

Damien scoffed. "Uh, boss, hate to be a pall, but I think everyone we can gather is currently here in this room."

Sin paused to look at Simi, Xirena, Damien, Kat, Kish, and Xypher. It was a pitiful number of defenders. But it was all the world had. "In that case, we need to seriously arm ourselves."

Damien crossed himself. "Hail Mary, full of grace—"

"What are you doing?" Kish asked. "You're not Catholic."

"Yeah but I'm feeling really religious all of a sudden and it seemed like a good idea."

Sin rolled his eyes. He looked at Simi and Xirena. "You two are our tanks." He glanced around to the others. "We'll have to guard them so that they don't get overwhelmed and brought down. If we lose them, we have no one who can help us."

Kat frowned. "Wait. I have an idea . . . You go ahead and arm everyone. I'll be right back."

Sin opened his mouth to argue, but before he could speak, she was gone.

Kat flashed herself to Olympus, onto her mother's balcony. Luckily, Acheron was still sitting on the terrace, looking incredibly bored.

He gave her a chilling look. "Are the Dimme out yet?"

She gaped at the unexpected question. "How did—"

"I felt the vibration. It's a sensation I've felt before the last time they almost went free. And to answer the question in your mind, you'll have to ask Artemis. I can't leave here until she dismisses me."

That sucked. "You've got to be kidding."

"Oh I never kid about Artemis. I promised her I'd sit here and do nothing so here I am doing nothing. Much like a really tall, bored guard dog. Personally, I'd rather be throwing myself onto an electric fence—be about the same, I think."

Kat growled low. "Where is she?"

"Still with her father."

She leaned her head back and cursed at the ceiling. She hated having to go up there. "All right. Sit tight and I'll go talk to her."

He laughed. "Good luck."

Kat quickly flashed herself outside the main hall of Zeus's temple where the gods gathered to party. She stayed in the shadows as she got the lay of the situation. Apollo was off to the right with Ares and Demeter while Athena sat with Aphrodite and Nike. Hades was in a corner with Persephone while Zeus laughed with Hermes.

Luckily, Artemis was alone, drinking from a two-handled goblet. Music filled the air as other gods frolicked, danced, and laughed.

Moving as carefully and silently as she could, Kat worked her way over to her mother who jumped in surprise as she realized Kat was there.

"What are you doing here?" Artemis snapped.

"I need to talk to you."

Artemis glanced about nervously. "This is a bad time."

She had *no* idea. "I can't stress the importance of speaking to you. Now."

"Katra . . ."

"Please."

Artemis glowered at her before she pushed herself up from the table and walked her outside to the gardens. "What?"

"I need you to release Acheron."

She laughed, then sobered. "No," she said firmly.

"Matisera, please. The Dimme are about to break free and if I can get him out, he can help corral more Charontes and—"

"Are you insane?" she hissed. "Have you ever seen what happens when the Charonte are set loose? No, you haven't because you're still alive. They're like unleashing locusts with piranha teeth and there's no stopping them."

"But Acheron could control them."

"And he could get killed which is one thing I will never allow."

"What about me?"

"You'll be fine."

Kat was completely appalled, but she was also determined. "I need his help."

Artemis waved her hand. "Leave the humans alone and don't worry about them. We can always make more." And with that, she turned and left.

Kat stood there with her mouth hanging open. She couldn't believe that was all her mother had to say. *We can always make more.*

Why was she even surprised? What, honestly, had she expected? It wasn't like her mother was going to suddenly wake up and be Mother Teresa.

Disgusted, Kat flashed herself back to Sin's penthouse. He gave her an expectant look.

She held her hand up to stop him from speaking. "Don't even ask."

"Typical Artemis response?"

"I said don't ask." Her heart heavy, she walked over to the weapons he'd laid out on his bed and picked up a small crossbow which at the moment, she'd have liked to shoot into her mother's evil heart.

She'd no more lifted it, than a bright flash illuminated the room. She turned, ready to fire at the source of it.

Until she saw Deimos . . . and fifteen other members of the Dolophoni.

She couldn't have been more stunned to find her grandmother there.

Sin stepped back, his face suspicious. "What is this?"

"Back up," Deimos said sincerely. He pinned Kat with that dark, deadly stare of his. "I heard what you said to Artemis . . . and her response. We're not all so cold."

One of the females smiled. "Besides, fighting is what we do best."

Sin considered it for a second before he held his hand out to Deimos. "Welcome to the battle."

Deimos inclined his head before he shook Sin's hand. "For the record, this doesn't mean I like you."

"Ditto."

As Sin started for Kat's map to show them the layout of the cavern, D'Alerian, M'Adoc and M'Ordant appeared.

Kat was even more stunned than she'd been with Deimos.

"You have room for three more?" M'Adoc asked Sin.

"Sure," Sin said. "We can always use more fuel for the pyre."

Kish snorted. "For the record, I don't burn well."

Xirena ruffled his hair. "Trust me, human, all of you burn well."

"That's right," Simi added. "The Simi can ignite most folks and fry them up extra crispy."

Kish sighed. "Lovely."

Ignoring their exchange, Sin ran over the plans with everyone. "The good news is, they haven't had time to round up as many humans to sacrifice. I'm hoping that whatever they did to speed up the clock, they didn't know about."

Damien grimaced. "What if they did it on purpose?"

"Let's be positive, shall we?" Kat said in the voice of a kindergarten teacher, "Let's pretend that we're all going to survive this."

Kish grinned. "I'm with Kat. I like her plan. A lot."

After glaring at him. Sin clapped his hands to get everyone's attention. "All right, kids. We're going to a party where they don't like us very much. Everyone know what they're doing?"

"Not a clue," Kish chimed in happily. "But I think certain death and dismemberment is in my forecast, followed by light rain of guts and flayed skin."

"So much for being Mr. Positive, huh?" Damien laughed.

"Let's see how you're laughing when they toss your butt out in daylight."

"I think I can handle it." Damien stepped forward, but Sin stopped him.

"You need to sit this one out."

Damien glared at him. "Bullshit."

"No," Sin said, his tone determined. "Kish is right. It's daylight and I'm not willing to take that chance."

Still, Damien wasn't sold. "We'll be underground."

"And we'll be blasting holes in the walls. If someone hits the right place, daylight and dead Damien."

A tic started in Damien's jaw, but he ultimately conceded. "Fine. But remember when they kick your butt, I tried to save it."

Sin clapped him on the back before he surveyed each member of their team. "I wish I could think of something inspirational to say to all of you. Some great speech to send you off to battle with, but as I look around—"

"All I see is people going to die," Kish wailed.

Kat laughed. "Pretty much. But if we have to check out, let's take as many of them as we can." She moved to Sin's side and took his hand in hers. "You're not alone, babe."

He squeezed her hand. "Thank all of you for being here. Mankind may not know about you, but I know they're grateful. Now let's go kick demon ass."

CHAPTER NINETEEN

It was one thing to plan an attack, but an entirely different matter to implement it.

Kat stopped them before they could span out and start toward the chamber where the tomb was. "I'm going to do some quick recon. Let's see if they know the seal is breaking and are waiting for us."

Sin held her hand for a full minute. He stared at her with every part of his heart in his eyes, shining there for her to see. "Don't you dare get hurt."

Kat grinned playfully. "You keep talking like that and I'm going to think that you actually like me."

"I love you, Katra, and I don't want to bury you."

She knew exactly how hard it was for him to say those words. The fact that he said them before so many witnesses . . .

Nothing had ever touched her more. "Don't worry, I'll be back to torment you before you can even miss me."

"You better be. Without you, I might actually manage to grow an ego—May the gods forbid." He kissed her quickly, then sent her off.

Kat changed to her Shade form to float through the winding caverns unseen and unheard. Everywhere she went, there didn't seem to be much activity. The demons didn't appear to be gathering their forces at all.

"When should we start rounding up the humans?"

She froze at the sound of a sharp, feminine voice coming from a room just ahead of her.

She approached it carefully, then peeped around to find Kessar and a woman lounging before a fire.

"End of the week," Kessar said. "No need to have them here any sooner. I hate listening to them whine and cry. Mewling, pathetic creatures."

Kat felt a giddy rush. He had no idea the seal was broken . . . Oh this was good. Finally, some luck for all of them.

Smiling, she took a step back.

And bumped into something solid.

Kat's heart stopped beating as she reached around and touched an arm. *Please be one of us, please be one of us . . .* She turned slowly, hoping to find Xypher or one of the others.

It wasn't.

It was a tall male demon who eyed her like the roasted turkey on a Thanksgiving's Day buffet. He shouldn't be able to see her, and yet somehow he did.

"Kessar! We have a spy in our midst." He reached for her.

Kat vanished instantly and returned to Sin and the others. "Houston, we have a problem. A demon spotted me and is calling for help."

Sin cursed.

"But," she added quickly, "the good news is, they don't know about the timer speeding up."

Deimos met Sin's gaze. "With any luck, they'll think Kat was alone."

Sin nodded. "We need to split up to keep them from learning how many of us are here." He turned toward his servant. "Kish, stay with Simi and Xirena and follow me and Kat. We're headed for the tomb to stop the clock."

"We'll divert the demons," Deimos said. "And raise all manner of hell."

"Thank you."

Deimos inclined his head to Sin. "Are we all ready?" He looked around at his brethren who all appeared to relish the coming fight. Letting out a blood-chilling war cry, he and the rest of the Dolophoni ran through the caverns.

Thank the gods they weren't on a snowy mountain top with all that noise. There would be an avalanche for sure.

M'Adoc put one finger in his ear and waited until they'd vanished. "I hate their dramatics . . . and the decibel level."

Then he and D'Alerian and M'Ordant headed after them at a much more subdued pace.

Kat looked around. "Where's Xypher?"

"He went to keep an eye on you."

"I didn't see him."

"That's because I was doing recon of my own."

They turned to see him looking pale.

"Where did you go?" Sin asked.

"Zakar. I know why the clock is ticking and you're not going to like it in the least. They embedded the lock in his chest."

Sin felt sick at the news. "You're kidding."

He shook his head. "I assume that whatever spell makes the lock work—"

"Caused it to accelerate. Zakar is part demon and god. The combination must have been what caused it."

Xypher nodded.

Kat squirmed at the thought of poor Zakar and the pain he must be in. "Can we get the lock out?"

"You can look, but I don't think so."

Sin's face was harsh, cold, and furious. "Kessar's paying me back for his brother's death."

"No," Xypher said, his voice thick, "he's paying Zakar back for helping me. Bloody bastard."

Kat put her hand on Sin's arm to comfort him even though she knew he was past that. How could a simple touch alleviate the pain he must be in?

"Take us to him," he said raggedly.

Xypher did.

Sin felt his face go pale as he saw his brother on his knees next to the tomb that held the Dimme. Dressed only in a pair of jeans, Zakar was slumped against the stone with his hands chained apart.

He ran to his brother's side. "Zakar?"

Zakar's face was contorted by pain as he met Sin's gaze. Sympathetic agony tore through Sin. He'd give anything to spare his brother this.

"You realized what they've done?" Zakar asked.

"Yes."

Zakar's golden eyes bored into him. "Then kill me and stop it."

Sin shook his head. There was no way he could do such a thing. "I can't kill you. You're my brother."

"Kill me, Sin," he said from between clenched teeth. "I'm not worth saving. End my suffering."

"No."

His breathing labored, Zakar looked at Kat. "Tell him, Katra. We don't have time to argue. The demons are already fighting the others and they'll be here shortly. I can hear them. Tell him to kill me and stop the release."

Kat hesitated. How could she tell Sin to kill his own twin? It would be the worst sort of cruelty—which was no doubt Kessar's plan.

It would kill Sin to hurt him. Out of all the powers she had, why couldn't she have had one to stop the . . .

Kat paused as an idea struck. "Wait. I have a plan." She went to Zakar to study how the lock was embedded in his chest. The sight of it made her cringe. Kessar had gone out of his way to make it as painful as possible.

Forcing the bile down, she met Sin's hopeful gaze. "Simi can pull the lock out and I can heal the wound instantly."

"Are you sure?"

She nodded. "Absolutely."

Sin cupped Zakar's head between his hands. "I believe in you, Brother. You stay with me and we'll get through this."

Zakar's eyes were filled with hope as Simi moved toward him. She seized the chain from his back. "This is going to hurt you a lot. I'm sorry for that." Then she jerked it free.

Zakar let out an echoing scream before he fell forward, into Sin's arms. Blood poured from his mouth and back.

Aching for both of them, Kat took Zakar from Sin and let him slump against her. "I've got him. Go reset the lock."

As soon as Sin reached for it, she placed her hand over Zakar's back and closed her eyes to heal him. She wouldn't have long to revive him or it would be too late.

Before Sin could insert the Rod, the lock flew from his hands.

Kat cursed as she realized her powers weren't working either. Zakar wasn't healing.

A feeling of dread consumed her. This wasn't right.

And in that instant, she knew what had happened.

Kessar.

Turning, she saw him standing in the doorway with the lock in his hand. "You didn't really think you could win this easily, did you? That you'd send your conspirators to attack my demons and I wouldn't know where to find you? For shame."

Sin ran at him, but Kessar slammed him down without even touching him. He did the same as Xypher tried to attack. "I have the Tablet of Destiny and you have no powers."

"Bullshit," Xypher snarled. "I stole it from you." He pulled a medallion from his pocket.

Kessar laughed as he held his arm up to show a small, identical medallion hanging from his wrist. "Do you really think I'd be so stupid? Had you really taken it, I would have chased you straight to the halls of Olympus to reclaim it. As I said, you have no powers now."

Xirena scoffed. "I got mine."

"And the Simi has hers."

But before they could even move toward him, Kessar stepped back and sealed them into the room. The sound of scraping stone echoed around them and slammed shut with a resounding crash. Kat ran at the door, but it was a solid slab of stone in the way that would take an elephant to move.

And it wasn't budging. Damn it!

Kat let out a disgusted breath. "I can't believe this. We're trapped in here, with the Dimme, while the lock is on the other side." She turned toward Sin. "How long till our powers are back?"

Sin looked as ill as she felt. "A few hours according to last time."

"Sweet," she said sarcastically, "and we have how long till the bitches awake?"

"Less than two."

She mimicked Mr. Rogers's voice. "Can you say screwed, boys and girls? Yes, I thought you could."

Sin ignored her as he went to Zakar's side. A muscle worked in his jaw as he pulled his brother to him and held him quietly in the darkness.

Kat wanted to cry for him. Her heart heavy, she moved to stand by his side and gently rubbed his shoulders. "I'm so sorry, Sin. I didn't know it'd turn out this way."

"I know."

But it didn't change anything. Zakar was still dead and they were trapped. Kat sank to her knees to hold him while he held his brother.

"Akra-Kat?"

She turned at Simi's call. "Yes, sweetie?"

"The Simi is going to get akri to come and make it better."

How she wished it were that easy. But her father was as trapped as they were. "I've already tried that."

Kish studied Simi for a minute. "Why don't we send the demons out to get the Rod and bring it back to us?"

"They can't stand alone against the number of demons outside," Xypher said. "They're two against thousands. It would be a slaughter."

"I'm going to get akri." Simi vanished.

Sin didn't speak a word at all. He just held his brother and looked as if his heart had been ripped out, too.

I *don't understand* your moodiness."

Ash rolled his eyes as he stood in front of Artemis's settee with her glaring at him. "I'm not moody, Artie. I'm usually pissed whenever you're around. This is nothing new to you."

Before she could respond, Simi appeared.

Artemis curled her lip. "Oh get that out of my temple before it wets the rug."

"You don't have rugs," Ash reminded her, unamused by her attack on Simi.

"The floor then."

Simi hissed at Artemis.

Ash ignored the goddess and turned to Simi. "Hey baby, what do you need?"

"Akra-Kat is in trouble, akri. Them demons have her caught and she's got no powers. They're going to let the really mean demons out to eat her."

Artemis stood up and came forward, her face white. "What do you mean she has no powers?"

"They got this medallion that sucks all the powers of a god away and they used it on Akra-Kat. Now they're going to kill her."

Before Ash could move, Artemis vanished. An instant later, she reappeared. "You might need to come with me."

"You think?" Sin would tear her apart. But Ash needed verbal confirmation from Artemis before he acted. "You're releasing me from my promise?"

"Yes, now help me protect my daughter!"

Kat *looked up* as a shadow fell over her. Her heart stopped as she saw Acheron. "You're here."

Using his thumb, he pointed to Artemis over his shoulder. "Nothing like a bear worried over a cub." He frowned at the sight of Zakar in Sin's arms.

Sin laid his brother down as he saw Ash and Artemis, but to his credit, he didn't attack the goddess.

"What happened?" Ash asked.

Kat swallowed before she answered. "Kessar killed him. I was going to heal him, but my powers are gone."

Ash met Sin's agonized gaze. "Don't worry, Sin. You've lost enough. I'm not going to see this happen to you again." Kneeling on the ground beside the body, Ash placed his hand over Zakar's chest. Two heartbeats later, Zakar gasped as his body seized. He lurched forward, coughing.

The relief on Sin's face was tangible. "Thank you, Acheron."

Ash inclined his head before he took the rest of the cavern in.

"Can you stop the Dimme?" Kat asked hopefully.

Ash rubbed the side of his face as he considered everything. "I don't control the Rod. It's not Atlantean. Only Sin or Zakar can stop them."

Sin helped his brother to his feet. Zakar appeared to have a bit of trouble breathing, but he was alive and that was all that mattered. And with every breath he took, he seemed to get stronger.

Sin met Ash's gaze. "We need our powers."

Ash turned to Artemis.

She stared at the men blankly. "What?"

Ash's irritation with her was more than apparent. "Kat is a Siphon. Even weak, she can take powers. One of us is going to have to share with her and the other will have to get the Rod from Kessar and return with it here."

Artemis screwed her face up. "I'm not touching that demon. He's disgusting."

"Then you'll have to share a few powers with Kat . . . and Sin."

Artemis fumed. Everyone who knew her knew the goddess didn't like to share anything. "Fine. But who will protect her if you fail to get the Rod?"

"Simi . . . and trust me, I won't fail."

Kat wasn't quite so confident. "What if Kessar takes your powers before you get the Rod?"

Ash smiled wickedly. "I'm going to hope the Tablet can't take all of my powers. I should still have enough juice to do some damage."

Kat didn't like the sound of any of that. "Hope? This isn't the time to be hoping."

Ash winked at her. "This is a perfect time for hope. The more dire the situation, the more you need it."

Sin snorted. "You know something's going to go wrong."

"Probably." Ash's silver eyes were twinkling as if he relished the thought. "It always does."

Artemis folded her arms over her chest. "I don't like this plan. I want one where my powers stay inside me."

"There's no other plan and not really enough time to think of one." Ash indicated the tomb with a jerk of his chin. "You'll have a better time negotiating with Apollymi than you will with them. The only one who can contain them is Sin and he has to have his powers back to do it."

Kat gave her mother her best pout. "Please . . . we need you. *I* need you."

Artemis reluctantly held her hand out to Kat.

Kat smiled at her mother, grateful that she was being reasonable for once. "Thank you."

"You better be thankful." Artemis cast a hostile glare to each one of them. "All of you."

Sin wasn't quite so accommodating when Kat tried to touch him. "Are you sure you're not reversing this and taking what little powers I have left to give to Artemis?"

She more than understood his fear. Even so, she couldn't resist teasing him for it. "Guess you'll have to trust me, huh?"

Sin hesitated. Deep inside, he was terrified of touching her now. Kat could kill him. Not just physically, but if she betrayed him . . .

There would be no way back and he knew he'd never recover. He was more vulnerable now than he'd ever been before. All the centuries of betrayal were there and they wanted him to run for the door.

But as he looked at her, his heart truly believed she would never hurt him again. Not intentionally.

It's now or never . . .

His heart thundered in his chest as he took her hand in his and waited for her to betray him.

Kat closed her eyes and summoned her failing powers. She felt the small electrical charge that went through her as she sorted through her mother's powers to find the ones she'd taken from Sin all those centuries before. Once she found them, she let these from her back to Sin.

Artemis jerked back. "You're weakening me too much."

Sin was frozen as he realized that Kat hadn't betrayed him . . . more to the point, he had powers he hadn't felt in thousands of years. And it felt *damn* good.

Kat had returned to him everything she'd taken. *Everything.* He had his full god's strength back. Lifting her hand to his lips, he kissed her knuckles.

"Hey!" Acheron snapped. "If you want to keep that mouth attached to your head, I suggest you put some distance between it and her skin."

Sin laughed as he pulled back. "Sorry." He turned to Ash. "I'm ready to battle."

"Good. Let's do it."

Ash *could feel* the blood pumping through his body as he and Zakar, who was disguised as Sin, headed toward the fighting. The smell of blood was thick in the air and it permeated his head. He licked his lips in anticipation of what was to come.

The blood lust inside him was ferocious as it begged for a taste of what he smelled. It was a beast that lived inside him that was forever hard to leash, especially in battle. It craved nourishment, reminding him how long it had been since he last fed. He should have taken a small bite from Artemis before he set out on this quest.

But it was too late now.

He entered the main cavern chamber. The Dolophoni were still standing . . . at least all but two who lay on the floor. M'Adoc was in one corner, eliminating two demons with one sword stroke.

Ash met D'Alerian's gaze before a demon lunged at him and D'Alerian killed it.

Two demons moved to attack. Ash's incisors grew as his body was thrown into battle mode. He grabbed the first demon to reach him by the throat in one hand and slammed him to the ground, then spun to catch the other. The beast inside wanted to rip the demon's throat out. But he chose a more humane death. He shot a bolt between its eyes.

"Kessar!" he shouted, leading Zakar through the fray as he spotted their leader in the back.

The humor on the demon's face melted into disbelief as he saw Acheron there. He reached for the medallion on his wrist and held it up, then chanted in Sumerian.

Ash laughed as he felt his skin turning blue. "What makes you think that ancient mojo's going to work on me?"

Still, Kessar chanted.

Ash reached for the medallion, then cursed as it burned him. He'd forgotten that the emblems of other pantheons didn't play well with him. Not that it mattered. Pain was one thing he could deal with. Closing his hand over the Tablet, he ground his teeth against the searing agony of it burning against his palm and fingers.

It was sucking his powers out of him. But he still had enough left to do damage.

Snatching the Tablet, he tossed it to Zakar, then head-butted Kessar who staggered back.

Kessar let out an evil laugh as he caught himself and straightened.

A bad feeling went through Ash. "What are you laughing at?"

The demon straightened before he leaned against Ash to whisper in his ear. "By bringing Zakar back and handing him the Tablet with your blood on it, you just opened the tomb to the Dimme. Congratulations, Apostolos. You are the harbinger of Telikos . . . the end of the world."

CHAPTER TWENTY

The rumble of the tomb went through Kat like an electrical current. She and Artemis staggered back into Kish whose eyes were as wide as possible as even the walls around them vibrated. Pieces of the ceiling shook loose and fell while the sound grew louder. She met Sin's gaze to see the confirmation of her fears on his face.

Kat laughed nervously. "Please tell me the cave just has a little indigestion."

But as it rumbled again and she heard a piercing shriek from inside the tomb, she knew the truth.

The Dimme were coming out.

Kat tensed, ready to battle as she saw the wiggling feminine fingers that appeared in a crack in the stone. They had long, black fingernails that pushed against the opening, trying to enlarge it.

"Get back," Sin snapped at all of them.

"I'm powerless," Artemis said. "I can't fight against a demon since I gave someone—" she glared at Kat—"temporary loan of my powers. At least it better be temporary . . ."

Kat shook her head. Yes, she'd given Sin his powers back, and taken some for her own, but she would never take away her mother's. They might disagree from time to time, but at the end of the day, she loved her mother more than anything.

Sin smiled as he gave Artemis a meaningful stare. "I think we found our sacrifice to them."

"Oh poo," Simi said petulantly, "we can't let the heifer-goddess die. Akri will die too if he can't eat from her." Her eyes flaming, she put herself between Artemis and the tomb. "C'mon, Xirena, you gots to help the Simi protect the bitch-goddess."

Xirena let out a disgusted snarl before she took up a position beside her sister.

Kish moved to stand next to Artemis. "Looks like the safest spot here for a human who doesn't want to get eaten."

Artemis raked him with a sneer as Xypher came to stand between Sin and Kat.

"Any game plan?" Xypher asked Sin.

"Don't die."

"I like it. Simple, bold. Impossible. Works for me."

Kat scoffed at his sarcasm. "What are you bitching about, Xypher? You're already dead."

He laughed. "You know, for once, it's good to be me."

Kat only wished she shared his status. She looked at Sin. "Any words of advice on how to kill these?"

"Not a one. It took three of us to trap them last time . . . trap, not kill because we never could figure out how to do that. They're nasty buggers."

Great. She couldn't wait to meet one.

All of a sudden, something crashed behind them. Kat turned to see Acheron entering the chamber with Zakar and the rest of their group.

"Seal the door behind us," Ash ordered Deimos.

Kish scowled at them. "Um, not to be argumentative or anything, but didn't we have to fight to get that opened?"

A female Dolophonus gave him a duh stare. "Well, if you want to leave it open and let all the demons in—"

"Close it, please."

She smirked. "I somehow thought you'd agree."

Deimos and his twin brother Phobos leaned against the rock that sealed the door. They were bloody and panting, as were the rest of them.

"Well," M'Adoc said as he wiped blood from his bruised brow. "At least there are only seven of these."

"Who are about twenty times worse and stronger than the others," Sin added.

"Oh goody," Kat said excitedly, "how it evens out." Deciding she was through with the games, she flexed her arms out and manifested blades in her hands as Zakar came forward. Sin handed him the Rod they'd taken from Ishtar's tomb.

"Simi," Ash said sharply. "Take Artemis to Olympus."

Simi let out a noise of aggravation. "One day I wish you'd just let me eat her."

"Simi . . ."

"I'm going, I'm going," she grumbled before she complied.

Sin passed a repugnant look at Ash. "Did you have to do that?"

Ash shrugged. "Forget the Dimme. If she dies, you'd have to fight me in my true form. You ready for that?"

"Not today. I'm a little battle worn."

Ignoring them, Zakar put the Rod into the lock. When he tried to reseal it, the Rod shattered. "I think we waited too long. It won't close again."

Kat eyed the Dimme fingers that were pushing at the crack. "They're awake and steadily chipping the stone down."

"What the hell kills a Dimme?" Xypher asked.

They all looked at each other as a deep green glow burst out of the tomb. The gallu demons outside were now pounding at the door, trying to shatter it. The Dimme were screaming louder, breaking away more of the stone.

How did someone kill something that was invincible? The question chased itself around in Kat's head until she was dizzy from it. And as she looked back at the tomb, a new thought occurred to her.

Kat turned to Sin. "I think we're asking the wrong question. Forget killing them. How did you trap them last time?"

"Three Sumerian gods and a chant."

Kish sighed. "Too bad we only have one out of the three."

"No," Ash said. "We have three out of three. Zakar, Sin, and Katra."

Sin froze as he caught Ash's meaning. It was brilliant. By saving Kat's life, he might have saved the entire world. "The blood exchange."

Ash nodded. "Kat shares Sumerian blood with you now. She can function as the third god."

Sin smiled as he met Kat's hopeful gaze. He looked at Zakar and for the first time, he truly felt they might survive this. "Do you remember how we locked them down?"

"Yes, but the Rod's broken. We need something else to use as a key."

"Will the *sfora* work?" Kat asked Sin. "It can move forward and back through time."

He wasn't sure, but it was worth a shot. "I think it will. All we can do is try."

Kat pulled her necklace off and handed it to Sin. "What do we need to do?"

After handing Zakar the *sfora*, Sin stationed her to the middle of the tomb while he moved to the far right and Zakar to the far left.

As soon as they were in position, Sin began chanting in Sumerian. "I am the one, the guide of the demons of this earth.

"We summon the forces that created us and gave us birth.

"To all that is here now and before.

"We protect and guard with our core.

"To the lives of others we are giving.

"Forevermore we will protect those who are living." Sin spoke the words twice before Zakar joined him.

Kat held her breath, trying to focus on and learn the Sumerian words as she watched the Dimme's hand slide further from its hole. The pounding of Kessar and his army echoed even louder as she joined their singing.

Any minute now, one, if not both, groups of demons was about to break into the room with them.

The *sfora* turned bright red.

"Zakar!" Kessar's voice rang out in the room. "Free the Dimme!"

Zakar faltered in his chanting.

"Stay with me, Brother," Sin said, his voice eerily calm.

Still Kessar shouted at Zakar to help them.

Zakar lowered the hand holding the *sfora*. His voice grew weaker as the Dimme laughed.

Kat looked to Sin.

"Don't move," he warned her. "We have to stay where we are for it to work."

Zakar was breathing more heavily now as Kessar continued to order him to free the Dimme.

"I won't let you control me anymore," he said from between clenched teeth. Sweat beaded on his forehead as he struggled for his freedom. "I am not yours. I won't betray my brother. Not again."

C'mon, Zakar, she whispered silently. *Don't fail us*.

Most of all, she prayed he didn't fail himself.

But as she watched, she saw the demon swelling up to take possession of him and it terrified her.

Quicker than she could blink, Ash moved to stand behind Zakar and whisper something in his ear.

All of a sudden, Zakar's eyes turned completely white. He raised his hand with the *sfora* and began chanting again with renewed fervor. Kat was desperate to know what was going on, but didn't dare break her own chant to ask.

A loud wind whipped through the room. It was so strong the Dolophoni were sliding into each other. Xirena tucked her wings in. Kat's hair whipped around her face.

It felt as if she were rooted to the floor and while it could pull at her hair and clothes, it couldn't budge her. The Dimme were pounding for freedom, their screams mingling with the chanting.

More light suffused the room as the gallu broke through the door.

"Attack!" Deimos shouted, running to engage them. Total chaos broke out as the gallu assaulted their group while Kat, Zakar, and Sin continued to drive the Dimme back.

The *sfora* turned brighter an instant before one Dimme escaped.

Kat had to duck as it flew at her head, but she held her ground.

"Let it go," Sin said. "Just keep chanting. Seal the tomb on the others and then we'll deal with her."

Kat stayed focused even while the others were fighting virtually on top of her. She watched as the tomb finally began to knit itself closed. Time seemed to slow down before the Dimme cries were finally silenced.

Covered in sweat, Zakar pressed the *sfora* to the lock and sealed it before he collapsed on the ground.

Kat was about to go to him until she saw Kessar from the corner of her eye. Before she could even blink, he turned aside one of the Dolophoni and lunged at Sin, stabbing him in the back, straight through his heart.

She couldn't breathe as she watched in horror. "No!" she cried.

Kessar laughed evilly.

Sin's eyes widened an instant before he sank to his knees. It was then she realized Kessar had taken Sin's sword that had been forged by Sin's people. It was the one thing that could kill the gallu and it was also able to kill Sin . . .

Her vision clouded by fury, she blasted Kessar with a god-bolt from her hands. And then she hit him with another and another until she had him pinned to the floor. She was so intent on him that she missed the other demon who ran at her back and knocked her to the ground. Kat sprang to her feet and turned on her newest attacker. She manifested a dagger in her hand and lunged for the demon. It dodged, then tried to bite her. Kat swept its feet out from under it, then plunged her dagger between its eyes.

She rose, looking for Kessar to kill him too . . . Unfortunately, she didn't see him. But she did see Sin writhing in a pool of his own blood.

Terrified, she ran to him. "Sin?"

He was shaking as she pulled him into her arms. "I've got you, baby," she whispered, placing her hand to his wound. Kat whispered as she tried to heal his wound. But it wouldn't close. How could that be? "I don't understand . . ."

"It's a Sumerian weapon," Ash said as he knelt beside them. "One designed to kill their gods."

She looked up at him and did something she'd never done before. She begged. "Heal him, please. I'll do anything."

"I can't, Katra. Not from this."

"He can't die. Don't you understand? Please . . . please, Daddy, help him."

Ash's heart broke as he heard the desperate love in her tone. Kat was willing to do anything to protect Sin. He remembered a time in his life when he'd felt that way about Artemis. And that love had turned on him and ruined his life. It had left him shattered and vacant. Lost and damned.

He could give Kat the knowledge to save Sin, but would Sin be like Artemis and cause her pain? Would she look back on this moment in time and curse it the way he did his own past? Would she hate herself later for this one desperate moment where her entire world was the one she loved and nothing else mattered except keeping Sin close to her?

Don't interfere with free will. She wanted Sin. Who was he to stop her from choosing to make a sacrifice for him?

Ash controlled fate. But the human heart was its own master, right or wrong. Good or bad.

Dread, agony, and love warred inside him as he clenched his teeth. What should he do? Protect his daughter from a future that might or might not happen or give her the one thing she wanted most?

But in the end, he knew he had no choice. The decision was hers to make, not his. Life was a series of choices made and the consequences that followed.

Please don't let this hurt her. Don't let her regret her love the way I regret mine. Please . . .

Taking a deep breath, he spoke. "Give him your powers, Kat."

She scowled at him. "What? I don't have the power to heal myself."

"I know. But your powers are from the Atlantean and Greek pantheons. They're not Sumerian. Those powers will negate the sword blade. It will save him. Trust me. But you'll have to give away your powers permanently."

Kat couldn't breathe as she heard those words. She'd never been without her powers . . . it would leave her defenseless. Vulnerable.

"Don't, Kat," Sin said, his teeth chattering from the pain of his wound. "Don't weaken yourself for me."

Those words cemented her conviction. Her heart pounding,

she leaned over and kissed him. And as she did so, she summoned her powers from deep inside and let them leave her to fill his body.

Sin's head swam from the sensation of her gentle lips and from the power that suddenly filled him. He lay there unable to breathe as every sight and sound were amplified. He'd known Kat was powerful, but the magnitude of her powers hit him hard.

What she'd given up . . .

For him.

The fact that she'd never abused so much power or hurt anyone with it. It was mind-blowing and it made him love her all the more.

She pulled back to look at him.

Sin cupped her face in his hands as he stared at her in wonder. She was truly the most beautiful soul he'd ever encountered. "I love you, Kat."

Her eyes twinkled with mischief. "I know."

Invigorated, Sin pushed himself up. Kat stood to his right and Ash to his left. The instant they were on their feet, the demons retreated. All those who were able to vanished.

"Oh come on," Sin taunted. "You cowards."

But there was no sign of them now.

Deimos wiped his hand over his cheek as his comrades finished off the demons who were wounded and dead. "Did anyone happen to see where that Dimme went?"

No one had an answer. One by one, they all had to admit no one had seen her leave.

Deimos let out a heavy breath. "Well this sucks, huh?"

Kish scoffed. "Not from where I'm standing. If we lived, it's a damn good day."

Xypher nodded. "He does have a point. Trust the one person in the room who is currently dead."

Sin moved to Zakar who was still trembling and sweating even though he was standing.

"The demon is still in me," he whispered.

"I know." Sin pulled his brother against him. "And we're not going to let it win."

Kat looked around at the damage. There were demon bodies everywhere. The Dolophoni who were wounded were cauterizing their wounds. She was grateful they'd been able to confine their battle to this cavern.

But would they be able to do it the next time? "Can one Dimme end the world?"

Sin stepped back from Zakar. "Not as easily as seven could. Besides, she should be easy to spot. She won't have any social skills and she's hungry."

Kat hoped he was right. "When they attack do they convert those they bite?"

Sin shook his head. "No. They just kill."

"Well that's one thing I guess."

M'Adoc came forward to address Sin. "We'll patrol dreams, watching for the gallu to turn up."

"And I'll warn the Dark-Hunters, Chthonians, and Squires to watch for them," Ash said.

Kat sighed at the carnage. "I guess that's all we can do. That and clean our wounds."

"Yeah," Kish said, "but we saved the world just now. You have to feel good about that."

Sin agreed. "I do. But I'll feel a whole lot better when he find Kessar and his crew and the Dimme and eliminate that threat entirely."

"Believe me," Kat said, leaning against him, "we'll all feel better."

Sin laced his fingers with hers before he spoke to Ash. "Can you locate them?"

"No. They're off my radar. The best defense we have against them is you."

Without thinking, Sin put his arm around Kat. As soon as he did, he saw the look of warning from Ash.

Ash crossed his arms as he approached them slowly. "You ever hurt her, god or no god, I'm going to kick your ass."

Sin laughed. "Don't worry. I'd die before I let anything happen to her."

"You remember that, and you'll have a long and pain-free life."

Kat smiled as love for both of them welled up inside her.

One by one, the Dream-Hunters and Dolophoni left.

"Xypher?" Kat called as he started to leave too.

He turned toward her.

"I'll speak with Hades immediately to get you your freedom."

Xypher curled his lip. "Human for a month. I can't wait." But buried in that disgusted tone, she heard the underlying hope and anticipation.

With a nod to them, he vanished.

Ash held his hand out to Xirena. "You ready to return to Kalosis?"

"Am I ever. The human world just has too many humans in it for me, which wouldn't be bad if I could eat some. As it is, it's just too cruel to be taunted this way. Let me go back to my shopping room."

Ash paused. "I'll check in with you guys when I can. In the meantime, you know where to find me."

Sin turned to Zakar, "C'mon, Brother. Let's go home."

Zakar shook his head. "I think I need some time alone."

Sin frowned. "Where are you going?"

"I don't know. The world's changed . . . and so have I. I need to find my place in it again. Don't worry. I'll be in touch."

Kat felt the sadness in Sin as his brother vanished. "He meant what he said. He's not out to do harm."

"I know. It's just hard to see him leave like this." He leaned his head against hers. "I only hope he finds what needs."

Kat patted his ribs before she left his side to retrieve the *sfora*. She closed her fingers around it. It looked so small and insignificant, yet it had held back the destruction of the world. "Well, we averted this crisis. I can't wait to see what comes next."

Kish stepped out from the shadows. "Um, guys, can we go home now?"

Sin took her hand. "Yeah, we're going home."

Kessar stood back as he watched the remnants of his people. They'd suffered an atrocious blow today. But they weren't defeated. Even though this was a hard situation, there was still hope.

And hope had seen him through worse times than this.

Leaving his people to tend their wounds and set up their homes, he wandered through the new caverns they'd found to use in just such a case.

But honestly, he was tired of hiding. If they were to venture out, they would need an ally. One they could depend on who was just as angry and bloodthirsty as he was.

One who hated humans as much, if not more . . .

As Kessar paused in the lowest part of the cavern, the old adage played through his head. My enemy's enemy is my friend.

Drawing a circle on the ground, he filled it with the image of a dragon . . . an ancient symbol of a cursed race that had once been their enemies.

War made such strange bedfellows.

"Strykerius!" he shouted, summoning a different kind of demon from its home.

A thick smoke appeared from the circle to form the image of a man Kessar hadn't seen in centuries. Tall and well-muscled, he had short black hair and a nasty attitude that more than matched Kessar's.

Stryker looked at him with cold disdain. "I thought you were dead."

Kessar laughed before he removed his sunglasses to show Stryker his red glowing eyes. "I'm alive . . . and we need to talk."

EPILOGUE

One month later.

Kat snuggled closer to Sin as they lay entwined in bed. There was nothing she adored more than feeling his hard muscles against her naked body. If she could, she'd spend eternity right here.

But they'd been in bed for almost fourteen hours and sooner or later, they'd have to get up to attend to business in the casino . . . and the business of patrolling for gallu.

They still hadn't found the location of the Dimme. But so far, the demon hadn't gone on a rampage. Kat wasn't sure if that was good or not. She was glad the lone Dimme wasn't killing humans willy-nilly, but it must be killing someone in order to survive. And it would continue to do so until they located it.

Sighing, she heard Sin's cell phone going off again. "Damien," she said, recognizing the ring tone.

"Probably." Sin rolled over to rub noses with her.

She wrapped her body around his and moaned at the wonderful sensation of him on top of her. "Aren't you going to answer it?"

"Eventually. First I have something I want to do."

She gave him a wicked grin. "I thought you already did that."

His gold eyes burned into hers as he stared at her as if he could eat her up. "Not yet." He pressed his lips to hers.

Kat sighed at the taste of him until she felt the electric surge of powers moving from him to her again. She tried to pull away, but Sin held her close until she felt every bit of her old power.

Only then did he release her. His gaze searched her face and body as if afraid he'd harmed her. "Did it work? Are all your powers back?"

She nodded.

He let out a relieved breath. "Good. I've been trying to figure out how to do that since you gave them to me. You know it's not easy to control all that power."

"Yes, I do know." She cupped his cheek in her hand. "It's how I accidentally depleted a certain Sumerian as a young woman and almost killed him."

"That was what I was afraid of doing with you. I didn't want to hurt you, but I want you back as you were."

"Why?"

"Because I love that about you and I don't want to take anything from you. I only want to make your life as great as you make mine."

Warmth filled her at his words. "So I guess this means that you've abandoned all your quests to get back at Artemis, huh?"

A devilish glint appeared in his eyes. He only looked like that when he was plotting something. "No, not entirely."

"What do you mean?"

He shrugged before he nipped at her lips. "I've just found a better form of vengeance on her."

"And that is?"

His eyes glowed warmly as he locked gazes with her. "I want to see the look on her face when you tell her she's going to be a grandma."

Kat laughed. He was absolutely evil, but that was what she loved most about him. "Then get dressed, my sweet, and we'll go make your day."

More thrilling titles available now by Sherrilyn Kenyon from Piatkus . . .

THE DARK-HUNTER COMPANION

Sherrilyn Kenyon's Dark-Hunter Companion is essential reading for anyone who has recently made that once-in-a-life-time deal with Artemis. Packed with insider knowledge and secrets mankind are rarely privy to, it's also a valuable guide to the Dark-Hunter series for lesser mortals. It includes a Dark-Hunter directory, a handy reference guide to Dark-Hunter and Greek mythology, useful tips on dealing with daimons and squires, lessons in conversational Greek and Atlantean; there's even a section on how to handle unexpected visits from ancient gods . . . The companion also includes a brand new short story from every Dark-Hunter's favourite writer Sherrilyn Kenyon.

978-0-7499-4095-9

DARK SIDE OF THE MOON

'Ravyn Kontis is most definitely not human. He'd been born into the world of nocturnal predators who commanded the hidden magicks of the earth – who ruled its darker arts – and he had died as one of their toughest fighters . . . Now he walks the earth as something else. Something soulless. Something ferocious and even deadlier than what he'd been before . . .'

Susan Michaels is a reporter on a mission to resurrect her professional reputation. And she only has to brave her cat allergy at a local animal shelter to follow the lead that could get her off the tabloid beat forever. But she gets more than she bargained for when she inadvertently adopts one of the cats . . .

As soon as she gets home the cat turns into a gorgeous naked man. Ravyn is entirely unique – a Were-Hunter who became a Dark-Hunter as well. Suddenly, Susan is pulled into Ravyn's mysterious world – one full of danger and magic. And, despite the way he makes her sneeze, despite the danger that swirls around him, she can't resist him . . .

978-0-7499-3687-7

THE DREAM-HUNTER

In the ethereal world of dreams there are champions who fight to protect the dreamer and there are demons who prey on them . . .

Arik is such a predator. Condemned by the gods to live for eternity without emotions, Arik can only feel when he's in the dreams of others. Now, after thousands of years, he's finally found a dreamer whose vivid mind can fill his emptiness.

Dr. Megeara Kafieri made a reluctant promise to her dying father that she would salvage his reputation by proving his life-long belief that Atlantis is real. But frustration and bad luck dog her every step. Especially the day they find a stranger floating in the sea. His is a face she's seen many times . . . in her dreams.

What she doesn't know is that Arik has made a pact with the god Hades: in exchange for two weeks as a mortal man, he must return to Olympus with a human soul. Megeara's soul.

978-0-7499-3797-3

UNLEASH THE NIGHT

'It's a predator eat predator world for the Were-Hunters. They trust no one. Love no one. Not if they want to live. Set up a little over a hundred years ago, Sanctuary is the only place where all species are forced to get along. It is a safe haven for misfits and refugees, creatures who had been thrown out of their clans for all manner of reasons.'

Wren Tigarian was taken to Sanctuary as an orphaned cub, where he grew to adulthood under the close scrutiny and mistrust of those around him. Many regard him as an abomination – a forbidden blend of two species – he has become a loner, shunning both Were and human company alike. Until that is Marguerite D'Aubert Goudeau walks into his life.

The daughter of a prominent US Senator, Marguerite hates the socialite life she's forced to live. Still, she has no choice except to try and conform to a world where she feels like an outsider.

The world of the rich and powerful humans is never to meet the world of the Were-Hunters who exist side by side with them, unseen, unknown, undetected. To break this law is to call down the wrath of the highest order.

But in order to protect Marguerite, Wren will have to fight not just the humans who will never accept his animal nature, but the Were-Hunters who want him dead. It's a race against time in a world of magic without boundary that could cost the two not just their lives, but their very souls . . .

978-0-7499-3630-3